PODEVIN AND THE QUEEN'S DEATH

NIGEL OAKLEY

Paperback ISBN: 978-1-915981-75-2
Ebook ISBN: 978-1-915981-76-9

Published by Resolute Books
www.resolutebooks.co.uk

Cover design by Liz Carter at Capstone Publishing Services
Interior design by Amie McCracken

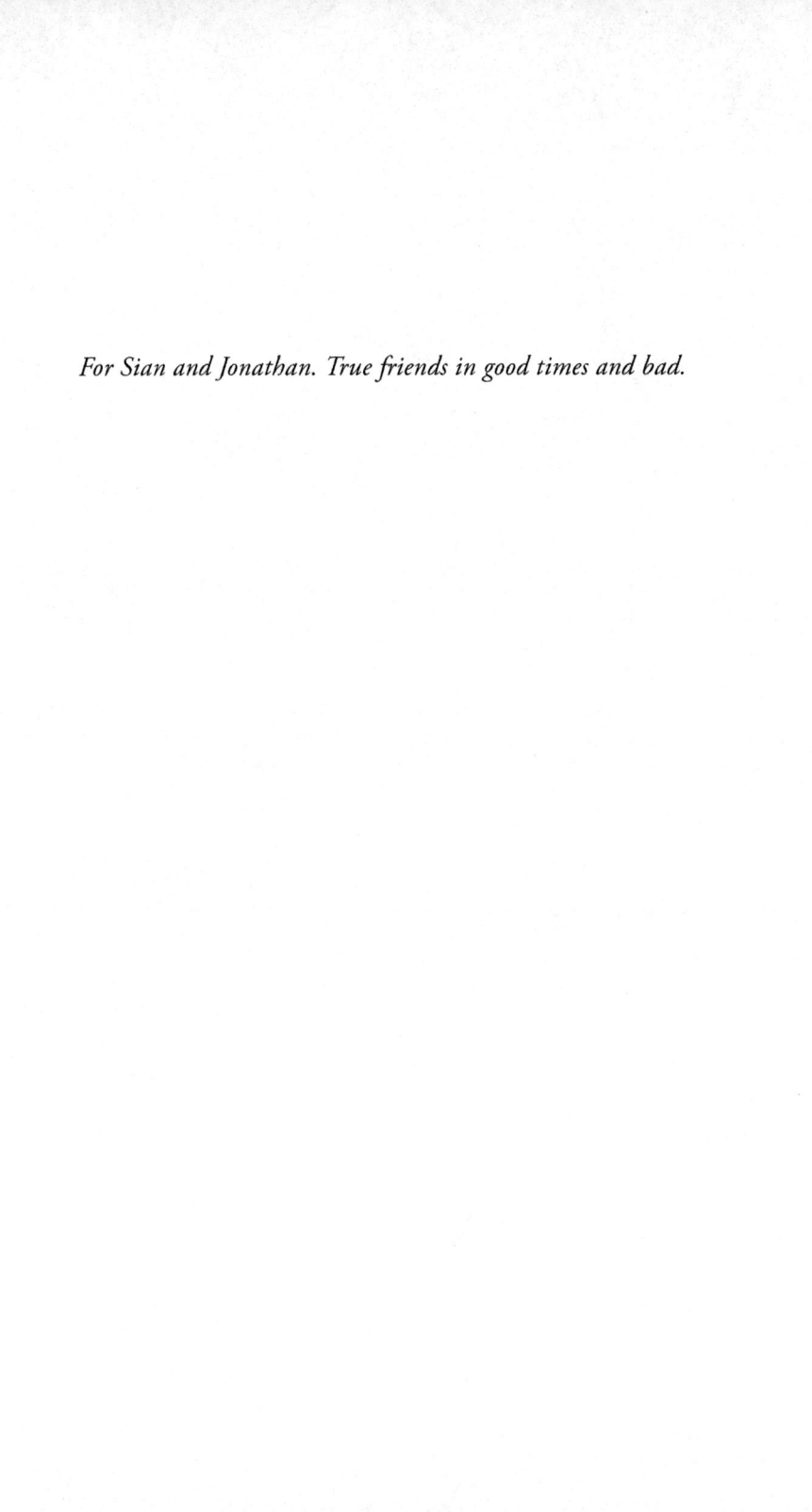

For Sian and Jonathan. True friends in good times and bad.

Podevin's Bohemia

Drawn by Jaromir
Clerk to King Wenceslas
(Not to scale)

Mělník

SAXONY

Stará
Beleslav

Labe

Budeč

Levý Hradec

PRAGUE

THE
MAGYARS

Vltava

Tetín

Characters

Anglo-Saxon

Athelstan—deceased, King of England

Beatrice, Hilde—ladies-in-waiting to Emma

Edmund I—King of England, half-brother to King Athelstan, killed in May 946

Edred—King of England from May 946, brother to Edmund

Emma—Princess of Wessex, Athelstan's half-sister, married to Duke Boleslav of Bohemia

Matilda—Princess of Wessex, Emma's older sister, also half-sister to Athelstan, married to King Otto of Saxony, died in January 946

Geraint—captain of Emma's bodyguard

Brother Mark—former warrior, now a Benedictine Monk, Emma's chaplain

Bohemian

Alexandr—son of Podevin and Lyudmila, aged 7

King Boleslav—King of Bohemia, took the throne after he assassinated his older brother Wenceslas (see book 1 of this series), He is father to:

Duke Boleslav (also known as Mladenic: 'the youngster')—heir to the throne and Emma's husband

Boleslav III—Emma and Duke Boleslav's son

Blanik—Prague Castle Constable and Podevin's tutor under Wenceslas, now fled to Saxony

Cesta—a Bohemian warrior, a particular favourite of King Boleslav (was present at Wenceslas's assassination)

Dalimil—chef at Prague castle

Edith—Emma's daughter, aged 10

Lyudmila—Podevin's wife

Maria—Lyudmila's daughter by Tugumir, 16 years old

Mikael—knight

Podevin—former page and bodyguard to King Wenceslas (also his second cousin)

Pribyslava, 'Priby'—abandoned as a child, adopted by Podevin and Lyudmila, aged about 18

Radslav—Duke of Kourim, Budec and Tetin; an old warrior, loyal to the Premyslid family

Sven—Priby's biological brother, Podevin's sworn enemy, a captain in the Saxon army

Tugumir—former Duke of Budec, deceased, Podevin's older half-brother on their mother's side, part of the group who killed Wenceslas, Maria's biological father

Vaclav—son of Podevin and Lyudmila, aged 9

Wenceslas—deceased, former King of Bohemia

Saxon

Bernard, Wolfgang—soldiers in Count Johan's troop

Dietrich, Kurt—courtiers at Augsburg

Heinrich—Duke of Saxony

Jan—squire to Count Johan

Johan—count and captain in the Saxon army

Liutgarde—Princess, daughter to King Otto and Queen Matilda, aged 16

Otto—King of the Saxons, married to Anglo-Saxon Princess Matilda

Others

Emma of Melnic—Duke Boleslav's second wife

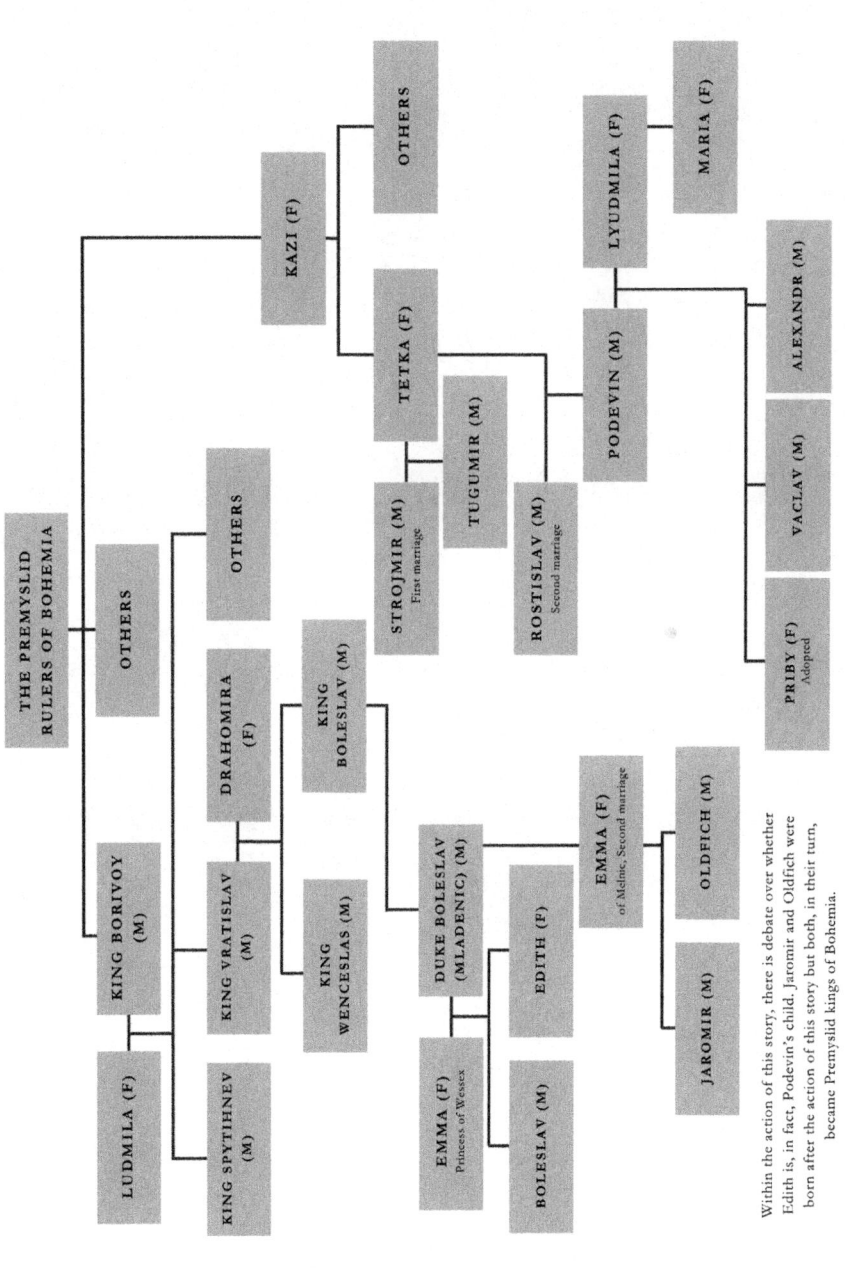

THE PREMYSLID RULERS OF BOHEMIA

KING BORIVOY (M)

LUDMILA (F)

OTHERS

KAZI (F)

OTHERS

KING SPYTIHNEV (M)

KING VRATISLAV (M)

DRAHOMIRA (F)

OTHERS

TETKA (F)

LYUDMILA (F)

STROJMIR (M)
First marriage

TUGUMIR (M)

PODEVIN (M)

MARIA (F)

KING WENCESLAS (M)

KING BOLESLAV (M)

ROSTISLAV (M)
Second marriage

PRIBY (F)
Adopted

VACLAV (M)

ALEXANDR (M)

EMMA (F)
Princess of Wessex

DUKE BOLESLAV
(MLADENIC) (M)

EMMA (F)
of Melnic, Second marriage

BOLESLAV (M)

EDITH (F)

JAROMIR (M)

OLDFICH (M)

Within the action of this story, there is debate over whether Edith is, in fact, Podevin's child. Jaromir and Oldfich were born after the action of this story but both, in their turn, became Premyslid kings of Bohemia.

Chapter 1
Duchess Emma Plans a Hunt

In a normal year, the memory that the penetrating frosts of January extended well beyond their allotted thirty-one days, would have lingered long amongst people dependent on being able to sow crops as soon as they could. For Duchess Emma, who started the year as Prague's castle constable and ended it as a runaway from a nunnery, the year of our Lord 946 lived on in her mind as a year of disaster, loss and retribution.

When February forgot to bring both rain and any warmth, the future was a closed book. King Boleslav's rushed departure after the Christmas celebrations was testament to another Magyar raid across the border. Whatever might have been going on in the east, in Prague Castle and in the forests surrounding the city, all was quiet. Not peaceful, but quiet. Being fellow Christians, the Saxons could be assumed to keep an informal winter truce during the whole period, but as Christmas had receded into the past, all that would now hold them back was the frozen weather. If a horse slipped on a solid, icy road and broke a leg in falling, that would be disaster enough; but if it brought down a knight with it, who ended up being unable to fight, that was a whole different story.

So, if the guards on the palisade wall, or on look-out from the castle towers, spent more time blowing on cold hands, or seeking warmth from the few braziers dotted around the place, their captains—provided there was some evidence of patrolling and the horizon was being watched—would not make too much of it.

Inside the castle, in Duchess Emma's chamber, domestic life had been more tense than usual. King Boleslav, on his departure eastwards, had left his son in Prague; and that son, Duke Boleslav, was still here, 'checking the books.' Duke Boleslav was the reason Emma had travelled all the way from England. Although four years older, she had been selected as Duke Boleslav's bride. Neither, despite a living son and daughter, had ever been happy with the situation. Emma preferred it when her husband was anywhere other than Prague. Sitting in her chambers, with her lady-in-waiting Beatrice combing out her hair, Emma took a deep breath. In the polished metal mirror, she saw Beatrice smile.

'What?' Emma said.

'Begging your pardon, madam. I was just thinking about tomorrow.'

'The hunt?'

'And the fact it will put more tangles in your hair. We ladies will freeze, trying to follow you, and that's another fact.'

'Would you prefer to be stuck inside, by a smelly brazier?' Emma smiled in her turn.

Beatrice was one of the very few people she had left with whom she could talk openly. There had been so many deaths, and partings of ways, over the years since she had come to Bohemia as a callow fourteen-year-old, furious at the thought of being married off to a little boy. The ten-year-old—everyone had called him Mladenic, 'the youngster,' back then—had grown up, but had never moved out from the shadow of his father.

The door crashed open, startling both of them. Beatrice gasped and dropped the brush. Emma grabbed a knife from the dressing table. She turned. And her shoulders fell. She breathed out, forcing herself to relax. The visitor was her husband, with half a dozen guards arranged behind him. She should have realised that only he, or his father, could have bypassed the guards on her door without a fight.

'A typical unfriendly welcome, I'd say,' Duke Boleslav said, striking his hands-on-hips pose.

'Husbands don't usually visit their wives with armed attendants,' Emma said.

Not only did Boleslav have a sword strapped to his side, but his attendants were liberally arrayed with swords, pikes and battle-axes. She noticed Beatrice, with infinite stealth, pick up the brush. As a mere lady-in-waiting, she had sunk into a curtsy on recognising their visitor. Protocol dictated that, as the senior person in the room, only Duke Boleslav could allow her to get to her feet, but he showed no sign of acknowledging her presence.

Emma stood and half-turned towards Beatrice. Her husband had only been in her rooms half a minute and already she was annoyed. In another moment, she would be telling Beatrice to—

'Oh, on your feet, woman,' Duke Boleslav said. 'And clear out! I have things to say to this one that don't concern you.'

Beatrice flashed a worried glance at her mistress. Emma stuck the knife in her belt—it was better than nothing and she was not going down without a fight.

'Mark and Geraint,' she muttered under her breath.

Beatrice's gaze dropped as she gathered herself to leave the room, but her minute return nod was enough to tell Emma the message had been understood. Her chaplain and her chief bodyguard would know within the minute what was going on. Though she would have questions for the guards outside her door later on: why had they not reported to their captain as soon as the duke turned up?

Boleslav waited until Beatrice had left before opening his mouth again, but Emma spoke first: 'So, it takes seven of you to deal with one of me, does it? What have you got to say that requires all these witnesses?'

'You be careful. My father isn't here. Unless you're going to tell me you're with child?'

'You know that's impossible. A husband has a duty to perform first.'

Boleslav's eyes blazed. Emma noted a couple of the younger guards in his retinue flickered a half-smile before remembering their duty. She had slept alone for years. One living son, one living daughter, in that order. And a stillbirth. The dead child had been a boy. Emma had been left alone ever since.

Her husband was speaking again.

'You're getting old. Your chances of producing any living child are falling by the month. Especially when you insist on performing unladylike acts.'

Emma groaned. She knew what was coming. Tomorrow's hunt was not happening. Females on horseback were considered unladylike in this country. Despite not being told, she sat. It was ridiculous.

She put on her best simpering smile and said, 'Come along, husband, tell me what's on your mind.'

'You will be pleased to know, I have inspected the kitchens and found their stores depleted. So, I have decided to allow the hunt tomorrow—on certain conditions.'

Duke Boleslav had to stop speaking as raised voices sounded from outside the room.

'Let us through, in the duchess's name.'

'Access denied—in the duke's name. No-one goes to the duchess on pain of death!'

'The duchess is castle constable here. Anyone who threatens the constable in her own castle, dies.'

There was a sound of weapons being readied.

'So, husband, either stand your men down, or be responsible for yet more deaths of your own men.' Boleslav was about to respond when Emma continued, 'And we'll see what your father makes of it afterwards, shall we? I'd advise you to be quick—or shall I shout I'm being attacked? There are seven of you—all armed against protocol.'

Boleslav had started breathing heavily, as he always did when thwarted in his plans.

'All right!' he yelled. 'Let them through.'

'And send your guards away—how many have you got out there?'

Boleslav shrugged, would not look at her.

'How many?'

'Twenty.'

'You brought twenty guards, just to come to see me?' Emma stood, raised her arms, then let them fall to her sides.

The chamber was now crowded. Brother Mark, arms folded inside the generous sleeves of his habit, stood a little apart. Geraint, battle axe at the ready, was by the side of the door—any person trying to enter with hostile intent would meet a rapid and sticky end. Mikael was there, too. Emma noted Boleslav's hostile glare at him: Mikael had come to court as part of the duke's retinue, but it had been Emma who'd trained him and so won his loyalty. It had been the king, no less, who had approved Mikael's transfer to Emma's personal body-guard.

Her husband raised a shaking finger at her. 'You don't hunt. You are meant to be a woman, so do only womanish things. If you go tomorrow, you will ride a palfrey, and follow behind the hunt. The kitchens will be restocked by our forester—you'd better send a message. What's his name? Krok? He will be here by first light tomorrow and he will be your companion. On foot!'

At that, Duke Boleslav turned on his heel and left. His armed guards, with no orders, hesitated, before the most senior of them jerked his head at the door and they, in no particular order that Emma could see, filed out of her room, leaving her alone with her men.

For a moment, there was silence as Emma absorbed Boleslav's last speech.

'But … the forester?' Mikael burst out, confused. 'He supplied all the Christmas meat; he comes every week with what he can get—how can he supply us again when he gave us everything he had two days ago? There's his own family to feed.'

'I'm afraid it's worse than that.' Mark reached into his belt, extracted some folded parchment from his purse and handed it over. Emma took a moment to read it.

'Two boars? Two boars! He's not supposed to hunt boar, anyway. What is this? The hunt is supposed to get those. And, even if he kills the boars, how does he get them to us?'

'He uses his cart, doesn't he? And his packhorse.'

Emma nodded at Mark's words. Of course, 'Krok' had his horse and cart. She'd been the one to give them to him when it became clear he was becoming their chief supplier of meat. That was in the days when the war with Saxony was a hotter affair than it was now, and hunts had to be low on her list of priorities. Scraping together armies to fight off Otto's troops had been the order of the day. Emma shook her head—she had to think. How much of her husband's words to accept, what could be safely ignored, and what would cause a fight—and a bad report going to his father, the king of Bohemia—if she failed to do as she was bid?

'Is there anything else?' she asked, before trying to make her decisions.

'You have two guards who aren't as loyal as they might be.' This came from Beatrice, who had joined the party in Emma's chambers once Boleslav had taken his troops away. 'They might have been standing at the door, but their weapons weren't going to be used.'

'I thought they'd been disarmed,' said Geraint, 'when the duke arrived.'

Beatrice shook her head. '"About time the bitch"—begging your pardon, madam—"was sorted out," was what I heard as I left. I don't think they knew I understood Czech,' she added, in Anglo-Saxon, prompting Emma and Geraint to nod quietly.

At Emma's nod to him, Geraint left the room. At best, there were two men who'd be on cleaning duties for the foreseeable future. They all paused while Geraint did his shouting at the two men, and they were marched away to the dungeons.

'Why don't we all sit,' Emma said, 'and do some thinking?'

Once they had done her bidding, Emma continued, 'How much do we know about this visit to the kitchens? It's hardly "checking the books," is it?'

'Apparently, the kitchens have to account for everything coming in and going out. The "scraps to the poor" policy has been, er, scrapped. Unless the poor pay.' It was Mark who stepped in with the information.

'Why wasn't I told?' asked Emma.

'It happened this morning. Dalimil would have come to you, but was specifically told his place was in the kitchens and he was to remain there. There's a guard on the doors.'

'We have barely enough to guard the walls, and he's putting guards on the kitchen doors?' Emma sighed.

Mark spread his hands.

'As soon as you leave here, send them back to their former duties— on my authority. My husband will no doubt be checking somewhere else tomorrow—unless he's coming on the hunt?' Emma looked round, and the grins and shakes of heads told her all she needed to know. She continued: 'He's going to prioritise the scriptorium—he has to if the king really does want a report.'

'He goes there at night.' This time, it was Mikael who interrupted. Emma stared at him, and he nodded. 'Yes, madam, most nights, his guards have to pretend not to notice him. It seems he goes to read some special reports. I don't know what they are, but he sneaks out, is gone for an hour, sometimes longer, and then comes back.'

'When does he sleep?' Emma muttered, then turned to her chaplain and adviser. 'Mark—that's one for you. You know all the clerks, don't you?'

'Most of them,' Brother Mark replied. 'But I think we have other things to worry about. Mainly "Krok."'

'Ah.' Emma flushed. 'He's supposed to be my companion tomorrow.'

'And that is both the worst idea your husband's had, and the one he is most likely to be watching out for if it is not followed.'

Emma looked round the room. The guards on the door, after Geraint's discipline and removal of the previous guards, would not say anything, but she planned to lower her voice anyway. Of those around her: Beatrice knew, Mark knew—Mark knew everything— but could Mikael be trusted? She stared at the man who had been her first Bohemian bodyguard, and found he was smiling back at her. She made her decision. She stood, beckoned to her three companions, and retreated to the back of the room. They stood in a huddle.

'Those who don't know, will have heard rumours.' She glanced at Mark, but he was nodding encouragement. 'Rumours to the effect that the king's forester, this "Krok," isn't all he is meant to be.' She lowered her voice even further, then leant forwards to the others, who obligingly leant towards her. 'His real name is Podevin, and he was Wenceslas's page, bodyguard and friend.'

'Who owes the duchess his life,' Mark put in, using an equally low voice.

'There was a real Krok, who was the king's forester, but he died and Podevin took his place and his name.' Emma opened her mouth to continue her confession, but Mark forestalled her.

'If I may, madam?' he said. 'This Krok, or Podevin, lives in the forest. He has a wife and children and has learned to be content.' If Emma heard an edge to Mark's voice at this last statement, she was the only one—the other listeners did not react.

Mark carried on: 'If, of course, any of the rumours are substantiated, then not only is the duchess's life in danger, but also that of her children.' Now Mark had everyone's attention.

'The rumours only ...' Mikael stuttered to a halt.

Mark smiled. It was grim.

'It is more a case of what the duke, or his father the king, would seek to make of it. And whether, at that time, there might be an alternative way of securing the succession. And, yes, we could discuss ideas on the lines of: "is it worth it, just to sort out who's going to get the throne?" But I think we need to address the immediate situation.'

'Which is?' Emma asked.

'Tomorrow. I think we'd better fall in with the duke's plan.'

Now Mark had surprised Emma. Part of her thrilled to the idea of spending a whole day with Podevin. Her mind leapt to the last time she had been alone with him in the forest—but that had been the summer, and they had both been younger, much younger. Emma wondered if Podevin had kept his figure; she knew her waist had thickened after her pregnancies and the often-enforced lack of exercise. She was vain enough to check her mirror, but she knew there were lines on her face that hadn't been there before, but no grey hair yet, not even when her next birthday would be her thirtieth—

'Madam? Madam! Are you listening?' Only Mark could use that sharp tone with her.

'What were you saying?'

Mark pursed his lips. 'I was saying, one of us needs to get the message to "Krok" and help him get the supplies here in the morning. Especially if we are not to be responsible for him having to slaughter both his remaining sows.'

'Yes, yes,' Emma said. 'Good idea.'

'I was also suggesting I go,' Brother Mark said. He over-rode Emma's puzzlement. 'Madam, you need every man loyal to you who can wield a weapon. I would suggest a double guard tonight. And I'd recall Hilde to your side, as we don't even know who Beatrice's relief is!'

'I can stay,' Beatrice said.

Unlike Hilde, Beatrice was still single. But Mark was right. It was a siege mentality, but if the duke decided that Emma, by forcing him to retreat from her rooms, had insulted him, and he wanted his wife to die, then tonight would be as good a time as any to do it. They all knew how Duke Boleslav reacted to being thwarted.

Mark's own cell, it was too small to be called a chamber, was too far away for him to be of any help in an emergency anyway. But, before he had become a monk, he had been a warrior in his native Northumbria, so he could help with hunting in the forest. Even so, by the time Mark arrived at the forester's home (and assuming the man was home, not out on one of his many duties), and delivered the message, there would not be much light left to mount a hunt. Boars indeed! When Podevin/Krok had lived his life in the forest being specifically told there was one animal he could not hunt ...

Emma allowed Mark to leave them to work out how they were going to cope with all the extra bodies in Emma's chambers. Preferably while not raising her husband's suspicions any higher. She reminded him that, once he was back, he needed to try to find out what was, and what wasn't, going on in the scriptorium.

Chapter 2
Troubles in the Forest

'Oh, you stupid animal. Move!' Lyudmila jabbed at the sow again. Harder this time. The sleeping pig grunted and opened one small eye. 'Move!' she yelled again, and waved her staff.

At last, there was a reaction. The sow rolled onto her front, lumbered to her feet and, mouth agape, charged her owner. Lyudmila just made it through the gate, which was closed behind her by Priby. The sow slammed against it, but with both women leaning on the other side, the gate held.

After a pause, Priby banged the bucket of slops against the fence, and the sow followed the noise until the bucket was emptied into its trough. Priby had stretched over the fence in order to empty the bucket. She straightened her back, which was always her weakest area. While the sow ate her extra rations—the first bucketload of food had gone into the trough with no reaction from the sleeping animal— Lyudmila opened the pen and crept up to the farrowing bed. Three dead piglets, squashed by their mother, lay there. The bed was soft enough for them to have been all right—if their mother had got off them quicker. But she had decided she would lie there, and that had been it. Now there were only two left alive, and one of those was the runt.

Lyudmila sighed. Some days, life just felt like one upset after another. Podevin had taken both boys with him to sort out the traps. The traps should not need sorting. What they were going to do was practise becoming knights. Vaclav knew more about fake sword-fighting than he did about living in the forest—and what was he more likely to end up spending his life doing? Lyudmila didn't care what Duchess Emma might, or might not, have said to Podevin on one of their so-called chance meetings. She knew the actual price paid, and the way real life worked. Podevin's dreams for the boys were even affecting Maria. Instead of doing her chores, she had invented some story about needing to go to the castle and had disappeared as soon as she had her distracted father's permission.

There had been a row. Starting with Lyudmila asking her husband where Maria had gone.

'She's with you, isn't she?' he'd said.

'No. She's off to the castle. With your permission.'

'So that's what she was asking?' But Podevin failed to notice Lyudmila's concern. He turned away. However, his wife hadn't finished:

'You don't need all those weapons to check the traps, surely?'

So it had gone on. In the end, she had screamed at him to take the boys, but not to be surprised when they came back home to find no meat in the pot.

Lyudmila and Priby looked at the three dead little bodies: two of which could have grown up to give them plenty of pork for next winter, and one of which could have produced litters of her own for them in the future. They heard the thump at the same time and rushed to the pen. The sow had finished her food and decided she needed a rest. The runt had escaped, perhaps because it was too small, or too quick, but the other piglet was struggling under its mother's bloated belly. Ludmila reached for the leather strap that held the gate closed, but Priby put a hand on her arm.

'Wait,' she said.

The piglet was thrashing from side to side, but with each jerk, more of its body came out from under its mother. Eventually, with one last convulsive pull, its back legs also appeared. However, it did not seem to hold any grudge against the big beast that had just tried to squash it, as it turned to latch onto a swollen nipple and began suckling. After a few moments' hesitation, the runt realised its brother, or sister, was not going to attack it, so also came up for a feed.

'Two is better than none, I suppose,' said Lyudmila, 'but what's going to happen next winter, I have no idea.' She looked to the other pen: that sow hadn't produced a single piglet.

'Let's worry about the rest of this one first, shall we?' said the ever-practical Priby.

They both looked up as they saw a figure approaching them down the path.

⌖

Mark helped them bury the little bodies: the thought of putting them in the pot turned Lyudmila's stomach. There was little enough for him to say, given the news he brought with him. He was also unhappy with Podevin, when he finally came back from 'checking the traps,' carrying all those weapons.

Podevin came back alone. He had to admit what he had really been doing—though it was clear that he hadn't been checking any traps, or why had he needed to send his sons on a race around the forest afterwards to check those same traps?

'Look,' he tried explaining, 'I can't ever get back into court life. I know that. But my sons are also of royal descent. Maybe that blood is somewhat diluted—'

'Thanks very much!' interrupted Lyudmila. 'So my peasant blood is no good for you, is it?'

'That's not what I meant,' Podevin said, but whatever else he was going to say went unsaid.

'Podevin,' said Mark, 'are you sure it's just your bloodline prompting this training? Or a supposed half-promise by a person in authority? As much as she might like to help, I don't think Emma is in a position to give you what you want. For one thing, how is she supposed to explain why she is helping these children, when there are so many others? Others whose fathers are soldiers, guards, castle servants. Do I make my point?'

Podevin opened his mouth, and shut it again. When he did speak, it was to ask a different question of Mark: 'Why are you here?'

As Mark explained, including the bit about Duke Boleslav expecting two boars, Podevin's thoughts tumbled over each other.

He remembered the last time—so long ago now—when Emma had gone hunting, and been alone, and had found him, and ... Lyudmila's cough brought him back to the present. Her look was one of pain and, worse, understanding. Mark was looking at him oddly as well.

All right! he thought, *I'd love to spend time with Emma, just her and me; but we're both older now, and not stupid.*

'You really think it's a risk? Me and Emma out in the forest—in these temperatures?' He grinned at the other two adults, for the moment leaving Priby out of the conversation.

'It may be a little on the chilly side, but don't think you won't be watched,' Mark said, to Lyudmila's silent agreement. 'Duke Boleslav may decide the king's forester could be replaced.'

After a pause, during which Podevin noted Lyudmila and Priby in murmured conversation, they changed the topic of their discussion to fulfilling Duke Boleslav's orders. Whatever happened, they had to turn up at Prague Castle with a load of meat—more meat than Podevin had to supply even for Christmas—or no doubt the forest home would get more, and much more unfriendly, visitors. Podevin remembered the pit. It was the easiest way, wasn't it? Both Mark and Lyudmila knew the story of how the pit had been dug to trap a deer, but, due to Podevin's interference, they'd ended up bringing home a boar.

'If we can get one boar, then it's better than none. It's not been used for a while, so I hope it won't take too long to get sorted,' he said, after Priby had been told the tale.

Podevin's screaming run down the path, being chased by a boar, and only escaping because he'd been able to jump the pit, a feat the boar could not emulate, had happened months before they had found the injured Priby abandoned in a tumble-down hut. Mark's medical knowledge, and Lyudmila's practical care, had brought the girl back to reasonable health—and, for want of anyone else to fill the role, Lyudmila and Podevin had ended up becoming her adopted parents.

The forest had not quite reclaimed the pit, but there was enough soil and debris to dig out. Then, they needed sharpened stakes— hopefully, the beast would fall onto them and it would be a clean kill. Finally, they had to cover the pit over with branches and bracken.

And hope. In the fading light, Lyudmila set out for home. Although Maria should be back by now (where *had* she been?), the boys were expected home, and their mother felt she ought to be there to meet them, even if what they brought with them was now more likely to be going to the castle, than into their own pot.

The three remaining people knew anything and everything that came along the path needed to be shot and taken up to the castle. A deer was first. It presented its flank, and Podevin put an arrow straight to its heart from his position hiding in the trees. It was the work of a couple of minutes to drag it out of sight, and the humans hid themselves away again downwind from the pit. They waited. The afternoon noises of the forest resumed.

Boars aren't so easy to kill. Which is why pits are dug. Did it sense the pit, or maybe it thought there might be a tasty morsel to eat just at the side of the path? Either way, the first boar delicately trod around the pit. It stood and stared at exactly the spot where Podevin was readying his arrow. He felt he had no choice: wasn't he under orders to bring two boars to the castle by dawn? The arrow struck and pierced the boar's throat, but failed to kill it.

'Stay there!' Podevin yelled, breaking cover, brandishing his spear.

The boar charged. The spear crunched onto bone but was borne backwards as the animal still did not collapse. Podevin slipped, rolled, grabbed at his dagger, but Mark was there with his own weapon. The boar had slowed enough for its head to be grabbed, and its throat opened. Its lifeblood gushed, and finally it sank to the ground.

'And I wonder why everyone laughs when they hear the tale of how I ran away down this very path all those years ago!' Podevin rose to his feet, groaning, and moved to retrieve his spear. However, his joke fell flat. Priby was staring at the animal with horror on her face. Mark had also frozen in place.

'She's in milk.' Mark said, his voice dull.

'She can't be,' Podevin said. 'Our sow was early, but she's been fed all winter.'

'She's in milk,' Mark repeated.

'Oh, those poor piglets!' Priby said. 'We must find them.'

Podevin thought, for all of ten seconds, about arguing the point—there was a second boar they needed to kill. But he knew the conventions of the hunt: if you could avoid it, you made sure you were not killing a mother, especially one that was feeding its babies with its own milk. Nothing sentimental about the convention: it was a way of trying to ensure there were animals big enough to hunt next year. However, the swollen nipples on this dead animal's belly gave it away. Given that baby wild boar followed their mother when she went foraging, it could be hoped these little ones were not too far away.

That they were not too far away proved to be the case, but the four little animals—obviously terrified of the humans who had just killed their mother—were not about to trot obligingly into Podevin's arms. Priby, on the other hand, merely had to crouch down, hold her hand out and make clucking sounds. Her cloak became their temporary nest.

Again, any thought of hanging on—surely, with the light fading, now was the best time for another boar to come down the path?—was obliterated by circumstances and daughterly determination. Determination backed up by Brother Mark. Priby and Mark decided the best chance for the wild piglets was to be adopted by the domesticated sow back at the forest homestead. It was also a good opportunity to take what meat they had back home, so it was not pinched by any marauding wolves.

Three people, one dead deer and one dead boar ought to be easily transported, even if Podevin had not had the foresight to bring the cart or carthorse. However, add in four squealing, wriggling piglets and the fact of Priby's bad back, and there was some thinking to do. Could Priby's cloak be tied tightly enough to prevent the baby boars escaping? Might she then be able to take one end of a sapling which had been felled and use it as a means of carrying the dead mother boar: its forelegs and hind legs being tied to the sapling for just such a purpose? In the end, with the cloak also tied to the sapling, and Mark taking the heavy (rear) end, that was what was done. Podevin had to cope with heaving the deer over his shoulders by himself—an operation he had done before, though not with an audience: so, of course, he made a hash of it. Eventually, and before a cloak-less Priby started shivering too much, they were ready.

ↄ⌒

Podevin trudged homewards. He was not really listening to Mark and Priby's conversation. He gathered Mark was concerned for Priby's back—weren't they all?—and was telling her to say if she was hurting or getting tired. Priby's mind was clearly on the little piglets, who would be hungry by now. Mark muttered something Podevin didn't catch, but they were closing on their home, with its welcome fire.

They put the meat onto the cart. It could be butchered at the castle, as there was a limit to what Podevin was prepared to do, or have done, on such short notice. When they returned, the boys' rabbits would have to go on there as well. It appeared that Maria had returned, glowing, but refusing to say where she had been, what she had done, or whom she had been with.

After a quick word of explanation for Lyudmila, Mark and Priby went into the pen and relieved the sleeping sow of her two remaining piglets. They then spent a long while rubbing domesticated piglet against wild one: tummy to tummy, back-to-back, side to side. All six juvenile animals were then returned to the sow. Podevin didn't watch; he was too busy getting himself ready to go back to the pit.

It was decided he would go alone but would come back later, whether or not he had secured another boar. As Lyudmila pointed out, there was no point in him being too tired to walk alongside the duchess while she watched the hunt.

Maybe it was his lucky night, or maybe he was being lulled into a false sense of security, but before he had gone a hundred yards, he had another deer. No, it was not a boar, but if a boar had gone into the pit, he could get that first thing tomorrow. Yes, he knew what the duke had said, and what he had written, but since when did hunts actually leave at first light? Besides, you could not hurry carthorses—and theirs would not go anywhere without breakfast.

He carried the second deer back home and explained his thinking.

'Quite right,' Mark said. 'And I'll do my best to prepare the ground. It'll either be two deer and one boar, or the other way round.'

'Or two and two, surely?' Podevin pointed at the loaded cart.

'If the duke gets his two boars, I think you lot should have the second deer for yourselves. We do not starve at the castle. You know you aren't the only person who provides meat for us?' Mark heaved himself away from the pigpen, where six piglets were feeding well. 'There you are, Lyudmila.' He grinned. 'If they stay too wild, they'll grow fast enough to make decent meat next winter. Either for you or the castle.'

Mark took his leave, saying he was sure the boys would be back soon. He picked up the stout sapling they had used to carry the boar and strode out into the fast-gathering dusk. It would not be much good against any attacking wolf, or boar, but Mark had refused any more conventional weapon. Mark would trust to God. Podevin watched him go.

Chapter 3
Podevin's Sons
Meet the Saxons!

In the silence after Mark could no longer be seen or heard making his way back to the castle, Lyudmila took one look at Priby, shivering, but still staring at the piglets, and started on her husband:

'You know Priby's back is giving her trouble, yet you let her take the heavy end—and can't even see when she needs a rest. She's practically on her knees.'

'We had to get back before dark. And Mark took the heavy end.'

'She shouldn't have had to take either end! And where are our boys?' Lyudmila, hands on hips, had gone into battle mode.

'Look!' Podevin took her tense form into his arms. 'I'm sorry. If I'd known what today was going to turn into, I wouldn't have taken Vaclav and Alexandr out in the first place. I didn't ask for Mark to come here with his news. We should have had days to get more supplies ready to go to the castle. But we don't. In just over an hour, I've managed to kill two deer and a boar. That's not too bad in my book. So, what if the boys are taking their time—they're boys! They'll be home soon.'

Lyudmila was not having it. She shook herself free. 'Don't you get all reasonable with me! You need to realise what is going on here—and it has nothing to do with your stupid idea about anyone being a knight. I'm taking Priby into the hut and giving her some valerian root for the pain she is so clearly in. And while I'm doing that, you,' a finger jabbed into his chest, 'are going out there and finding our sons. Don't come back without them. And when you do, we're having a talk about Maria—who thinks she no longer needs to play a part in this household.'

Podevin turned to see Priby still standing by the pig pen, both hands grabbing at her back and tears in her eyes. He could not even mutter an apology before Lyudmila put her arm round her adopted daughter's shoulders and guided her inside, leaving him standing there with only a dead boar and two dead deer on a cart for company.

℘

The dusk outside was turning into full darkness and Podevin could muse no longer. Vaclav pretended he didn't mind the dark, he'd stay out all night if he could; but Alexandr, at only seven, was more honest—on the other hand, he would be unafraid to state his wish to be home. They were boys, accustomed, it must be said, to finding their way among the forest tracks. Podevin, unable to change his clothes, nonetheless went to the hut for his new cloak, the one that coped with his broader shoulders. He tugged at his leggings; the rip would have to await a repair. His waist was getting broader too: Lyudmila complained about that, but as she didn't cut down how much food she cooked for him, there wasn't much he could do.

He picked up his bow and made his way to the gateway—the gateway that should have been closed and barred an hour since—and towards the forest. This time, he had not gone fifty yards when he heard a sound coming from the wrong direction. The boys were barred from going west, towards Saxony. It was Lyudmila's prohibition, but one Podevin had to agree was sensible. It ensured the lads were always well away from any possible raiding activity. Not that any Saxon 'border raids' would get this far into Bohemia. Any Saxon party coming this far into enemy territory would have to by-pass the town and castle of Budec and, depending on their route towards Prague, the similarly defended Levy Hradac. Anyone seeking to avoid both those places would have to make their own way through the forests and would be most likely to lose themselves before they found Prague.

Podevin, worrying that the Saxons had decided to violate the precarious peace, stepped back into cover and readied his bow. This was wrong. This was something blundering its way towards his home. He glanced back to his homestead, where he could see Lyudmila and the two young ladies he had raised as daughters in the open space. So much for leaving him to go and find the boys. It was too late to tell them to step back into safety and close the gate. Then his sons erupted into the clearing, running full pelt: Vaclav, his long, nine-year-old legs outpacing his brother. Even in the moonlight, Podevin could see the ashen face, the eyes wide with fear, the mouth open as he gasped the frozen air into his lungs.

'Whoa! What is going on here?' he said, causing Vaclav to stop and scream. Alexandr, coming up behind, crashed into him and they both fell.

'I don't want to die! I don't want to die!' Vaclav was moaning, repeating the refrain.

'It's your fault! You said we could get to the Saxon Road! And you shouted at them!' Alexandr, his high voice catching, started pummelling his brother, his tiny fists striking wherever they could reach.

'The Saxon Road, eh?' Podevin said, standing over them, but making no effort to intervene in the scrap. 'What did I say about the Saxon Road?'

He saw three shadows at the entrance to their homestead and waved. No need to be shooting arrows just now, but it rather looked as if there would be no rabbit stew tonight.

✧

The boys, alternately scolded and cuddled by their mother and their older sisters, were scrubbed clean and their faces dried of tears. Podevin, having done a stealthy patrol around the whole homestead and finding nothing untoward—though he promised Lyudmila he would conduct another patrol at dawn before he set off for the castle—sat and waited until they were presented before him.

'Rabbits?'

Silence. Two boys, looking and no doubt feeling very small, gazed at the ground just in front of their feet.

'Look at me.' Podevin waited until both his sons had raised their eyes to meet his: 'Did you even get as far as checking the traps? Or were you too busy doing what you had been told not to do?'

'No! We got rabbits!' Alexandr started, before his brother jabbed him in the ribs to shut him up.

'Vaclav? If you don't want your brother to tell me, it had better be you, hadn't it? I assume it was your idea?'

Vaclav gaped at him, as if he was thinking how could his father have guessed? Podevin almost laughed aloud: hadn't he known his son since the day he was born? Who was going to lead the pair into trouble? Which of his sons always, but always, leapt first and thought afterwards—if he thought at all?

'Vaclav, either you start talking, or it's bed. And I'll get the story from Alexandr.'

In fits. In starts. And with his brother chipping in, the story emerged. As they weren't hunting, they—'It was Vaclav's idea!'—decided to run all the way round the traps. Podevin conceded it was a good way to keep warm on a cold day and could have given them time to have a snowball fight, if there had been snow in any of the clearings.

'I do hope you weren't thinking of going out onto the hill in front of the castle.' There was nothing wrong with their mother's hearing, even as she sorted out supper—the meat would not be fresh rabbit, but something salted and dried from their stores. The silence that greeted her interjection was all the answer any of the four older people needed.

'So, where did you go? Did you follow my patrol route?' Not that the boys should have ever followed him, but he had to ask.

'Oh, we know where you go. We went farther down.' So much for them not knowing where he went!

'You mean towards Saxony?' Podevin asked, still doing his best to keep his voice mild.

The answer was yes, even if Vaclav did try to cover up Alexandr's mistake. Until they'd met the Saxon party, it had all been fun—an adventure. 'Mum's always saying we should go out on adventures!' The two of them used the cover of the trees and bushes to see what was going on, what Daddy was looking for.

Daddy was annoyed with himself. He was a key part of Duchess Emma's look-out system, just in case anything started happening before she was officially aware of it. Now something had happened, and Podevin had been too busy to notice.

'They were stopping—and talking—I just wanted to hear what they were saying! Alexandr's German is better than mine! But you tripped over! So they started running for you! You only had to keep quiet!' Vaclav's exasperation at his brother's clumsiness might have been understandable, but his willingness to risk his brother's neck in a foolish attempt to bring better news was less so. However, there was a question Podevin had to ask first:

'Did you hear what they were saying? Any of it?'

Alexandr nodded. 'They said they didn't see the point of their assignment. Their chances of killing the duchess were slim, and the sooner they went home, the better. Then the man on the horse shouted. I was trying to step away when I tripped, and they saw me!'

Alexandr's tears threatened again as he relived the fear of fully-grown, fully-armed men coming after him and his brother.

'You didn't have to throw the rabbits at them!' Vaclav continued.

'You didn't have to shout at them!'

'Enough!' Until that moment, Podevin had not even raised his voice, but Vaclav's stupidity was beyond endurance. He leaned towards his eldest son: 'Even if, even if! I had told you to go that way, you do not try to take on grown men by yourself. And if you insist on putting yourself in danger, you do not endanger your brother's life on your own whim!' A thought struck him. 'Are you going to tell me what happened when your brother threw the rabbits?'

Another silence. This time Podevin didn't wait: 'Alexandr?'

'They ducked! Two of them fell to the ground! Then they stopped to see what it was, and picked them up. So, we ran away. I'm sorry—I couldn't think what to do!'

'In other words,' Podevin turned his attention back to Vaclav, 'your brother gave you both time to get to your feet and run away from the danger you'd got yourself into. Yes?'

A reluctant nod.

'Right. We will talk again later. I need to know everything you can remember about these men. But for now, you'd better get up to the table.'

With all four children—though calling Maria and Priby children was hardly fair—at the table, Podevin went to assist Lyudmila.

'What are we going to do about Vaclav?' she hissed. 'He's ten next year—and full of your tales about being a knight.'

'Dear, even as a knight, he's supposed to think! Before he gets himself into trouble he can't get out of.'

He received no reply. They sat down to eat in silence.

Suppertime was rescued by Priby starting to talk about her adventures rounding up the new piglets. Sixteen-year-old Maria chipped in with a tale about having to avoid a boar while she was out; if she'd known that they now needed them, maybe she could have told them where it was. Podevin didn't believe her, and he could see Lyudmila had her doubts, but by mutual unspoken consent, they let the tale stand—for now.

After a further talk with their father, both boys promising never to do it again, they were put to bed. Once she was sure they were asleep, Lyudmila went over to where Podevin sat staring into the fire.

'You're going to have to find these people, aren't you?'

Podevin nodded. 'Just keep those lads in, will you? I don't want them following me.'

It was a change to the duke's plans for him—and he would miss that time with Emma—but his duty was clear. There were enemy soldiers on Bohemian land, and he was the nearest person who could find out what was going on and report back. Any general, any duke or king, would surely see that?

'Don't worry. We'll keep them safe.' Lyudmila nodded towards Maria and Priby, busy with their chatting in the flickering light of the fire, as it was now too dark for any chores.

Despite his thoughts of the morning, Podevin smiled. Perhaps it was because they were already older when he came into their lives, or maybe because Lyudmila didn't tell him half of what went on, but he felt it had been so much easier raising two girls. He didn't catch what Priby said, but, in the firelight, he noted Maria's blush.

'Do you know what Maria was up to today?'

'How old is she?' Lyudmila was talking in riddles.

Maria was, they both were, young ladies, he supposed. There had been talk of finding them places in Emma's entourage at the castle, but Podevin had not pushed too hard. If he was honest, he wanted to keep them both by his side for as long as possible. He heard Lyudmila sigh.

'She's old enough to be married! Why do you think she's going back and forth to the castle?'

Podevin turned and stared. 'Without my knowledge? I'm—'

'Not going to do a thing without us both talking to her first! If you can't make the arrangements, the girls will take matters into their own hands. You castle folk might expect to keep your daughters on a short leash, but those of us who work the land are more used to making our own decisions. If Maria's made her choice, I suggest you be gracious about it!'

'But …'

'But she has royal blood?' Lyudmila shook her head. 'Her mother was, and is, a peasant. A peasant who was taken against her will, by her lord.'

Podevin tried to stop his wife. He knew all this. He also knew that Lyudmila's lord had been his own half-brother, Tugumir, and their shared mother was of royal, Premyslid, descent. So Podevin and Tugumir were second cousins to the dead King Wenceslas, and the very much living King Boleslav. Lyudmila ignored his attempts to stop her speaking.

'So, what does that make Maria: a third cousin? Come on, Podevin! How many royal bastards marry well?'

'Very few.' He had to admit it.

If it was true that Maria had royal blood, she was a second cousin's illegitimate child, and it was also true the current royal family had shown no interest whatsoever in providing for her. Mark had made it clear: Emma had enough on her plate. Making Podevin's sons knights might be beyond her. So, Podevin trying to bargain for advantageous marriages for his adopted daughters would get nowhere. Perhaps

Maria sorting things out her herself was a better way—but he still wanted to know who the young man was!

'If Maria has a young man, what about Priby?'

'She's close, that one. For all she's that bit older, I haven't seen any signs of a romance. Maybe she's taking her time. Not every girl wants to flee the nest.'

'Especially one found after her own family ...' Podevin stopped.

He, Lyudmila, the long-dead Krok, and Brother Mark, had all been involved in Priby's rescue. Her biological father had been dead, her mother and brother had fled; and the injured Priby had been left behind. There were still scars on her back, and the continuing weakness, to show for it. Podevin shook his head to clear it of his thoughts. Once this immediate crisis was over, he really must sort his family out. Anyway, the girls didn't give him trouble, he didn't have to worry they would be following him tomorrow—and it was time for bed.

Chapter 4
The Saxons Come Hunting

Podevin woke with a start, knowing he'd been woken, but not knowing by what. He lay still in the darkness, listening. Something was snuffling around the fence. There was nothing unusual in that; they lived in a forest, but this was no deer, wolf or boar. This was some person, or persons. Silently, Podevin slid out of bed, shrugged out of his nightshirt, grabbed his belt, and threw his cloak over his shoulders. He blinked, forcing his eyes to get used to the darkness. His feet fumbled for his boots—no point in treading on a thorn—and he reached for his dagger, sliding it into the sheath on his belt.

'What are you doing?' Lyudmila's voice, sleepy but aware of his absence from her side.

'Shh!' He leaned back towards her so his mouth was close by her ear. Silence was imperative. Her eyes instantly open and aware, stared at him in fear.

'There's someone outside. I've got to deal with it. Leave the rest sleeping, but above all, don't make a sound.' She nodded.

His bow and arrows were waiting for him by the door. Lyudmila closed it behind him. If hostile eyes were peering through the fence, they did not need to see any shadows inside. Podevin could see a bit better in the moonlight, but still took a circuitous route to the gate.

A hunting arrow through the heart at point-blank range is, to look at it positively, a quick way to die. The man, dressed in Saxon black, was reaching over the gate to lift the leather strap Podevin used to hold the gates closed last night. All anyone had to do was unhook the strap, lift the gate up out of the depression in the ground where the post slotted in, and pull. The system was designed to protect them against unwanted animals, not humans. They were so far from the border that consideration of an attack aimed at his home, especially a surprise attack, had never crossed Podevin's mind. Even after Vaclav and Alexandr's excitement, he had not seriously considered there was anything to do until morning. All this morning was supposed to be was a scouting trip to assess what was going on. It had to be, at best, a small group of Saxons who'd lost their way, hadn't it?

From his vantage point just on the other side of the gateway, Podevin had fitted the arrow, drawn the bowstring and loosed it through a gap in the wooden slats without any thought other than stopping the attacker. There was a grunt, a pause, and the man fell back onto the frost-encrusted ground. Caution made Podevin duck out of sight behind the gate, trying to peer through into the moonlit night. Dawn must come soon, but was this man alone, or had he friends out there?

'Wolfgang? What's going on? Aren't you inside yet?' German, not Czech, but Podevin understood it well enough. It was he who had taught his sons and adopted daughters the language.

Couldn't the other man see what had happened? Inspiration struck Podevin. He called softly, muffling his voice with his cloak: 'Come here and give me a hand.' He fitted another arrow, waiting. Then, out of the corner of his eye, he saw movement. Damn! To get a clear shot, he was going to have to open the gate, move through it and fire along the fence.

'Wolfgang?' The voice was closer.

The man had come from round the corner, which explained why he hadn't seen his friend fall. Podevin made up his mind. In two seconds, he'd unhooked the gate and pushed it open. Bow at the ready, he stepped out, but maybe the other man was more suspicious than his friend as his crossbow was up and ready to fire. Podevin felt the bolt whisper past his face on its way to goodness knew where. He slipped on some ice as he ducked, dropping his bow. He couldn't see it! Podevin scrambled to his feet. The other man lowered his bow in slow motion, reached to his left shoulder and snapped the quiver before his hand went to his waist where his sword was ready. But Podevin, in the approaching dawn light, was charging, yelling, his cloak slipping from him, and his dagger in his hand. He ducked under the man's swinging sword, and thrust upwards into the unguarded throat, his charge meaning the two men collided and fell.

Silence. Apart from his breath coming in gasps, it was deathly quiet. Podevin rolled off his adversary. The man would never move again.

'And what would you have done if there had been any more of them?' His wife was behind him, and she was furious. 'You criticise Vaclav for running headlong into danger without thinking—like father, like son!' She grabbed hold of him and hauled him to his feet. 'Are you hurt? That's blood!' A cursory wipe and a lack of wincing on Podevin's part told her the truth. 'Your sons told you there was a gang—a gang! Not just a couple of men! What were you thinking?'

That word again: thinking. Podevin was, in the midst of all this, trying to do just that. It was difficult with Lyudmila's remonstrations. He did try to justify his headlong rush to kill the second man as a matter of surprise, but that only set his wife off again.

'A crossbow and a sword! And you just had a dagger?'

In vain did Podevin point out he was the one still alive. Besides, if there had been more, there would have been a reaction to the two men's deaths. There hadn't even been the sounds of anyone running away. So, the question was: where were the rest of them? Were they renegades, deserters from Otto's forces; or had they been sent by him on a specific quest—perhaps to probe Prague's defences? Had these two exceeded their orders? What was their plan? He could follow their tracks back to where they'd come from and find out. He had to. He bent down to pull his arrow from the Saxon's shoulder.

His plan was met with a flat refusal from Lyudmila.

'But we have to move quickly! If we don't find out what's going on, how do we warn the castle?' he said, desperate both to make her understand, and to get on as soon as possible.

'And leave me alone here with the children? No, thank you, Podevin. What am I supposed to do? Go and be your substitute with the duchess?'

'Go to Prague and see Mark while I go after this gang.' Podevin missed the inference that there had been orders. The one thing he was supposed to do today, was go to the castle. His wife was looking at him.

'You're going nowhere.' The fury had left her voice, but there was something else: was it humour? There was nothing funny about this and Podevin was about to explode when Lyudmila said, calmly, quietly: 'Why don't you look down at yourself. You lost your cloak in your headlong rush ...'

There was a leather belt around his waist, which he'd used to sheath his dagger. And he was wearing boots. Nothing else. Lyudmila had found time to clothe her body but, with her hair uncovered, she could hardly go to Prague as she was. Podevin shivered.

'Shall I get dressed first?' he said.

Whether it was relief, or the amusement caused by Podevin's lack of clothing, they were both grinning as they walked back to their home, hand in hand.

☙

Circumstances alter cases. Podevin could not see how the duke would insist on him going to the castle, instead of investigating the Saxon incursion—after all, he was a trained tracker, so who better to find and report back on the enemy? If he knew Emma, she would be all for charging out of the gate with her troops, heading for the last known sighting. Which in turn was why Vaclav and Alexandr would be going to the castle to give their account. (No, their father agreed, they didn't have to say they were being naughty in going that far towards the border on their hunt for rabbits ... though they might then have to explain the lack of rabbits on the cart ...) Given what the family was going to report, a hunt would be a foolish activity, no matter how much everyone might have been looking forward to it. It wasn't as if the frost had let up, so it was still unsafe to go charging around on horseback. It was not always a brilliant idea to go rushing around on foot: people could slip up as well.

The plan was finalised over breakfast. It had to be hoped the duke would understand. Instead of going to the castle, Podevin would track the rest of the party.

'Alone, Vaclav,' Podevin said as his elder son tried to object. 'I need you and Alexandr to look after the girls and get them to Duchess Emma and Brother Mark safely. Can you do that?'

Vaclav puffed his chest out and nodded, not noticing the amused glances between his sisters. Podevin and Lyudmila returned to outlining the plan. They would first visit the pit, getting as close as they could with the cart before doing the last part on foot. Lyudmila had Podevin's spear, in case whatever was in the pit was not dead. Provided they could do it safely, they would get whatever it was, out of the pit and—

'Not me!' Maria declared. 'I'm not going to the castle all muddy! I'll mind the cart.'

'Your sister has a bad back,' Podevin reminded her. 'You'll help your mother.'

Maria opened her mouth to respond, but in the face of both parents glaring at her, she closed it, though her arms were folded across her chest and her face was lowered so they did not notice the mulish expression. Podevin did, however, wonder about the best dress. Had she been wearing it yesterday? He could not remember.

After a pause, Podevin reminded his family that Brother Mark would know what to do, and he would be expecting the cart and its load of meat—even if the exact order could not be fulfilled in the given time. Yesterday, Podevin had decreed they were not sacrificing one of their only two sows to Duke Boleslav's whims. Besides, there ought to be something in the pit.

Podevin was to track and observe the gang, to see what their plan was. Vaclav and Alexandr were sure it wasn't an army, so there was no invasion. But the Saxons were up to something, or why was even a small party of soldiers so close to Prague? And how had the scouts been able to track his sons through the night?

Or had they been there all night? And just waited until the hour before dawn to attack? Podevin's blood ran cold at the thought. Or was this forest dwelling just the first one they had come across? Given that both men were dead, Podevin could not ask them—but he had the feeling it was them or him and his family.

'Did they know Duke Radslav's away and Prague's defences are minimal?' Maria, of late, did not usually contribute to family discussions, and the tone she adopted, one of I-know-something-you-don't, caused everyone to stare at her.

'Are you telling me your gentleman friend—be quiet, Podevin!—is in a position to give you that sort of information?' Lyudmila said.

'Yes! He told *me* all about it,' Maria said, looking defiant.

'And why didn't you tell us? You do realise you put us in danger.' Podevin was ready to explode.

'It was my secret! I wasn't to tell anyone! You can't tell me what to do. And, anyway, if those stupid boys had done what they'd been told to do, the Saxons wouldn't be here!' Maria stood. 'I'm going to the castle—by myself. You lot can do what you like.'

'Sit down!' Podevin thundered. 'That's enough, young lady!'

Silence reigned.

'You are all going to the castle. Together,' he said, forcing himself to speak calmly, 'Now isn't the time, but your mother and I will be having words with you, Maria, before you are very much older. Including what and when you share what you might find out.' He paused. 'For now, we have to sort out the aftermath of your brothers' little adventure, don't we?'

Perhaps that was a little unfair, especially on Alexandr, but it had the desired effect of restoring peace. However, before anything else was done, there was a grisly job for the adults: there were two bodies to dispose of. Podevin still had to get his arrow out of the first body: a wooden shaft might be easy enough to replace, but the metal barb was a different matter. However, it was not something to discuss here and now.

Podevin did not argue when Lyudmila insisted the boys—and the girls for that matter—were kept away from the results of Podevin's defence of their home. Even if the youngsters were less experienced in the art of warfare than he had been at a similar age, Podevin and Lyudmila understood the rest of the Saxon party would not hang around forever waiting for their scouts (if that's what they were) to return, so time was of the essence.

Once young stomachs were full, a quiet apprehension settled over the family. There had been no fire this morning. Alexandr was not the only one to stumble in the semi-darkness. Podevin couldn't do anything about the lack of light; the sun would rise when the sun would rise, and he hoped everyone would get warm moving through the forest.

However, Lyudmila was not about to leave her home in a state where she couldn't come back to it if this was a false alarm. All the animals were going to be fed and watered so they could survive a day or two. The fence was to be checked, and the gate barred against intruders as best they could: a couple of stakes bashed into the ground once they left would have to do. Both sides of the gate—anything to make life more difficult for an intruder.

'No, Vaclav. Mummy will reach over the gate and hammer the stakes into the ground that way. You girls, as you're taller, will have to hold each stake for her. You understand?'

The nods were mute. The seriousness of the situation had sunk in to all their minds.

'You'll tell Brother Mark everything. And apologise to the duchess that I cannot do as she commands. Yes?' Five pairs of eyes looked at Podevin offering silent consent. 'Mark will know what to do. And I will get to you as soon as I can.'

Chapter 5
A Trip to The Castle

Wolfgang's body did not want to give up Podevin's arrow. He had to use his dagger to make a hole in the corpse's padded jerkin, other clothing and chest, big enough to prise the barbed metal away. He'd done it often enough on deer and other animals. But butchering a human body was different. The job done at last, he knew he could not hand the weapon over to Lyudmila to clean. There was a stream nearby he would pass on his way. By instinct, he tested the point of the arrow. Still sharp, so it would not need filing. He could set out. Rather, he could set out once he'd hidden the body. He knew a thicket. It was far enough from their compound for any smell of decomposition not to reach their home, and, he hoped, too much of a thicket for animals to drag it out into view before ... he preferred not to think about that. If all went to plan, they would all be back soon and able to give the two men a proper burial.

Despite the cold, Podevin was sweating with the effort of removing Wolfgang's body. He trudged back home to collect his weapons. It was just getting light; individual trees and even some branches could be discerned by the naked eye—in a winter forest, greys and browns often predominated against the shiny greens of a holly or evergreen ivy. Podevin shook himself; every moment of delay was a moment wasted. As he turned to check where the two Saxons' tracks led from, Lyudmila appeared, carrying his own jerkin. She held it out to him.

'Maybe I should ask Brother Mark to get you some armour?' she said as Podevin put the jerkin on and then grabbed his cloak. She hugged him. 'Don't do anything stupid, you hear? You're on your own. You can't take them on by yourself!' He nodded, but she hadn't finished. 'We need you here, you understand?'

He nodded again, not trusting himself to speak, with his whole family there too. He gave each girl a hug,

'Don't let Maria do anything silly,' he whispered to Priby. 'Not until I get back, anyway!' Then it was the boys' turn: 'Just look after everyone, and I'll be back.'

He picked up his bow and arrows, along with the bloodied one. Hiding it from his family's view, he waved with his free hand and walked away, heading to the stream. He knew he should stop to check where the tracks came from, but his best guess would have to do until he was out of sight and he could concentrate without them looking at him. If he was out of sight, he knew Lyudmila would have an easier time corralling them all, getting all the remaining jobs done, and setting out to find Brother Mark—and Duchess Emma.

Podevin knew the direction his sons had come from. He knew what they had said about where they had been and, unless they knew the forest better than he did, the enemy would not move far once the sun had set. With the arrow cleaned, wiped dry on his cloak, and back in his quiver, he circled around until he picked up their tracks. Two men, moving slowly, often stopping, but they must have … yes! Podevin knew what they had been up to: they were tracking his sons. Their eyes must have been sharp, but even in moonlight there would have been several stops along the way. He presumed the Saxons had known, or guessed, the two boys would run to their home. But what was so urgent that they were sent out to track his sons by moonlight? If they had waited until daytime, the whole force could have moved up to attack.

☙

Old Bracken plodded down the track at his own pace. Not even Priby, walking beside him, talking encouraging nonsense, would make him speed up. Rather than divert the carthorse from the pathway to Prague, Lyudmila decided to do the rest of the journey to the pit on foot.

Vaclav, on realising where they were when Lyudmila stopped the cart, decided to drag his brother off to check nearby traps. The two of them jumped off the back of the cart and, before their mother could stop them, ran off into the scrub.

'What about the Saxons!' Lyudmila yelled.

She saw Alexandr hesitate, but Vaclav grabbed him and they disappeared. Therefore making sure they were not available to help getting any animal, if there was an animal, out of the pit.

Maria had stayed in the cart. She said nothing. Not even when Lyudmila begged, not even when she pointed out Priby had a bad back. In the end, worried about losing time, she and Priby went to the pit, carrying the spear. The pit had done its job; that is, its original job: both women looked down at the dead deer. Lyudmila found herself hoping the death had been quick. There were no signs of a struggle. Holding on to a convenient root, she clambered down to the deer. It had gone into the pit front feet first, so its chest had met the wooden stakes. Lyudmila had to get her shoulder to it, to force it off the wood. She managed to push it to the side of the pit and, with Priby hauling from above, they shoved and heaved the deer out of the pit.

It was a buck. Heavy. Neither of them was going to be able to carry it by themselves. Podevin's spear came in useful. It saved them having to find a sapling. There was a bit of an argument over who would get the pointy end, but, after Priby had pointed out they would probably have to rest at least once on the way to the cart, the two women lifted the carcass onto their shoulders and plodded their way back to Maria.

'Right. Those boys aren't back, so they can make their own way,' said Maria, as soon as Lyudmila and Priby managed to get the kill onto the cart with the rest of the meat. She even picked up the reins, ready to goad Bracken into movement.

'We wait!' Lyudmila said. 'This is not all about you, young lady.'

'But we're supposed to be there before first light. And it's well after that.' Maria duly flicked the reins, and Bracken lurched forward.

Lyudmila stumbled. She had been in the process of getting onto the cart.

'Maria—stop the cart. *Now!*' she said, hissing her words.

Maria hauled on the reins. Bracken shook his head. Priby, having had no chance to get on the cart, had to run to his head and hold on to make him hold up. Behind her, as she whispered to the confused beast, Lyudmila clambered up by Maria and jerked the reins from her hands. There was no point in saying anything, as Maria simply folded her arms and turned her back.

Silence.

'I'm going to live at the castle,' Maria said, still not looking round.

'That's what you think, my girl,' her mother replied.

It was an uncomfortable five minutes. The boys did return, holding two rabbits. At first, Vaclav was inclined to be proud of himself, but their mother's 'Perhaps you might like to explain to the duke why we were not at his castle on time? You think he will be impressed by two rabbits?' dampened all excitement.

It was a very sombre family that turned Bracken's head towards Prague Castle.

When they arrived, they were waved through the gate. Priby was walking by Bracken again. The old horse had plodded up the last slope even more slowly than normal.

'Get a move on! The duke's been wondering where you are!' the guard on the gate called out as they passed. 'Shall I give it a prod with my spear?'

'That won't be necessary,' Lyudmila replied, flicking the reins again as she directed Bracken towards the castle kitchens.

Head down, the carthorse complied with his mistress's instructions. The courtyard was not exactly full—the garrison had been depleted by the king in his rush back east to deal with the Magyars—but there were plenty of people who had to make way for the horse and cart.

Dalimil was waiting. That the king's chef was there at the kitchens was no surprise. It was the fact that the duke was there as well, which brought them all up short.

'You're late,' Duke Boleslav snapped. 'And where's Krok?'

Priby turned to look at Lyudmila, who swallowed, preparing her reply.

'If it please you, sire, my husband had to go and track some Saxons. Two of their warriors attacked our homestead before dawn.'

Lyudmila was concentrating so hard on her own story, she nearly missed the duke's response: 'Why am I surrounded by idiots? They weren't supposed—' He stopped. 'I gave clear instructions. Utter incompetence.' Another pause while people looked at each other, wondering what was going on. The duke spoke again: 'Get off that cart. I want to see what you've brought.'

The rest of Podevin's family duly dismounted, Priby remaining at Bracken's head. Maria seemed to be distracted, glancing up under her eyelashes at one of the captains, swaying from side-to-side, flaunting herself. It could not have been more obvious, but Lyudmila was attempting to explain to the duke about all the deer and the solitary boar.

To no effect.

'I ordered two boars, and for Krok to attend here at daybreak. It is past daybreak by hours.'

'But the Saxons, sire. Surely …' Lyudmila faltered to a halt.

'We saw them. They chased us! There's a whole lot of them,' Vaclav said from her side.

'And how do you know they were Saxons, boy?' Duke Boleslav leaned down towards Vaclav, who shrank back into his mother's skirts, but there was no escape. 'Hey? You have proof? What was it? An army?'

Tears starting in his eyes, Vaclav shook his head. Another pause. The duke straightened.

'So, what we have here, is a disobedient forester who cannot fulfil a simple order, and sends his women and little boys to explain his wilful treachery!'

There were gasps at that, not only from Podevin's family. The king's forester might have not fulfilled his orders to the letter, but calling it treachery shocked the duke's listeners.

Bracken whinnied, so Priby stroked his nose, trying to keep him calm.

'As immediate punishment—and to make up for the lack of sufficient meat—You! Kill that horse.' Boleslav pointed at his captain, the one Maria was flirting with.

Priby moved to block the man's approach.

Dalimil spoke up: 'My lord. The meat will be tough.'

'Then give it to the servants!' Boleslav said. 'Get on with it!'

The captain moved and, as Priby did not move in her turn, a gauntleted hand smashed across her face, making her fall. Bracken reared, but it was no good. The captain's troops rushed in with spears. Lyudmila held her sons close so they did not see what was going on. But they could not help hearing Bracken's dying scream. From her position on the ground, blood pouring from her nose and mouth, Priby saw the grin as the captain's sword made it into the carthorse's throat. Spears were pulled from Bracken's chest and side with a squelch.

'Well?' The captain turned, not to the duke—who, despite having ordered and watched the killing, now presented his back to the spectacle—but to Maria: 'Not going soft on me, are you?'

Maria took her hands from her ears, straightened up, glanced at the newly dead horse which had thudded to the ground, and then at Priby.

'Of course not,' she said. 'She's only a peasant girl. And the horse was useless anyway.'

'Get up,' the captain said to Priby. 'That was just a tap.'

'All right.' There was a new voice by her side. Dalimil was crouching down, helping her to her feet.

'And chop that cart up for firewood. If they've no horse, they don't need a cart.' The duke had not finished. 'Captain, get your troops ready for the hunt.'

'So, we are still going on a hunt, are we? Despite knowing about a Saxon incursion?' Emma had arrived.

'It's nothing to do with you.'

'I'm castle constable. What goes on here, especially within the castle walls, concerns me.' Emma noticed Priby. 'Who did this? This cannot have been necessary.'

'I did. I was carrying out the duke's orders. That peasant tried to stop me.' The captain made no move to defer to Duchess Emma. 'If I was wrong, show me my fault.'

With Boleslav standing there, also defiant, Emma paused.

'I see. Dalimil, take Priby to Brother Mark. He and my ladies will care for her. You, captain, tell me, are you part of Duke Boleslav's retinue, or part of my castle garrison? Think carefully on your answer.'

'Your garrison, madam.' The reply was smooth. 'However, the duke always outranks his wife. And I had no indication that you would think differently—madam.' The captain stood, confident.

The duke tittered, pleased by events. Priby, with Dalimil's arm about her, looked on.

'And how many carthorses have I killed—or had killed? How many peasant families have I deprived of their living on a petulant whim?' On these last words, Emma turned to face her husband. 'This was, as I said, unnecessary. This family now needs a new horse. And a cart, if what I heard as I arrived here is true. Does my lord have spares? Or would he prefer the whole of this castle to starve because it can no longer be supplied with meat from the forest? It's a long time before the next harvest.' Emma's voice had grown stronger as she made her speech. By the end of it, no-one in the surrounding area could fail to hear.

Duke Boleslav opened and closed his mouth. The captain, still standing by the dead horse, looked more isolated as his willing helpers shuffled backwards, less sure of themselves.

Emma looked around. She took in the frightened faces of Vaclav and Alexandr. Lyudmila bowed her head as the duchess's gaze passed over her. The troops were still. The duke had started chewing the side of his thumb, not saying a word.

'Captain, you are aware of the call for reinforcements to go east. Were you and your troop selected to go?' Emma asked.

The captain shook his head.

'You are now. Or does my husband wish to disobey his father's order?'

Duke Boleslav shrugged. It appeared he wasn't bothered. If the captain was able to hide his reaction to the news, several of the soldiers ranged behind him gaped. Their reaction was ignored.

'And, by the way, captain. Until you depart, this family are to be treated as my guests. Which means, captain, you defer to them, not the other way round.'

'I—I am to defer to women? Peasant women? And children?' The captain was clearly appalled.

'As a married man, I would expect you to be used to that.' Emma smiled. Her own husband scowled at her inference.

As Priby was led away to see Mark, she watched Maria's face register open-mouthed disbelief, which descended into anger as she screeched, 'You said I was the first!'

'The first one who claimed to be royal, you bitch! But you're just like the rest. A peasant only too eager to get her clothes off!'

'I'm not a peasant!' Maria replied, but under her breath, as Priby was led by her.

The two girls shared a glance, and it was Maria who turned away. Emma had ignored the disruption. She turned to Vaclav and Alexandr and crouched down to their level.

'You saw Saxons, yes?' Emma asked the boys. At their nod, she grimaced. 'How many? As many as them?' She pointed at the captain's troop, who were making their way back to their quarters, presumably to pack.

'About,' came the response, 'but we might not have seen them all.'

'They were supposed to be hiding. They had their orders,' Boleslav muttered, but then froze. Horror was written all over his face as Emma's head snapped round to look at him.

'You *arranged* for a Saxon incursion?' She stood and took two steps towards him as she tried to work it out. 'And you wanted me to go hunting, but to be alone with—' Emma caught herself, as she had been about to spill Podevin's name.

Her husband smirked.

'You'll be fine. It's a tale made up by two little boys, who got lost in the forest and were afraid they were going to be told off by Mummy and Daddy. That's it, isn't it?' The duke again leaned towards Vaclav and Alexandr, who shrank back. Duke Boleslav straightened and looked at his wife. 'I thought you were going hunting?'

Emma rose to her full height.

'Oh, yes. We're going hunting. But we're pausing long enough for me to get changed. We're hunting Saxons.'

Emma all but drove Lyudmila, Vaclav and Alexandr before her to her quarters, where she called for her armour and explained their presence, and their need for a new cart—and carthorse. Maria had disappeared. Perhaps she had followed Priby to see if she could comfort her adopted sister? Emma did not have time to worry about the girl now—whatever she might have done. She had to get her forces out into the forest to deal with an unknown number of Saxons. An incursion she had not known about, but her husband had. That was another conversation for later. She did not even want to think what the king would make of all this.

Flinging herself out of her rooms, she descended to the court-yard, where her bodyguard was already assembled in full battle array. Geraint and Mikael between them had arranged everything—though, truth be told, apart from a sudden preponderance of battle-axes, there was not much difference between preparations for a hunt and for warfare. Emma's palfrey had been changed for her destrier, who shook his mane. Even the warhorses had caught the mood. Duke Boleslav, she noted, had disappeared.

Chapter 6
Hunting the Saxons

What would Podevin have done in the Saxons' position? He had spent a decade in the forest, but he could still remember his early military training when he was page and bodyguard to King Wenceslas. If he was leading a small force in hostile territory, which had been discovered by two small boys who had run away home, how would he have reacted? Assuming the assignment could not be abandoned—the force was too small to attack Prague Castle, so it must be some sort of information-gathering exercise—he would want to find, and, yes, eliminate, those boys. Though sending soldiers after them so they ran, helter-skelter, for cover was probably not the best approach. A pretend hail-fellow-well-met and we-have-some-hot-food-here might have achieved better results. But these were soldiers, weren't they? And, Podevin suspected, they weren't all scouts. Which probably meant the main force, such as it was, would wait where it was until the scouts returned. Which meant a camp. Which, in turn, by this time, well past daybreak, would mean noise. The bigger the force, the more noise—they would assume they could deal with any peasant out early enough to blunder across their camp. But would they assume there was someone tracking them down, someone who understood their chatter, and moreover, someone who was not at all happy to know they had tried to kill his sons?

He was already farther down the road to Saxony than he had been for a long time. He could see the smoke from a camp fire rising in what must be a clearing on the other side of the road, but he was not yet near enough to hear what was being said. If it was the Saxons, had they posted a guard on the road? Podevin wasted half an hour disappearing into the forest to emerge at different points so he could check all the likely places where he would have posted a guard, before he dashed across and ducked into the brushwood on the other side.

'Where are those two dunderheads? Boy! Why isn't my horse ready!'

Burly and scarred, the old soldier, heavy with chain mail, sat on a log beside the fire. He was chewing on a meaty bone, ignoring the bits of food sticking to his grey beard. The frown, and the relaxed way he sat there while everyone else was standing, showed he was used to command, but, Podevin reckoned, he was not used to operating in enemy territory. That the fire was in the middle of the clearing was evidence of that. As was the fact they had set up camp, in a clearing, without a guard—or how had Podevin got so close? He counted eight. A patrol, no more. Also, for all his waiting, there was no suggestion this group of Saxons was part of any bigger force.

The boy, a lad no bigger than Alexandr, was struggling with the warhorse's saddle. Podevin watched as he finally shoved the thing over the horse's back. None of the others moved to help him, though they were all looking in the boy's direction. The horse, its reins attached to the branch of a tree, shook itself as the weight of the saddle descended on its back. Only a frantic grab by the boy prevented it from sliding off.

'Useless!' the old soldier said.

He jerked his thumb at one of the other soldiers, indicating he should help the boy. The slow way the soldier stood up told Podevin this wasn't the first time. Nor was the blow the soldier gave the lad as he passed him. The boy didn't move out of the way, even though he must have known what was coming. There must have been tears in his eyes, and Podevin could see blood from a split lip, but the boy made no effort to raise a hand to his face. The captain—if that was what he was—watched impassively.

'My lord took you on as a favour to your father,' he said. 'By now, you should be a competent squire, not a waste of space! We're moving out!'

'But, sir, you said we'd wait for Wolfgang and Bernard.' It was the soldier by the horse's head who spoke. He had detached the reins from the branch, and had been calming the animal. His crossbow rested by the tree trunk.

'And what do you know?' The captain heaved himself to his feet. From his hiding place, Podevin saw nervous glances between some of the other soldiers. However, the captain was ready to be gone, with or without his two dunderheads. 'Get everything ready! We're meant to do this quickly! We're to find this Anglo-Saxon whore—she goes hunting often enough—and get her back to Duke Heinrich.'

'Though God knows what Otto will do with her—when he gets her from Heinrich—he prefers them compliant!' The soldier by the tree hadn't bothered lowering his voice, but all he got was a glare and:

'You watch it. Remember where your loyalty lies.'

With King Otto of the Saxons, Podevin wondered, or this Duke Heinrich?

Further conversation was halted as everyone, including Podevin, heard a sound, an unnatural rustling from something too big to be a boar. Without thinking, Podevin fitted an arrow into his bow and tensed. Now what?

Even as that thought flitted through his brain, a man emerged from behind the camp. He had a bill-hook raised above his head, running at the nearest soldier, who reacted too slowly and went down as the scythe slashed into his neck. In seconds, the camp descended into chaos as screams and shouts filled the air. Podevin had time to sight his arrow and send it into the back of a second soldier—the one who was now nearest to the intruder. It was instinctive. The man, the countryman, the farm worker, whatever he was, was yelling. He was yelling in Czech.

'You bastards! You killed my family! My children! My wife! Butchered by you!'

But what chance did one peasant have against the six remaining, trained, armed soldiers? The boy was the only one not moving; he was holding the horse's reins—his helper had tossed them to him as he grabbed his crossbow. This soldier was bright. Unlike the rest of them, including the captain, he was not heading for the visible threat, but was glaring straight at Podevin. Podevin had no choice. His second arrow pierced the man's throat. Then it was his turn to yell and break cover. The peasant was surrounded. If nothing else, Podevin needed to distract the enemy. The third arrow went wide. Shooting while running wasn't a good idea under any circumstances. Podevin stopped and knelt, so his fourth arrow found its target.

It was too late. All that was left was a bloody mess on the ground of what had once been a man. Now Podevin was exposed and running out of arrows. On the other hand, the four soldiers were also exposed. One. Two. The third foot soldier dropped to the ground. Sensible of him, but his armour-clad captain was contemptuous. And there was the boy, of course, but he was holding the horse, a dead man at his feet, just watching.

'All right, you Bohemian scum! Are you going to fight? Come on!' The captain was standing, swinging his battle axe back and forth. As if it was a toy.

Podevin only had a sword. Unless he could distract the man, or run. If he ran, which was the obvious way to stay alive, he would have to go back not knowing what was going on. Besides, the Saxon captain had a horse. A horse, any horse, can outrun a man. Even in a forest. And there was a man on the ground who was not dead, so he could reach for his weapons. Running was not an option. Podevin stood, carefully rubbing his left hand along the ground before closing his fist.

The soldier on the ground was staying there. He was not even looking in Podevin's direction. The captain was the dangerous one. Sword against battle-axe. A jerkin-clad peasant against an armoured knight. A forester against an experienced, battle-hardened warrior. Not much to choose between, really. Would the boy, still frozen to the spot holding the horse's reins, have bet against his master winning the fight? But peasants don't know how to fight fair. They move lightly on their feet as warriors flail with their axes. They move close, only to dart away again, out of danger. And then, at the right moment, they fling dirt into a warrior's eyes so he cannot see the sword coming for him. Except Podevin's sword did not need to draw any blood.

The captain sank to his knees and keeled over, a crossbow bolt in his back. Only then did Podevin realise the chain mail stopped just below the captain's shoulders. The boy, his feet on a log to give him the height he needed, and his face a terrified mask, peered at Podevin over the back of the horse, the weight of the crossbow on its back. Why the animal, even if it was a trained warhorse, had stayed still, Podevin did not ask. Nor did he ask why the boy had chosen to shoot his own captain—unless he had been aiming at Podevin and missed? Both fighters had been in the boy's line of sight. He dragged the crossbow off the horse's back and dropped it to the ground as if it had become too heavy for him. Then the boy half-stepped, half-fell from his log, and retched.

For the moment, Podevin left the boy alone. Including the captain, there were seven dead Saxons. He approached the eighth, the one still lying on the ground. The man's bloody sword had been flung into the undergrowth. Still no movement. Podevin prodded the man with his own borrowed, but as yet unbloodied, sword.

'If you want to live, start talking,' he said in German.

Nothing. Podevin shrugged, raised the sword above his head, ready to bring it down.

'No!' The man rolled over, reaching for his dagger.

It was his last move. There was only the boy left. A boy who was still standing by the horse, having recollected the reins. A boy who had tears streaming down his face, vomit on his chin and who had soiled himself.

Podevin surveyed the carnage around him. He was, after all his years of hunting in the forest, a good shot. Which was fortunate for him. What Lyudmila would say, after what she had told him this morning, was another question. He looked up at the boy and spoke in German.

'I'll not harm you. Do you know why you came here—into Bohemia?'

The boy started gabbling. Podevin caught the names 'Matilda' and 'Emma.' He tried not to react as the boy babbled on about the Saxon troop stealing to make themselves richer. The boy dropped the reins and reached for a bag; he began searching in it. The contents flew here and there as the boy tried to find what he was looking for. In a few strides, Podevin reached the boy's side.

'You're all right. What are we looking for?'

'Orders. We had our orders.' The boy started on a different bag.

Gently, Podevin stopped him. He pointed into the forest. 'There is a stream over there. It'll be cold, but go and get yourself cleaned up. Take some spare clothes with you. I'll look for the orders.'

He watched the boy—he must try to get a name from him—hesitate his way into the trees and bushes. Even a castle-raised child would hear the gurgling stream soon enough. That is, if he hadn't had to go back and forth collecting water for all the rest of the troop; in which case, he'd know exactly where the nearest stream was. Podevin settled down to a systematic search for these orders, and some decent wood to build up the fire.

☙

The boy took his time, but he did reappear. His new leggings were a touch too large for him, but they were clean. Podevin beckoned the lad over but, before he spoke, he took a surreptitious sniff; the boy had washed thoroughly.

'Why don't you stand there? Where you can warm up.'

'Why are you being nice to me?'

'I don't kill people when I don't have to.' He'd spoken gruffly. He already had qualms about that last death. For all his brain argued he'd had no alternative, another part of him wondered what Brother Mark would make of him killing a man already on the ground. He shook himself. 'You don't seem upset by what's happened here.'

'It's war. People die in war,' the boy replied with a shrug.

'Did your captain say that?'

'You mean Count Johan? Yeah.'

Podevin nodded. He had to think things through. He was also aware he was risking getting cold. He had sweated under his clothes during the fight. His knee was damp, as was the front of his jerkin, where he'd been in contact with the frosty ground. What was he to do with the boy? In theory, to hide what he had done, he should kill him. But he'd already said he wouldn't do that, and the boy seemed to trust him.

'What's your name?'

'Jan. What's yours?'

The hesitation was minimal. 'Krok,' said Podevin.

He'd made his decision; Jan was going home. The only alternative was captivity in Prague Castle—and, whatever promises Emma might make, a Saxon captive would not be treated well there. Especially one who hadn't the sense to stand up for himself. Or the means.

'Haven't you any family? They talked about your father.'

'He's dead. I was supposed to take his place.'

'No-one else?'

The child was beginning to sound like a Saxon version of himself, already motherless when his own father was killed fighting for King Wenceslas over twenty years ago.

'I have an aunt. But she's a farmer's wife,' Jan said.

Podevin sat back on his haunches. So far, both of them had been crouched down, hands towards the flames. Over the years, Podevin had discovered, unlike the girls, it was so much easier to talk side by side with his sons. If they didn't have to face you, they found it easier to talk about the stuff they found difficult. Unless, of course, he needed to face them to make sure they were telling him the truth.

'Why is that a problem?' Podevin asked.

'I'm supposed to be trained as a warrior.'

'But you're not, are you? You were more worried about the horse than joining the fight.'

Podevin watched as Jan wrestled with his thoughts.

'Had that man been a fighter, and not a farmer, he would not have attacked your friends the way he did,' Podevin said into the hush.

A breeze filtered its way to the camp, fanning the flames, which rose and fell again. Jan looked at his Bohemian captor.

'But you're not dressed like a warrior.'

'No, I'm not. But I did the training. And I've had to kill before.' That was true enough, even if it had been a long time ago. 'But you, Jan, have to get back home. I'd take the horse, if I were you.' It still stood where it had been left, with its saddle fitted.

'But it's Count Johan's horse!'

'He won't be needing it again. You ride for your aunt's house. Your uncle will need all the help you can give him, even in winter, won't he?'

'He treats me better than this lot ever did. My aunt even likes me.' A smile almost flickered across Jan's face.

'Do it. I have the orders you brought, so Otto will find out soon enough what happened—his little kidnap party failed and was annihilated.' Podevin stumbled over the last word. 'You were all killed. No-one will be looking for you.'

'Can I take some of the food?'

'Of course.' Podevin was surprised by the question.

Jan was so clearly not used to thinking for himself. He could see why the boy was condemned as useless, but he could only hope, surrounded by his family, he could learn to be a farmer.

❧

Jan left. Although he looked tiny on the war-horse's back, the animal accepted his gentle guiding and trotted away. Podevin had told the lad to take the horse off the road if he came across anyone—anyone— along the way. A Bohemian border patrol would take him captive at best, and a Saxon one? Podevin did not like to guess what they'd do to one who had run away from his master. Even if that master was dead. Throughout their conversation, neither of them mentioned who had actually done that particular deed.

Podevin sighed. He had a job to do. Several bodies to hide from the road. A message to take to Prague. And his own family to placate— especially his wife.

Although Jan had taken plenty of supplies with him in the saddle-bags—he might as well appear at his aunt's farm well provisioned— there was much to tidy up and carry away. Before that, however, Podevin realised he, too, was hungry. Surrounded by bodies, he ate Saxon supplies until his stomach stretched against the waistband of his leggings. Then, it was back to work. Podevin spent a good half an hour simply hiding provisions by securing them to bare branches, keeping them away from roving animals (he could come back later and take them home). There was a convenient tree—probably uprooted by one of the recent winter storms—to bury the Bohemian farmer who'd been hacked to death, but that was the only burial Podevin bothered with. There were parchments to carry safely to a new destination. By the time all had been sorted to Podevin's satis-faction, it had started snowing again.

It was as the afternoon light was starting to fade that he heard it. They were approaching from the west. He clambered up a tree. Partly to hide, partly to have a look. There was no stealth from those approaching. It was stop and start, and start and stop. Was it Saxon reinforcements? Come to find their renegade troops? Or were they just reinforcements? Podevin did not know. All he knew was they were approaching fast.

They charged into the clearing. A whole vast troop of them, a mixture of armour and weapons and nationalities. The leading horse-woman pulled her horse up short. It reared, but she held her seat and calmed the horse. Podevin dropped lightly to the ground. The horse-woman flung her reins to the nearest warrior, who had come up by her side, and dismounted in a flurry of excitement.

'Podevin! You're safe!'

Podevin froze, as did Geraint. There was nothing to be done as Emma approached him, arms wide. Being hugged by someone wearing chain mail and a sword belt—complete with sword and dagger—when all you are wearing as armour is a padded jerkin—is not as pleasurable as might be supposed. In fact, when the hugger squeezes tight, it can be downright painful.

'Madam. Please! I was uninjured, but now I am not so sure,' Podevin said, trying to strike a light tone. She released him.

'Lyudmila will be pleased—when she hears,' Emma said. 'But what happened here?'

As the troops dispersed, checking for any signs of life, Podevin told his tale. For Emma's ears only, he told her how their captain had died.

'The lad won't run to King Otto?' she asked.

Podevin shook his head. 'He's had enough of the Saxon court, of being a fighter. Besides, what would they do? Probably kill him for not dying on the field of battle.'

'You're happy for him to go? He could have been aiming for you.'

'If he was, he missed. And I'm grateful for that.'

At that point, Geraint came up. 'Madam, I fear you made a mistake. They're all talking about it. You called him,' he jerked his thumb in Podevin's direction, 'by his real name.'

He paused to let the implications sink in. Podevin was dead and buried under a woodland chapel. Podevin had been Wenceslas's page and bodyguard. The Good King Wenceslas, who had been assassinated by his brother ten years ago, and whose page and bodyguard had been trapped and hung in these very forests after this Podevin had killed one of the knights who had assisted in Wenceslas's assassination. The (new) king's forester was a man called Krok. If the men had never seen Podevin close up, they knew the man who had gone tracking the Saxons was the king's forester, and they knew this man had frequently been seen at Prague Castle, delivering supplies from the forest: whether those supplies were wood for the fires or meat for the kitchens.

Emma stared at Podevin, her mouth a perfect O and there were tears standing in her eyes as the implications sank in.

'It was bound to happen, madam,' said Podevin, trying to shrug off the disaster. 'And it was good to know you were worried. When this all started, if you had told me we would keep up the pretence for ten years, I would have taken that. Saxony, I suppose?'

Some of it was bravado, but Podevin was surprised at how calm he felt. Sooner or later, the past would catch up with a person. He had survived facing a whole gang of warriors, but he could not survive having his name known. Because someone, sooner rather than later, would talk. It would not matter how, or when. Emma's greeting to Podevin would be reported back to her husband. A husband who was already suspicious.

Emma's face had gone white. She looked around. 'Some have left?' She put it as a question to Geraint, but she already knew the answer.

'I could hardly send Mikael after them to kill them, could I? We need all the troops we've got. This could still be an advance force.'

'I think, if you read these—they look very much like orders to me.' Podevin handed over the parchments he had found.

'Yes.' Emma handed them straight to Geraint. 'But the priority now is to get back to Prague. As quick as we can. Anything to prevent—' She stopped whatever it was she was going to say.

Podevin could guess. Anything to prevent her husband deciding his suspicions were confirmed. Anything to prevent the duke sending someone to kill Podevin. Whatever happened now, he did not need telling he could not go to Prague Castle himself.

Emma put her foot into the stirrup. She looked back at Podevin.

'I'm sorry. Truly sorry.'

She mounted up and, without a backwards glance, led her troops out of the clearing, leaving Podevin on his own. By the time the noise receded into the distance, they were cantering down the Saxon road, heading for Prague—and the potential for more trouble.

Chapter 7
A Jealous Husband?

'Well, my dear. Did you track down these Saxons? And did you find your forester—this peasant you seem so concerned about?'

Duke Boleslav was standing in the open gateway, impeding Emma's entry. Hands on hips so his cloak flared out either side of him, he looked up at her, his head slightly to one side as if he was appraising an underdone side of beef. She had become bored with his games a long time ago. Fortunately, the king had also despaired and given her, and her alone, the jurisdiction of Prague—though quite what King Boleslav was playing at in leaving his son here for so long was, at present, beyond her. More to the point, she needed to dismount and converse with him.

She took her time and, of course, when she dismounted, she placed the horse between them. He sighed. He shifted his weight from one foot to the other. But she still did not hurry. She gathered the reins and stood at her horse's head. It was as if she was addressing the dumb animal rather than her husband.

'Yes, my lord, we found the Saxons, didn't we?' She stroked her horse's nose. It blew out a snort, telling her that, like all the animals, it wanted its stable, its feed and some water. The humans were hungry too, and the duke's behaviour was not helping.

'So, you found them. How—er—how many?'

'We found eight bodies—that's right, Geraint?'

'Yes, madam. Eight. All dead.'

'Eight! That's all? There should have been more.' Once again, Duke Boleslav had spoken before he thought and, once again, his face registered stupefaction.

'Perhaps, my lord and husband,' Emma said, starting forward and leading her horse, who was only too anxious to get to his stable, 'you might like to explain how you know so much about this incursion and the size of it?'

She passed him by, keeping her mount between them. The others followed. The duke had to step aside as they came through the gate. With so many horses not being too careful where they put their feet, it was inevitable the duke was splashed with mud. Emma heard his 'ughs' and 'yucks', but did nothing about it. She handed her horse over to a groom and prepared to go to her apartments.

'Where are you going?' The duke was running, actually running, towards her.

'To change,' Emma said.

'No, you're not. At least not until I have all the orders.'

'What orders?' She stopped and faced him. How much did he really know about all this, and what was going on? She realised she was in no way going to give him those orders until she had seen them. Out of the corner of her eye, she could see Mark and Geraint in conversation. Those two would be waiting for her.

'The orders the Saxons had. What were their orders?' The duke was going puce with rage. He even stamped a muddy foot.

'I don't have any orders,' she said. Which was the truth, in its own way—though Brother Mark might disagree.

Silence. How far would her husband push it? He must have been on tenterhooks all day, wondering what she had found out. So far, she had discovered nothing, as she hadn't read what Podevin had found. Podevin! She remembered and froze; she looked down and forced herself to breathe deeply. She realised Duke Boleslav had not mentioned Podevin. Her brain started working again.

'Maybe, husband,' she said, 'those Saxons had merely been told what to do? A secret mission with nothing written down. Now, if you'll excuse me.'

She made to carry on towards her rooms, but Duke Boleslav grabbed her by the arm. She saw his fingers tighten. As if he could inflict physical pain through her chain mail. She merely glared at him.

'You went into that forest because of your lover. You're no lady, if you prefer a peasant to me. No.' He continued over her half-formed objection, 'And if you say he's no peasant, I will have to conclude the rumours are true. Saint Podevin does not lie under the chapel, but lives—and my own wife prefers a traitor to her husband.'

He released his grip on her arm.

'Think about it,' he said. 'Remember, I've worked it all out.'

'Oh, as if I haven't thought about anything else,' Emma said, furious not least because her husband had decided to have this row in the courtyard, with everyone standing around, watching and listening. 'Shall I remind you I fought a duel against your champion when these rumours were put about? Put about by you yourself—something you had to admit to your father, if you recall. Yes, I have dealt with the forester, like I deal with all the people who supply this castle and its people with food, clothing and everything else. And is that so surprising when I am castle constable and that is my responsibility? I have not been with child these past years because you, my lord, have not seen fit to visit me—not even when your father, the king, orders you to stay here.' She allowed a pause to build, one which Duke Boleslav did not seem willing to fill. 'Have we finished this conversation?' she asked.

Not waiting for a reply, she resumed her interrupted walk to her own chamber, where her ladies awaited, and where Mark and Geraint—and possibly Mikael—would join her.

She was at the steps when he called, 'Duchess Emma.'

She stopped, waited, but, as there was nothing else, she continued.

'I have something you might be interested in.' His words brought her to a halt again. 'From your brother, or half-brother, I can't keep track of your Anglo-Saxon royals. About your dead sister.'

'My sister's dead? Which one?'

'Didn't you know? King Otto of the Saxons is in need of a new wife.'

'Matilda? Matilda's dead?' She was back across the courtyard, hand outstretched for the parchment Duke Boleslav was holding, but he held it out of her reach. She could have grabbed it, but that would have involved an unseemly tussle. All she could do was wait.

'Are you quite sure those Saxons had nothing in writing?'

Wordlessly, Geraint marched over to the duke and duchess, and handed over some parchments to Emma. She glared at him, but he appeared unmoved. Behind the duke, she could see Mark gesturing.

'Ah! So, you did find something after all. Shall we swap?' Boleslav said in his sweetest tone.

With a sigh, Emma held out the parchments to her husband, who grabbed them. She did not let go.

'I believe you said "swap", husband?' Emma could do sweetness as well.

Only when she could hold on to the missive from England, did she release her hold of the Saxon documents. Duke Boleslav scuttled away towards the scriptorium—surely it would be full of clerks?—but Emma was beyond puzzlement at her husband's antics. She looked around.

'Has nobody any work to do?' she said as blank faces avoided her eyes.

Warriors who needed to tend to horses and then themselves. Kitchen staff who needed to prepare meals. She even saw some of those very clerks from the scriptorium huddling in a corner before dashing back to their shadows and parchments. The only people who did not move were Brother Mark, Geraint, and her ladies, who had gathered outside her chambers—though what good they could have done, had the altercation with the duke turned out badly, Emma did not know.

When she was satisfied the castle was returning to normal late afternoon busy-ness, and she could see the gates being closed and barred for the night, Emma resumed her walk to her quarters.

❦

She had forgotten. She had left orders that Podevin's family should be regarded as her guests while she was away. Somehow, because she knew there were no more Saxons trolling through the forest, Emma had assumed Lyudmila would have taken her children and gone back to their forest home. As it was, she found her chambers very crowded. Beatrice and Hilde were doing their best to entertain Vaclav and Alexandr. Lyudmila and Priby—who had some sort of poultice or plaster across her face—were sitting, doing nothing apart from staring out of a window into the gathering darkness. Maria was standing by herself by the fire. And two other ladies-in-waiting, whose names Emma had not bothered to learn as they had been imposed on her by her husband, were keeping themselves busy by wandering round checking on everyone's conversations—no doubt ready to report anything scurrilous to their master.

The first troops back must have reported to Duke Boleslav, mustn't they? Yes, they had, according to Mark; they had said all was safe and the Saxons were dead. However, the duke had not seen fit to pass on the message. Mark could have done so himself, but the duke had decided that, if Emma wanted that peasant family to have a horse and cart provided for them, she would be the one to decide whether the horse and cart chosen were acceptable. With Emma unavailable, Mark had decided it was better if the family was kept out of the duke's way.

'Yes, all right, Mark. I mean, you were right. But now that means they have to stay the night. You—and you!' She pointed at the two new ladies-in-waiting. 'Go and find some accommodation for them. *Suitable* accommodation for my guests,' she added, as the girls showed hesitation.

Mark smiled. Emma had made sure she was surrounded by Anglo-Saxons, or Bohemians loyal to her. As the ladies-in-waiting left, they passed someone on their way in. Emma tensed, but it was Mikael.

'My lady,' he said, sketching a bow and having taken account of who was in the room (and who wasn't), 'may I remind you? It is as we feared. The duke is aware that you embraced—'

'Podevin,' sighed Emma.

Mikael half-smiled in a gesture of appeasement. 'Podevin, and called him by that name.'

'And is no doubt putting the worst possible construction on it.'

'What construction should *I* put on it, my lady?' Lyudmila's voice was quiet, but Emma realised she deserved an answer.

She also realised everyone was standing—and had been ever since she had come into the room. She was still in her armour.

'I need to change,' she said—she also needed time to think how to frame her words to the wife of the man she loved. 'And we need food. Gentlemen, you can retire and sort that out, if you will. Beatrice and Hilde …'

Her Anglo-Saxon ladies knew the drill. The men left, taking Vaclav and Alexandr with them. Maria had barely moved, but Emma had not the time, nor the patience, to deal with Podevin's family's squabbles just now.

♥

'Why don't we all sit down? No, Lyudmila, you sit next to me.' Emma, clad now in a more comfortable dress, her hair tamed and covered, every inch the princess she was born to be, patted the seat next to her.

There was a pause. Emma waited while everyone sat. She knew she didn't have long. If Mark and Geraint (never mind two hungry boys) turned up at the kitchens saying the Duchess Emma wanted food, Dalimil would make sure food was provided, and quickly. But what Emma wanted to say, the fewer people heard it, the better.

'Your husband, Lyudmila, is safe at home. The duke will not do anything tonight—he won't do anything that puts himself at any personal risk, nor will he do anything without his father's express permission.' Emma paused. That had been the easy part. She swallowed. 'You will know I was fond of Podevin. We were thrown together by King Wenceslas while I waited for the duke to grow up so we could be wed. Of course, in another life, Podevin and I may well have wed—we're of an age—and raised many little dukes to come after us … why are you smiling, Lyudmila?'

'I am sorry, madam, but if I didn't know better, I would say you were there years ago when Podevin said much the same thing about "another life" to me. That was just after Krok had died, and your chaplain, Mark, had decreed Podevin was to step into Krok's place—in all aspects of his life—and, well, I knew I was, at best, his second choice.' Lyudmila stopped.

Priby had come close and was curling herself at Lyudmila's feet. The two women clasped hands and smiled at each other before Lyudmila continued.

'If you had told me, when I fled Budec after Tugumir took me on the eve of my wedding, that I would end up married into King Wenceslas's family, even if he was only a second cousin, and I would have had ten happy years with that man, I would have taken it and been thankful. But it's come to an end, hasn't it?'

Emma nodded and looked down. Ended by her own stupidity. It was no good thinking some sort of ending would have happened sooner or later. There was to be no resumption of the conversation. The door opened, and Lyudmila was distracted by her two excited sons telling tales of the 'absolutely enormous' kitchens and the 'piles and piles' of food being brought up for them all to eat.

Everyone, apart from Maria, and Mark, who had chosen to absent himself, tucked in with relish.

Chapter 8
The Return to the Forest

Staying away from all the main paths, Podevin trudged his way back home in the fading light. It was turning cold again. He found himself hoping Emma had arrived back at the castle safely, and none of the horses had slipped on a pocket of ice or a frozen puddle in the road.

If it hadn't been for Emma's husband demanding meat from him, and this unexplained Saxon incursion, he would not have removed his family to the safety of the castle. Had they been home, they could have left overnight and taken the path to Saxony. Could they, would they, find Blanik—Prague's castle constable under Wenceslas who now fought for the Saxon king? Either way, alone, he was not going to risk being out in the darkness. Never mind the wolves and the boars, the endless war meant a wanderer could not be sure the next hollow tree, the next bend in the track, did not hide a desperate outlaw who owed loyalty to neither side.

While his reactions were quick, and he had done well earlier that day, Podevin knew his life had hung by a thread. Or a misfired arrow. Or a lucky shot from a crossbow fired by a lad barely able to hold the weapon. As he removed the extra stakes and entered his silent home, he had to shake himself. He also had to light the fire. He shivered, but he needed to think. Once again, he had killed men. Once again, he had survived—but what for? Was he going to have to get involved again, with the thoughts, the plans and schemes of others for whom his life meant nothing?

After a sleepless night and with no other orders, he was now making his way to the edge of the forest. He had his borrowed sword strapped to his side, his bow and arrows with him, and his dagger. But the Prague castle guards had crossbows and the castle approach was in the open. Or they could open the gates to him and then kill him. He had to assume they knew who he was, but he still had to see his family. He dithered. To advance and be recognised, or to hide away and hope? The gates were open. People were going in and out. Carts were doing the same. One was even coming down the slope with a whole family on it. The woman was driving it, with a man beside her, and four young people in the back. It wasn't their cart; it wasn't their horse—it was going too fast for that—but those people looked familiar.

As they came closer, with Lyudmila unerringly guiding the cart along the paths to take the quickest way to their forest home, Podevin stepped out in front of them. Not too close, and not too sudden, in case the horse shied, but there were things here that puzzled him.

'Greetings, strangers,' he said, 'and what news from the castle?'

Lyudmila pulled on the reins and the cart came to a halt. Before she, or Brother Mark, could say a word, Maria scrambled out of the back of the cart.

'I'm going for a walk—*alone*,' she said. The last word was added as Priby—who seemed to have something wrong with her face—moved to follow her.

Lyudmila's head had turned to see what was going on, but Mark laid a hand on her shoulder and murmured, 'Leave her,' before turning back to Podevin, who was watching all the drama in complete bafflement.

'Just as Maria is walking, so will we, Podevin. There is much to explain.'

'And I hope you explain my views, too,' Lyudmila said as she flicked the reins. Mark drew Podevin aside as the cart rolled past. There was a half-hearted wave from Alexandr as the cart disappeared round the bend, to which Podevin responded.

'So. What's been going on?' He turned to Brother Mark.

'I'll explain on the way.' Mark indicated the road out of the forest towards the castle.

'You can't be serious. They know who I am.'

'But because of what you've done, Emma needs to see you.'

'Forget that! It's because of who I am that Duke Boleslav and his father want me dead.'

'True, but not just now. Things have happened to change circumstances.' Mark paused.

'What things?' Podevin said. 'Look, if you want me to risk my neck going up there, you need to start talking, and talking fast. Including why Priby has some sort of poultice on her face.'

Mark sighed. 'She has a broken nose from trying to stop your old carthorse from being killed …'

In fits and starts, not least because of Podevin's interruptions, Mark told the story. Mark had to insist Podevin did not try to find the captain who had hurt Priby because Emma had sent him (and his troop) to fight the Magyars under King Boleslav. 'Besides, you might find yourself in the middle of a row between your daughters,' he finished. Then, he had to explain that the captain in question was the captain Maria had been seeing.

'Why didn't you stop it?'

'I assumed you knew. And, besides, I think I would have hardly been welcome if I had interrupted anything.'

They emerged from the forest and started on the slope down to the stream, before the rise all the way up to the castle. From this moment on, they could be seen by anyone looking in their direction from the castle wall. But Podevin stopped anyway.

'I'm needed back there, aren't I? I need to talk to Maria.'

Mark shook his head. 'Not now. Lyudmila understands. She doesn't like it, but she understands. Your life is in danger—which means we have to sort things out. Again.'

'From being called by my own name and a hug?'

'If you want to put it that way. But also, from a husband with a suspicious mind …'

෴

Once they had driven the new cart back home, unloaded their provisions, cleaned out Bracken's stable, persuaded their new carthorse to retire to that stable, and made sure all the rest of the livestock had been fed and watered, Priby could see Lyudmila was exhausted. Maria had been no help. It was clear she had arrived back first, as the gates were left open, and she was found in her bed, with her back to them, refusing to respond either to entreaty or to command.

The boys rushed off to practise shooting their new arrows with their new bows. There was an argument; it turned out Vaclav was better than Alexandr, and he started crowing about it, saying his brother would never be able to shoot a deer from even two paces. Priby had to step in to point out Vaclav was older. That's all—just older. She told Alexandr he would get better as he grew older, and, as he would have more time to practise, he would probably be a better shot than his brother was at the same age.

Of course, Vaclav tried to object. Priby sighed.

'All right, Vaclav. Tell me what is wrong with what I just said.'

Vaclav looked at his feet.

'Nothing to say? Good. So, both of you can go and collect your arrows, then come back to help your mother with sorting out everything for your meal—unless you would prefer to go without?' She added the last words as she could see Vaclav—again—wanting to object.

Lunch was quiet. The boys concentrated on their food. Maria ate next to nothing. Lyudmila appeared not to notice but, afterwards, as Priby gathered the bowls ready to take them to the stream for a wash, Lyudmila laid a hand on her arm.

'I'll get the boys to check the fence—to keep them from getting into any more mischief. Can you please take Maria with you to check all the traps, including the pit if you like, and bring back anything killed? She won't talk to me. Something's wrong—I want my little girl back.'

Priby looked at her adopted mother. There were grey circles under her eyes, and lines on her face that had not been there before.

'I wouldn't ask this of you, if I could think of another way.'

Priby nodded. Lyudmila, perhaps wisely, left the homestead, leaving the girls alone together.

૭৲

'Oh, all right, then. If I must.'

It was not reluctance, but Maria's attitude could hardly be called enthusiastic. Before, the girls would walk side-by-side, listening to the forest. The birds chattering, the breeze in the branches, noticing the tracks. Now, Maria walked behind. Priby tried to point to a deer spoor leading them farther into the forest.

'I'm not a peasant. I shouldn't be doing this.' Maria's comment stunned Priby.

'I wasn't saying you were. I was only pointing to a track. We all know deer tracks. Including Dad,' Priby said.

'He's not your dad. And he isn't mine. My father was duke of Budec and Tetin—who that man, the man you call your father, killed.'

Priby turned around and grabbed Maria by the shoulders. 'What is all this? We know the story. Your actual father took Mum from the fields and—' she searched for the right term, '—violated her without her consent or desire. Dad raised you as his own. And you know it!'

'Only through guilt! He didn't have to!' Maria shook Priby off. 'You deal with the traps. I'm not doing peasant work again. I'm going to the castle. He's got to marry me.'

'Didn't you hear Duchess Emma? Your captain's married already.'

'I never said he was my captain.'

'Oh, come on, Maria. It was pretty obvious when you seemed more concerned about his fist than my broken nose!'

'You shouldn't have been in the way!' Maria shouted. 'But you're just a peasant—so what do you know?'

Priby refused to rise to the bait, merely saying, 'You were born a peasant to a peasant mother, in a peasant's hovel, and you were raised by a peasant—and when he died, you were raised by an outlaw. Hardly a matter of pride, I would have thought.'

Maria stepped close enough to hiss, 'My father was a duke. My captain will look after me as is fitting to my station. He's waiting for me. Thanks for bringing me this far. I'll make my own way from here.'

By the time Priby could think to repeat, 'But he's married,' Maria had darted out of sight through the trees. Priby knew there was no point in going after her. Though what she would say to Lyudmila, she did not know. She sighed. She turned to go back to the homestead, but then stopped. They had to check the traps—she had to check the traps. It would give her time to think, even if it could not change the story she would have to tell when she made her solitary way home.

Chapter 9
Letters, Letters

'But what was I supposed to do? Just let him be killed?' Podevin tried reasoning with Emma about the Czech farmer who'd charged into the Saxon camp. Despite Podevin's worries about being recognised, there had been no issues at the castle gates. He and Mark had been shown straight into Emma's rooms. They were meeting in private, which meant Emma had some say over who was there: her Anglo-Saxon ladies, Geraint and Mikael, but she could not count on the guards' loyalty. Geraint could shout and berate the soldiers who guarded her door forever, but he and she were still regarded as Anglo-Saxon interlopers. Ever since her husband had been present in the castle, if she insisted on having the doors closed for a meeting, the guards would be inside the door—'They can hardly intervene if anything gets nasty, if they're on the wrong side of the door, can they, my dear?'

There had been no point in telling him in all the years he had been absent, no-one had tried anything. If guards were there to guard the door, that was what they guarded, wasn't it? In the end, it was easier to keep the doors open, their voices down, and retire to the far end of the room. Even if it meant being that bit farther away from the fire.

'He was going to be killed anyway.' Emma was clear in her focus. 'What if you'd been killed, or even just injured?'

'I wasn't, and I found the information you needed about the raid. You have got it?' Podevin said, suddenly unsure.

'No,' Mark said. 'The duke has it all. And he's taking it all with him, when he goes east. Unless he's destroyed it.'

Podevin held up his hand. 'Excuse me. Duke Boleslav is going east? Why?'

'His father needs yet more reinforcements against the Magyars,' Emma said, as if it was of no importance. 'We all know that.'

'I didn't,' Podevin replied. 'I live in the forest, remember?'

Emma rose to her full height, Mark stepped forward. 'The point is,' he said, 'no-one saw fit to tell Emma the king wanted his son leading those reinforcements.'

'So? That's good, isn't it? For us, I mean,' Podevin said. 'Though you might have waited until he was gone before bringing me here.'

'Shh!' hissed Emma at Podevin's raised voice. She paused. 'We're trying to tell you now.' She nodded at Mark, who took up the tale.

'I found King Boleslav's orders in the scriptorium.' Mark sighed. 'I've been getting slow in my old age. Predictable. So, I surprised them. Hradek was reminded who he served. And told me why he no longer needs me as translator.'

'Translator?' said Podevin. He knew Hradek was in charge of the scriptorium, but why Mark, on top of everything he did for Emma, should need to work there as well, was beyond him.

'From Anglo-Saxon to Czech. When anything came from England.'

'Or my sister in Saxony,' Emma said. 'I've left Hradek in his position—for now. But it seems there's been a spy in the scriptorium for a long while. The duke has known about Matilda's death for weeks.'

Podevin opened his mouth, but Mark raised his eyebrows and muttered under his breath: 'Queen Matilda of Saxony? Emma's sister? Remember?'

Podevin remembered. It was so long ago when he was Wenceslas's page, and he had to witness Emma's parting from Matilda in Augsburg, and they had swapped rings. Emma must be thinking about the same incident, judging from the way she was twisting her sister's ring about her own little finger. She noticed his look and stopped. She glanced at the guards, who appeared to be minding their own business, perhaps realising their lives would be more comfortable if they were loyal to the duchess who was present, than the duke who was shortly to be absent.

'Never mind the scriptorium, we have another problem,' Emma said. 'Show him, Mark.'

Mark silently handed over the parchment Duke Boleslav had traded for the Saxon orders. It was short, and to the point.

We have heard with sorrow of the death of Matilda, Queen of Saxony, and offer you our deepest condolences in the sad loss of your sister. We trust you are well and look forward to hearing from you in due course.
Your brother,
Edmund, the first of that name, king of all England.

Podevin handed it back to Mark. What could he say? Queen Matilda had been over thirty; if she had been with child or had gone down with any of the many diseases that struck without warning, even queens don't live forever.

'I am sorry to hear this, madam,' he said, hoping the formal words would count for something, but Emma waved him into silence.

'She's been killed. Just like you and I, Podevin, were to be found and killed. I could have been kidnapped—apparently, after the king, I'm our most dangerous general—and taken to Otto "to be used as he pleases," but my death would not be viewed with disfavour. On the other hand, your death was expected.' Emma had paused at that point. 'I think that's a fair summary of the documents from Saxony.'

'But you said you had to hand them over to Duke Boleslav,' Podevin said.

'You really thought, while the duke and duchess were in dispute, her servants would not be able to guess what would happen? And we'd do our best to thwart … certain people?' Mark glanced at the door as he amended his final words.

'You read the documents before handing them over?' Podevin put it as a question, but light had dawned. He didn't need everyone's nod. However, not every question had been answered. That he, especially now his identity had been uncovered, was a target, was a given—

though how Duke Boleslav had been so sure before Emma's error, was another matter—that Boleslav hated his wife, and would have her killed if no blame attached to him, was also a given, but why had the Saxon queen been a target? Emma had risen, retired to the far end of the chamber, reaching into the wooden chest, the one she'd brought from England, the one which held her most precious items.

'What I don't understand is why you're so convinced it was murder,' Podevin said as Emma returned to them, her attention on the parchment she held in her hand.

'"*If this is my last letter to you, and the next you hear is my death, I shall have been murdered*—"' Mark opened his mouth to interrupt. But Emma, remorseless, carried on reading: '"*I fear my husband is bending his ear to wild counsel telling him to conquer all lands—Frankish, Polish, Bohemian, even the Papal lands to the south—that he can be a second, and better, Charlemagne. He does not see that, even as he does this, there is no guarantee his successors will hold it.*" Shall I go on?'

'That was from Queen Matilda?' Podevin asked.

'It came with all the Christmas wishes of peace and goodwill from the Saxon Court to ours. A private message, delivered separately, later. After it had been in the scriptorium,' said Mark, sharing a glance with Emma.

'I suppose we're lucky it wasn't intercepted more permanently,' Podevin said, thinking back a decade to when Emma's messages to her sister never made it out of the Prague forests. He'd been the one to show Mark the charred remains. At least Matilda had found a trustworthy messenger.

'We must find the culprit!'

'And do what, madam?'

Suddenly alert, Podevin stiffened. Mark never used formal address towards his mistress in private, but if Emma noted his change in tone, she ignored it.

'Avenge her, of course.'

'What good will that do?' Mark's voice was low, each word spaced out.

'For one thing, stop any other princeling getting similar ideas!'

'Your husband already has the idea. Someone in Saxony with the ability to send an armed gang across the border, already has the idea. We are fortunate the duke has been sent east.'

'So, we just sit here? Do nothing? What about this?' Emma waved the parchment.

'It may be Otto is investigating. It may be Otto isn't happy. But whether he is happy or not, what do you think will happen if we go barging in, demanding answers?'

Mark paused. There was no reply. So, he continued, 'What do we know? Actually know? Is Otto in mourning? Has he arranged another marriage? Is he just off on campaign and—I don't know—merely annoyed he hasn't a ready-made regent to take over in Augsburg because his queen is dead?'

'Otto has mistresses,' Podevin blurted out, recalling the conversation he had overheard in the forest. Not that they'd said the word 'mistress' aloud, but 'prefers them compliant' was a strong hint the Saxon king behaved like his Bohemian opponent in one respect at least.

'Podevin can go,' Emma decided, as if she'd heard nothing of Mark's concerns. 'Unlike you, Mark, he is unknown in the Saxon court. I mean, he's unknown here! You haven't forgotten how to be a courtier, have you? Living in that forest for what? Ten years now?'

'No,' said Podevin, daring to interrupt, 'I'm not leaving my family. You don't know the whole story.'

'Matilda's dead!'

'So—very nearly—was I and my whole family! Why do you think I sent them here yesterday?'

'I think Podevin has a case, my lady,' said Mark in his quiet, but firm, way.

'But those parchments you brought—they said they were to take me back to Saxony for Otto. Like some damned parcel—you men are all the same!' Emma said. She turned and approached the table and chairs. She sat and, after a pause, her extended arm gave permission for Podevin and Mark to sit as well. Mark leaned forward to place his forearms on the table. Unlike his mistress, he had read the parchments thoroughly.

'Emma. My lady. We clearly have a dangerous situation here. We know what your letter from your sister said. We know, from the documents Krok brought us,' Podevin looked up as Mark intoned his fake identity, but Mark just shrugged before continuing, 'we know that small band of Saxons had a mission, which included kidnap *if possible*. And maybe Count Johan was arrogant enough to think he could fulfil that part of his mission if you went hunting. But how often do you hunt alone?' Emma flicked a glance in Podevin's direction. Mark noticed and straightened his back. Yes, there had been that one occasion when Emma had 'discovered' Podevin fishing, but that was over—for both of them. Mark cleared his throat.

'Our priority, as I see it, is to make sure there are no more raids like this one. I know Otto has trouble in other parts of his realms, so we don't think he can send an army just now; but he clearly knows we have our troubles in the east too. His is the bigger empire.'

'I can't keep patrols out all the time—not in winter.'

'No, but you can have patrols along different parts of the border. Change the routine. Have it so Otto does not know where his patrols might meet yours. Count what's-his-name clearly knew when and where to get past the patrol, the one patrol, and get close to Prague. Perhaps it is fortunate the young lads found them.'

'It was nearly very unfortunate for all of us,' Podevin put in.

'And I thank God it turned out well. I am assuming we have time.' Mark changed his tone. Business-like, he stood, nodding a brief bow to Emma as he did so, but he needed to pace as he thought. Podevin waited, knowing his role was to listen and come up with all the objections he could. He wondered what he would be expected to do. Going to Augsburg was not in *his* plans.

'We have to find those Saxon bodies, check them and bury them,' Mark said. 'The count will be wanted, even if no-one else is important enough. The horse is gone, you say?'

Podevin nodded; he still thought he'd done the right thing in letting the boy go. In his judgment, the boy might have known about their assignment, but no more than what was in the orders he had found. Besides, he did not want that child's maiming or death on his conscience. The adults killed in a fair fight, or killed before they could kill him, they were bad enough ...

The plans for the next few days were sensible enough. Podevin would get himself home and keep his head down. Just because Duke Boleslav thought he knew who Podevin was, it did not mean (yet) he was necessarily a wanted man, given what he'd just done to keep Emma, and the country, safe. Podevin thought he had argued well enough that he did not need to be sent to Saxony—and certainly not as Podevin. He breathed a sigh of relief and prepared to listen to the remaining plans. He was less likely to be recognised if he left at dusk anyway.

There would be a diplomatic letter sent to Augsburg, the Saxon capital, telling them of the failure of the mission and demanding redress over the threatened capture of the Bohemian princess. Podevin had demurred at that point: Emma was an Anglo-Saxon princess born and bred, but in Bohemia, and as far as Saxony was concerned, she was a mere duchess. He had demurred, but not pushed the point. It would, he was told, give the two countries something else to argue about with letters going back and forth. Which would be in Bohemia's favour. The more time spent arguing in letters, the less time they would be doing any actual fighting. Because if Otto was serious about kidnapping Emma (why he would be bothered about Podevin was an issue laid aside for the moment), it was obvious King Boleslav would pack her off; away from any possibility of both capture or playing any part in running the country.

'And that would please Boleslav the Pious no end!' Emma fumed.

'Boleslav the Pious?' Podevin asked, thrown by the expression. He knew the king of Bohemia was called Boleslav the Cruel—behind his back—but who was the pious one?

'My darling husband has discovered the Christian faith,' Emma spat. 'And now he thinks all we have to do is pray and all our troubles will disappear. He even asked Mark to become an abbot at a monastery he wanted to set up.'

'Don't think it's quite "me,"' murmured Mark. 'Besides, I suspect Bohemian monks might prefer a Bohemian abbot.'

'He only did it to upset me,' said Emma. 'At least we were able to persuade his father that spending money on monasteries was not a good idea at the moment.'

'Yes, castles are more practical in a time of war.' Mark was grinning.

'Anyway, I thank you for your loyalty, Mark.' Emma stood, forcing Podevin and everyone else, to scrabble to their feet as well, but she was coming round the table towards him. She placed a hand on his shoulder, leaning close enough to whisper, 'As I thank you for yours, Podevin. I will remember your bravery in taking on those Saxons as long as I live.'

Hell and damnation! Why did that smile get to him—still? After ten years, all she had to do was smile in that special way she had, and his heart lurched as if he was some love-sick youth. Then, before he could react, or even correct her to say it had been his own family uppermost in his mind when he had set out the previous day, they heard the screech from outside. Another row was going on in the courtyard.

'You promised! You said I could go with you!'

'Maria!' Podevin was up and heading for the door.

'Stop him!' yelled Mark. The guards reacted, and Podevin had two spears poised at his belly.

Mark, Geraint and Mikael came up to him.

'Boleslav is out there. If he—' Mark broke off, tried again. 'You stay here. We'll see to it.'

'He's right, Podevin,' Emma said. 'I'd better stay here, too. The duke is taking extra troops on my say-so. I really don't need another confrontation.'

'You bastard! I'm no peasant!' Maria's voice came to them again. Mark, Geraint and Mikael left, not quite running. Mikael ordered the guards to follow them. With a quick glance at Emma, who shooed them onwards, they did as they were told.

Chapter 10
Maria's New Job

The scene in the courtyard was chaotic. Everyone was waiting for Duke Boleslav to make his appearance. Maria had caught hold of the bridle of the captain's horse with her right hand, refusing to be shaken off. He was leaning forward from the saddle, hissing at her. She was red-faced, yelling.

'You promised! You said I was the one for you! You said—'

Mark and Mikael approached, leaving Geraint with the guards.

'Is this your lady?' Mark asked, as if he didn't know Maria. He stood a couple paces away from horse and rider, on the other side of the horse's head. Mikael had gone up to Maria, trying to get her to calm down.

'No. It is not! She's just some whore who thinks she can take advantage of a man who is only doing his duty.'

'And if I told you her father was a guest of Duchess Emma? And if I told you the duchess is not impressed by your continued violation of the castle's peace? And—'

'All right! Fine me! But first you'll have to find me, won't you, monk?' The captain spat the last word, but he had not finished, 'I'll soon be out of Duchess Emma's reach. And I don't intend to come back. Certainly not for a peasant whore.'

Mark opened his mouth but was forestalled.

'Oh, dear. Are my wife's lackeys causing more problems? We do need to get going, you know.' Duke Boleslav had decided he was ready. He wandered over to his heavily guarded litter and was helped into it.

'Well, don't just stand there. We're going, aren't we?'

Trumpets fanfared, drums beat, and horses shook their heads as the company made their way out of Prague Castle. Maria's captain jerked his reins out of Maria's hand; Mikael caught hold of her to prevent her tripping, and dragged her out of the way. A horse side-swiping you, or placing its hoof on your foot, is not an experience to be endured if it can be avoided—and the captain was in no mood to be bothered if his horse did either of those things to the young lady to whom he had so recently been murmuring sweet nothings.

Maria's face lost its furious red hue as she gazed at the empty gate. Mark and Mikael said nothing as they waited for her to realise her beau was gone for good. Eventually, when it seemed they were the only three left in the courtyard, Mark spoke.

'Shall we take you in to see your father? I'm sure he'd like to see you.'

'My father is dead. The man you call Krok is an outlaw who killed my father. And this Krok should be dead. And so should anyone who helped him.'

'Including your mother?' Mark said, as, despite Maria's protestations, they led her to Emma's apartments.

∛

Given what had so recently been said outside, it was not a happy reunion between Maria and Podevin. Until she was reminded that she was in the presence of the duchess, Maria was inclined to be surly. However, under Emma's questioning—Podevin having given up in exasperation—Maria admitted she had been coming to see the captain in secret for months. All she had to do was approach the castle wall at the right time and give the password.

'Which is?'

'"A Premyslid, a Premyslid."'

'And then you'd be let in?'

A shrug.

'He's much older than you. Surely, you realised he was bound to be a married man.'

'But he said he wasn't! He did!'

'How did his men react when he said he wasn't married?' That was Mikael. All of them were listening. They were seated round the table; the kitchen had supplied sweetmeats and beer—wine for the ladies, should they so wish. Podevin could see Maria, for all her protestations about not being a peasant, was having to watch Emma closely to see how she sipped her wine, and how she broke her food into small pieces before popping it into her mouth. How she wiped her fingers between moving from food to drink. How it was the right hand (not the left) that a person ate with. At home, Lyudmila had not bothered with such refinement—often, by the time the family sat down to eat, they were too hungry to care beyond hands being clean and mouths not being overfull if anyone wished to make a comment.

Maria paused at Mikael's question. Somehow, some aspect of his tone—curious, no notion of censure, enquiring—had got through to the girl.

'They smiled. But none of them said anything!'

'They wouldn't, would they?' said Emma, reaching for another sweetmeat. 'Being under his authority—and didn't we see this morning how he dealt with those who were in his way? How is Priby?'

'Broken nose. I set it,' Mark said.

'Painful,' murmured Emma.

It was Mark's turn to shrug. 'Nothing else to do, except use a poultice to help the swelling. The loose teeth should be all right if she doesn't chew anything on that side of her face for a few days.'

Distracted from Maria's predicament, Podevin demanded to be told what had happened to Priby. Mark had not mentioned teeth before. While Emma, Mark and Mikael informed him about what his family had endured, and how Emma had made restitution, if he noticed Maria talking with Beatrice and Hilde, Podevin ignored it. As he finally managed to make sense of the confused tale Emma told, with interruptions from all the others, he realised it was getting late; he needed to take Maria home. No doubt Lyudmila would have something to say to her wayward daughter, but, with her beau's removal to the east, hopefully it was one incident over. Tomorrow was another day.

Except it seemed Podevin was to go home alone. Maria was going to learn how to be a lady-in-waiting.

'If she is so set on becoming a lady of the castle, why not? It'll be nice to be able to add to the ladies I can trust,' was Emma's comment. 'I'm sure Beatrice and Hilde will train her well.' She leaned towards Podevin. 'Sometimes, it might be good to let youngsters have what they want?'

Was she thinking back to when the two of them were young? When, had they been asked, they would have requested a different future than the one which was now playing out? Podevin looked into those hazel eyes, eyes he remembered being less careworn than of late, and thought hard. He looked across at the girl he still thought of as his daughter. Yes, she'd come out with some words she should not have said. But what about him at a similar age? The things he'd said when he—a castle brat himself—had first been told he was to live *as a peasant* in the forest …

'All right, if it's what she wants,' he said, and received his first hug from Maria in months—before she remembered herself, and tried to un-hug him and curtsy to Emma, all in one movement. Very clumsy, but a light-hearted moment to ease a parting.

⁓

The next day was back-breaking and soul-destroying. The trouble with burying the dead, even enemy soldiers, is that they become people. Trinkets are found that show they had lives, hopes, dreams—and even cowards can have sweethearts. Even cowards who pretend to be dead while their comrades die around them, and a young boy is left to fire a crossbow.

'Did he have to be killed?' Mark said under his breath as they heaved this last body into the pit they had spent hours digging.

'He was pulling a dagger on me. At the time …' Podevin could say no more. Of course, Mark had reached for the action that most troubled Podevin, the last man he killed, but now was not the time for his confession. Yes, at the time his blood had been up and he felt it was kill or be killed. Now it was too late, he could think of alternatives. There was rope enough in the camp—never mind at home. He could have tied the man up and brought him to the castle—though how he'd have kept him overnight was another question. The man would have needed to urinate, if nothing else, and be fed and watered. And someone like him would have to be watched constantly—as a prisoner, the man would have been keen to escape, and to kill Podevin on his way out. He might, once back in Saxony, have even told how Count Johan was killed, leaving the boy, Jan, in an impossible position.

Logic still told Podevin he'd had no real choice. But, as he listened to Mark's prayers, other emotions battled within him. On a previous occasion, when he had been talking with Mark about not being keen to join in King Boleslav's battles, Mark had simply said having your own family changed your priorities. Despite what had just happened, Podevin no longer saw himself as a warrior. Nor was he a king's page whose duty it was to die for that king. He had other responsibilities now. Other people to care about.

Until two days ago, when the war became personal and he'd had to use skills he had forgotten he knew, he'd been happy to keep away from any fighting. The arrows were one thing; a forester must also be an archer if he was to provide meat for his family—or the local castle. But the way he was able to use his dagger? It worried him that he found killing so easy. Perhaps he did need to talk with Mark, who used to be a warrior but now was a monk.

For the moment, it was another of Podevin's forestry skills that was needed. Where had that Bohemian peasant farmer come from? Presumably from finding his dead family. Even on winter ground, there were tracks, which he followed to a flimsy homestead, now destroyed. A woman with her belly slit open. Two children: one impaled, one hung. Neither an easy death. Podevin would never know where the father had been at the time of their demise. He dismissed the theory that the man had run away. Such cowardice would be unlikely to produce that mad, angry rush at his family's killers. And what they were looking at now was butchery. Podevin's lament about the killing he had done lessened at the sight. He insisted it should be he who laid both children next to their mother in the makeshift grave. He wished now their father could lie with them, but, as Mark pointed out, making the castle guards find and dig up the body, then bring it back to his family, would be asking too much when there was so much else to do.

Chapter 11
Diplomacy

The Saxon reply to Emma's letter came several days later. It wasn't just one messenger on horseback either. This was a proper diplomatic event. Outriders, cavalry to the fore and behind, and the diplomat reclining in his litter as he was borne towards Prague. All right, they were travelling under a flag of truce, but as Podevin watched them from behind the tree line as they made their way through the forest, he doubted that friendliness was high on their agenda. And, with both Boleslavs—father and son—absent from Prague, how was Emma going to cope with this intrusion?

Decisively, was the answer. That very afternoon, bringing Maria on a visit home, Brother Mark arrived to find a training session going on. In order to stop the boys becoming reluctant to go out, Podevin had, on the excuse he didn't want the ducks being continually scattered by the boys running about, brought them outside their enclosure for their lessons. The ground was clear of trees and bushes; he'd seen to that over the years, though there were old roots and tussocks of frozen grass ready to trip the unwary.

'No, Vaclav! You might be stronger than Alexandr, but most of your opponents will be stronger than you. You have to learn to move, get out of the way. In a real battle, they won't use wooden swords or battle-axes.' Podevin shook his head. He knew Lyudmila didn't want either of her sons to leave home, but their older son wasn't interested in forestry or farming, that was certain.

Anyway, they had a visitor, so Podevin called an end to the session and conducted Mark into their homestead. As soon as she saw Podevin with Mark, Priby rose quietly from her mending. Podevin looked at her, wondering what was going on.

'If you've left the boys alone, they'll be arguing already. Someone needs to sort it out,' she murmured as she passed him on her way outside. Being very careful with a new, green, fur-lined cloak, Maria, without asking permission, chose to sit with the adults. Podevin glanced at Mark, but getting no guidance there, chose to let it go.

'Emma wants you at the castle. There's a job for you,' Mark said, accepting the drink Lyudmila gave him. He smiled his thanks.

'If you stop being a forester,' said Maria.

Podevin studied her. Shapely and pert, she had her mother's good looks, but there was a shimmering sheen of discontent about her mouth that had not been lessened by her days in Prague Castle.

'For a time,' Mark said gently, 'but you be careful how you speak to your father.'

'He's not my father. He's my uncle. Half-uncle.'

'That's enough, Maria,' Lyudmila interrupted. 'If you can't think of anything better to say, you can help me with supper.'

Receiving no support from Mark or Podevin, and sighing dramatically, Maria stood and went over to the fire with her mother. Mark turned his head to gaze at Podevin and raised a questioning eyebrow. Podevin shook his head.

'She doesn't appear to have changed. Perhaps she should come home,' he said.

'There's something she's not telling us. I don't think—nor does Emma, in case you're thinking I wouldn't know—she's mourning her captain. But she's learning fast—very fast. She's almost never out of Beatrice's company. At least Hilde can escape to her home.'

'Oh, dear. She isn't being a bother, is she?'

'She's a little "aware" of her position, but that's just something she'll grow out of. If she wants to, she can make an excellent lady-in-waiting one day.'

'She isn't still going on about her royal blood, is she?' Podevin grinned.

'Actually, it's your royal connections we need,' Mark said.

'I'm sorry?' Podevin said.

Mark took a deep breath: 'It seems Duke Heinrich of Bavaria has heard about your recent exploits—no, he doesn't know who killed his "diplomatic emissary travelling under a banner of truce," but he does "expect both a full explanation and notification that those responsible have been punished to the full extent of the law."'

Given Maria's too obvious listening-in, Mark refused to divulge any further information other than that Podevin was to come to the castle, it was an order from Duchess Emma and she expected him to obey at once. Emma had also decided Maria could spend a day at home—with her mother.

꿍

'All right. Are we far enough away from home?' Podevin asked, as they came to the edge of the forest. 'And who's Duke Heinrich, anyway?'

'Come on, Podevin! Do I need to say everything twice? Duke Heinrich is Otto's younger brother. And, like another younger brother we know, would much prefer to have an empire of his own.' At Mark's words, Podevin could not help but think of Boleslav's assassination of Wenceslas. Boleslav now had a kingdom but was having to fight all-comers to keep it. 'As for you,' Mark continued, 'Heinrich is demanding an "appropriate emissary" to return to Augsburg to explain this "outrage."'

'You're sending me to the enemy camp to explain why I killed Count Johan and his band of marauders? People who'd killed anyone they found along the way? Who nearly killed my own sons?' Podevin had stopped walking. 'No, thank you! I'm going home.'

'No, you're not. You'll hear me out. And you'll hear Emma out. As far as I'm concerned, if you breathe a single word about what you did, you're crazy and would deserve everything they did to you. Count Johan was "a true and trusted servant" of the duke.'

'But not of King Otto?' So Podevin had fought Duke Heinrich's men, not King Otto's.

Mark smiled, but it was grim. 'Quite possibly, so we have to be careful. We also don't know how much king Boleslav, rather than his son, knew about this.'

'A plot from Boleslav the Cruel? Or Boleslav the Pious? Oh, great! So, not only will I not know what undercurrents I'll be dealing with in Saxony, I won't have any idea what's going on here. You need a proper diplomat, not some forester who's been in hiding for the past ten years. Besides which, I've done some thinking too: those Saxons had orders to kill me. So, what's going to happen when I turn up at their capital city? I get killed.'

Podevin made to turn about, but Mark grabbed him and forced him round so they were face-to-face. 'Listen, Podevin. Firstly, those particular Saxons were told to "kill any companion" with Duchess Emma, not "Podevin, the king's second cousin." In other words, they weren't after you specifically. To that extent, you're safer in Augsburg than you are here. Understand? Like it or not, *we don't know* whether you're in danger here. This has to work.

'Quite apart from the fact we don't know how many people— apart from Duke Boleslav, who was already suspicious—think they know who you are, having been a forester is what recommends you. You'll be looking at the whole thing with fresh eyes. And you will be updated as best we can. Emma has been doing some thinking. And, of course, as a cousin of the king—sorry, duke—of Bohemia, you'll have enough weight to your embassy to be heard by Duke Heinrich, and Otto himself.'

'You're assuming I'm going?'

'You're still walking by my side, and we are over the stream that divides the castle mound from the forest.'

'Only because you told me I couldn't go home until after I discussed this whole stupid plan with Emma!'

Podevin fell silent, watching his shadow, long and dark in the brightness of a low-hanging winter sun. The ground was still sharp with frost, but away from the trees, the crunching under his feet was from half-hard grass, not dried leaves. The two men came to the gate, which was open, but guarded. Brother Mark nodded at the guards who nodded back. They did no more than glance at Podevin. He was used to being anonymous. Besides, even when he had come by himself, it was Mark he had called for as his guarantor.

As before, their way into Emma's presence was smooth. They were expected. They were on time. Podevin did find himself feeling a little annoyed that Emma and Mark knew him so well they could guarantee not only that he would come to them, but how long it would take for him to turn up.

'Thank you for attending us, Podevin.'

'It was my duty, madam.' Even in her own chambers, they both used formal words, but both were smiling. They were attended by Hilde—it seemed Beatrice had a day off as well as Maria—and Mikael. Geraint was patrolling the walls.

'We've done some thinking,' Emma said. 'Everyone else involved in Wenceslas's assassination has either been pardoned, done penance, or is dead. We do not think the king has any further interest in pursuing vengeance over something that happened so long ago. Especially not when that person can be, has been, of use to him. And where the king leads, his son will follow.'

'"We?"' said Podevin. 'Who else has thought this through?'

'All of us,' Mikael put in, 'even if some of us are not as confident as our lady here, that everything will follow so smoothly.'

Suddenly, Emma stood. 'Look. I'm sorry! I was so relieved you weren't dead.' She was staring at Podevin. 'I'm sick of pretending I don't care. That my world must consist of saving Prague from the next attack.'

Podevin had stood as well. Tears shone in Emma's eyes. Neither could make a move. Neither could unsay what had been said, and neither wanted the moment to end.

Mark coughed. 'A cloth for my lady's eyes?' He addressed Hilde, who rushed to obey.

Mark took it upon himself to move Podevin to the table. Once she had finished with the cloth, Emma joined them.

Most of the documents lying there, Podevin had seen before. There was a summary of the documents from the raiding party—Podevin realised Mark must have written that up. These documents, given she did not have the original, just Mark's summary, Emma had been careful not to mention in her note to Saxony. There was Matilda's letter to Emma, the one which had caused such consternation on news of the Queen of Saxony's death. And there was the new note Podevin had not yet seen. The one brought with such fanfare and ceremony. The one insisting there had been no evil intent in the previous incursion—only they didn't call it that—and that Emma herself, 'or someone of equal or higher standing in the kingdom,' should return with their emissary and give the explanation.

Podevin began to get the idea. 'Are we going to pretend that I'm of equal standing to you?'

'No,' was Emma's considered response, 'because it wouldn't wash with Duke Heinrich.'

'I thought King Otto ...'

Emma shook her head. 'I got that out of their ambassador before I sent him packing. Oh, no,' she said in response to Podevin's intake of breath, 'I wasn't going to send anyone with him, and certainly not go myself. Leave Prague without a general?'

'But isn't Duke Radslav ...?' Podevin said. For years now, Duke Radslav had been Emma's stand-in when she was indisposed. The old duke of Kourim, Budec and Tetin (the old man seemed to collect titles) had been a general since before Podevin was born—as he had cause to know. Duke Radslav was not Podevin's favourite person.

'You've not heard? He's on his sick bed, not likely to survive.' Mark shook his head. Mark was a gifted healer, using remedies from all sorts of places, but his biggest gift was knowing when something, or someone, was beyond his skill. If Mark had lost hope, there was not much to do except pray.

'He's an old man,' said Podevin, louder and more bitterly than was wise.

'And you still need to make your peace with him.' Mark's voice was firm.

There was a pause. Emma and Mark shared a glance Podevin could not interpret.

'So, it can't be Duke Radslav, can it? It has to be you,' Emma said, her hazel eyes looking directly into Podevin's own. 'Unless you would prefer me to go?'

Podevin looked away from the well-known face. A face he'd come to love when they were teenagers, thrown together by international politics and Wenceslas's whim. Emma was now a married woman and a mother twice over. But it was still the face he had once loved, that he loved still. Their youthful passion, he told himself, had spent itself against the rock of Wenceslas's assassination and Emma's marriage. There had also been the tiny matter of the death sentence hanging over Podevin for simply being Wenceslas's page and bodyguard. They had been caught up in a fantasy ...

Chapter 12
Families, Families

Podevin had a wife. A wife who had given birth to his half-brother's daughter. A wife who was a peasant, born and bred. The Podevin who had been raised in Prague would have scorned such a match, but he had learned to be content with his lot, with his family. However, court life, court politics, was intervening and he, like it or not, was being asked—commanded—to play his part once again.

'I'll have to see what Lyudmila says. And I have to be sure she and the children will be looked after.'

'Podevin, this is your chance to be pardoned and readmitted to court. What happened in the forest was incidental; neither Otto nor Heinrich will care—Count Johan's death is just an excuse. Your family will be perfectly safe. Besides, I thought you wanted your sons trained up as knights?'

'Regardless,' Mark interposed, 'we will do everything we can to keep them safe while you're away.'

'Nevertheless, I will consult with my wife. Just as you have consulted with your husband and the king.' Podevin stood his ground and saw the glance between Emma and Mark. 'What's that? You have not consulted?'

'Of course not, weren't you listening earlier?' Mark said, 'We need to show you can be—and have been—of use to him. He has hundreds who can kill a few Saxons for him. You come back having completed this diplomacy, you come back with a peace treaty so King Boleslav can concentrate all his forces on the Magyars—even better, come back with a peace treaty so that he and Otto fight on the same side against the Magyars—and you will have to be accepted.'

'And Lyudmila? Where does she fit into all this?' Podevin looked at Emma, standing there, surrounded by people constantly, but so alone. 'Even if I succeed, if I lived here alone, how long before the rumours started, before someone remembered a time when Wenceslas ruled and a young boy was asked to look after a princess lately come from England? I think it's more complicated than you think.'

'No,' Emma said as Mark made to speak. 'No. Podevin's right. But I'm doing what I can with what I've got. Do you have any idea of the fragility of my position? I have a husband …' Emma leaned on the table and lowered her voice to a whisper. Podevin was forced to bend forward to catch her words. 'I have a husband who would have me killed, but for his father. And my father-in-law is so capricious, that if I make a wrong move—like visiting the enemy camp …' She let the thought drop. She straightened. 'It has to be you. It has to be you as who you really are. My risk is announcing your restoration to your fortune and "good odour" before the king has granted it.'

'You mean he doesn't like having decisions taken out of his hands?' Podevin said. 'And there's no guarantee Boleslav the Pious won't send assassins after me. I won't always beat the odds. But why now—why the rush?'

'Because Duke Heinrich has an army on the border he's just itching to unleash. That was his diplomat's threat: do as you're told, or face the consequences.'

'It's February! Not even spring.'

'Nevertheless.' Mark quoted Podevin's word back at him. 'Listen to me, Podevin, if you won't listen to your princess.'

Podevin raised his arms in a gesture of frustration. It had nothing to do with not listening to Emma, or Mark, for that matter. It had everything to do with the thought that decisions had been taken involving him, but without consulting him, and he was expected to drop everything and desert his family a mere matter of days after they had all faced extreme danger. Not to mention he was now expected to risk his life to sort out other people's problems. He was not altogether sure he wanted to move back to the castle anyway.

He listened to Mark. He listened to Emma. With an army on the border ready to be used; with Boleslav, father and son, in the east facing yet another threat from the Magyars; with Radslav—the kingdom's best and most experienced warrior—on his deathbed; with Prague so shorn of troops that Emma had barely enough to man the castle if she sent out any more patrols, there weren't many options available. She could hardly travel to Augsburg herself: what would her husband say? What if, despite all the honeyed words, she was captured and held hostage? (*Thanks*, thought Podevin, *what if that fate befalls me?*) However, an emissary had to be found who could command attention and was close enough to the royal family to be heard—and who Emma could trust.

'The field is small, Podevin. Whatever I do is risky. We don't even know how far Heinrich is operating with his brother's consent.'

'He's rebelled before, and been forgiven, but he's not normally left in charge of Saxon policy,' Mark said.

'So, where's Otto?' Podevin opened his mouth for the first time in a while.

Mark shrugged. 'He moves around all the time. Putting down one rebellion after another. Our best guess is out west, over to France. Unless he's in Italy.'

'The other thing is, we have to be quick,' Emma put in. 'Our embassy is expected within the week.'

'Will it be as grand as the one that came here?' Podevin asked.

'I will give you as many troops as I can.' Emma sounded tired, but she smiled. She had sensed Podevin's acceptance of the situation—no matter how reluctant.

'I will consult Lyudmila. And I will go to her with your plans to keep my family safe,' Podevin said, his tone making it clear this was his condition.

'I'm sorry, Podevin,' Emma said, 'but things here have been rather desperate. Shall I tell Mark to come with you?'

Podevin shook his head. In Mark's presence, he thought Lyudmila might bridle more at being forced to agree.

☙

He was right. But because he now saw it was the only option they had, Podevin could not refuse Emma's plea, Emma's plan.

'We'll find a way,' Podevin said to his wife. 'Your daughter is already a lady-in-waiting. And the boys are old enough to become squires.'

Lyudmila looked at him. 'If that's what they want.' She paused, and changed the subject. 'Since when have you had any training as a diplomat? Using sugared words when you'd prefer to blast them to hell?' Lyudmila came to the nub of the problem as she saw it.

'I did spend my boyhood in Wenceslas's court,' Podevin said.

'And you've spent all your time since you came to the forest telling me how you'd have preferred him to have said what he meant.'

That was an exaggeration, of course. They had talked about other things, but pointing that out would only get him a 'you know what I mean' from Lyudmila. He tried explaining what he was to do: present Emma's letter explaining the Bohemian point of view, tell Duke Heinrich how his troop of men under Count Johan had behaved, and show there had been no flag of truce when he—rather, when a Bohemian patrol—had surprised them in their camp.

'Why, in the name of all that's holy, did she have to call you Podevin?' Lyudmila burst out. 'She spent ten years making sure we all called you Krok—after the man who died in your place, after the man who is buried in your chapel—she, and her damned chaplain practically made sure even Maria and Priby never called you by your own name, in case it gave the whole game away.'

Lyudmila could no longer sit still. She walked away from him, still gesticulating. Then she turned, hands on hips, facing him again.

'Some game! Even though they're all loudly proclaiming your death by hanging, even though I cannot mourn my husband—barely even allowed to go to where he's buried—and I have to pretend my new husband, who hardly married me for love, is my old husband.'

Lyudmila strode to the pot and snatched up her ladle. She started thoroughly mixing whatever was in the pot. She hadn't finished.

'Every single time you leave me here, there's me never knowing until you come back through that gate if someone hasn't recognised you and killed you. And there's you, just carrying on as if this were all normal.' By now, her shoulders were shaking. A tear or two actually dropped into the pot.

'Love.' Podevin stood, and moved behind her. He put his hands on her shoulders and guided her body back until he felt her weight against his chest. 'My wife,' he said, 'mother of my sons. Whatever I once felt for anyone else, I love you. Why do you think I didn't agree to going to Augsburg until I had spoken with you? No,' he continued as he felt his wife stiffen, 'I am not happy Emma called me by my name. But she, like everyone, is playing for high stakes. If she loses, she dies too.'

'But she wouldn't lower herself to come to live in the forest, would she?'

Lyudmila straightened and put the ladle aside. She turned, rested her head on his chest and sighed. There was silence. Emma? Live in the forest? Maybe she could have enjoyed that sort of life. Podevin thought he could have enjoyed that sort of life with her; but, really? A princess living as an outlaw? Hardly.

'Do you really have to go?' Lyudmila asked.

Podevin sighed. 'Would Emma have me killed? I doubt it. But there are others who would. You know we have both enjoyed our time here. But, love, it was always dangerous.' Lyudmila froze. Podevin changed his words. 'Risky, then. Sooner or later, someone would wonder who I was. Emma has a husband who does not love her. Who is looking for excuses. Who, we think, tried to set up a situation where I would be killed. Do we wait for death to come looking for me—for us? Or do we try this?'

'Leave it for now,' Lyudmila said. 'I need to sort supper. Go and find Priby and the boys.'

'Maria?'

'She's gone back to the castle. I'm surprised you didn't see her on your way back.'

'When did she leave?'

'I didn't see her go. She wasn't here to do any work. You noticed the dress, the cloak?'

Podevin nodded—not that he'd really noticed, other than that Maria looked very smart.

'The sleeves, Podevin, the sleeves. All nice and wide, plenty of material that would dangle in any muck or water, or whatever. Maria could sit and talk. She could not do anything to help. I don't know her anymore.'

This time, the tears flowed. All Podevin could do was hold her while she wept. Children grew up, it was inevitable. They changed. He might wish he had said nothing about her background, but he could not change the past. Perhaps Maria becoming a lady-in-waiting was for the best. If she wanted to put on airs and graces, then … why not? At least Emma could keep an eye on her.

☙

The next morning, breakfast was disturbed.

'There's someone at the gate,' said Priby.

'Saxon?' Lyudmila whipped round to face the gate.

'Hello there! It's only me! Brother Mark.'

The monk's voice had the boys rushing to the gate to prise it open between them. Priby went to help but ended up just closing the gate after them as the boys were too busy telling Mark about their father's new job.

'I asked if there were Saxons at the gate just now. You might as well be.' Lyudmila's greeting was sharp, but the monk merely said 'Ah!' and sat down. Politeness, and her husband's look, forced Lyudmila to offer food and drink. The food was declined, but the drink accepted. Mark sipped, said 'Ah!' again, but this time in appreciation, and set the cup down.

'Let me guess. You don't like the idea?' Mark reached for his cup.

'That's right.' Podevin sat down beside the guest. 'Priby, why don't you go and sort the animals—the boys can help you. Off you go!' he added as there were instant signs of resistance on the part of the boys. However, with Lyudmila also insisting, they left the men alone, and all went outside.

A pause. Mark finished his drink. He set the empty cup down.

'A slight change in plan. You have twenty-four hours. That is, Podevin, you leave tomorrow morning, and you—just you—are coming back with me now. You need to be dressed and equipped.'

'What's happened? Another letter from Saxony?'

'Another missive, but not from Saxony.'

'I don't understand.'

'Boleslav's coming back from the east.'

'Well, that's all right then. Emma can talk to him and he can decide what to do about the threat.' Podevin ground to a halt as he realised Mark was shaking his head.

'Not the king. The duke. It seems the king wants Prague reinforced against Heinrich, so he has detached the least useful part of his force and sent it west "to reinforce our capital and our borders against our former overlord." He also wants to know how Emma allowed a Saxon force to get so close to Prague. He has been told—contrary to the report she sent—that some of the Saxon forces got away.'

'But why?' Podevin broke into Mark's flow of words. 'Why believe his son instead of Emma? Surely after ten years, he knows who to trust?'

Mark shook his head. 'He fears she's gone soft. The idea that a captain, and his whole troop, should be punished for hitting a peasant and, in the process, overruling her own husband. It's not good because she did it in public—that's what the king finds … difficult.' Mark paused. 'She gets to keep her title, but, given Emma "allowed" a Saxon force to get so close to his capital, the land around the castle is her husband's to patrol and keep safe.' Mark spread his hands. 'Something is going on.'

'But—but how come all this has happened so quickly? How did the duke get to the east and back so fast?'

Mark swallowed. 'Messengers on fast horses? We should have realised King Boleslav would never really want his son with him. Anyway, he's not back yet. We have time to get you sorted.'

'He's not going without his breakfast,' Lyudmila said, from behind them. 'You'd better join us. But while you eat, you can explain what's happening to the rest of us.'

'Oh, you can stay here,' said Mark as they both turned round.

'So, he goes and leaves us defenceless. That's the plan, is it?'

'No. I—we—have thought again. The best way forward, we now believe, is to get the boys away to,' unusually, Mark hesitated and took a breath, 'to Budec. We know Radslav is there, and, yes, he's dying, but he still regards you fondly and has said he will train the boys—and his son will follow his father's orders. It might be better, and they might be comforted, if Priby goes with them. Prague is the only alternative, and given the situation, Maria ought to go with them as well.'

'So, I stay here, all alone?'

'No, you come back and forth to Prague castle, with me, or one of the guards I choose.'

'Why not Geraint?' Podevin named the captain of Emma's personal bodyguard—one of the few other people who knew about their home in the forest.

Mark shook his head. 'He's leading the escort to Saxony, but it might well be one of the other bodyguards. Someone personally loyal to Emma, anyway.' Mark brought his hands together. 'It won't be for a couple of days. Three at the outside, to get everything sorted and you can all move away from here.'

'Three days. Does today count as day one?' Mark's silence gave Lyudmila her answer.

'In effect, four days.'

Mark still hesitated. 'It depends.'

'Hang on,' Podevin said, 'if my family aren't going to be safe, why should I go anywhere?'

'You're going via Budec. Duke Radslav wants to see you. No!' Mark held up a hand to stop Podevin's exclamation. 'Your children are going separately. This is between you and him.'

'But me! Why should he want to see me? Why should I want to see him?'

The one man Podevin had not been sorry to lose sight of, had been Duke Radslav, the man whose conduct on the battlefield had meant Podevin's father had died in that battle—leaving Podevin an orphan at seven years old. Duke Radslav had then rebelled against Wenceslas, who had duelled with him, won, and … forgiven him. Wenceslas had ever after expected Podevin to do the same.

Chapter 13
The Duel with Duke Radslav
A.D.923

The whole thing was stupid. As Podevin grabbed the few things he might need for his journey to Saxony, via Budec, his mind went back to that duel between Radslav and Wenceslas. His father had been killed because Duke Radslav hadn't withdrawn his forces as he'd been told by his king. If Duke Radslav had withdrawn his army at the right time on the day of the battle with Prince Otto (as he then was), King Wenceslas would not have been in danger, Podevin's father would not have had to protect his king, and Podevin's father would still be alive. Podevin had hoped this duel would sort it out, that Radslav would pay the price for his crimes. But that is not how it worked out. Wenceslas ended up forgiving Radslav for his rebellion, and for his failure to follow orders. It wasn't fair.

ᘓ

Podevin remembered it all too well, for all he had only been nine years old at the time. He had been riding Whitesocks, his first pony. They were leaving Prague on a nice summer's day, when the late harvest was being gathered in, and were going to cross the river Vltava on their way to meet Duke Radslav. Whitesocks plodded on while her rider was going over everything in his head: hold the reins with your left hand—first finger over the right rein so you're gripping it between the first two fingers, then the left one goes between, *between*, the last two fingers. You only need to rotate the wrist to steer your pony, and pull back smoothly, *smoothly*—don't jerk—to halt. Now, the standard goes in its slot on your saddle and the horse takes the weight; you keep it upright—that's straight up, Podevin! And you stay on the horse because you're using your legs; don't rely on the stirrups. Have you understood that? So why can I see daylight between your knees and the saddle?

Podevin glanced up and tried to keep his right arm relaxed but still holding the standard vertical—there were plenty who'd regard it as an evil omen if he didn't keep hold of it. The shaft was solid oak, polished until it gleamed like a newly dropped acorn covered in dew. His hand was hot beneath the leather glove, but he set his face forward as he'd been told—just moving his eyes to make sure he was to the right, but his pony's head no farther forward than his king's stirrup.

Wenceslas had just passed a light comment—something trite like it being a good idea to use stone in buildings, not just bridges—to Blanik, who was riding on his left. Podevin hoped Blanik would be pleased with his riding. He glanced across at his tutor; Blanik was fully armoured—he too was riding one-handed, but that was because he would need his right hand free to use his sword. Podevin prayed desperately that he wouldn't let Blanik down, that Blanik would still be alive at the end of the day, that no-one would be hurt—now he was getting frightened by his own thoughts.

Then, just as they got to the middle of the bridge: 'Die, Wenceslas!'

Podevin turned his head sharply left to peer over his shoulder, the standard wobbling. He saw Blanik had also turned, but his expression was not surprised. One or two of the other horsemen had also glanced behind and up towards the shout. Wenceslas didn't turn. He rode on, but Podevin had seen Boleslav leaning over the parapet, his smiling mother beside him. No doubt, were all to go well, it would be explained away as a joke, or a perverse encouragement, but it didn't feel like either.

'If you want a peaceful life, don't have a brother.' Wenceslas's calm recitation of the old saying was loud enough to reach Podevin and Blanik.

'A little obvious, sire, even for him,' replied Blanik in an effort to match his monarch's tone.

'But I have no doubt it would not have been said without our mother's express permission and approval.'

'She didn't look cross,' blurted Podevin. Then blushed into the silence. He heard Wenceslas clear his throat.

Wenceslas was looking down at him—the amused smile reached the dark blue eyes. Podevin, despite himself and the awareness of his awful duties, smiled back.

'Shall we trot for a bit?'

Without waiting for an answer, Wenceslas touched his spurs to his horse's side. Podevin suddenly had to concentrate hard as Whitesocks increased her pace without waiting for his command and threatened to bounce him out of the saddle. Gripping with his knees, he managed to rise and fall with the pony's motion. After a few minutes, mindful of the jogging men behind them, Wenceslas slowed them back to a walk, but there was no more conversation.

The tramp and thud of the men-at-arms became more measured at the slower pace—and it could be heard even over the horses' hooves. A hundred horsemen in a castle courtyard looks like a lot, but they didn't look so many now they were coming out into the open. Podevin thought there were loads of men-at-arms behind the horsemen, but he'd heard Blanik's worries. Every time one of the scouts came back riding on their sturdy, shaggy ponies, the news seemed to get worse.

Podevin was off to his first battle—one where he had a role, not just to watch. Pristoprim was just a little village by a stream. The stream flowed south from the wooded hills, laughing its way through the pines, then the birch, and the oaks and sycamores, before gurgling out into the pastureland and the crop fields. Then it met the mill and surged under the paddles. The energy partially abated, the stream broadened to a brook and curved around the village before wandering off towards the town of Cesky Brod.

There was one mill, one smithy and a few huts with enough land to keep the occupiers from starvation over the winter—provided they were left unmolested. However, soldiers weren't too fussy where they got their food and, by the time Wenceslas's troops arrived, most of the livestock had been roasted over open fires. Whatever Duke Radslav's plan, Pristoprim was as far as he got before he met his enemy.

Podevin could hear the birds tweeting and chirruping. The stream still forced the water-wheel round, the constant splash of the water as it heaved against the paddles. Even the smells of the newly turned loam reminded Podevin of an alternative life. One he would, at that moment, have traded all he had to be part of. Then, out of the stillness, came the caw of a raven. Blanik glanced up.

'Trust them to be here. They're hoping to be picking over bones by nightfall!'

'Not mine, I trust!' Wenceslas smiled. Then, to Podevin: 'You can loosen your grip on that standard—there's hardly a breeze!'

Finger by finger, Podevin opened his hand. He also loosened his grip on Whitesocks' reins. She shook her head. Then came another silence.

The meadow had a gentle slope. No doubt, when the village children played it would be fun to run down it, squealing, kicking aside the poppies, and coming to a halt just before the stream that gurgled its way towards the mill. But the children were being kept well away today. If they were here, they would be peeking out from behind bushes, risking parental wrath in their desire to see what was going on.

The challenger was there first. His forces were arrayed at the top of the slope. Their camp must have been a little farther off, as Podevin only saw the men-at-arms, the companies of horsemen, and the archers. If this was to be decided by numbers, Wenceslas should give in now. Radslav was marching up and down in front of his men. Every now and then, he swung his axe, as if testing its cutting power.

Wenceslas turned his horse from the track and rode onto the open ground. The rest of them followed, silent now. Blanik left his place at the king's side and turned to arrange the men so they formed up as one long line with the few mounted horsemen at either end. Podevin remained with Wenceslas, but he was nervous, he wanted someone to talk. He wished the king would say something, and not just look at Radslav pacing up and down, up and down his lines of troops— there were so many of them. Hundreds and hundreds. The little party at the bottom of the slope would be annihilated at the first charge. But it was so quiet. So quiet that Podevin could hear the bees in the buttercups, the birds in the trees. Swallows darted overhead, still catching all those pesky midges. Whitesocks shook her head again. This time, Wenceslas didn't even turn his head. His horse might be better trained, but even it pawed the ground.

At last, Blanik came back. Wenceslas must have been waiting for him. Slowly, he dismounted. Blanik dismounted as well. Then, like they had rehearsed in the courtyard, Podevin turned his pony away. He walked her ('You don't trot, canter or gallop. Walk!') to the middle of the line, where he turned her to face up the hill. He was the only one moving. Everyone was watching. Blanik half-turned his head. Podevin knew he'd started to sweat; to have Whitesocks trip over a tussock of grass now would be so appalling it didn't bear thinking about... but he thought about it. ('Look ahead, Podevin. You're on duty, remember?') He glanced left and right. He was in place. The groomsmen, like the men-at-arms, had marched up to the king and Blanik. They would take their horses to the back of the line. White-socks whinnied, the sound carrying over the whole meadow. Then silence returned. Podevin tried to relax. His job was done. His pony was in the line. The standard was being held high and fluttering in the breeze. All they could do was wait.

Wenceslas and Blanik were talking to one another. Then the king started walking up the slope. As Wenceslas approached Radslav, Radslav stopped pacing back and forth. Wenceslas stopped a respect-able distance away: out of reach of Radslav's lance, in case the duke of Kourim should want to spear him with it. Podevin watched the two men. Radslav was in full armour, and the day was already getting hot. He had his lance, his axe; a long sword hung in a sheath attached to his belt, and there was a dagger. His shield was across his back. Wenceslas had his light sword, a dagger and only his mail shirt and his shield for protection. Podevin knew Wenceslas was taller than Radslav, but it didn't look like it from where he was—Radslav was still higher up the slope.

'So, mummy's boy, you've come to be killed. You are not, and never have been, my lord. You do not have, and never have had, the right to tax my land and my peoples. I am lord of my lands, and I will rule how I choose.' Radslav paused, but not for long. 'And when I've killed you, I will take over your lands, and rule them how I choose as well!'

'Not if I have anything to do with it!'

Podevin started. He hadn't seen Blanik walk over to him—he'd been concentrating so hard on Radslav's bellow. Podevin saw Blanik shift his weight from one foot to the other. Blanik was normally so calm, so sure... But now Wenceslas was speaking.

'My lord, we have heard your complaint several times over these past two years. We note that you do not refer to the help we have given you in the past, nor that you have sworn fealty to my father and his successors—'

Wenceslas got no further: Radslav roared the word 'Traitor!' and threw his lance.

'Move!' hissed Podevin, knowing that his king couldn't hear him, but tensing up just the same.

Although Wenceslas was no more than a few yards away from his opponent, he watched the lance fly, without moving a muscle. Perhaps he could see that it was going to miss—either way, it was Podevin who winced as the lance buried itself in the ground no more than a few inches away from Wenceslas's right foot.

Wenceslas still hadn't drawn his sword. But, at last, he moved. He went to the lance and worked it out of the ground; then he broke it across his knee and threw the pieces away. But now Radslav was charging at him with his axe at the ready. This time, Wenceslas dodged … and tripped his opponent. Radslav went sprawling.

At this, one or two of Radslav's knights broke ranks. Only a step or two. But immediately, Blanik signalled to Wenceslas's knights and they, too, started riding forward. Podevin was in the middle, holding the standard. His first battle!

'Stop!' This was Wenceslas. 'We'll sort this out, man to man.'

Radslav's knights, seeing that their duke was heaving his way upright, retreated to their line. Blanik held up his hand. His knights stopped. Podevin stopped. They did not retreat. They had closed the gap with Blanik, but Wenceslas was farther up the hill. Blanik took a step backwards, so he could be heard, then moved to the side, every move matched by the knight supporting Radslav. Blanik stopped, but Podevin noted he'd put himself in a position where he'd be better able to lead Wenceslas's troops—more central—but Radslav's second was more to the left of his army: would that help? Radslav still had more troops, and they'd be charging downhill. Silently, Blanik's groomsman appeared with his horse. Blanik nodded at the man, but did not mount up—yet.

Podevin went back to watching the duelling men. Quite what had happened to the axe, he wasn't sure, but both men had now drawn their swords. Perhaps Radslav thought he'd have a better chance now they both had similar weapons, but he didn't change tactics. Another shout, another charge, and another dodge from Wenceslas. Radslav's sword thudded into the ground. Angrily, Radslav pulled it out and turned to face his opponent. Now both men had their backs to their adversary's forces. Radslav had to charge uphill, but the result was the same. Even at the bottom of the slope, Podevin could hear the cries of 'coward' and 'stand your ground' from Radslav's men.

With his light armour, Wenceslas continued to dodge out of the way. Radslav wasn't standing quite so upright; was he beginning to tire? Podevin hoped so. Not least because the crowd backing Radslav started booing Wenceslas, demanding that he close with Radslav 'like a proper king.' On the other hand, Blanik, Podevin could see, was looking worried.

'He'd better not listen to them!' Podevin muttered.

Radslav caught Wenceslas and swung a mighty blow at his head. Wenceslas went down, but, as he did so, he thrust his sword at Radslav's legs. Radslav jumped to avoid the blow and also crashed to the earth. Podevin gasped. The knights were tense too. But, with a bit of an effort, Wenceslas stood first. And he still had the sense to face his opponent. Radslav couldn't get up. Wenceslas still had his sword. Radslav froze. The point of Wenceslas's sword was at his throat. Not taking his eyes off Radslav, Wenceslas beckoned to Blanik, who walked up the hill. Wenceslas didn't move, his sword didn't move, Radslav didn't move.

'Stay where you are!' Wenceslas had his hand up, but it wasn't directed at Blanik. One of Radslav's knights had tried to approach, but Wenceslas had seen him.

'It's all right,' growled Radslav, as Blanik approached Wenceslas. 'I know the rules.'

Careful to keep out of the way of his king's sword, Blanik moved towards the fallen duke. Radslav's heavy sword lay just out of reach. Blanik picked it up and beckoned to Podevin. Podevin walked Whitesocks and the standard up towards him, stopping when Blanik gestured. This hadn't been in the plan. Podevin was puzzled, but tried hard not to show his confusion. Blanik speared the ground with the sword, just by Whitesocks's side.

'Now, Duke Radslav, no sudden moves,' said Wenceslas—and Podevin realised that the king was puffed as well, 'but show my second where your dagger is.'

It was a command, and Radslav shifted slowly, so the right side of his belt could be seen. Wenceslas moved round, more to Radslav's left—with his sword at arm's length, Radslav could not get him. Unless he threw the dagger, but Wenceslas had thought of that.

'Right then, thumb and one finger, draw it slowly.'

Radslav did as he was told.

'Toss it aside.' The dagger went the way of the sword, and Blanik duly collected it.

Radslav's knight had folded his arms. They all watched and waited for the inevitable outcome. Podevin wondered why Wenceslas was dragging it out, but the king, rather than act, spoke.

'Do you acknowledge my overlordship? Over all your lands, castles and people?'

Radslav nodded. Then, to his surprise Wenceslas put up his sword and helped Radslav to his feet.

'Sire!' said Blanik.

'What?' said Podevin.

'I don't understand,' said Radslav.

No-one understood. Why would a king forgive an over-mighty subject who'd defied him, challenged him to battle, and tried to kill him?

Both the Queen Mother and Duke Boleslav looked disappointed when Wenceslas returned to Prague with his former enemy by his side. All that could be said was that, until Wenceslas died and Radslav made the instant decision to serve his successor rather than fight, the duke was often top of Wenceslas's list when he wanted an ally by his side. Radslav even made friends with Blanik. Podevin just had to accept the new situation and say, in his prayers, that of course he forgave Radslav for any part in his father's death, and try to get on with the duke as best he could.

Chapter 14
A Final Talk

Mark's words broke into Podevin's thoughts.

'Maybe he wants to hear you say "sorry" for all the hate and bitterness you've held against him all these years?'

Podevin turned and glared. 'He killed my father.'

'He did not. It was a battle where your father was a casualty of war. And you need to stop behaving like a child.'

'Podevin, you are going to have to sort this out. For your children's sake, if not for mine.' Lyudmila's voice was soft, almost inaudible, but did what Mark's comment could not.

Podevin sighed, his shoulders slumped.

'Let it go, Podevin.' She used his name again. 'People die. Your mother died, so you told me, before you even knew her. Should I be bitter because my Krok died so you could live?'

He could have argued that was a low blow. Krok was injured a long time before he chose to walk to his death pretending to be Podevin. The past weighing heavy on him, all Podevin could do was nod, but he carefully did not commit himself to doing, or saying, anything once he arrived at Budec.

'Leave us, Mark. I want to say goodbye to my husband,' Lyudmila commanded. Then, suddenly practical, 'What else does he need from here?'

'Nothing. His forestry skills will be redundant in Augsburg, I fear.' Mark had already stood.

Podevin had the feeling their guest also wished this was all different, could have happened differently. Could have not been so rushed, so forced. He knew this was a chance for him to be a part of things again, not on the edge, but his life on the edge had been all he had known for years. Until a week ago, when war, diplomacy and the castle, had intruded so violently, so unexpectantly. Podevin didn't even know if he was up to the challenge. However, he and Lyudmila were now alone, and he could hear Mark's voice chivvying and encouraging the boys—they were so young to be pitched into dangerous waters—in their chores.

'Come here.' Lyudmila, surprising him again, had her arms open wide for a hug.

They embraced. In the flickering light of the fire, she held him tight for what seemed a long time. All he could do was hold her while she held him. He had no words: what could he say? See you soon—when he didn't know how long he would be gone? Or even if he'd come back at all?

Finally, she pulled away to hold him at arms' length.

'If I never see you again, I want you to know this: I have loved you these past years with every fibre of my being. I know you did not choose me, and you would not have chosen me under any other circumstances, except that you had to hide here and pretend to be someone else. But know ...' Lyudmila put a finger on his lips to stop him talking. He could see the tears standing in her eyes, then she swallowed, and carried on. 'Even if you repudiate me, or forget me where you are going, I won't regret these past years, or my sons and daughters raised here with you.' She removed her finger and moved close for a kiss. He could taste salt.

But what could he say? Mark was outside waiting and, as he was the one who had forced the marriage on Podevin, he could not say in Mark's hearing that Lyudmila's assertion was untrue. He chose action: Podevin embraced his wife and kissed her again.

Only then did he whisper, 'I love you,' into her ear.

He did not know if they were merely cheap words, easily said, easily forgotten; or whether he meant them. He no longer resented her, that was true. He could accept that none of this was her fault, but since when did a king's cousin—even a second cousin—wed a peasant?

He stepped outside, said his goodbyes to his sons and to Priby. The boys were full of excitement and anxious to be off on their adventures. So it was with little apparent regret that they waved Podevin off with Mark towards Prague Castle. Having said their goodbyes, and on Lyudmila's instruction, none of them came with them through the forest.

ↂ

It was all very well, but Podevin had been a forester for so long now he had forgotten how to be a courtier. At one time, knowing his place was instinctive. As a king's page, you were by his side. If he was being the king's (second) cousin, that was also easy: you deferred to anyone closer to the throne by blood, anyone else, from third cousins down, deferred to you. Other dukes? It rather depended on the duke, and how far they were in the king's favour, but a neck bow to each other at about the same time usually sufficed.

Except this time, Podevin was visiting a duke on his death bed. A duke he had never trusted, for all the people around him had declared Radslav to be one of the good ones. At the entrance to the bed chamber, Podevin held back, watching as everyone, but everyone, deferred to the gaunt, white figure on the bed. In unfamiliar, bright flowing robes, Podevin straightened his back and advanced into Duke Radslav's limited line of sight. Three paces before the bed, he stopped. He bowed from the waist. Was he supposed to stay there and wait for the command to rise? He wished Brother Mark had told him what to do, but Mark, like all the others involved in this plot to reintegrate him with the royal family (for that was what it was, even if ostensibly they were saying they just needed to send a diplomat of appropriate standing to Saxony), assumed he knew it all. Out of the corner of his eye, Radslav's right hand jerked on the bed cover. He took that as his permission and stood erect, looking down at the former warrior.

The terror of Bohemia's enemies was now a shrunken, spent force. His body was wasted. But the eyes still shone, they still stared, they still commanded. Radslav gestured with his hand for Podevin to approach. His knees touched the counterpane. The hand gestured again. Podevin leaned forward.

'Come to gloat, have you, page?' Radslav's quiet words, forced out as if they cost the speaker enormous effort, could have been an insult, but there was humour in those eyes.

'No, my lord duke.' What else could Podevin say? But what other reason could he have for being in Radslav's presence—he'd dreamt of the duke's death often enough.

The duke's eyes shifted away from searching Podevin's face. 'Leave us,' he said.

'But, my lord, he is armed!' The voice came from behind him, but the words were true enough.

As part of his new outfit, he had a sword belt. And a sword belt carried a sword and a dagger. Without a word, Podevin unbuckled the belt, turned, held it out to the room.

'Come on, take it. But I'll want it back when this is all over.' Perhaps the aura of command had not completely left him, as a servant scurried forward, bowed to him, and took the belt.

'Now I am no longer armed, is there any objection to doing your lord's will?' Podevin asked.

The room emptied. Podevin noticed Brother Mark raise a questioning glance, not at him, but at the figure in the bed, before he also left the bed chamber.

Radslav appeared to be gathering his strength, but his first words were a surprise.

The duke pointed at the far side of the room. 'Bring that stool here.' And, once Podevin had complied, 'Sit.'

If Radslav moved his head to the side, he could now look Podevin in the eye. They were now, especially if Podevin leaned forward, on a level.

'You always blamed me for your father's death, didn't you?' Radslav said.

Podevin opened his mouth to deny it, but what was the point? Instead, he nodded.

'Sorry about that. Rostivslav was a good man … A good fighter. He knew what he was doing.'

'So did you. You knew the plan. You knew you were to withdraw your forces after that first rush. You knew—' Podevin stopped as Radslav's hand jerked on the covers.

'I also knew Wenceslas was young, untried in battle. All battle plans change while the battle is being fought. But,' the hand moved again to prevent Podevin interrupting in his turn, 'but I had forgotten Blanik. Boleslav missed a trick when he condemned him rather than pardoning him.'

'You forgot Blanik?' Podevin asked.

In those days, very few people argued with Blanik: constable of Prague Castle, formidable general in his own right, though never a duke.

'It would have been his plan. He never minded giving ground to further his overall cause.' Radslav's smile was grim.

'But you did?' Podevin put the question with a half-smile on his face. This was almost like two old men discussing a past joint enterprise.

'A lot of battles are push and shove. And who gives first, ends up running away as loser.' Radslav spoke the truth, which is why Wenceslas had won the battle.

The Saxons assumed the withdrawal was the beginning of the rout and reacted accordingly, not realising the Bohemians were waiting for that precise reaction. Prince Otto had done well, but not well enough to win.

'Not for the first time, I disobeyed orders.' The man in the bed grinned, and then coughed.

He gestured at a goblet on the side table. Instinctively, Podevin grabbed it and helped the old man drink. There he was, left hand holding Radslav's head, lifting it gently from the pillow so he could use his right hand to guide the goblet to the all-but-colourless lips. The drinking over, he lowered Radslav's head to the pillows again and replaced the cup on the table.

'Thank you,' Radslav said. 'Where were we?'

'You were disobeying orders,' Podevin said, 'before you rebelled.'

'On Drahomira and Boleslav's orders, I might add.'

Podevin thought back. He had been nine years old, so could not be quite sure he remembered everything exactly, nor how much his memory had been affected by what he had been told. But he knew he had never heard that Wenceslas's mother and brother had told Radslav to rebel. There was another thought.

'But if you were ordered to rebel, why didn't they support you properly? Send you troops, that sort of thing?'

'Because what they wanted was a duel, not more battles. You forget, Wenceslas was popular and King Henry's friend at the time. Henry of Saxony would have destroyed any rebellion to put Boleslav on the throne.'

'So, it was all politics?'

'It was all politics. And they got the wrong result from the duel.' Radslav smiled grimly.

'Tell me, if you were following Boleslav's orders, why did you become so loyal to Wenceslas?'

'I owed him my life.' A weak movement of the shoulder sufficed for a shrug. Radslav, however, had not finished. 'I'll tell you this, what to do when Wenceslas died was the toughest decision of my life. Blanik would have fought, but Henry was dying. We'd have lost everything, including our lives.'

'Blanik nearly did.'

'Blanik fled in time.' Another smile from Radslav, the consummate politician. 'Look at me, Podevin.' The former page did as he was told. Radslav looked at him from the centre of his bed. 'No matter what any of this lot says to me, I'm dying. I still don't know everything I did wrong. I am sorry your father died before his time, but there is nothing I can now do to change that.'

Maybe Radslav was going to say more, but another bout of coughing, worse than before, erupted from him. Once again, Podevin helped with the goblet.

This time, he managed to find the words.

'I'm sorry my father died, too. But I'm also sorry for the bitterness I held against you all this time. I'm sure I could have learned from you. Go your way in peace.'

'That's not what this is about. You're off to Saxony because Emma asked you. But it isn't Saxony you have to worry about.' Radslav paused.

Podevin nodded. He knew what the duke was going to say, that King Boleslav would never grant the pardon. He'd have to do what he could and accept that—maybe another forest somewhere?

But Radslav, as if guessing Podevin's thoughts, gasped out, 'Not the father, the son—he's the underhanded one! Now go. Just live your life. No more regrets—yes?'

This time, Podevin could not be sure, but was Radslav's hand raised in dismissal, or blessing? Either way, Radslav was exhausted, and there were many gathered at the doorway, looking in. They included Mark and what looked like a priest. Podevin looked down at the man in the bed. His breathing was very shallow. Podevin beckoned them in.

☙

In the end, when Radslav breathed his last, Podevin was not there. Mark had hustled him out of Budec castle, reunited him with his entourage, under Geraint's captaincy, and sent him on his way to Augsburg in double quick time. The reasoning was, there might be a spy in King Boleslav's pay who would report Podevin's presence in Budec, so Podevin must be hustled away. There had only been time for Mark to hand over one last item. It was a ring. One which had never left Emma's finger since she had exchanged it with Matilda when they had parted all those years ago. Matilda had just been married to the then Prince Otto, and Emma had been about to start her journey to Prague. A tearful exchange; and now the ring was in Podevin's possession as proof of his good intentions.

Only hours later, a messenger was sent after him with the news of Radslav's death. Podevin's conversation with him had been the last Radslav had held with anyone, apart from a few muttered words heard by his priest. It was a quiet, thoughtful diplomat who approached the Saxon border. Though why Radslav should think Podevin must be more wary of Emma's husband than her father-in-law, he had no idea, unless it was the delusions of a dying man. It was King Boleslav the Cruel who held the power, who had the authority to have Podevin killed. For all his petty vindictiveness, Boleslav the Pious was not going to do anything without his father's permission.

Chapter 15
On the Road to Budec

'His father still calls him "Mladenic," you know.'

'His father?'

'King Boleslav himself.' The first guard nodded, slow and secret.

He even tapped the side of his nose to his companion, before the two of them noticed Mladenic's wife was too close to be ignored and snapped to attention as Duchess Emma left her apartments and made for her warhorse.

Emma smiled to herself. She had heard the guards' mutterings and was glad. As far as she was concerned, her husband was still 'the youngster.' She was on her way to Budec; she had work to do.

Unfortunately, they met his train, his troops and transports on the road before they could turn off towards Budec. She was on horse-back, riding with her bodyguard. She explained that, with Radslav dead, and three sons still living, unless the will could be sorted peaceably and quickly, there would be civil war to contend with. Mladenic didn't see it that way.

'I've come to take over from you, so you need to do as I say!' He was looking up at her from the comfort of his litter. 'It won't do them any harm to sit and stew for a few days. I need you to tell me what you've been doing to aggravate the Saxons so that they've put a whole army on the border.' He waved a parchment at her. 'Daddy says so.'

Daddy? *Daddy*! Really?

'And you dismount in front of me!' Once she had completed that, and curtsied, but before she had a chance to defend herself in being on the road, he started again. 'And, if you are to be seen with me, you don't wear hunting attire—you will stop all this pretending to be a man.'

'Sire, I'm the one, if you recall, who is castle constable!' she said through gritted teeth.

'But you're no longer to leave the castle! I'm in charge of the lands all the way to the border. You let a patrol get almost to the gates! It's not good enough. I've talked to Daddy about it—and the Saxons.'

'Husband. You said I would be dealing with it.' Mladenic just smiled as Emma continued, 'That patrol was destroyed before it could do any damage to our castle or our person.'

'Wife. That's not what Daddy thinks. Especially as Duke Heinrich knew all about what happened. Daddy isn't pleased with you.'

The horses' breath was still showing as steam against the savage winter branches of the trees. The ground was a dull green, or brown where it had been ploughed last autumn, in the vain hope of planting a winter crop. Even the sky frowned a dull grey cloud cover on their meeting. Before Emma had worked out who it was clomping down the road, Mikael had been ready with his sword and barked orders for close formation. She'd found time to be impressed, though wishing Geraint could have been there. Mikael, being Bohemian born and bred, would be better for the possible negotiations over Duke Radslav's will. Of course, once they knew who they were faced with, swords were sheathed and orders for close formation countermanded.

'You always called him "Father" before. If you called King Boleslav anything. What's going on?' Emma tried her most reasonable voice.

'Nothing that you need to bother your pretty head about.' Mladenic snapped his fingers. A liveried servant came running up. 'My cushions! They need rearranging.'

There was no further conversation while this was done and the blue-lipped servant was sent off with no thanks but a wave of a hand.

Emma commented about the retreating servant, 'That thin costume might look good, but if it doesn't keep them warm, it won't help in keeping them.'

'What? Oh, the livery? The best silk. My friends think it looks wonderful—especially on these boys.'

Emma held herself in. She knew Mladenic wanted an explosion; he was sneaking a look at her from under his eyelashes. Posing.

'My daddy,' he said, when at last he realised she was not going to attack his friends, not even verbally, 'said the two of us could be a little informal now. Given the help I have been to him recently.'

Suspicious, but no further forward, Emma reverted to the reason she was on the road, insisting, or trying to insist, that Budec needed to be their next stop. Not Prague.

'My orders are for Prague.' Mladenic flung himself back on his recently rearranged cushions. 'So, unless you can magic up some new orders, that's where we are going. And you, my darling wife, will do as you are told.'

The 'darling wife' was having extreme difficulty in not drawing her sword, and using it to pin her husband to his cushions, when there was a shout from ahead of her.

'A horse! A horse!'

Servants panicked, pack horses were dragged off the road, Emma's shout of 'How many?' was ignored, and Mladenic frantically drew the curtains of the litter, crying, 'Don't let them get me!'

Emma remounted her horse. Mikael came up, sword already drawn for a second time that day, along with the rest of the bodyguard. Progress was slow, as they had to weave their way through all the strongboxes of material and equipment Mladenic had presumably thought necessary to bring with him on his journey. That and servants rushing hither and thither, trying to get out of the way, but often being very much in the way. Her husband's own bodyguard was only obvious by its absence.

Once past the mess, Emma's bodyguard moved into close formation beside her. She drew her sword. This was more like it. Warriors beside her, facing the enemy head on. Just like when the Saxons had attacked Bohemia all those years ago. Responding to no prompt she was aware of, her horse lengthened its stride. Mikael and the rest of the bodyguard kept up. All grim-faced but ready for whatever was round the corner.

A horse. One solitary, cantering horse was round the corner. The lone rider was brave enough—she had to give him that.

He managed to shout, 'I'm the king's messenger! On his authority, you must let me pass!' while trying to control his rearing mount and drawing his sword. He managed to bring his animal in hand, and it came to a stop in the middle of the road, but he held his sword ready.

Emma held her own sword high while using her other hand to rein in her horse. Her party came to a walk, and then a halt, just out of reach of the messenger's weapon, which was still held ready. She sheathed her sword, unsure whether she was relieved or not that there would be no battle. Mikael and the rest followed her lead. It was the fact that this one horseman had caused so much panic in her husband's party that disturbed her the most. Where was his bodyguard?

'Just one messenger? With no escort?' she asked.

'The king made the assumption his lands were safe to travel in,' the messenger said. He did not sheath his sword. 'He assumed I would not be dealing with bandits.'

'He thinks we're bandits, Mikael.' Emma smiled with her mouth, but the humour failed to reach her eyes. 'Perhaps we'd better disabuse him.'

Mikael took a glance at the young man, who'd stopped waving his sword around. 'If we were bandits, ma'am, don't you think we'd have killed him first, rather than stopping at the mention of the king's name?'

'So, who are you then?' the messenger asked.

'Have you never been to Prague? Do you not recognise the Duchess Emma?' If Mikael was grinning before he saw the messenger's response, he had to stuff his fist in his mouth when the messenger sheathed his sword, dismounted his horse and knelt in front of Emma, stammering his apologies, holding out the missive he was carrying.

The message, admittedly, was addressed to Duke Boleslav but, given she'd been the one to have to defend her husband from this supposed attack, Emma didn't bother to point out her husband was just around the bend in the road, hiding in his stationary litter.

Emma broke the seal on the dispatch. She read the contents. She grinned. She looked down at the messenger, still on one knee.

'Are you meant to take back a reply?'

'At once, my lady.'

'Then you may assure the king his instructions will be carried out to the letter. Though, I advise you to say that this message was delivered to the duke—which it will be—rather than the duchess. Off you go.'

The messenger mounted his horse and, with a final salute, turned and headed back the way he had come.

The king's message was that Duke Boleslav, heir to the kingdom of Bohemia, was to sort out Radslav's funeral, and his will. Of course, Mladenic complained. He complained that Emma should have handed the message over with the seal unbroken. He complained that sorting out wills was the sort of thing an ordinary clerk should do as part of his job. The duke of Kourim, Budec, Tetin and so on and so forth, was rumoured to have split his large domains between his children—children, not sons. However, King Boleslav wanted the will checked over. King Boleslav wanted to make sure there would be no over-mighty subject in the future. But, on the other hand, Duke Boleslav was warned not to offend any of Radslav's heirs, male or female.

Mladenic also complained that he'd been on his way—not, given the time he'd taken, that Emma could see that he had been hurrying in any way—to Prague to sort out the latest mess that Emma had got them into. Emma reminded him it was the Saxons who had crossed the border, not her. The response to that was that Emma was too prone to act on her own initiative, without consulting her husband. She said there had been an incursion. She said her sister had been killed. She said there was a plot against her person.

'Oh, please! If only that last was true, and both you Anglo-Saxon females could have been killed! What freedom for Otto and me!'

'You make very free with your thoughts—husband.'

Emma's terse reply must have broken into his thoughts, for he merely glanced up at her and said, 'Did you say something?'

He was still in his litter. Emma still rode beside him. When she had returned to him after taking, and reading, the message, she had found there was a guard, of sorts. Foot soldiers. It might be a partial explanation for the slow progress Mladenic had made, but weren't the soldiers supposed to know what to do in the event of an attack? It turned out their leader was one of Mladenic's friends, who was riding in another litter. His excuse was, he had emerged to see a troop of cavalry going forward to face the threat, so what was needed was to secure the duke's life. Therefore, he ordered his troop to surround Duke Boleslav's litter to make sure no-one attacked the duke. And, as it had all worked out well, what was the problem? In the face of Mladenic agreeing with his friend, there was not much Emma could do.

With the new orders—and Mladenic decided that, yes, those orders did come from his daddy, so he had better obey them—they had to turn the litters, the pack animals with their carts (those that hadn't been taken off the road in the recent panic) and everything else, round on the hard, cold, pitted, lumpy road. Or, in those places where the sun had reached, the muddy, puddly, pitted, lumpy road.

Turning a cart with attached carthorses on a narrow road is a job not for the faint-hearted, nor for those who suffer from a lack of patience. The bushes and dead trees either side of the road, and brown, muddy fields beyond that, where a cart might sink to its axles in seconds, did not help. Neither did Mladenic, who was heard to moan that if only the messenger could have slowed down so they would have been too close to Prague to change direction that day. Or speeded up so they could have taken the road to Budec before the turn-off to Prague. After all, Radslav was dead, so he wasn't going anywhere. However, as Emma took pleasure in reminding him, according to the dispatch, he, Boleslav junior, was to represent his father at the funeral and sort everything out. Oh, and had he read the bit about his father expecting a full report?

❧

At least, once they arrived at Budec, Mladenic behaved. He was gracious, he murmured all the correct words to the grieving family. However, the man in the coffin dominated the whole place as if he were still alive. Radslav had been at Emma's side at the first battle Boleslav had fought against the Saxons, so she found herself surrounded by people remembering the duke. Talking about what a fighter he was. Some even ventured to mention, very quietly and not in Duke Boleslav's hearing, his role in the two battles against Saxony. In the first, he said his father had clearly told him to commit his troops as soon as there was a need for them. Which he did. Surely it was obvious, if his troops hadn't been there, taking on the Saxon cavalry, then Emma and Radslav's scratch force—which they'd brought up from Prague without orders—wouldn't have been able to smash into the Saxon reserves, swinging the battle in Bohemian favour.

Of course, Emma had needed to tell him, 'You don't put infantry in open country to be trampled on by highly trained horsemen.'

It did not help the relationship that Emma had been praised by the king for 'destroying the reserves.' Actually, what she had also done was capture the supplies and looted treasure. Money. It was all about money.

The second battle had been worse. Again, without orders, Emma had found a load of archers, who were shooting arrows at the enemy from the woods. Her husband had professed not to know they were there, so when he ordered his troops to help by marching them alongside the wood … That time, Emma had been furious with him for nearly losing them the battle. And she didn't care who knew it: she had his father's backing, what was he going to do about it?

Duke Boleslav, in all his finery, his fox furs, his ermine cloak, his beringed fingers, moved with studied elegance to his allotted place in the chapel at the funeral. Emma knew, if he'd had his way, his wife would have been nowhere near him, but that wasn't protocol, it was not proper. So, she was in her rightful place, by his side. At least, with a solemn service going on, they didn't have to talk to each other. However, she knew she was going to have to try to work out what her husband had been up to. She was beginning to feel a little odd, as if there was a level of play-acting to her husband's attitude. He was being himself—only so much more so than she remembered. The whole 'daddy' business seemed to have been dropped, but that didn't prevent Emma from getting a sinking feeling in the pit of her stomach.

Chapter 16
The Duke's Will

But first there was the will. It was always the will. The eldest wanted everything. The other sons wanted their fair share. They all had tales about what their father had said to them, what he had promised them—sometimes on holy relics—but if it was not written down, there was, or there ought to be, nothing to be done.

Except the king had devolved the power to change Radslav's will to Emma's husband. A duke's will does not have any power against the will of the monarch. She watched as, all day, people came and went with different stories, different ways of telling him what he must do. It was quite clear Radslav's unmarried daughters must be deprived of their inheritance. It was obvious their brothers would decide what dowry they should have—assuming they married at all. Surely, Duke Boleslav knew, if he or his father needed the new duke of Kourim on his side in his wars against the Saxons or the Magyars, then it was obvious, given the old duke had never split his lands, that the whole estate, including Budec and Tetin, must be kept whole? But surely, he also knew, if he needed competent commanders in the field, and decent tax revenue from all the former duke's estates, then they must be broken up and given to those sons named in their father's will?

In the end, Duke Boleslav exploded and demanded to be left alone in the great hall while he thought and made his decision.

'But, your highness, you need help to sort out what the estates could yield. It is very complicated.' Emma was not sure, but she thought it was some clerk who had spoken.

'Are you saying I'm stupid? Or is it more that you've been taking more than is your due for yourself?' Boleslav waited. There was a babble of noise. 'Silence! I thought I told you to leave?'

'There are so many documents, your highness. You can't possibly understand. I know I don't.' That was the new duke of Kourim, the one demanding to get his hands on the lot.

Boleslav stood, placed his fists on the table—a table covered in parchments from all over Radslav's estates—and yelled, 'Leave me!'

Silence.

'Go on. Go!'

Emma was amazed; she was sure his father would not have to repeat himself like this, nor would she—certainly not in Prague.

Finally, in dribs and drabs, they left. Until only she remained. She was sure he really did not want her to stay, but how was he to make any decisions without her? He sank back into his chair as she, unbidden, wandered up to the table. She even picked up a parchment and looked at it. Standing there, she frowned at the figures.

'You know,' Emma said, mildly for her, 'this is rather complex.'

Boleslav reached across and grabbed the sheet from her hands. 'Receipts from Budec,' he said. He scanned the page. 'Not complicated at all, really. It's obvious these don't add up. Someone's been fiddling the figures. It's the same for all the estates. What I need to know is how far back it goes, and who has been benefitting. Then I can sort out the will.'

'No,' Emma said, contradicting him was a way of life—all right, he had surprised her with the way he could scan a page of figures—but there was so much he missed about ruling people. 'The will has to be sorted today. Or you'll have a rebellion on your hands—and I don't think your father will be happy about that, will he?'

'He won't be happy about his taxes going missing either,' Boleslav said. 'And they can wait. If they rebel, they lose any chance of getting their lands—easy!'

'If you tell them they'll lose their lands, that will make them more likely to take up arms, not less.' Emma was standing, hands on hips, and she could feel the red spots on her cheeks showing again.

She saw him stare at her with distaste. Last night, he had accused her of 'not knowing how to dress like a lady,' but not even her masculine attire 'could disguise she no longer had the body of a slim girl.' He knew she still rode, still hunted, still galloped across the fields in pursuit of her prey, like some hoyden or demon. And she still practised fighting with her bodyguard, despite knowing he opposed all such practices. She knew he hated this impenetrable part of her entourage. He couldn't have expected the few remaining Anglo-Saxons to report to him, but she knew, because they told her, that his agents were rebuffed by the Bohemian recruits to her bodyguard as well. However, for some reason, the days when Mladenic had only known what she chose to tell him appeared to be over. Little things, like him knowing Geraint had left Prague Castle, were giving her cause for concern. Emma tried to concentrate; she knew she was right about this. Here could be grounds for a rebellion.

'So,' he said, 'where is your bodyguard?'

'And, why, your highness, should I need my bodyguard?' Another time, she would have been flippant, but why was Mladenic, her husband, wanting to know where her bodyguard was?

'You'll need your bodyguard to deal with all these rebellions. If you're quick, you can just have all Radslav's heirs killed off and we can take his inheritance for ourselves.'

Oh, he was just being stupid again.

She took a breath. 'And then we'd be facing an even bigger rebellion from all your father's other vassals, worried about not being able to pass on their inheritance. Do you ever think things through?'

She was so lucky they were alone. She regretted that last comment, as soon as it left her mouth. It was no way to talk to him. She started searching for the will. Mladenic made a grab for it but was too late. She seized it and wandered off across the room with it. It was, thankfully, neither long, nor too complex. She could almost hear him fuming while she stood there, by the window, her back to him, going through the will, clause by clause.

At last, she turned, and brought back the will. He held his hand out for it. A normal wife would obey her husband and give him what he clearly required. Not Emma. If he could play games, so could she. She sat down on the table, on the actual table, without his permission and just out of his reach, and looked at him.

'It works. Radslav has split his lands to avoid a fight. Duke of Kourim, Budec and Tetin. He has three remaining sons, who all get dukedoms. There are subsidiary lands for his two daughters, which make excellent dowries, given who their intended suitors are.'

'Given their father is dead, it's for their brothers to decide their dowries,' Boleslav pointed out.

'Husband,' she said, as patiently as she could, 'their father has decided. It's in his will. All we have to do is call them in together, tell them what is what, but also tell them you will be sending auditors to each of their estates and everything had better be sorted, and accurate, or the king will be branding them traitors for withholding tax. That, my dear, will concentrate their minds long enough for them not to worry about rebelling.'

If calling him 'husband' stuck in her throat, 'my dear' was worse. However, he thought there was a problem.

'Why should those bits of land be dowries?'

She stood up and said, 'Shall we glance at the map?'

In the course of the previous day, Emma had put her finger on the pulse of the love affairs and matrimonial prospects of Radslav's family. She wasn't sure if Mladenic really knew, or was busy pretending he'd known all along. Either way, he had to agree it was sensible for the allocated lands to be added to the future husbands' lands in both cases—instead of Radslav's heirs having to guard fingers or promontories of their land poking into the neighbours' holdings.

Emma then felt she had to point out, given his father would want a report sent to him as soon as possible, it made sense to sort the whole will out as soon as he could. Of course, once it was clear that Emma, the castle constable of Prague, was behind the decision, even the new duke of Kourim had to bow his agreement to following his father's will. All the heirs affixed their seals. And why not, given they were already gathered in one place, organise a double wedding for their sisters? Possibly a bit close after a funeral, but, with everyone here, it made sense ...

It made sense to Emma, anyway. She wanted these dowries allocated before any brother decided to risk stealing one while the king, the duke, or she herself, were busy elsewhere. One wedding had already been postponed because of Radslav's illness, the other had been in negotiation. It was Emma who oversaw the final, nitpicking resolutions, Emma who persuaded the priest to agree to the double wedding. It was Duke Boleslav's job to give the brides away to their respective husbands, thus symbolising the royal blessing on the marriages, and the agreements which went with those marriages.

⁌

However, all this, including the double wedding, took time. The few days promised to Podevin's family stretched into two weeks. Maria, taking advantage of her new status as one of Emma's ladies-in-waiting, managed to suggest Priby, Vaclav and Alexandr would be better off if they stayed with Lyudmila. With everything being so rushed, under the impetus of King Boleslav's orders, Emma had travelled to Budec without the youngsters. She had promised they would be brought to safety later. However, Maria argued her siblings would be just as safe remaining in the forest, which they knew, instead of being placed with strangers—strangers who, moreover, had other things to think about—seemed reasonable at the time.

So, Emma had agreed, not knowing that, during those weeks, Boleslav—King Boleslav—had returned to Prague. Messages from Augsburg, which had bypassed Prague and Budec, and so had not reached Emma, meant the king of Bohemia had another problem on his mind. He could have done without another crisis, especially one fomented by the younger generation operating without his knowledge or permission. Now his own emissaries were travelling back and forth to Otto.

Emma knew he was not a patient man; her mistake was in thinking her battlefield experience and expertise made her position unassailable.

Chapter 17
Augsburg

'The duchess said we were to get to Augsburg with all speed. What are they going to do if they see us at the edge of the forest like this?'

'Assume we're waiting until the gates are opened in the morning to approach?'

Geraint, like Podevin, was on horseback, staring at the fortress, which was their destination. It was not fully dark, but they could see the gates were shut. Against this closure, there was the fact, as Podevin pointed out, they could still see—therefore the Saxons could see them.

'This is ridiculous. Do you really want to sleep on cold ground, or would you prefer a feathered bed? I know what I'd prefer. And this lot?' Podevin pointed back to their guard.

Twenty horsemen, none of whom had been asked to come on this little trip away from home, family and friends. The hasty packing, the inadequate provisions, the inability to ask for shelter in hostile territory, and a constant need to be on the alert. Nobody had slept well over four days and nights. In bad weather, it had been easier to keep moving. They had come to Augsburg, only to find the gates shut against them.

There were a few murmurings behind them.

Geraint shook his head. 'I hope you're right,' was all he said.

'We have a flag of truce. We won't unsheathe our swords—or anything else,' said Podevin, noting the battle axe hanging from Geraint's saddle. 'And we'll take our helmets off.' Podevin suited his actions to the words. 'Besides, we have our credentials from Emma.'

'Aye. But they have to read them first, don't they?' Geraint said, but Podevin had already urged his horse forward at a fast trot.

In the greying dusk, the Bohemian party moved up to the high gates surrounding the Saxon capital. On top of the wall over the gate, there were guards with crossbows and spears. Podevin smiled to himself. He remembered a time, long ago, when he had come here with Wenceslas. It was here he had first met Emma. And now he was returning as her ambassador. Peace could and would be assured. Wasn't ten years of war long enough?

'There!' Podevin said. 'They're opening the gates.' He smiled at Geraint, then looked back and was puzzled at the reaction: helmets were hastily being placed on heads, weapons seized.

'No defence!' he shouted.

Thud! Thud! Crossbow bolts buried themselves in the turf. Geraint was yelling, too, except his word was 'retreat' as cavalry—lots of cavalry—surged from the gate. All armed, all armoured.

'We come in peace!' Podevin yelled.

Podevin's horse reared. Had it been hit? He was thrown. He landed hard on the ground, surrounded by horses. A blow to his head. Without his helmet, he felt blood. What was going on? Saxon shouts. Geraint seemed to be standing over him, giving him time to get to his feet, even as the man's blood dripped on him.

It's all right, Geraint, I'll just sleep here, the ground is not that cold, after all, Podevin thought. *Oh? Oh, that's ok, you sleep on top of me. It's no problem. It's gone very quiet …*

❧

Podevin woke. Tried to open his left eye, and found he couldn't. It was still dark. Except it wasn't; there was a very small window, high up, letting in only a small amount of light. He tried to move. For some reason, he appeared to be chained up.

What had gone wrong? They had come to Augsburg; they had approached the gates. Geraint yelling something.

Podevin had merely acted on his orders from Emma. Which were, get to Augsburg, demand to see King Otto—or Duke Heinrich if Otto wasn't there—and get this sorted out. How could Heinrich expect her to take kindly to a kidnap attempt? Didn't he know her own half-brother, the former king of England, had tried that trick? And, while Podevin was there, Heinrich had better give a very good explanation for Queen Matilda's murder. In some ways, this, as the trigger for all that followed, was more important.

Podevin was not altogether sure he shouldn't replace the word 'murder' with simply 'death,' but that was as far as questioning his orders had gone. He had been so determined to get to Augsburg as soon as possible, get his mission over with, and return home, that not even Geraint's caution could sway him. Oh, well. He was sure it would all be sorted out. He was still a bit tired.

ℭℨ

He stirred. He seemed to have been asleep. During the day? With his one good eye, Podevin looked about him. His senses were confused. Only last night—or was it earlier in the day?—he had dreamed he was back in Bohemia, living with Krok (who was somehow alive again), Lyudmila and Maria. Priby, Vaclav and Alexandr were also there but, unlike the others, those three were as old as they were today—the others were as Podevin remembered them from before Wenceslas had been assassinated. Even in his dream, he and Lyudmila had rowed before he left on this mission.

'Don't tell me she hasn't got anyone else to send because I won't believe it!'

Given that was exactly what Podevin had been told, he was stymied. Brother Mark would have been the obvious choice: he knew the language and he knew Emma. However, there was some reason, which had sounded good enough at the time, but now the dreaming-Podevin starting questioning, which was all about how royal he was. He was not born to be a forester! He was born to be a duke, a warrior—look how well he'd done in dealing with that whole Saxon patrol!

Besides, the yearly cycle had become predictable. He was on top of his work as the king's forester and, allow him to be honest with himself, he was getting fed up with being Krok. He was even more fed up with being dead, with a chapel built over him. They were calling it Saint Podevin's and it wasn't just Lyudmila and her daughters who left flowers to mark the spot where life had been choked out of the broken body that now lay at peace under the soil. He should, he knew, be grateful to Krok—there had been no more than one, possibly two, winters left in the man when he'd allowed himself to be hanged.

Podevin's thoughts went to his sons. He had been trying to train them up to be warriors. Vaclav enjoyed the training more than his brother, if he was honest. But, sooner rather than later, he was going to have to petition Emma to take the boys under her wing to get them some proper training. If he got out of this mess alive. Oh, yes, this didn't look like a bedroom—more a sort of prison, dungeon even. What was the plan again? Have another snooze? Good idea.

❦

Later that day, he was woken and dragged, none too gently, to the captain's quarters. Tired, hungry and thirsty, he was left in front of the captain's desk, until a report came back. The report said there were half-a-dozen Bohemian dead, and the rest had fled back towards the border. The chief bodyguard's head was unceremoniously dumped down on the floor before Podevin.

'Recognise him?' a voice asked in Czech.

Podevin, still groggy, stared into Geraint's dead eyes, and nodded.

'That's what's happening to you, peasant!'

'Peasant!' Podevin said, struggling upright, becoming aware of a painful head as well as the fact he could not see properly. When he blinked, he could focus on the captain, sitting at a table and eating what looked like a very hearty breakfast—or was it lunch, or even supper? The table was sturdy, the legs carved from oak. There were mats on the floor and tapestries hung on the walls. There was even a fire in a grate, and the room was pleasantly warm. For a lowly captain, this man had done well for himself.

'Yes, "peasant"!' the captain, said. Then for the benefit of the soldier who had given the report, he switched to German. 'This man, this pretend emissary, once found my family in the forests around Prague. I was a mere boy at the time, and he, as a fully grown man, was able to beat me senseless, molest my mother. My father and sister died. Mother and me only just made it out alive. I don't think he expected to see me here.'

The soldier dutifully laughed at the weak joke, but made no comment. Podevin fumed but decided the captain—he knew he'd remember the name of Priby's brother soon enough—would not be interested in his protestations about what had really happened.

About how he and Krok had found the family of four in the forest, brought them food, found the father injured and dying in a shack with the daughter, Pribyslava, trying to comfort him, even though she was injured herself. Injured in trying to protect her father. Injuries conspicuously absent from her brother. All Podevin had known, to this point, was that Sven—that was the name!—had fled with his mother to Saxony, taking all the food and leaving his father to die (unless he had been already dead), and his sister to fend for herself with nothing. Podevin and Lyudmila had raised Priby as their own and, even as he stood there, trying not to collapse, pretending not to understand the conversation going on around him, Podevin realised he was glad Priby had not been forced to go with her brother, no matter how well that brother had done in Otto's service. However, he did have a question.

'How did you recognise me from the battlements?'

'What? Oh,' Sven leaned back in his chair, 'I didn't. Not then. We have orders to kill or capture all Bohemians. So that's what I did. But we knew you were on your way, Podevin.'

'What! How?'

Sven laughed. 'As fast as you find our spies, we replace them with new volunteers. Besides, I knew you as soon as I saw you close to. You're a liar, a spy, and a traitor!'

Another soldier appeared. 'I have orders.'

'Well?' Sven said, clearly annoyed at the interruption. 'Out with it!'

'The captive is to be kept alive until he can be presented to the princess.'

'What! Who says so?'

'The duke, sir. Just in case there is something in the letters he had with him.'

Podevin breathed a sigh of relief. Maybe he could even get a message back to Emma.

'And how did the duke see the Bohemian dispatches?' Sven stood, fists at the ready.

The man blanched but stood his ground. 'Your orders, sir. Duke Heinrich was to be found and informed. He, um, he didn't quite believe the Bohemians would be able to send a force to attack Augsburg. So, although he can't be present in person, his niece can.' The man paused. 'The duke is leaving very soon for the border for the routine inspection … If you wish to speak with him yourself, captain?'

There was a silence. The captain sauntered round the table. He faced Podevin, shoved him so he fell. Then he shrugged.

'The pretty princess is only a girl. We can manage her. She'll agree to getting this peasant hung, and having a message sent to Prague soon enough. No-one attacks me and gets away with it!' For good measure, Podevin received a booted kick to the stomach. 'Take him back to the dungeons!'

ↇ

It was from those dungeons that Podevin, half-starved—his rations were bread and water, and not much of either—and very thirsty, was dragged a week later. He was roughly scrubbed, allowed to drink some water, which he gulped down readily enough, and dragged up several flights of stone steps to be presented to the princess.

With his head ringing, and nothing to help his eye to heal, it had taken time for Podevin to realise this was purely personal on Sven's part. If it had been anyone else on the battlements that night, they'd have been let in. And Geraint would not have died—died defending him.

While it is always dangerous to underestimate your enemy, it helps to know he is there. Too late now, but how could Podevin have known Sven had made it to Saxony to become a captain in Otto's army? The boy had done well, but his previous meeting with Podevin had obviously festered. And what about his mother? There had been no mention of her; was she still alive even?

Sven was not going to listen to Podevin under any circumstances. He had recognised Podevin, that was clear. Podevin could only assume he had seen him in the torchlight as they approached Augsburg's walls. The last time they had met, Sven had been a spotty youth, trying to defend himself and his mother with a blunt blade loosely tied to a stick. It had been an easy matter to disarm the lad and get him to the ground. From his dungeon, Podevin could have told him he had a living sister—one who was, moreover, a beautiful young lady, even if the scars on her back would always be there. But would there be any point?

Chapter 18
Trial and Retribution

The room was stone built, warm with braziers burning every few paces, and a huge fire by one stone wall. There were tapestries on the walls, furs and other rugs carpeting the floor. Very comfortable. Podevin's feet were unshackled, so he could walk, but his hands were roughly tied behind his back, his head wound still troubled him and seeing was not as easy as it might have been.

The Saxon guards lifted their spears and brought the butts down from behind him, onto the back of his knees. Podevin's legs buckled and, unable to help himself, he fell onto his face. The ropes around his wrists were pulled tight as the guards 'helped' him into a kneeling posture. He was still shuffling, trying to get comfortable, as the lady came into the room. Assisted by her ladies and her gentlemen, Princess Liutgarde processed up to the dais and sat down.

'Yes?' she said.

'I have a message from—' The cuff to the side of his head stopped Podevin.

The captain of the guard stepped forward and bowed. Snapping back to attention, he handed over the letter.

'The spy was carrying this, ma'am. We decided to show you—before his execution.'

'And the ring!' Podevin said. 'You took the ring!'

His knowledge of German clearly surprised his captors, but the captain, after one alarmed look at his prisoner, focussed his attention on Princess Liutgarde.

Who raised an eyebrow as she took the letter in her left hand. 'You decided, captain? And what's this about a ring?'

'My apologies, I phrased it clumsily. As for a ring, ma'am, we all know these people say anything, steal anything.'

There was a pause. The princess opened the letter. Podevin glanced up as something caught the light. The princess's fingers were visible. He squinted, trying to focus with his good eye. Could it be?

'It's like the ring you're wearing, ma'am.'

Another blow. This time, Podevin tasted blood.

'You'll address her highness with proper respect if you value your life!'

Podevin shook his head to clear it; he'd said ma'am, hadn't he? But who cared? 'As you've already said, I'm going to die today, why should I bother? She's not my princess!'

'Enough!' Princess Liutgarde was sitting straighter and the guards snapped to attention. She looked at Podevin. 'Describe this ring.'

Podevin paused, swallowed, and concentrated. 'Gold,' he said, 'fairly thick, but made for a small finger, with three stones. One bigger in the middle, green. Two smaller ones either side—clear or white in the sun. Inside the ring, the letter "M" is engraved.' Podevin stopped as the princess stood.

She glided down from the throne and came close. She held out her hand, where the ring glittered on her little finger.

'Like that?' she said.

'Different colour stones, ma'am, but yes.' Podevin swayed on his knees.

The guards steadied him, the princess's nearness seeming to remind them they had some duty of care.

'Captain?'

'Ma'am?'

'Find his ring.'

'But ma'am?'

'Now, captain.'

Podevin smirked. He knew exactly where the ring was, but how was Captain Sven going to get it out of his pocket and to Liutgarde without letting on? However, Podevin had underestimated his jailer, as Sven marched out of the hall and could be heard bellowing to other guards to search the dungeon, '*Now!*'

After a brief space of time, during which not even a princess could start fuming, Sven was back, holding the ring, which was handed over to Liutgarde with due ceremony. However, the explanation was murmured so low that Podevin had no chance of hearing what was said. Sven was left at attention while Liutgarde reread the letter. A single letter? There had been more than one, hadn't there? Podevin's knees ached, but two hands on his shoulders kept him in place. The princess glanced at him, the ring, the letter. She had whispered conversations with her gentlemen. Her women chattered amongst themselves, stealing glances at him and, once or twice, daring a comment.

Having been ignored for long enough, Sven stepped away from the dais: 'I'll take him away then—the spy.'

'No, captain, you won't,' Liutgarde said. 'As a guest of this court, he will come under Kurt's jurisdiction. He needs to be properly clothed, fed and—how long did you say he'd been with you?'

'Long enough.' Podevin provided the reply, earning yet another venomous glare from Sven. 'And I still haven't seen Blanik.'

'General Blanik can vouch for you?' The princess held up her hand to stop any reproach coming Podevin's way for speaking out of turn.

'He was my tutor, ma'am. Back in Wenceslas's time.'

'Captain.' The formal politeness froze all friendliness.

Podevin felt the guards stiffen.

'Yes, er, ma'am?' Sven said.

'I'm waiting for your explanation.'

'The general is checking our western border security, ma'am. He hasn't been in Augsburg for a month. And you, yourself, ma'am, have been dealing with Councils of State in the absence of your father and—your father.' Sven had stumbled.

Podevin knew there was a brother, a prince, as well as an uncle, but it appeared the uncle was patrolling the border with Bohemia 'to prevent any further incursions' and the prince was with his father.

After a pause, Sven continued with spurious confidence. 'We brought the prisoner before you as soon as time permitted.'

It was, Podevin conceded in his own mind, a brave try.

'My father has no horses? There was nobody able to carry a message to Blanik? And there was no-one you could speak to who could, in turn, speak to us?' Liutgarde's gesture took in all her attendants.

Sven kept his mouth shut.

'You, captain, will go yourself to give Blanik my message and require him to return here. You will return with him.'

Sven turned and gestured to Podevin's guards, his final mistake of the day.

The temperature of the words coming out of Princess Liutgarde's mouth dropped below zero. 'I thought I made it clear; the young man is to remain under Kurt's protection—not yours.'

Sven left, taking the guards with him. The princess turned to one of her men. 'Dietrich, get a message written for the captain to take to my father. The king needs to hear about this.'

'It will be a pleasure, ma'am.' Dietrich bowed and marched out. His glance, as he passed Podevin, was friendly—there was almost a smile.

'Kurt,' Princess Liutgarde said, 'you'd better take charge of my aunt's emissary from now on. Get those ropes off him and, before he dines with us, make sure he is appropriately dressed—he'd better have a bath as well. And get his eye seen to.'

Appropriately dressed? He had arrived appropriately dressed. Just not at an appropriate time—though Podevin still wondered how he was supposed to know that. All he knew, he'd gathered from his dungeon. Even in a dungeon, you can hear things, especially when people don't think you can understand them. Guards are forever gossiping. He'd heard Blanik's name more than once.

The danger most to be wary of, is the unseen one. The impression he had made on Princess Liutgarde was favourable, he knew that, or she would not have chosen to accept his story. He'd even picked up enough from his visit to the great hall to realise Sven was not exactly popular with the young lady. Had Sven's assumption she would do what he said, that she was 'manageable', come across in his attitude? That was idle speculation, but what he knew was the guards' relief at the prospect of Sven's absence from Augsburg.

Or rather, the muttered, 'Better make sure he doesn't choose to take us with him,' he'd heard from the two guards holding him before they, and Sven, were ordered to hand him over to Kurt, Augsburg's chamberlain.

If your own troops don't want to accompany you, it says a lot about your popularity—or lack of it.

Podevin realised his great piece of good fortune was that Queen Matilda had given her ring, or rather Emma's ring, to her daughter and that daughter had recognised the description of the ring Emma had taken in exchange. But, with Queen Matilda dead, Podevin could not be sure how his mission would be received. However, at least he was to be spared any further contact with Sven.

At dinner that night, the food was heavy but plentiful. There was wine, but Podevin was careful; in his forest home, they usually drank beer, and mostly small, twice brewed, beer. Lyudmila was sparing with drink. As far as she was concerned, if people were thirsty, they could drink from a clear, sparkling brook. As a young man, Podevin had been more used to strong drink than he was now. He would rather face the taunts of being a lightweight than suffer from having said too much at table.

However, very little was said at table, or afterwards. In the end, he asked Kurt what was going on.

'We await the arrival of the general. Then, you will be questioned.'

'Do we know how long that will be?'

A shrug was the only reply. Podevin kept his eye on Kurt, his good eye; the left one was bandaged up—the best that could be done until the swelling went down.

Kurt eventually opened his mouth again. 'The general is elsewhere and her highness has commanded him back—besides, it would be foolish of her to present you to his majesty without having your credentials checked.'

'Tell me,' Podevin was curious, 'how did Blanik end up as a general in the Saxon army? He's a Bohemian.'

'When he arrived here, we were at peace. But he has a Saxon wife, Saxon children, Saxon land. And he is good at winning battles. Otto almost trusts him.'

Podevin's head snapped up. 'Almost?'

'Your Blanik has never been sent against Boleslav. You do know we keep getting more and more men offering their services?'

He hadn't known, but Podevin was not surprised. Too many people observed travelling the road to Saxony and not enough coming back. He had reported this to Emma, but the only information he'd received by way of response, via Mark, was that Boleslav regarded them as traitors whose land was forfeit to the crown. Podevin hadn't recognised many landowners on the road; more often, they looked like landless peasants who, having had their meagre possessions trampled over, or their money taxed until there was none left, had decided to flee. Or else they were merchants who suddenly found themselves without goods or a shop to sell them in.

Or they could have been people like Krok and Lyudmila, who, if a raiding party found their home in the woods, would have had to flee until it was safe to return, gather what possessions they could salvage, and head to the nearest safe place. Which would have been Saxony, wouldn't it? And if Otto was prepared to pay his soldiers a decent wage, any fit, able-bodied man would join up. Anyone who didn't know German could learn it quickly enough once they were surrounded by people speaking that language all day.

However, Podevin wanted to keep the conversation going.

'Does Blanik still do training?'

'Yes, but he's a bit more on his guard these days.'

Podevin was all attention. 'What happened?'

It was a few years ago now, Kurt told him, but after a Saxon 'reconnaissance in force', not only had there been prisoners, there had been a minor flood of refugees. The able-bodied males had been selected for fighting in the west and Blanik, given he knew how to speak their own language, trained them.

'He trained them too well.' Kurt's mouth rose in a grim smile. 'One group of them decided to take Blanik on. It was close—if the guards on the ramparts hadn't seen what was happening as soon as it began, well … let's just say, you'd have to be very good to kill six when you only have blunted weapons.'

'But didn't they have blunted weapons too?'

'Somehow they'd all acquired the real things.'

'Did you ever find out what their plan was?'

'No. In the heat of battle, they were all killed. None of them surrendered. We assume King Boleslav sent them. He denied it, of course.'

'Of course,' replied Podevin, taking a sip of his wine.

So, the king of Bohemia hadn't changed. Spying and assassination had always been his stock-in-trade. Podevin did wonder how this gang of six had stayed together, and what sort of hold Boleslav had over them. Maybe it was the old trick of holding their families' hostage or, more in keeping with his past, the promise of release from prison or execution. Unbidden, Radslav's dying words came back to him. The old man was wrong; it was still the king that Podevin should worry about.

From Podevin's point of view, however, there was another worry— another thing he hadn't thought of in his headlong flight into trouble—this meant there were spies at the Saxon court. If Boleslav had known Blanik was here, someone must have told him. Maybe he needed to be even more cautious than he had been before. Perhaps Podevin should assume his presence in Augsburg was already known to Boleslav, and he was wondering who this 'Podevin' was. Podevin had been here several days, but he still had not had a chance to put his mission, Emma's questions, to anyone who mattered, if you excluded a sixteen-year-old princess. Suddenly he was nervous. If they waited too long, Emma's plan would fail before it had a chance to begin!

'Tell me, will Blanik have been told why he's being asked—or commanded—to return here?'

Kurt smiled again. 'Of course.'

However, that was as far as he would go. Which bits of Emma's letters had been copied and sent out, or whether it was a mere summary, or whether it was a case of them waiting to see if Podevin passed muster before taking any account of the letter, Podevin had no idea. However, before he could become too worried, it was time for him to be escorted to his room.

All very friendly, all very courteous, but it would take a very stupid person not to realise there was a double guard on his door—a double guard who did not appear to be present anywhere else.

Chapter 19
Under Attack

No castle is ever totally silent; there are guards on the move, checking the battlements, checking the gateways, checking the prisoners. Not all the prisoners were in the dungeons. Podevin's bed was comfortable, and he was not only clean of body, but had clean clothes as well. Kurt had sent another doctor to treat his eye that evening. He was fortunate—this man, a small fussy individual from the town, told him he did not usually come out of an evening. The splinter had missed the actual eye, the skin around the wound had filled with pus but, once the wound was drained of the dead material and dressed, the doctor held high hopes of a full recovery. His other head wound was to be bathed daily until it too recovered. The man, making a lot of finicky comments about how 'anyone could have seen what was wrong', left him. Podevin was alone.

Alone, but not in peace. Unlike in the dungeon, where a creaky door would alert him to anyone accessing his cell, this room had doors that opened on noiseless hinges. In the forest and without his wounds, Podevin would have slept. His mind was attuned to the natural sounds of the countryside night; owls could screech, foxes bark and wolves howl, and he would have slept on. But the slightest scratch at the gate and he would be alert even before his conscious mind had registered the potential alarm. In this external comfort, despite the guards or possibly because of them, he tossed and turned behind the bed curtains, hearing things, seeing things in his mind's eye, waking in the darkness drenched in sweat, imagining all sorts—

including the destruction of his forest home and all in it while he was away.

A mere lightening of the darkness, away on the other side of the room. A hint of a draft across his face. Apart from his knife, which was more use for helping him eat than anything else, he had no weapons. Why would he need a sword or battle-axe as a guest of the princess? A step onto a rug. Yes! Someone was here. Now fully alert, but aware he needed to be at least as stealthy as his opponent, Podevin began to gather the bed covers together. If he bunched them up in the middle of the bed, maybe in the darkness the attacker would go for them instead of his victim, who was now sliding out from under those same bedclothes and onto the wooden floor. Damn! The chamber pot! Had he made a noise? He moved his foot away—at least he hadn't put it right into the pot. There was a cabinet at the bedside, with his knife on it, but it was the on other side of the bed. Had his attacker known this? Podevin, still moving as if he were tracking deer in the Prague forests, slid, inch by painful inch, out from underneath the curtains, keeping his breathing steady.

In the expanse of the room, he could hear the intruder as a floorboard creaked. The two of them froze, Podevin assessing his options: door or opponent? If he could get out the door, he could raise the alarm, but that thought assumed the door was not locked. If it was, Podevin would be faced with an attacker who had locked them both in. He was going to have to close with his assassin in unarmed combat. It was just like when he had confronted Tugumir ten years ago but, since then, he had grown older, he'd had no practice—and now there was no time.

Podevin had crept to the end of the bed and the shadows had shifted; maybe the dawn was letting some grey light through the curtained window, but he saw a shadow raise an axe and bring it crashing through the bed curtain onto the centre of the bed.

'Bohemian spy! You'll never talk with the king!'

The shredded curtain enveloped the attacker, who nevertheless was able to step back in an effort to free himself from the clothing. But Podevin had leapt on him and was reaching for his belt—there must be a knife or sword he could grab. The two of them fell back onto the bed. A wrenching sound as the slats, unused to the force of a battle-axe, followed by the weight of two grown, desperate men landing on them, gave out and sank to the floor. Fighting curtains, bed linen and each other, they rolled apart. Podevin recovered first, finally grabbing his knife, but, as he turned, he realised the other man had drawn his sword.

'What's going on in there? Open up!'

Podevin moved, but the attacker, now visible as a guard, blocked his way.

'I don't think so.' The man was speaking Czech.

'Who are you?' Podevin asked.

'That doesn't matter. Sven will reward me.'

'Are you sure about that?' But Podevin was backing away as the other man feinted with his sword.

'Oh, yes. Very sure.'

With Podevin's back now against the wall, he raised his sword. Podevin leapt, his left arm grabbing the other's sword arm as he thrust with all his might at the man's throat. He had no other place to aim for; there was no guarantee his puny knife would get through the leather jerkin, or far enough into the man's stomach to stop him.

There was a crash as the door gave way and guards piled into the room. Podevin collapsed under the forward pressure of his assailant and lost his grip on the arm that held the sword, but his right hand was warm, sticky and wet. It was not his blood.

−

'I'm not sure I should be happy about being a man down.'

Kurt had thrown a cloak over his nightshirt. Servants were running around, making sure both Kurt and Podevin were comfortable and nourished. Podevin had been supplied with a bowl of warm water so he could get himself cleaned up. His borrowed night attire had been removed and he had dressed in the previous night's borrowed clothes. The other three guards had all been discovered asleep. Drugged. Podevin's would-be assassin was dead. As the only surviving witness, Podevin had thought he might have a problem explaining himself, but the axe buried in the bedclothes and the fact a fully-armed guard was on top of the esteemed guest, told its own story.

Kurt, however, did seem somewhat perturbed that one of his guards should be so easily overcome by an unarmed guest.

'Dammit, I'm supposed to train them!'

'Yes, sir, but for guard duty—"advance and be recognised"—not for assassination,' said another man, whom Podevin took to be Kurt's second-in-command.

'Alright, but there will be an investigation. Even without the princess in residence, there would be an investigation! And you say, he said he was doing it for Sven?' Kurt's attention returned to Podevin.

Podevin nodded. He had already given his version of events three times. The first to the rescue party who'd crashed through the door, the second to the second-in-command who had come rushing from wherever he'd been on duty, and the third to Kurt, whose rooms they were now in.

Sven was now a wanted man—at the very least, he had allowed his enmity for the princess's guest to overcome her clear orders—but, as he had been sent off to get Blanik, he was not around to be asked about the night's work. It was to be hoped General Blanik would appear soon.

Chapter 20
In Mark's Dispensary

'What are you doing back in Prague, Maria? I thought you were in Budec with Duchess Emma.'

The forester's daughter, turned lady-in-waiting, jumped at Priby's voice, nearly dropping the stoppered pot in her hands.

'I could ask you the same question,' Maria said, replacing the pot on the shelf. It seemed it was not what she wanted.

'Oh, come on. You know we always come to Mark's dispensary before we go home. Besides, I need to get some valerian root.'

The wooden hut was dingy, though warm—the fire told them Mark was not far away—plenty of herbs hanging up from the rafters, other herbs and ointments in bottles. Brother Mark's skills ensured he was always in demand.

However, Maria did not seem interested in Priby's need for valerian root. She was too busy scanning the shelves herself, looking for something, though it was clear she did not know what it—whatever it was—looked like. If Priby was waiting for her to ask about her mother, or the rest of the family, she would apparently wait in vain.

Instead, Priby repeated her question.

'The duchess needs new dresses for the weddings,' Maria said, after the pause had stretched to breaking point. 'She sent me to get them. I clearly have a good eye for colour. That's what she said.'

'So, you're doing well as a lady's maid?'

'I'm her lady-in-waiting. The only Bohemian lady in her inner circle with Beatrice and Hilde. People notice me.'

'Well, you won't find any dresses in here. Just a few herbs,' Priby said. 'And our mother is well. The boys are fine. Thank you for asking.'

Maria sniffed at Priby's pointed statements, but otherwise showed no reaction.

Priby continued, 'Though we're all having to work quite a bit harder now you and Dad have left.'

'And if I hadn't sent you back, there'd only be one of you,' Maria said. 'Hire some help, then. It's not my problem.'

'What's not your problem?' Mark ducked into the entrance and greeted both girls.

'Just something trivial,' said Maria. 'More to the point, where have you been?' she said, putting yet another pot of herbs back on the shelf.

'Out,' Mark replied, though Priby noticed his frown at Maria's rudeness. 'But what are you doing here?' Mark was looking at Priby, but Maria interrupted.

'I need rue, dill and asarum. And tansy, mullein and feverfew.'

Maria had turned from where she'd been peering at Mark's medicines, and Priby was puzzled at the way Maria had reeled off the list. Were these requests from Emma and her ladies at Budec? Surely they had healers there?

She watched as Mark moved to his prie-dieu, his prayer desk that doubled as a seat, and sat, looking at Maria. In moving, she saw he had deliberately placed himself so that, until she shifted position, he would see her sideways on. Light dawned. Priby, too, looked more closely at her sister. In her new court attire, which no doubt suited her face and figure, these clothes, if they were not getting tight just yet, would be getting very close-fitting around the middle soon. The swelling was slight, but it was there. Mark gestured to Priby, then nodded towards Maria.

'Oh, Maria,' she said.

Mark sighed. 'Your captain, I suppose?'

The silence resumed.

Mark shook his head. 'Maria, the course of action you are seeking to pursue is very dangerous. Life-threatening, even. You are young, fit and healthy. There is no reason why you should not produce a healthy, living child. Your mother would help raise it, I'm sure. As would your sister.'

'Of course!' Priby said, anxious to be friends again. 'We can still live in the forest—all of us. He, she, will be part of the family. Mum might be cross to start with, but you know her, she'll come round—'

'And, after a time, you could, if you still wished, resume your role as a lady-in-waiting to the duchess,' Mark put in.

'Dammit!' Maria stamped her foot. 'He's married. I can't have his child. I need to get rid of it—he doesn't want it.'

'Are you sure about that?' Mark asked.

'Are you going to give me the herbs or not?'

'No,' said Mark. 'They're too dangerous without supervision and, anyway, I don't suppose you can even tell me which you take internally, and which you bathe in, can you?'

Maria opened her mouth, then closed it again. Priby realised, if her own information was limited on how to stop a pregnancy, Maria's was not much better. However, before she could say anything else, Maria flounced out of Mark's herbarium.

As she ducked out of the door, Mark called out, 'I'd avoid the king at the moment, if I were you. He's on the warpath against your master and mistress.'

There was no reply. All they heard was Maria's retreating footsteps, and some muttering about, 'I'll show you.'

Mark turned to Priby. 'Valerian root? Your back's still bad?'

'Only when I do too much, but everyone has to pull their weight now. Even Vaclav's helping—not willingly, but he's helping.'

'You didn't need to come here by yourself with the cart, though,' Mark said. 'Did the kitchen maids make you unload it all by yourself? Surely not.'

Priby nodded. 'The king is feasting tonight. Everyone was busy. They did take the deer, though. I've never seen Dalimil get venison from the cart to the kitchen table to be prepared and then on the spit so fast!'

Mark grinned and reached for one of his ever-ready pots.

'Mark.' Priby forced herself to speak. 'You do know Mum's worried. I don't think she's sleeping. Vaclav can shoot straight enough, but we've no idea if he could kill a man—he's only nine! Alexandr can't seem to see what's in front of him half the time, and me and Mum can't do much. I know Emma's wielded a battle-axe, but—with my back?'

Mark gave her the herbs she needed. 'Nobody's invading just now, or Emma wouldn't be at this double wedding.'

News from Budec had filtered down the tracks and bridleways, the streams and currents, and found its way even to the homestead in the forest. The family there tried to be glad for the nobility and for Maria's ringside seat, but Maria, it seemed, was too busy to write even a few lines. And Priby did not know quite how she would tell Lyudmila either about Maria being pregnant or what she wanted to do about it.

She stood, eased her back. Thinking about problems like that didn't help them go away. She supposed all she could do was slip in the news that she'd seen Maria with everything else—along with it being obvious the king was around. No-one, apart from Mark, had time to stop and chat.

Mark took her out to the cart and their new carthorse. He peered in the back. 'Nothing? Not a single loaf?'

'Dalimil said next time,' Priby said.

Mark shook his head.

'The king's not going to miss some bread and vegetables, is he?' He strode off to the kitchens and returned quickly with some supplies.

Not the freshest, maybe, but sufficient for a family for a week and, with a sack of oats for their new horse, Priby was able to amble her cart homewards before the light faded.

Chapter 21
The Forest Home
Changes Hands

'Get your stuff together! Whatever you can carry—and get out!' Mark flung himself from his horse and charged through the gate, yelling at Priby. 'Where are the boys? And your mother?'

It was mid-morning, well past breakfast, but not normally the time for visits. But Mark was there, demanding answers.

'Vaclav and Alexandr are dealing with the traps. Mother's just tending the pigs; she's taken them to the forest. She'll be back soon,' Priby said, her voice trembling.

'Right, let's hope we can wait for your mother. We'll find the boys in the forest.' Mark took a deep breath. 'I've come to take you away. Just go and pack what you can. But we haven't long!'

'Haven't long to do what?' Lyudmila stood by the open gate, the one Mark had left wide open in his haste. 'Has your beautiful peace plan come to nothing?'

Brother Mark looked up just as a whooshing sound came from down the track and Lyudmila sprouted a red coloured shaft in her chest. Mark leapt up, ran to the gateway and caught Lyudmila as she sank to the ground. It was a spear. A spear expertly thrown. Yards away, Sven had still to move from his position on his own horse. Surly defiance on his face, he lifted his bow from where it had been lying across his back, and fitted an arrow to the string, though he didn't draw it back.

'I can kill anyone I find here—the king says so,' Sven said.

'This is not what he meant! I know, I was there—remember?' Mark spat from his kneeling position, but then Lyudmila moved—she was alive!

She gripped the sleeve of his habit.

'Shush!' he said. 'I can get help.'

Lyudmila shook her head. 'Just tell ...' She tried to swallow, but blood ran down from the corner of her mouth and dripped unheeded to the ground. 'Just tell Podevin I always ... I always ...' Then her head sank back, the grip on his sleeve relaxed, and she was dead in his arms.

Mark forced himself to breathe: in and out, in and out. He should have moved as soon as he saw this man, but he'd wanted to be sure. Sure that the king would really act, that Podevin's job really was on the line. And he had not expected this man to arrive so quickly.

'Stand up.' Mark didn't move. 'I said, stand up!'

Sven had dismounted and walked the few yards separating them, his family—at least Mark assumed it was his family, a grey woman covered in grey garments, and a couple of scrawny children—coming into sight in a horse-pulled cart. They stared at the body in Mark's arms.

Mark laid Lyudmila on the damp earth, trying to put her on her side so the spear could do no further damage—she would feel no more pain, no more oppression, nor inner conflict about being wed to a man from a higher social rank. Then, with a glance at Priby, whose mouth was wide in terror, but from which no sound came, Mark stood, putting himself between her and Sven. Sven, who was somehow in high favour with King Boleslav, despite arriving from Saxony, despite having nothing to tell but spiteful tales. Sven who had spun those tales to the king, in his presence, causing Mark's flight out to the forest. Mark knew this man was an enemy, but realised there was so much he did not know. He struggled to keep his voice even.

'You were given the right to tell the people here to move. That's all.'

'Why should that bother me? I know who you are, monk. Not even half a man. You're not worth killing. Clear off! I have work to do here.'

'No.'

'So, I have to waste an arrow on you, do I?'

'You kill the duchess's confessor and confidant, and I wonder how long you keep your job.'

'Yeah? As if bodies don't disappear! As if your Emma knows you're here. As if she matters anymore.' But Sven still had not drawn back his bow.

'Sven?' Priby, unseen by Mark, had come up behind him and was looking at the man.

'And who are you?'

'She's your sister, Sven—are you going to kill her? You did find her inside "your" home,' Mark said. He was struggling to remain calm, but knew he had to, if he was to get Priby and her brothers out of here alive.

'My sister is dead.' Sven had barely a glance to spare for Priby. 'That bastard Bohemian killed her.'

Mark interposed, before Priby could respond. 'Not so, Sven. If, by that bastard Bohemian, you mean Podevin, he, Krok, Lyudmila and I all went to that hovel, found your father dead, Priby by his side, and you and your mother gone.'

'She was dying—we had to get away from the infection!' At least Sven was engaging in the discussion now.

'She doesn't look dead to me.' Mark knew he was treading on dangerous ground but, if Sven had come here determined to kill, then risks had to be taken.

Not just by him. Ignoring his outstretched arm, Priby took a deliberate step in front of Mark, and another, until she was in front of Sven. She pushed aside his bow and arrow and, being as tall as he was, looked him in the eye.

'You did nothing. You let Mummy tell you what to do. You didn't even wait for Daddy to die. Something I had to watch all alone.' Priby paused, but not for long. 'And I'll tell you another thing—when Tugumir's thugs beat Daddy to a pulp, I know you were there! You just hid, like the coward you are. At least I tried to help!'

'And look what happened to you! I don't know what witchcraft cured you—but you shouldn't have lived—I saw your back!' Sven stepped back so he could ready his bow.

It would be a point-blank shot into Priby's chest. She did not flinch; she did not move. She kept her gaze looking straight into her brother's eyes. It was Sven who looked away and, if he did not let go of the arrow, the bowstring lost its tension.

'It was me, a Christian monk, who provided the medicines,' Mark said, 'and it was Lyudmila who provided her care. Whereas you,' Mark moved to Priby's side, 'ran away, telling stories. Like the story you told in the great hall.'

At that, Sven laughed. 'It was the truth. The truth your king needed to know. He has a traitor in Augsburg, one who your duchess has sheltered and lied about for ten years. And, if I suggested my role was larger than it was, who's going to say it happened any different? Whatever he does, even if he tries to come back here, Podevin's a dead man. Dead!' Sven noticed Mark looking at his family. 'You won't get a different story out of them—they weren't at Augsburg, for a start. They do as I say, if they know what's good for them.'

'They know what you'd do to them, do they?' Mark said.

The little group behind Sven had not moved during the whole scene. Apart from the occasional, flickering glance, they had not even looked in the direction of the family they were displacing from their home—as if seeing no evil made everything all right.

Into the silence, the two boys arrived. Somehow, even Vaclav had sensed all was not right, and the brothers had made no noise as they came up behind the Saxon family. Open-mouthed, they took in the scene. Birds still sang in the trees. Ducks waddled around the homestead, and the pigs grunted in the clearing. But, most of all, the body on the ground.

'Mummy! What have you done to my mummy!' Vaclav launched himself at Sven, fighting Alexandr, who was trying to stop him, trying to catch him before it was too late.

Sven whirled round and his arrow flew. The boys crashed to the ground together, even as Mark ran towards them.

Alexandr sat up, holding his arm, mouth open wide as he gazed at the arrow, which had gone straight through the flesh of his upper arm. Maybe the pain had not surfaced yet, but his face was a mask of shock. Mark, giving silent thanks the shaft had missed the bone, grabbed the bloodied arrow with both hands and, with one quick jerk, snapped it. The feathers dropped to the floor, the pointed end Mark drew through Alexandr's arm.

'I need cloths—wet ones,' he called.

Priby had abandoned the confrontation with Sven and was ahead of him in her thinking. 'I used the boiled water—it's all we had.'

Mark nodded his thanks. 'I'll just rip his sleeve off and wrap it tight. I'll deal with it properly later.'

Vaclav had scrambled to his feet but gone nowhere. Mark told him to stay there with his brother and not to move until told. He returned to where Sven still stood in the gateway. The brother and sister reunion was not going well. Priby's retirement from the confrontation was temporary. After her close-up view of Alexandr's arm, she swung round, marched back to her brother, and slapped him across the face.

'First an unarmed, harmless woman! And now a child. A child! You always were a bully and a coward—and you've not changed!' Priby hissed, her fury palpable.

Sven put his hand to his cheek.

'I can kill you all!' Sven said, sounding like the petulant child he presumably was when Priby had last seen him.

'So why haven't you? We only have a monk to defend us,' Priby said.

'You're not Podevin's brats—those two are!'

'And who told you that?' Mark needed to get in on the discussion.

Vaclav's looking after his brother did not seem very helpful. From the sounds, he was berating his brother for interfering.

'Oh, let me tell you, a lot more is known about this little set-up in the forest than you thought in Prague. Oh, yes; they know, all right! They know Emma has always been keen to come to the forest, and *so* keen to worship at that little chapel. *Saint* Podevin? Ha!'

Sven smirked at both Mark and Priby.

'They've known in Augsburg because Blanik told them. We even knew in Augsburg he was on his way. There's a new spy in your Duchess Emma's court! And King Boleslav knows in Prague where Podevin is, because *I* told him, monk. You weren't there for everything I told King Boleslav. I'm important. I have access to the king.'

'So, it wasn't an accident when you "recognised" Podevin, then. Was it? I wonder who told you?' Mark was thinking furiously, but Sven, belatedly realising he had let too much information slip, clamped his mouth shut.

'Podevin was under Emma's protection when he was hung by certain knights.' Mark spoke mildly, as if he was musing to himself, but his brain was trying to think things through. And, despite the situation, was now more interested than ever in keeping Sven talking. 'And there is a body interred in that chapel. I saw it put in there myself.'

'Oh, I'm sure when King Boleslav's loyal knights hung someone, they thought it was Podevin. But there's no proof, is there?' Sven, more interested perhaps in parading his knowledge than worrying about who heard about his supposed superiority, continued, 'Maybe your king is waiting until the right time. After all, England is very far away.'

'What do you mean?' Mark gestured to Priby not to interrupt.

'An appointed heir can be changed—maybe King Boleslav is waiting for a by-blow to grow up—and where would your precious Emma be then?'

'Princess Emma, or Duchess Emma.' Mark was getting fed up at Sven's presumption.

Emma had not been condemned yet. He even wondered, if Sven knew all this, maybe it was better to have him in the forest. Away from the castle. At best, Sven was merely giving credence to rumours, but it was worrying that these were the rumours he had heard all the way in Augsburg. All Sven needed was to hear the one about Emma's daughter and the fat would really be in the fire.

'A court is rife with rumours. There must be plenty in Augsburg. After all, Otto has only two children by his wife,' Mark concluded.

'King Otto is faithful! No-one says otherwise,' Sven said.

'Is this the same King Otto who presumably wants an explanation why there was an attack on Princess Emma's messenger—a messenger who was also, as he was flying a flag of truce, his guest?'

'His name is Podevin, and a traitor—I recognised him.' Sven shrugged. 'There will be others who want him dead. In Saxony and here.'

'Including you?' It was the wrong thing for Priby to say.

'Yes! And if I can't have him, I'll have his family! I have the right!'

Again, Mark moved to put himself in the way. 'Why? What had Podevin done to you?'

Priby was not about to keep quiet. 'He let Sven go uninjured—except to his pride! I was there. Sven had a spear. Podevin had nothing except his dagger. Yet it was Sven who ended up on the ground. I don't care what you told Mummy afterwards. I have eyes and ears!'

Mark wondered at that. Mark recalled how Priby had 'wanted to see' when they burned her father's body. Lyudmila had been as gentle, and as excellent a mother as she could, but there was no way round the fact that Priby's actual brother, and her actual mother, had left Priby to die. And now Sven was back, in good odour with King Boleslav, and taking over her home and life. What his Saxon wife and children made of all this, remained to be seen.

'Mark? Alexandr's wound is still bleeding,' Vaclav called. 'Do you need to check?'

'I think we need to get you all out of here,' Mark said.

'You're not taking anything with you,' Sven said. 'Under penalty of death!'

Mark did not bother to argue. There was a body and three young people to get away from here.

Sven, for the first time, appeared to notice Podevin's family was outside the enclosure. With an abrupt wave, he told his family to enter. Which they did, in silence and on foot; their horse and cart were left outside with no protection against wandering human being nor wolf. Mark did not hear a single murmur, even from the children, who could be no older than Alexandr. He wondered at their life.

Priby and Mark stepped back as Sven approached Lyudmila's body. He bent, picked up the end of his spear—the one not covered in blood—placed a foot on Lyudmila's back, and yanked. It took him three goes, with Lyudmila's arms and head flopping about, before he could persuade the head of the spear to return through her chest and out of her back. In the end, he stood, both feet on her back, both hands on the spear, and it, with a final sucking sound, released its grip on its victim.

'You lot! Deal with it!' Sven pointed at Lyudmila's body with the bloody spear as he walked into the enclosure and shoved the gate closed.

'If he doesn't show more care, that gate's not going to last long,' Mark muttered as he collected his horse. Thankfully, the animal had neither tripped on the dangling reins, nor moved farther than the edge of the forest.

It was an effort to get Lyudmila's body onto the horse's back. The horse and cart Priby had ridden home in yesterday were lost to them inside the enclosure. Mark did think about stealing the abandoned horse and cart—it would make their life easier—but thinking of the trouble Sven could raise if he did that, made him abandon the idea. However, persuading Alexandr to ride with his mother's body took time. The boy's wound had drained all colour from his face. He was trying to be brave but tears squeezed out of his eyes as Mark hoisted him onto the mare's back.

'We'll leave Mummy by the chapel, and then get you where I can give you something for the pain,' Mark said.

He wondered whether he ought to have had a word with Vaclav, but Priby was holding him tight by the shoulder. Mark remembered Vaclav's father at a somewhat older age and how he had whined, tried to avoid being in the situation he was in, and had put Krok in danger. All right, it had been a boar rather than a man armed with a bow and arrow. Mark could see he ought to have a word with Maria as well, when he could find her—for all her troubles, it was her mother who had just died. But they were all having to deal with a sudden, drastic change in circumstances, and the death of the woman they had all looked to for maternal affection and warmth. It would not be a restful night—nor for many nights to come.

Chapter 22
Blanik Returns

In Augsburg, it had been an anxious wait. It was presumed Sven had gone on his errand to find Blanik, and the two of them would return together so both, for different reasons, could be questioned. However, after a couple of days, rumours reached Kurt that both Sven and his lieutenant were not at their posts. Why was the lieutenant also missing? The whole company was paraded. Answers demanded. Answers, after some hesitation, given. Sven had not even been in uniform, not Saxon uniform, when he galloped out of the castle gates. His lieutenant had been in uniform, and he had been the one with the message for Blanik, but he was not urging his horse so hard. Not exactly in a hurry, is how one supposed humourist put it.

No-one else found it funny. No-one at all found the thought funny, when someone—it was never pinned down who—asked what Otto would make of all this. That Otto would be fully informed, was a given. That he would take kindly to one of his own captains fleeing to an enemy was a non-starter—if that was what Sven had done. Especially when it had been known this captain had exceeded his orders in trying to kill an emissary flying a flag of truce.

'He did approach the gates after they were closed,' murmured one courtier, as Podevin wandered round the great hall, trying to fill his days.

Podevin knew he was the 'he' they referred to. He lived with Geraint's death every day. At least the Anglo-Saxon warrior's head had been buried with his body. All in all, however, considered opinion in

Augsburg was that Otto would not be very happy. A gang of twenty or so? With sixty cavalry on immediate duty and hundreds more to be called on if that wasn't enough? The first thought, no matter what the time of day or night, should have been a parley. And if it was known, especially if it was known through intelligence from the Bohemian court, precisely who was being sent, then parley not battle was the obvious answer.

There were one or two people, Podevin assumed they were the ones with immediate oversight of the guards, who were being very diligent in their duties. Good—Sven had managed to keep him in a dungeon for a week, and no-one who ought to have been asking questions, had asked any questions. It wasn't as if people tried to break into Augsburg every night. In fact, for a fortress, it felt like a very quiet place.

Some of that quietness was, of course, because no meaningful information came Podevin's way. Messages were flying all across Otto's kingdoms, but the man himself was absent from his capital: on campaign. It did mean Podevin could concentrate on letting his eye heal. At least it no longer hurt when the doctor took the bandage off. Given Podevin's new status, the small man had been prevailed upon to return. The bone round the eye socket was cracked. That would mend, though he could not tell Podevin how much of his sight would return. He could see, but if he wanted to glance left, he had to turn his head—seeing clearly demanded his right eye. It might get better, it might not. The doctor felt it too dangerous to try probing. Even when he peered in with a servant holding a torch very close to Podevin's eye (and Podevin trying desperately not to blink), or when he was taken outside on a bright, sunny afternoon and told to peer up at the sun (with the same effect as far as blinking went), the doctor could see no damage inside his eye. The doctor was minded to leave well alone—and hope.

It was as dawn broke and the gates were opened for another day about a week later, that Kurt and the others had their wish, in so far as Blanik arrived, clattering into the courtyard. Sven's lieutenant had given his message, but then had begged leave to visit his family before returning to Augsburg, as his captain had promised. Not, of course, knowing what had been going on in Augsburg, General Blanik had been happy to grant the leave.

On the other hand, already annoyed at being expected to somehow know what was going on, he was angered further when he reached the great hall where Podevin was waiting.

'If you had read the entirety of your orders, we would not now be looking for a captain of the castle guard and his lieutenant!' Kurt berated.

Blanik exploded. His pock-marked face turning puce with anger. 'Who said anything about reading? I was given a message, that is all! And you had better be careful how you talk to me!'

Blanik must be tired, Podevin thought. Blanik was, or the Blanik he remembered, had been more diplomatic than that. Podevin had retired to the side of the room, a sort of ante-room to the main hall and, for the sake of something to do, was munching on some dried, over-wintered nuts and staring out of the window. He let Blanik reiterate his version of events about receiving, and acting on, his orders. He and Kurt worked out between them that Sven had been playing a cautious hand by getting his crony—there seemed now to be no question Podevin's would-be assassin was part of Sven's plot—to drug his fellow guards, enter Podevin's room and kill him.

With Podevin dead, Sven could return to Bohemia a hero; on the other hand, if Podevin survived the night, Sven was not in Augsburg, so could have had nothing to do with the killing, could he? There was only Podevin's word for it, but, during the attack on Podevin, the guard had let slip it was Sven he was working with. However, the word of the duke of Budec against that of a mere captain—*what was that? Duke of Budec?*

Blanik continued. 'And he is of Bohemian royal blood—you do know that, don't you? Although he was a bit young at the time, he could have married our queen's sister. It was quite the option favoured by both the lady and her chaplain, wasn't it, my lord?'

My lord! What game was Blanik playing? Podevin nearly choked on the nut he had just put into his mouth, only just managing to spit it into his hand and then place it on the table. He was here on Emma's behalf, not to take her kingdom!

'Oh, yes, Boleslav's takeover was not as smooth, or as trouble-free as he would like to pretend.' Blanik was still talking, and started pacing the room, so he could make his points more fiercely. 'As you know, even his own mother turned against him.'

'Yes, and we had another duke ready to take over by marrying into her family. We know all this, general.' At least Kurt was being more respectful by using Blanik's Saxon title.

'My half-brother would have been worse than Boleslav,' Podevin put in, thinking it about time he asserted himself into the conversation. He ignored Blanik's glare.

'There are those who say Boleslav is doing well to contain the Magyars in the east,' Kurt said.

'But he cannot do that while, at the same time, having to deal with Saxony as an enemy. Which is why I'm here,' Podevin said, drawing breath to begin Emma's complaints. But he was interrupted.

'It is Boleslav who has refused tribute,' Kurt snapped. 'Are you saying you, Podevin, would be a vassal? Accept Otto's overlordship?'

This was going too far! Never since Wenceslas's time had anyone in Bohemia even talked about Saxon overlordship of the whole territory—and even Wenceslas had secured brotherhood with old King Henry, so had still had considerable freedom of movement.

'I brought a letter. Which I understand her highness, the Princess Liutgarde, has seen,' Podevin said, even as Blanik said 'yes' to Kurt's questions.

'The letter, which *Duke Heinrich* has seen, does not come from Boleslav,' Kurt said, 'but from your Duchess Emma. It was sent as a plea to her brother-in-law. I do not see how King Otto would be minded to draw back, given all the insults he has suffered from Boleslav, unless he has a guarantee of future good behaviour from Bohemia's ruler—which only you seem willing to give.'

The emphasis on 'guarantee' immediately worried Podevin. He had to buy time.

'That letter also inquires after Queen Matilda. To us, her death appears,' Podevin paused, but realised he had gone too far now to draw back—besides, Emma's letter had been seen, 'suspicious as she was but two years older than Duchess Emma. Also, there is—or there was—the plot to kidnap Duchess Emma. For what reason, we cannot fathom, but we have the letters giving the orders.' He finally noticed

Blanik looking at him, making 'pipe down' gestures. Podevin paused. 'May I have a private word with my former tutor?'

Kurt indicated that the two of them could retire to the end of the room, where a bench and table waited for them.

'I need some sustenance,' Blanik said.

Servants scrambled to cover the table with food and drink. Kurt wandered off, but Podevin saw others still hanging around, well within sight. If they kept their voices down, what they said might not be heard, but their attitudes would be reported on, no matter how they reported, separately or together, on their conversation.

When Blanik finally had a full plate and full flagon in front of him, Podevin leaned forward. 'What the hell are you playing at? Emma trusted me!'

'Then she's a fool! And so are you. I'm keeping you alive. Do you have any idea how stupid your Emma's accusations sound here? Why would Otto kill his queen? And kidnap Emma? Really? Your message is ridiculous, which makes you … dangerous. And dangerous people don't live long.'

'For crying out loud, Blanik, if Kurt, or Princess Liutgarde, wanted me dead, I wouldn't be talking to you now!'

'So, Sven's a one-off, is he? You've been here more than two weeks— some of that time in the dungeon, I might add—Sven would not have acted without some sanction from higher up; even if they're keeping quiet now. If that guard had succeeded, it would have been, "Oops, sorry, acting without orders, we have your letter, we'll consider it—if Boleslav agrees to our terms." And Sven would be a hero.'

'You don't know everything. I've met Sven before!'

Finally, he had Blanik's attention. Podevin gave, as briefly as he could, an account of finding Sven and Priby in the forest, and Sven's flight with his mother. In return, Blanik told him that Sven had turned up as an orphaned young man, willing to join the king's guard.

'He has always spoken German, not Czech—even around me.'

'Could he be in league with Boleslav?' Podevin asked.

Blanik shrugged. 'Which one?'

'The older one, of course. The younger one only does what his father says.'

'And you want *them* to carry on ruling? I don't see either of them letting you live—whatever your precious Emma says. Don't forget, she's already chosen the Boleslavs over you once, hasn't she?'

Podevin stopped what he was about to say, confused. Emma had no choice. She had to marry young Boleslav, however he treated her.

'Your Emma has been constantly, consistently, loyal to the Boleslav branch of the Premyslid family. Had anyone discovered who you were, would she have risked her life to save you? She's got you out of the way, that's all. You really think we have not been watching from here? She did not have to win those battles for Boleslav—especially when her husband was doing his best to lose them. But she chose to.'

'She has children.'

'And the rumour is, not by her husband.'

'What?'

'And she killed one of her husband's bodyguards in a trial by combat.' Blanik concentrated on his food and drink while Podevin gaped at him, his thoughts in a whirl.

'Duchess Emma is not your friend, Podevin—whatever happened in the past. After all, when did she get hold of you? When she needed to use you. She needed a soppy, love-sick fool to do her bidding. A kidnap plot? Oh, really! And we know the queen died of the bloody flux. Information your Emma could have found out at any time.'

'She isn't my Emma.' Podevin was getting annoyed. Why did everyone know so much more than him?

'At least you accept she isn't yours—she's Duke Boleslav's.' Blanik went back to his breakfast, before raising his head. 'You work it out, Podevin. She sent you precisely because she reckoned you would be killed. Maybe she didn't know about Sven, or maybe she did. Did you even think your messages, your dispatches, were remotely credible? People die, Podevin. Even queens. Is there a single woman, of the appropriate rank, whom Otto has shown any sign of wooing? No!' Blanik over-rode Podevin's wish to interrupt. 'Podevin, you need to be the claimant to the Bohemian throne, one who is free to marry into Otto's family, thus tying the countries together in perpetuity. So, not only do we both get to go home, you get to live.'

'Hang on!' Podevin paused; he'd raised his voice. He leant forward again. 'I have a family, in case you've forgotten! I am pledged to serve Emma, even if I don't like the family she's married into.'

He stopped. Blanik was shaking his head.

'Like many men of your rank, you have a concubine. Who performed your supposed wedding service, Brother Mark?' Podevin nodded. 'Brother Mark.' Blanik emphasised the 'brother.' 'He is not a priest. He can't perform a marriage service. Your peasant woman will be perfectly happy with what you can do for her as duke of all Bohemia—don't call yourself "king" here,' Blanik added, before continuing, 'and you can make your brats knights. Your legitimate sons will come from Liutgarde.'

'Liutgarde!'

'She is Otto's only daughter. Legitimate daughter. Look,' it was Blanik's turn to lean forwards, 'Otto will declare you the true duke of Bohemia. We will lead an army into Bohemia—at least half Boleslav's troops will desert—and take over. You and Liutgarde start a new dynasty and you'll have an ally to take on the Magyars and any other enemies!'

'And Emma?'

'You're not still holding a candle for her, are you? All right, let me be honest. She's a better fighter than her husband, and a better general than her father-in-law … So, the chances are, she'll die in battle. But, if she survives, I'd send her to a nunnery. Her bloodline will continue through her niece.'

'She has children!'

'Children die too, Podevin. You've just been lucky with yours.'

Though, without Brother Mark, Podevin did not think Priby would have stood a chance. Her injuries from Tugumir's thugs would have killed her, had Emma's Anglo-Saxon chaplain not known how to heal her. And even if that same chaplain had not been able to perform a proper wedding service, Podevin had always felt married to Lyudmila. Yes, before that wedding, there had been the one time with Emma—but that daughter, Emma's daughter who had been born nine months later, was Mladenic's, she must be Mladenic's, she was accepted as Mladenic's—but Mark (again) had made it clear if he, Podevin, wanted to live, then he must accept he was not, and would never be, anything other than a forester. The (not just a) king's forester, guarding the forests around Prague, had his own cachet: no, he wasn't a knight, but his sons might be. No, he wasn't a duke, but he was still lord of all he surveyed. His family feasted on meat and fish as often as a duke's did, even if he did get his meat more often by trapping it. Also, even dukes had to be prepared to help with the harvest! What had Emma done in sending him here?

Podevin's musings were cut short as Blanik's words penetrated. 'Or I could kill you myself.'

His former tutor was staring at him across the table. The surrounding attendants also appeared to be on the alert; even the servants had tensed.

'So, what's it to be, Podevin? A dukedom, or death?' Blanik had stopped eating.

Podevin leaned back, staring at his old tutor, ally and, he had thought, friend. Blanik had changed, become harder: where was the man who had been prepared to die alongside Wenceslas? Podevin sighed. There was a time he'd have risked all to be duke of Budec, a time when he fantasised about being king of Bohemia with Emma by his side, a time when … But now he had a general with what looked like plenty of troops at his back—those attendants looked as if they could fight well. Even Podevin, who had so recently taken on odds of eight to one against, realised he would get nowhere in this situation.

'All right, Blanik. I'm not going to fight you. If the only way I can stay alive is to claim the dukedom of the whole of Bohemia, then so be it. But I get to be a part of all the plans, all the considerations—understand? I don't expect to find that you and Kurt and Otto have cobbled together something, expecting me to just go along with it. If I'm supposed to lead armies, I expect to know what is going on.'

Blanik shrugged, turned and gestured to one of the attendants, who disappeared through a doorway. Kurt must have been waiting on the other side, just out of sight, as he appeared within seconds.

'Just in time. The princess is on her way.'

Chapter 23
Duchess Emma:
Bohemia's Traitress

Although King Boleslav had accepted his son's excuse that they had to stay in Budec for the weddings, as soon as the marriage services were over, Emma chafed at her husband's repeated excuses for further delays. He also refused to countenance her leaving before him.

'The accounts have been checked and rechecked. Radslav's sons have all promised you that any monies owing will be repaid. So, what now?' Emma said.

'Now we wait to see if the new accounts balance properly.'

'Of course they will, if you're here to check them. Ever tried trusting people to do their jobs while you're not there?'

He stopped looking at the figures and turned his limpid gaze onto her.

'No,' he said, 'never.' Then he resumed his perusal of the new accounts.

When they finally left Budec, Emma was ready to ride ahead, but her husband insisted she return to Prague 'in a manner appropriate to her station'. Which would be in comfort and in style. In other words, by litter. She would be wearing appropriate, feminine, attire. As she was travelling with her husband, it was his bodyguard ...

'You mean the one that was so effective in defending you on your way here?'

'I was on my way to Prague. Besides, you charged ahead and left them nothing to do. Your lot will stay here.'

'They are my personal bodyguard—they go with me. Or do you want me to stay here as well?'

'I think you'll find I am in charge of all troops in the whole area around Prague and to the border with Saxony. So, I decide, and what I say, goes.' Mladenic stood in their rooms, checking his fingernails, infuriatingly calm.

'I am Prague's castle constable. I need my bodyguard with me.' Emma strove for a similar tone of voice.

She knew he was only doing this to infuriate her. The idea of separating a bodyguard from the body they were meant to be guarding, was ridiculous.

'Oh, you'll need a guard soon enough.' Her husband turned his back, so she barely heard his muttering.

This was too much. She crossed the floor, grabbed his arm and spun him round, to the gasps of both her ladies and his gentlemen.

'Get your filthy hands off me! You will pay for that.'

'Then arrest me! Lock me up—and then see how long it is before you lose this war.'

'It's not the war I'm worried about. It's how long I have to put up with you. Remember, you have recently been demoted—due to your own failure to keep the border secure.'

'They were dealt with.'

'"They" had almost arrived in Prague before they were apprehended. Which is not acceptable.' Mladenic held up a finely manicured hand. 'All right, keep your bodyguard—for now—but they stay well away from me!'

※

So, they had. They became outriders, crossing back and forth in front of the procession tramping down the track towards Prague. Weaving in and out of the trees, cantering back and forth. Keeping their horses exercised, was the excuse. Keeping their mistress amused while knowing her husband was infuriated by their actions, was the fact of the matter. There was another argument in the litter but, this time,

Emma was the calm one. She knew her husband would not want it to be seen by ordinary people that he had fallen out with his wife. She saw no problem with her troops, her bodyguard, behaving as if they wanted to make sure no-one was around wanting to attack her. In fact, that was rather comforting. So what if it 'looked untidy'? Mladenic sulked, while Emma enjoyed her mini-victory.

The days were getting longer, with a hint of higher temperatures in the sun at long last, now March had arrived. Once it had managed to rise up into the sky, a person caught out in it might venture to suggest it was getting warm. The birds were singing, establishing territories, and getting on with pairing up. Farmers had started worrying about their sheep, making sure their lambs were safe, and not being taken by wolves. Observers, human and animal, watched from the fields and forests, well away from the tracks, hoping the procession would pass through and not stop. If they stopped, the mass of humanity would need feeding, and watering. No-one, from the lowest peasant to the village headman, wanted that responsibility when it could decimate their stores, halve their flock or herds, and divert the workforce from sowing the crops.

Emma would have set out earlier, and risked doing the journey in one day, even if it meant arriving at her own castle as the sun was setting. But her husband had other priorities. Their journey took two days, but they were able to arrive at Prague Castle in what Mladenic called 'the proper order'. Emma had to concede that, as she had made sure the approaches to Prague and its castle were free of woodland, her bodyguard no longer needed to ride round in circles, making her husband dizzy. They followed the liveried foot soldiers into the castle courtyard.

Where Emma was arrested, while Mladenic watched. Mark and Mikael demanded to know what was going on. They demanded to speak to the king. They demanded to know what charge Emma was facing. They were rebuffed at every turn. Emma was to be confined to her rooms, on the king's pleasure.

⚬

'Well, my dear. We always knew you were not happy to be part of our family. But we did not expect such disloyalty.' The king's summons to the great hall had given Emma no time to prepare.

'I have never been disloyal!' she replied, stung.

"Silence! You do not interrupt me!' King Boleslav thundered.

Emma shut up, but the king said no more. He rose from the throne, while his son, seated beside him, smirked, happy to let his father preside over his wife's downfall. The king circled Emma. Mikael, she knew, was outside. Mark was somewhere else, but all of them were trying to work out what had happened. She had no information. How, she did not know, but somehow the king and her husband knew about her sending Podevin to Augsburg. But that was to discover why her sister had died—been murdered—and why there was a plot to kidnap her. At the time she had sent him on his mission, she was in charge. All right, maybe she should have consulted first, but really? Was it worth all this fuss?

'We have long suspected your disloyalty. Your frequent letters to the Saxon court, which we have only recently been able to read.' The king paused and smiled at Emma's gasp. 'Oh, yes, we know all the private tittle-tattle. But let me also assure you, your half-brother in England has much more important concerns than to worry about you—or your sister.'

It was a different half-brother, of course. Edmund had barely reached his teenage years when she left England, and it didn't help that he'd had to spend most of the last five years since Athelstan's death consolidating his rule. Edmund had accepted the official reason for Matilda's death, but she, Emma, was nearer. She had Matilda's letters and, by the time messages had gone backwards and forwards to and from England, months would have passed. No, she had been right to go ahead. It was just it had all gone wrong in ways she could not have foreseen. But the king was still spouting forth.

'And plotting to put your lover on my throne—sending him to Augsburg to have Otto announce him as duke of Budec, while you were in Budec itself, approving Duke Radslav's will.'

King Boleslav spread his arms wide in a gesture of disbelief. Emma watched her husband. He sat, hand over his mouth, his elbow on the side-arm of the chair, but he could not disguise the pleasure in his eyes. He had been plotting this. He'd been plotting for years. Emma's heart sank. By going ahead with her plan, she had finally made a mistake.

However, there was more, and it was worse. A loyal subject had come and told the king that Podevin had arrived in Augsburg. This subject had caught up with the traitor at the very gates of the Saxon city and fought him. Although his bodyguard had been killed, Podevin had claimed sanctuary within the fortress and Sven could do no more, other than flee to Prague with his family and throw himself on King Boleslav's mercy.

'Which I gave him, of course. Along with Podevin's old home and job. I mean, my dear, Podevin is not going to need it anymore. Your monk friend was here at the time and went rushing off. I hope he made sure there was no fussing. Traitors' families get no mercy.'

'Podevin's no traitor. He never has been, and never will.' If she was going down, she was going down fighting.

There was a chair for her, but, as no-one had told her to sit, she stood, back straight, listening to the words, thinking how to refute them. Though, with King Boleslav being judge and putting the case against her, she knew she was going to be found guilty anyway.

No Podevin. No Brother Mark. Not even Geraint. She had been surprised to hear of his death—she would grieve his loss later—now she had, somehow, to mount a defence.

'My lord. My lords.' Even now, she could not stop herself mocking her husband with an ironic nod in his direction. She knew he had something to do with this, but no idea what—as yet. Anyway, she must speak. 'Why is it that, after ten years of faithful service, you must accuse me now? I see no accusers, other than you and your son. In removing a Saxon patrol from your territory, show me my fault. In seeking to find out the reason behind the plot to kidnap me, show me my fault. In sending an embassy to Augsburg, while you were in the east, show me my fault.'

She took a deep breath.

'I have fought battles for you—won battles for you. Why should I now turn on you, when doing so would be to my own detriment? If— and I only say if—my emissary were to try to turn usurper, he would face me at the head of your western army. Or would you prefer to do without your best general—and that, my lord, is not my estimation, but King Otto's—and not even Podevin,' there, she'd said his name— again, 'would wish to do that.'

'No, because he's your lover!' Duke Boleslav said, interrupting.

Emma paused. How was the king going to respond to this? With silence? Then she would break it.

'I remember, husband, you made that accusation once before, in this hall. There was a trial by combat, which I won.'

'But you've had no living child since. God must be punishing you.'

There was another reason for her not getting pregnant, which surely the king could guess at, but there was a different argument she could use.

'If God was so upset with me, why did I not miscarry the child I was carrying at the time of your accusation? Why did that child live?'

'Girls don't count.'

Emma drew breath, there was so much more to say, but the king stood.

'Enough! You, madam, will go to your rooms—and stay there until I make known my further displeasure. Until then, your role as castle constable falls to me.'

She sank into a curtsy. She knew better than to push her luck, but she saw Duke Boleslav's look. He had been expecting to pick up the castle constable role. At least she had her rooms, she had her ladies. And, so far, she had her bodyguard.

Chapter 24
A Rebel
Contemplates Marriage

Across the border, Podevin found himself wondering about Emma. He thought about Lyudmila too—about to be repudiated after ten years. Wasn't this what she'd feared ever since Emma had leapt off her horse to give him that hug all those weeks ago? However, here in Augsburg, he was considered a single man—a single man about to be in possession of a whole kingdom (if he could win a few battles and ensure every other claimant to that kingdom was killed off)—in need of a wife. A wife, moreover, of an equivalent rank, if not an equivalent age.

Dammit, he'd grown to love Lyudmila. They'd learned to laugh together, even as they had to work hard in getting enough food to feed themselves and their growing brood. It hadn't all been blood, sweat and tears, had it? He shook himself. Here he was, in his furs and gowns—all borrowed, of course, but all appropriate to a person of his new rank. He straightened; Kurt and all the rest of them were being trumpeted into the great hall.

Afterwards, Podevin wondered whether Liutgarde was fully aware of what was being planned, at least as far as her own future was concerned. There was an official response to Emma's letter. Podevin pointed out he had brought more than one dispatch, but his worries were brushed aside. Sven would have destroyed them.

Either way, it was brusque. Queen Matilda might have been Emma's sister, but she was Otto's wife. Otto was in mourning for his wife who died, in the depths of winter, of the bloody flux. The Saxon king, in mourning his wife, had no wish, desire, or thought, of replacing the irreplaceable, with anyone—and certainly not with her sister, who was (as she was surely aware) already married. If the lady wished for peace, she should first of all turn to her own family and persuade them to make good on all the insults they had heaped onto Saxony. She should not seek to engage in diplomacy on her own behalf.

Had Emma's plan worked, it would have been Podevin carrying the message back. However, given the tone of the message, and the realisation that it meant Saxony was not pleased with Emma, Podevin was relieved—to a certain extent—that he was not expected to leave Augsburg.

On the other hand, he realised he couldn't leave Augsburg. As a rebel leader, as a duke from a foreign land, but without any prospects of his own, he was totally dependent on his hosts for anything and everything. Even his request to pen a letter to Lyudmila was turned down. ('Who'd read it to her?' had been the response. Podevin's reply that Lyudmila could read and write was ignored.) It was said a message could be sent thanking her for her past devotion and expecting her future loyalty once Podevin's campaign had 'reached a happy conclusion'. But, perhaps not to Blanik's surprise, Podevin declined the offer.

It was Princess Liutgarde who pointed out the potential human cost of this venture. What about her aunt's future, especially once her aunt's husband had been killed? She was told it was to be hoped that Emma would not seek to give battle when she realised what she was up against—but that was the men speaking. Podevin realised, for all that Blanik was in more contact with his former country than King Otto would have been happy with, he really did not know the Anglo-Saxon warrior woman very well at all. The Anglo-Saxon lady he had known most recently was Matilda, and she was so much more the demure, stay-at-home type.

Except when she ran the country on her husband's behalf. Over the next few days, in conversation with Liutgarde, Podevin began to hear a lot about the former queen of Saxony and what she had done. How much the demure act had been just that, an act; and how much was real, Podevin could not guess, but he began to appreciate, by the time Otto was king, Matilda had established a freedom of movement that allowed her to run the non-martial side of affairs. With her husband away, as he often was, the disputes, the tax affairs, the way the peasantry coped with food production, were all issues that came under Matilda's remit. Liutgarde had observed her mother's influence over her father, and was always, on the surface at least, prepared to defer.

Which was why, of course, when it became clear that the young teenager was to consider herself engaged to Podevin, rather than pointing out her father (by virtue of his not actually being present) had not given his consent, she made no objection, merely curtsying first to her uncle and then to Podevin.

'I shall enjoy attending our wedding at St Vitus's chapel, once you are crowned in Prague,' was all she said. It took Podevin a few moments to realise she had therefore deferred their wedding until he was duke of Bohemia, claiming the land of his birth by right of battle. Until that moment, no-one had said anything about when, or where, the wedding would take place. Podevin was being manipulated into allying himself with the most powerful, the most respected family in Europe, and he realised all it did was leave him with an empty feeling in the pit of his stomach. He found himself constantly wondering how much Emma and Lyudmila knew of his plans. It appeared he was drifting on a tide not of his choosing.

❧

The guard was still doubled outside his room, but the room was more sumptuous than even the one Kurt had provided. He was bowed to, deferred to, and agreed with, by all at court, except any occasionally visiting duke from other parts of Otto's extensive realms. He learned again to sit on his horse making polite conversation, while servants flushed out game ready for their betters to ride down and kill. Only for those same servants to take over the butchery and the carrying back to Augsburg for cooking, their betters taking over again when it came to the eating part. In Blanik's company, Podevin would ride out to check on western defences—not that the Franks, or anyone else, was giving any trouble. It was only the south-eastern lands that needed to be brought to heel. Duke Heinrich was prepared to be patient, in a limited way. Podevin did not have to rush into Bohemia with the first signs of Spring, but it did have to be this year. The way Blanik saw it, they had four months at best.

It was Dietrich-the-grey, the one sent to tell the Saxon king of Podevin's arrival, who urged caution. Not that the hotheads dared disagree with him to his face; Dietrich had been a formidable warrior and faithful commander under Otto's father. He reminded Podevin of a cross between Radslav and Brother Mark. It was Dietrich who reminded them all about the Magyars, with their different ways of fighting, their lack of understanding of the word 'treaty', and their indifference to the ways of Christianity. Not to mention how these Magyars, seeing the fight between Saxony and Bohemia, would inevitably seek to take advantage of the conflict for their own ends.

'Remember, my liege,' Dietrich pointed out to Duke Heinrich, 'it took the combined forces of your father and Wenceslas to check them before—and all that did was confine them temporarily behind their forests. Not even your father dared challenge them in their own plains to the north and east.'

Podevin understood. These men from the east came from the plains—lands where trees were scarce but grasses grew well. Barley and wheat and rye grew in abundance. Cattle could graze—and horses.

However, what Podevin wanted—needed—to get a grip on, was how Otto proposed to use his presence, his opposition to Boleslav, to help. He hoped the Saxon king would actually put in an appearance in his capital soon—and before he, Podevin, had to act. Surely, Podevin would need time to make sure people accepted him as king, or duke, over them? As to leading armies that the day before had taken to the field in opposition to him—that was not going to happen, was it? And Bohemia, ravaged as she was by the constant fighting on all her borders, was not in a position to seek to deal permanently with the Magyars, with or without Saxon help, was it?

In the forest, even when he had been at the edge of that forest, wasting yet more time gazing up at Prague Castle, wondering what Emma was doing, there had been people to advise him, people he could trust. Emma herself, for all their meetings were now jokes disguised in formal language—the princess and the woodsman—was able to say what she thought: chiefly that her father-in-law needed to stop thinking he could fight anyone and everyone. Thus far, Boleslav had the devil's own luck: in the thick of every fight, but not a scratch.

Podevin shook his head. Yes, back there, he had Emma and Brother Mark—but hadn't they been the ones to send him here in the first place? Podevin had never felt so alone.

Chapter 25
Podevin's Family
Move to Budec

Priby had never seen Mark so furious. Though was he more furious with Emma, or more furious with Boleslav?

'Both of them, Priby, both of them!' he said when she was brave enough to ask—furious with Podevin, even.

She and Vaclav followed the horse carrying their mother's body and a silently weeping Alexandr. Suddenly, Vaclav shook himself free of her hand, ran forward and grabbed hold of Mark.

'Shut up! Just shut up! And can't you see you're going too fast for Priby? You'll have to sort her back out as well in a minute.' Then, he too was crying.

Mark stopped. Held the horse. He looked back at Priby, who stumbled up until she was level with the rest of them. Before she could say anything, Alexandr made to get off the horse, 'So Priby can have my place.'

'You stay on there, Alexandr. You're wounded,' Priby replied.

'I'm sorry,' Mark said, 'I'm sorry. We're just a few steps from the chapel. Can everybody cope until then?'

It was a long hundred yards, but the chapel eventually came in sight. Horses don't normally get to crop the grass just by a chapel door while waiting for their next instructions, but this was not a normal day.

Inside, there was no bier to lay Lyudmila on, so Mark laid her on the floor, over where her first husband lay. He knelt beside her.

'Sorry, Lyudmila, but this is as close as I can get you just now. You will be buried with him as soon as I can manage … I am so, so sorry.' He put his hand to his face. Tears trickled through the fingers.

'Why are you sorry, Mark?' Priby put into words what they were all thinking.

'I told your mother,' Mark gulped. He could not look at them. 'I told your mother she would be safe. You'd all be safe in the woods. No-one would come for you. I never thought Boleslav would know so soon what we'd done, whom we'd sent. I never saw what he would make of it. What he would think.'

Finally, Mark looked up. Priby had her arm round Alexandr. Vaclav was standing as close as he could on her other side. Mark took a deep breath.

'And I am sorry for you. We must get you into the castle. And do it as quietly as we can.'

'Why?' said Alexandr.

'Because, after what happened today, we do not know who our friends are.' It was Priby who replied.

The eyes that looked into Mark's were sadder and wiser beyond their years.

❧

Emma paced her chambers. How had everything gone so wrong? Why couldn't Podevin have avoided Sven in getting to Augsburg? Why couldn't King Boleslav stop jumping to conclusions and making snap decisions? Like giving Sven the job of forester without even checking if he could do the job? Just because the forester wasn't there, it didn't mean he'd walked out of his job. And as for getting Podevin a pardon—that was completely out of the window now. Her idea was sound: when your enemy has the potential to send an army across the border, and you have no troops to meet him in battle, you send someone to treat with him. Standard tactics. And she had also sent to Boleslav—she was always sending messengers to King Boleslav.

She could do nothing. As if she was some sulky, obstreperous child, she had been confined to her quarters. Without Mark, without even her ladies. Emma kicked out at a stool, which went flying across the room towards the door and thudded against it as it began to open. Emma turned away, trying not to hop. Silk slippers were no defence against the sturdy wooden leg of a heavy item of furniture.

'Feeling better, now you've hurt yourself?' Mark picked up the stool and carried it back to its place by the fire. He then sat down on it and warmed his hands. 'It's cold out there,' he said, 'and you have four people to care for.'

'You are sitting in my presence.' Having someone to vent her fury on at that moment felt good. Mark did not react. He carried on rubbing his hands, then even stretched out his sandal-shod feet to the fire. It looked as if he'd gone out without putting boots on. He glanced up at her. She had her hands on her hips, glaring. As well she might. This was insolence beyond belief.

'You should, madam, have five to look after, but it's only four. And one of those is injured.'

'What are you talking about?' Emma deigned to move closer.

'Sit,' he said.

Something about his voice told her not to argue, but she chose to position her stool so she could look at the fire, not him.

'When were you going to organise the removal of Podevin's family to Budec? To the care of the young duke?'

'It wasn't necessary. There were no raids. They are just as safe there as anywhere else.'

'Lyudmila is dead, and Alexandr is injured. Shot by Sven's arrow.'

'But—'

'He didn't waste any time getting out there. They had a horse and cart. To claim his new property by any means necessary.'

'But there are documents to fill in, to be sealed.' Emma's shock was real. How could it all have happened so quickly? At least now she knew why Mark had not been around.

'Is the king likely to change his mind once Sven reports back there's no former forester in residence?' Mark said.

'You mean he just went there and started killing them?'

'Yes.' Mark's simple word did more to startle her out of her self-pity than any deliberate insolence.

'How did you know? Shouldn't he have waited?'

'Waited to have his revenge on Podevin's family? It might have been his only opportunity. If you want to hurt someone, really hurt someone, destroy something, or someone, they love.'

Emma looked blank. Mark had to explain who Sven was, what his story was.

'And I bet there was no fight outside Augsburg. Not like he said, either. Now what?' Emma stopped speaking again as Mark looked at her.

'You mean, no-one told you? A message was sent to Budec …' Mark understood. Emma's husband would have intercepted it.

'There is no easy way of saying this: Geraint wasn't the only one to die trying to stop Podevin being captured. They were outnumbered. They had to flee.' He stopped speaking, giving Emma time to think. They stared at the flames as the silence grew.

'What have you done with Podevin's family?' Emma asked.

'At the moment, two are in the kitchens, and one is in the infirmary—waiting for me. One is, of course, your new lady-in-waiting.'

'How did Alexandr get hurt?'

'He was trying to protect his brother who, in turn, was trying to attack Sven.'

'Send them to Budec. If I still have the authority—'

'You don't.' A new voice entered the conversation.

Both Emma and Mark rose to their feet to curtsy or bow, according to gender. The younger Boleslav strolled into the room.

'I was not aware it was custom, even in Anglo-Saxon realms, for males and females to consort together without any chaperones.' The duke paused, posed, looked at his fingernails, sighed, and resumed speaking. 'However, as it's an effeminate monk, I think I can, just about, excuse it. He can get about his duties. Now.'

Mark bowed again, to both members of the royal family, and moved to the door. Mladenic waited until he was in the doorway.

'Oh, and by the way, Brother Mark, your lady is no longer castle constable. That's the king from now on, and I am still lord of all the land to the Saxon border. And you'll need our permission to leave the grounds of the castle.'

'My lord, I have some young people—'

'I know. Do you really think my father and I would not be told? The king has decided to be gracious. I'm to tell you they're off to Budec. The duke there is to keep them under close guard. As hostages against the good behaviour of their father.' Mladenic smiled on seeing the reaction to his last words. 'Perhaps you, and the traitor, should have thought about that when you allowed him to go over to the enemy. Farewell, monk—we don't need you anymore. I want a word with my wife.'

Mark could do nothing other than bow yet again and retire. The guards, not members of Emma's own bodyguard, closed the door behind him.

'Are you happy now?' Emma turned away from her husband.

Every time Mladenic had any sort of military command, it had ended in disaster for Bohemia, so what the king was playing at was anyone's guess. Even if her plans had failed (she might as well use the word in her own head), what did Boleslav think she had been trying to do?

'Happy enough to have the decision of your future in my power. Oh, yes, your brother may have some interest, but not enough to argue with us when we point out your treachery,' Mladenic said.

'It is unfortunate that Edmund is now undisputed monarch of all England, is it not? My brother will have time to be interested in affairs over here—and in Saxony.' She still had her back to him.

'Oh, please! My dear. Don't you realise that has been thought of? I repeat, your treachery stinks to the heights.'

'I am no traitor!' Emma whirled round to face the husband she had hated, despised and loathed ever since she laid eyes on him as a snivelling ten-year-old brat. There were so many ways he hadn't changed.

'You sent Podevin, knowing he was Podevin, to Augsburg, the Saxon stronghold, so he could lead an army against us.'

'That's not what I did. You know that's not what I did.'

'What I know is irrelevant. What the king thinks is what counts. And he thinks you betrayed him. The only reason you're here in your rooms, and not in the dungeon waiting for death, is because he's having to consider what Otto or Edmund might do. As you have pointed out, aren't you lucky your brother has mastery of England and has fighters to spare?'

Emma supposed she should be grateful, but she was in no mood to accept her husband's crowing. She could not imagine what Edmund, king of the Anglo-Saxons, would do if she were executed, given he had done nothing she was aware of about Matilda's death. A death that had started all this mess in the first place. Her silence was annoying her husband; little Mladenic was pouting. She sighed.

'All right. This hasn't gone as well as I planned. But do you really think I would send someone to Saxony, thinking he would claim your father's throne? What's Podevin—assuming it is Podevin and he does come here to take over—going to have to do to your father, to you, to me?'

The doors opened. Both Emma and her husband turned.

'Yes?' she said.

'My lady, the king has sent your chaplain with a message for you, and your captain desires admittance, as do some of your ladies,' the guard said.

'Let them enter.' Emma spoke before Mladenic's 'Why?' was uttered.

'You're a prisoner! You don't make decisions anymore.'

Emma looked him full in the face. 'My rooms, my say-so. I thought you were objecting to the lack of female company when I had a man in the room?' She allowed a pause to develop. Mladenic did not fill it, so she carried on. 'Do you wish to stay?'

Without a word, he left. Wisely, the group at the door parted to let him through, though none of them, Emma noted as she sat at the table, bothered to do much in the way of bowing or curtsying.

It was an interesting, sad little group. Beatrice and Hilde, Brother Mark and Mikael. All with news, all wondering what was to happen next.

Mark moved first, handing over the parchment he had been given by the king. His smile was grim. 'It's not good, madam.'

She looked up at him. 'What about Podevin's family?'

'Being sent to Budec under guard, as the duke informed you. I have issued instructions for Alexandr's arm—it was all I could do.'

'Even Maria?' Emma said. Her companions looked at each other.

'What? Come on! Tell me,' she said.

'Unlike her adoptive father, Maria is in good odour with the king. It is due to her influence that her siblings are being treated so well. She is their guardian—they will be treated as she sees fit.' Mikael paused. 'The king wishes to reward her for her good offices when she was last in Prague.'

'She told him what we did,' Emma said. It did not need to be a question. It was too obvious. 'Well. She's no longer my lady-in-waiting—' Emma started, only to be interrupted by Hilde.

'I'm afraid she is, madam. On the king's orders. "There are no counsels to which she is not to be admitted." How he ensures that, given what we now know?' Hilde shrugged, and gave up the unequal struggle.

'But Podevin's her father.' Emma was incredulous.

'She's been saying for a long time, for months, that Tugumir was her father—the duke of Budec and Tetin,' said Mark. 'I, like Podevin himself, basically ignored it as the ramblings of a discontented silly girl trying to grow up before her time, a girl trying to make herself more important than she was. They should never have told her …' Mark shook his head.

Emma sighed. 'It's easy to be wise after the event.' She looked up at the sad faces. Everyone was standing, apart from her. 'Sit down. All of you, sit.' Then another thought. 'While I read this, Mark, send for some food, or are we all to starve here?'

Mark moved to the door to converse with the guards.

Which reminded Emma of something else. 'Mikael? Where is my bodyguard?'

Mikael paused in the act of sitting. He looked at his mistress. 'Disbanded, madam. Dispersed amongst the rest of Boleslav's troops. I am "allowed" to accompany you for your final days, then I am dismissed.' He paused. 'I refused to return to Duke Boleslav's … gaggle of entertainers.'

'I'm sure my husband was pleased to hear you say that.'

'I endeavoured to be more polite, madam, but, no, he was not pleased.'

'And the rest of them?'

'I ordered them to accept the offers they were given. Most of them are moving nearer to their homes, so the only issues are the remaining ones from your home country, madam.'

'And without Geraint ...' Emma paused, the parchment still unread. She missed the old warriors. Geraint and Radslav now both gone. She shook herself. 'What was offered to my Anglo-Saxon warriors, Mikael?'

'Dismissal with honour. A farm. Or a safe passage to return to England.' As he said this, Mikael passed a scrap of parchment to Hilde; Emma indicated the woman could read it. Beatrice and Emma shared a glance.

'Hilde,' Emma said, 'if you need to go to discuss things with your paramour—or is he your husband?—then do so. I would advise accepting the offer of land—you have both been gone too long from England to settle back there easily.'

Hilde bobbed a curtsy and was gone.

Emma looked at Beatrice. 'Do you need to go as well?'

'No, madam. Besides, there is no-one else to serve you,' Beatrice said.

'My other ladies have been dismissed?'

'By the king himself. He no longer needs their services.'

'He?' Emma asked.

Beatrice nodded, confirming Emma's long-term suspicions. She had been watched, all the time. Never trusted either by the father or the son. Could she have done anything to change the situation? She doubted it, not without changing who she was—and that was never going to happen.

She looked up at Mikael. 'What about you?'

'I think I had better stay here.' Mikael pointed at the door. Where Mark was waiting, the order for food having been passed down to the kitchens.

'Given what my husband has just said about men and women together in the same room ...'

'Your remaining ladies will be here as well, madam. And your chaplain.'

'All—here?'

Mikael nodded. 'You are confined to quarters. Those who chose to remain by your side, will do just that. Remain by your side.'

Mark moved from the door as food arrived. Emma had to shift the still unread parchment out of the way. She supposed it made sense: if you were a king, or a duke, constantly suspicious, constantly on edge, and thinking a member of your own family had—what phrase to use? She could not say 'betray', not even in her own mind. And she was no traitor—'gone against their wishes.' That would have to do. She'd not even done that deliberately or maliciously …

They needed to eat. And they needed to think.

Chapter 26
Emergency Medicine

Mark was not destined to eat with the rest of them that day. Just as he stood aside so the servants could enter Emma's quarters, a shout came from down the corridor.

'Help! Mark! Maria needs help!' Priby, who as far as Mark knew, should be well on her way to Budec by now, ran down the corridor towards him as he stepped out of the room.

His lips were forming the words, 'What's wrong,' when one of the guards stepped in front of her, used his spear to trip her up, and kicked her in the back, causing her to squeal in pain.

'What do you think you're doing? Back to your post.' Emma, like an avenging fury, had dashed out to see what the fuss was about.

But, instead of obeying, the guard had put his spear point between Priby's shoulder blades and forced her back down to the floor, her anguished face still looking up. Emma found the other guard's spear was at her own throat.

'I don't think so,' the first guard said. 'You, *my lady*, get back into your chamber—or she gets it. Move!'

Watched by Mark and Priby, Emma stepped backwards. Grinning, the guard followed. One step at a time, until he was inside. Mark turned, blocking Priby's view, so she did not, could not, see how Emma grabbed the spear with her left hand, pulled it to the side and yanked it forward, so the guard stumbled onto her dagger and sank to the floor. As she did that, Mikael, sword drawn, emerged from Emma's room, appearing as an avenging angel from behind Mark.

There was a clash of metal and the spear dropped; the guard, who, half-a-minute ago had been giving orders, now had his back to the wall, his spear on the ground, and was holding his gashed shoulder with his other hand. Mikael's sword was across his throat.

'I was only obeying orders,' he babbled.

'Orders to kick defenceless women in the back? Those were your orders? No—you don't call for help. Not if you value your life.' It was Mikael's turn to increase the pressure.

'The king won't be happy.' The guard gulped.

'Tell me something I don't know. Come on. While we eat, you're going to start talking.'

As Priby, for the moment ignoring the pain from her back, dragged Mark away, the first guard was led into Emma's rooms, stepping over the body of his former colleague.

℃

There was a crowd in the courtyard. No horses, but the litter was on the ground. Normally, the people in a litter would remove themselves before the litter was lifted off the back of the horses and everything dealt with smoothly, and normally. The curtains were drawn, but the sounds from inside were of someone thrashing around in agony. This time, the lady was in no state to remove herself.

The captain, it was said, had to order his whole troop to lift the litter so the horses could be removed and returned to the stables. The litter had been dumped, none too gently, on the ground, the troops all too ready to flee the scene of female agony.

'We'd not gone far when she started screaming,' Priby told Mark as they rushed out of Emma's rooms. 'She wouldn't let anyone inside the curtains. Not till I had a look—there's so much blood. On her hands, down there.' Priby pointed, a gesture of embarrassment, between her own legs. 'It's horrible. The only other thing she said was, it shouldn't have started so soon,' Priby added as the two of them pounded their way down the steps into the courtyard, where the litter lay by the far wall, near the castle entrance. 'She was supposed to be all right until we all arrived at Budec—I hope I did the right thing bringing everyone back here.'

Mark did not have time for a reassuring reply. Even now, they could hear that Maria was alternating between screaming in pain and screaming to be left alone.

'Back!' Mark ordered as they arrived. 'Go on, give us some space here.'

Thankfully, as healer, he still had some authority, so the crowd at least gave him and Priby some room.

'Where are the boys?' Mark asked Priby as he bent to peer through the curtain.

'I took them with me, looking for you. Left them with Dalimil in the kitchens. He said he'd look after them.'

Mark nodded. He wrenched the curtains apart. The scene was bad—only on the battlefield had he seen worse. Maria lay there, her skirts up about her bloodied waist. She wasn't dead yet, but he guessed what she had done. Despite her pain, Maria was able to glare at Mark.

'If you'd given me the herbs, this would have been over long ago,' she spat.

'Maria!' Priby said. 'I brought Mark to help.'

'Don't—need—help!'

'You'd rather be stuck on the road to Budec?' Priby said. 'You agreed to the return to Prague.'

'Anything—to shut—you up!'

'Well, you can shut up now. Unless you can tell me exactly what you took?' Mark said, peering round Maria, as if he were looking for something. As Priby looked at him, he added, 'If I know what she took, it'll be easier to counter it. She does not appear to have miscarried yet.'

'Too late!' came the cackle from the cushions. 'That bit's—too late. I threw it out!'

Priby looked again at her sister's bloodied hands. 'You didn't! You picked up the child and—' She could not finish.

She'd had so much trouble getting the soldiers to agree to turn about—in the end, she'd all but shoved the captain's face into the litter. Once he saw blood, feminine blood, he couldn't order the about-turn quickly enough. However, Priby also had to look after Alexandr and Vaclav, promising them food and warm beds, anything to keep them both from moaning as they walked back the way they'd come. Maria might have had a litter, but the three of them, as befitted their status, had been walking to Budec. Then there was the frantic trying to find Mark. Not in his herbarium, not in the kitchens—at least she'd been able to leave the boys there—Emma's room had been the last hope.

What was Mark saying? Moss? Mustard?

'I'm not moving her until we've got this bleeding stopped. And we need to get her to vomit up any remaining poison.' Mark dived off through the crowd towards his dispensary, leaving Priby to murmur what soothing words she could to Maria.

'Poison!'

'He says she's been poisoned!'

'Tell him!'

'No, you tell him!'

The whispers went round the waiting crowd like an autumn breeze stirring up dried leaves. By the time Priby looked, the watchful still-ness had returned. One or two people were crossing the courtyard, going about their business, but most stopped—Maria's misfortune, and it being in public, was the most excitement some people appeared to have seen for days. That, and Emma's arrest. Priby was doing her best to keep as many prying eyes as possible from her sister, when Mark reappeared, carrying a beaker full of liquid.

'Drink it,' he said, pushing it towards Maria. 'All of it. We've got to get the rest of that stuff—whatever it is—out of your stomach.'

Still Maria hesitated.

'Come on, Maria, you know Mark is trying to make you better,' Priby said, taking the cup from him and holding it to her mouth.

It didn't take long before Maria was retching. She held on to the side of the litter as yellow-brown-green liquid spewed from her mouth in fits and starts.

The crowd, having crept closer since Mark's words, had, until now, only retreated so far as to avoid being splashed by Maria's vomit, and had been craning their necks to try to see what Mark was doing down between her legs. Until they heard a new voice. And scattered to the four corners of the courtyard. Most disappeared into buildings.

'This lady, my servant, has been poisoned. I want to know by whom.' King Boleslav, not even wearing a cloak, but surrounded by guards, marched up to an isolated Priby and Mark. And their patient.

'Sire,' Mark said, not pausing in his work, 'once I have finished, I will report.'

'I beg your pardon.' The king held a hand up to stop a guard captain from dealing with the monk. 'You can report now.'

It was a mild voice, but Priby could tell it was a voice only just holding on to its temper. She glanced at Mark, but Maria was the one to look up. Priby had no time to wipe a face with vomit down its chin. Maria had also wiped a bloody hand across her face and her headdress had been dislodged.

'It's poison. I would not be here but for him.' A shaking finger pointed at the captain.

Priby recognised him. She supposed Maria told the truth, in that this was the married captain who had fathered her child. Maria was continuing, glaring at all the men surrounding the king. Her voice dropped, meaning even the king had to lean closer, his nose wrinkling in distaste.

'Witchcraft. He has allies in Budec—he made sure you sent me,' Maria said, to Priby's gasp. 'He said we could not both serve you, sire. I had to die.' Maria gulped, dared to grasp the king's shirt with her bloody hand. 'Ask him. Ask him how he survived the Magyar's arrows, when so many of his company did not. Now it's my turn to die.'

At that, she sank back onto the cushions and closed her eyes.

The king gave his captain a long stare. The captain could not meet his gaze. Boleslav then looked at the litter, and Mark's preparations.

'What is all this?'

'That,' Mark finally straightened up and pointed at the beaker still in Priby's hand, 'is to purge the remaining—poison—from her stomach. She is also losing blood. My skills are limited, but I have been using dried moss to soak up the blood, and I hope her body will heal. I can do little more.'

'Your God cannot cope with witchcraft, is that it?' Boleslav said.

Mark did not reply.

'Take her to the duchess's quarters. She will recuperate there. You will find out who the witch is in Budec, and report the name, or names, to me.'

'I'm not sure—' began Mark.

'Gretel,' said a weak voice from the litter. 'It is enough. She has won. With her captain, she has won.'

'Gretel. We will remember that name,' the king said. 'Oh, the duchess will make sure she has the best care. If she dies, so does the duchess—as do you.'

If the captain, who had been standing there, silent, thought the danger of death had passed over him, the king's next words disabused him.

'As for the one who poisoned her, who *did* survive when his former company did not ... let him be hanged.' Silence. 'Now!'

The king left, leaving the grisly task of executing the captain to others. If Priby did not notice much reluctance on the part of the king's troops as they dealt with the now screaming captain, she did catch the smirk on Maria's lips, and the compressed whiteness on Mark's. Priby did not need it spelling out; because of Maria's own calculated statements, Mark's life, Emma's life, and her own life, were on the line.

❧

In the end, the arrangements were fairly simple. Maria, with Priby as her carer, was to be transferred to a side room in Emma's apartments, and Mark was to keep a close eye on her. Vaclav and Alexandr—who, at long last, had his wounded arm seen to by Mark—were to share Mark's quarters and keep themselves out of the way as best as they could. Mark was also to send several servants to make sure Lyudmila had a decent, if quiet, burial. As Maria could not be moved, and the rest of them were not supposed to leave Prague (until they were all set to be removed to Budec), the memorial service had to be held in Emma's rooms.

Before that, Mark and Priby had to apprise Emma of what had happened.

'You will be advised not to repeat this, but Maria was with child. She is no longer with child.' Mark was sitting at the table, stuffing down a few mouthfuls from the meal he and Priby had missed, so was giving his report in between bites of food. 'If she swallowed poison,' he continued, 'it was by her own agency, and not witchcraft. However, you will not convince King Boleslav of that—he is all too ready to believe in dark forces, that one. I hold no knowledge of this Gretel, but I am guessing she was the wise woman Maria sought to buy her herbs from.'

'How does this Gretel come into it?' Emma asked.

'Maria named her as the witch from Budec, who helped the king's captain poison her.'

Priby was picking at her plate of food. She felt sick to her stomach. All she had done was try to help her sister, and all she had received in return was a death threat hanging over her and Mark. And two actual deaths being ordered by the king on Maria's say-so!

Priby looked up at Mark. 'If you're sure of all this, why didn't you say anything? People are dead.'

'People die all the time,' Mark said, 'and arguing with kings, unless you are sure you can prove your case, is not easy. We will pray Maria survives.' Mark went back to eating.

৩

Over the next few days, even as it became clear Maria was not about to succumb to her poisoning, the patient was tense and tetchy, especially with Priby. Maria seemed more worried about messengers than even Emma, but maybe Emma was more used to masking her feelings. However, three days later, a message arrived at Emma's rooms. She held out her hand to receive it.

'No, madam. It's for Maria,' the messenger said.

'I can give it to her,' Emma replied, surprised.

After her altercation with the guard, she had been treated with wary respect. Besides, no-one had yet dared to remove Mikael.

'I have my orders—from the king—madam.'

Emma shrugged and indicated the side room.

It took until Maria was asleep before Priby could gently remove the parchment from her grasp and read the contents.

She stepped out into the main room.

'Gretel is dead. As soon as she is well enough to make the journey, Maria can escort "the traitor's children" to Budec.'

'Well,' said Emma, 'she's got what she wanted.' She was met with half-smiles, shrugs and shakes of various heads.

'But at what cost?' murmured Priby.

Mark smiled at her. 'I fear there may yet be more to pay,' he said. 'But now we must get you all ready to depart. And hope your father doesn't make any mistakes.'

'Other than agreeing to lead an army into Bohemia?' said Emma.

Chapter 27
Rebel Leader? General? Prisoner?

'All right, Blanik. What's going on here?'

Podevin had endured enough of Blanik's evasions when he asked a simple question, not to mention the deference that scarcely bothered masking those evasions. For all intents and purposes, despite the fact he had now led a Saxon army—briefly, it must be admitted, but he had led an army, and led it to victory—and for all the luxury of his rooms, he might as well regard himself as a prisoner. It had taken days to get Blanik to visit him, and Podevin could tell his former tutor was uneasy.

'Nothing,' Blanik said.

'I don't believe you. You manipulated me into this situation. You recognised me as duke of Budec. You said—not me!—you said I wanted to rule Bohemia!'

'It's your only option, unless you want to die?'

'I'd been living in the forest for ten years! I had a life!'

'A life? Hiding away? Not knowing if you'd be discovered from one day to the next? We have a plan for you.'

'Do you want to share it? Does King Otto approve it?'

Silence. Podevin lay down on his bed. Blanik had chosen to visit him in his rooms after Podevin found out there had been yet another meeting without him. Kurt, Dietrich and Duke Heinrich had, however, attended. Podevin gestured round him.

'Sumptuous curtains round my bed, tapestries and floor coverings. And a wooden floor underneath, polished to such a shine so I couldn't get a splinter in my toes no matter how hard I might try. There's even a stone fireplace.' He sat up again. 'But I'd swap it all for the rude hut in the forest, with rushes on the floor and a central fire with a pot of stew over it—and not knowing whether it would be fresh meat today or something salted from the store!'

'My oath! You have changed!'

'But I haven't become stupid. My supposed fiancée: not here. My army: nowhere to be seen. My support from King Otto: non-existent as far as I know—I've heard nothing from him myself. Does the king of Saxony even know what's going on in his capital?'

Blanik looked up at that suggestion, but said nothing, leaving Podevin to carry on.

'Are my family to be rescued? No idea. Why am I even alive? They could take you and make you king of Bohemia if they wanted—really wanted.'

'Duke,' muttered Blanik. 'Anyway, I have a Saxon wife and family. We're not royal enough.'

'I'm a second cousin—that's all! Tell you what, Blanik, just tell them, I'm happy to be sent back. I'll take the message, if you like, telling Boleslav how much he owes. And take my chances. If you need a royal as *duke* of Bohemia, try Duke Heinrich.'

The sudden silence, the turn to look at him, told him he'd said something important. Podevin had just been sounding off. He was fed up of the endless rounds of meetings. Either he was a competent general, or he wasn't. Either he could lead an army, or he couldn't. Either his family was to be kept safe, or it wasn't. His brain caught up with him: how stupid had he been? It hadn't been about him at all. He was just a convenient scapegoat.

'It's Duke Heinrich, isn't it? He wants Bohemia. So...' Podevin stood as Blanik tried to interrupt. 'No, let me work it out—given I'm nearly there.'

Podevin paused again, this time to let Blanik deny his claim. There was no denial, so Podevin spoke.

'When we were sent to deal with those rebels—out in the west, I note, nowhere near Bohemia—that time you were "told" to see how good a general I could be: we led Franks, and other mercenaries, not Saxons. No-one has suggested you'd be beside me when I invade Bohemia, so it would be just me in the lead. I'd be taking on King Boleslav,' this time, there was no correction, 'and Emma. Whoever won, would be in a weakened condition, so Heinrich could come up behind and destroy any remaining forces, and be the only option for an exhausted land. There! How'd I do?'

'Guards!' said Blanik, turning to leave the room. 'Once I'm gone, no-one enters, no-one leaves, unless I—or someone senior to me—says so.'

The door slammed shut behind him.

☙

Podevin was back lying on the bed. Perhaps he was fortunate not to be back in the dungeons, but there were now two guards on the *inside* of the door, facing him. Before his escape attempt, they'd been on the outside. He mused silently. Maybe, ten years ago, he would have been able to fit through the window. As far as windows went, it was quite a wide one—more than an arrow slit anyway—but that was because (as had now been pointed out) it was a window onto the interior courtyard, not in the outer wall. So even if he made it out of his bedroom—and, by the way, the sheets he had knotted together still did not reach the ground—he would not, he now knew, have got much farther.

'And why, if I am an honoured guest, would I have not got much farther? It couldn't possibly be because I am actually a prisoner here? And everyone from the lowest guard to Duke Heinrich himself, knows this?' Podevin demanded.

Kurt had looked at him, but said nothing. Podevin had been seen trying to squeeze his way out, having tied his sheets to the bed post and thrown them through the window. (The bed had now been heaved to the far side of the room, away from the window—even less chance of an escape.) He had waited for dark, but the unusual movement had caught the eye of 'one of our ladies', who happened to be crossing the courtyard at that point. His attempt had been doomed. *And*, thought a sadder and wiser Podevin, *would those thin, silk sheets have taken your weight?*

Podevin continued to smile on the outside for the sake of the guards. He had also now been told Boleslav, far from pardoning him, had reissued his death sentence. He was an outlaw. Anyone finding him on Boleslav's lands could kill him with impunity. All this had been explained to him as if he didn't know what being an outlaw meant.

༉

Podevin's increased reluctance to engage with the idea of becoming the next duke of Bohemia, was met by Blanik pretending Podevin had not worked things out. Either way, it appeared that Otto wasn't about to hand him over to Boleslav. Otto needed his tribute. What Bohemia owed increased each year and, so far, only Podevin, or those acting in Augsburg on his behalf, had promised to pay. And so, of course, Podevin was told Otto was fully behind the idea of making Podevin the duke of Bohemia. There were other plans for Heinrich, so Podevin was not to worry about that. Not that he had much choice in the matter. Nor did he get to see any evidence of Otto's support in writing, nor was there any news that the Saxon king might turn up in person. Podevin had to be satisfied with the concession that he was now being invited to all meetings that concerned him.

Against that, Boleslav held Podevin's whole family in Budec—a message had been sent to that effect, with an obvious implication: behave, or else. Not that his Saxon friends and allies appeared concerned. Podevin, and only Podevin it seemed, wanted assurances they were all alive and cared for. Would he really have fled to Saxony without his family if he was planning to lead a rebellion against Boleslav? Did they really think he didn't care about the woman he had lived with for ten years? The mother of his children? It didn't matter to him that his daughters were adopted. However, no assurances were forthcoming. No messages, not even one from Lyudmila.

Podevin wondered how his children, used to running wild and free in the forest, would take to being transplanted to a castle and being expected to behave as young ladies and gentlemen. Especially somewhere the ladies' only value was on the marriage market. Podevin wasn't saying Maria and Priby weren't attractive enough—Priby's smile was enough to melt the hardest heart… Nor that Vaclav and young Alexandr could not be trained to fight. Despite himself. Yes, one of his sons would fight, but the other? He shook himself. Maybe Lyudmila was right and Alexandr would be better finding a different career.

As soon as a Bohemian delegation appeared—surely sooner or later, there would have to be talks?—no matter whom it included, Podevin decided his priority. He wanted news of his family and how they were doing in their newly socially advanced status, as well as their use as hostages. Other than for a vague desire for peace, he no longer gave any thought to Emma's plan. And, as for Queen Matilda's death—the catalyst for this whole sorry saga—no-one, but no-one, was talking about it. It was as if she had never been; even her regencies were being glossed over and Duke Heinrich's role emphasised. The duke's rebellion against Otto being another part of recent history that was not mentioned at the Saxon court.

Even though they were at Augsburg, it wasn't the Saxon court unless King Otto was present. The court was wherever the king was. Podevin did not need Kurt's explanation that Augsburg was merely one place where King Otto had a palace. The king would appear soon enough; for the moment, messages would be carried back and forth, and Podevin had to be patient. If the king wanted to see him, the king would call for him. Until then, he just had to sit tight. Unless he was told to go elsewhere.

Although he could do no more than go along with what he was told, as he strolled in relative—but these days constantly watched—freedom along the corridors, around the battlements, or even in the gardens, Podevin kept his eyes and ears open. He knew he was still a mere pawn in a deadly game. Only now he wasn't sure who was pulling the strings. Although Otto had not explicitly said Liutgarde was not to marry the Bohemian pretender, he had removed his daughter from Augsburg on the excuse that the lady needed to mourn her mother properly before thinking about her own future.

That Otto, in time, wanted control of the entire area was as obvious as Boleslav wanting Podevin's death. However, Podevin was picking up fast on court gossip and the back and forth of the squires and other messengers in their varying livery. He was beginning to wonder where Bohemia featured at all in Otto's schemes? Was it just a buffer against the Magyars who, as long as they didn't raid his own lands, he was happy for Boleslav to fend off? When Podevin had been little, the Magyars had been the monsters: painted men from the east who flew on phantom horses through the night sky, silent killers who came, destroyed, and left again—leaving no trace except for the dead and the dying. No-one could stand up to them, no-one could fight them. All you could do was flee, or hide and hope they didn't find you.

Though their ferocity made them more than tales to frighten children at bedtime, they could be contained. They could be beaten, provided you chose ground that was not advantageous to their bow-wielding cavalry. King Boleslav could beat them back across their border again and again, but still they returned, sometimes in snatch-and-grab raids, sometimes in stronger, destructive force, carrying away plunder in the form of cattle and slaves, and leaving only desolation behind them.

On the other hand, maybe Otto was cautious because of the two defeats he had already suffered at Boleslav's hands? Blanik was dismissive.

'Otto wasn't on the battlefield on those days. You wait, Podevin. When he's ready, Boleslav will have no chance. Nor,' he added ominously, 'would you.'

Another conversation terminated. Even Blanik had become cagey; that was when he was in Augsburg—which he usually wasn't. And still, no-one was talking about Queen Matilda's death. Podevin had tried: it was the reason he had been sent. However, in the end, Blanik told him bluntly, his efforts were not welcome and he could be disfavoured as the Bohemian exile very easily. 'Disfavoured' was a new word to him, but Podevin grasped the meaning and shut up. He kept his own counsel about his own plans.

Chapter 28
My Enemy's Enemy
is My Friend?

'Mark. What is the meaning of this? Podevin: a traitor!'

They were still confined to Emma's rooms within Prague Castle, but, with the departure of Maria, and news of the safe arrival of all Podevin's children in Budec, the atmosphere had relaxed. Whether it was coincidence or not, information had started flowing. Emma was even consulted on matters to do with the running of Prague Castle. ('Maybe the father has worked out the son hasn't the faintest idea what goes into running a place this size,' was Mark's considered opinion.) Mikael found he was able to call on more and more of Emma's former bodyguards—those who had not retired to run farms—to do duty at her chambers. Of course, they had also, and frequently, discussed their whole situation. Basically, as long as they were alive, and being treated well, there was hope.

'I did warn you it wasn't good news, my lady,' Mark replied.

Over lunch, Emma had found time to read the reply from Saxony. She flung the parchment down on a table between her and her counsellor. Brother Mark reached for the document and scanned it. Emma fiddled with her little finger, missing the ring she had given Podevin.

'So, Blanik recognised him and proclaimed him duke of Budec. It's what Podevin has always wanted,' Mark said, to gasps from the others.

'Not like this,' Emma replied, still reluctant to believe that what she had just been told by King Boleslav was true. 'Besides, Boleslav's not going to agree! In fact, it'll just be another excuse not to engage with Otto.'

'Are you sure it's Otto playing this game?'

Emma turned. 'Have you other information?'

Mark half-smiled. 'I am sure Otto wants a compliant vassal sitting in Prague. Podevin is of the royal line. If it turns out he is not lying under his chapel out there,' Mark waved his arm in the direction of the forest, 'then Boleslav is going to want him dead anyway. We sent him to Augsburg. Where Blanik now lives. Blanik owes no loyalty to Boleslav, does he? Podevin for King of Bohemia.'

'*Duke* of Bohemia if Saxony has anything to do with it.' Emma paused. 'But we cannot meet the Saxons in battle, not now they have everyone else on board. Why can't the bloody Franks rise in revolt, or the Danes, or—I don't know!—Lombardy!'

'You know, I seem to recall two young people fantasising about ruling Bohemia between them,' Mark said.

'Yes, yes! And our children after us … We grew up, Mark.' Emma noticed Mikael sitting silently, listening intently. Hilde and Beatrice were also still at the table.

'But only one of you has come close to rule,' Mark said. 'Anyway, this is all beside the point. We are confined here. Whatever dreams you had, you've lived your life as wife to the young Duke Boleslav.'

'And now they say I plotted against them.' Emma stood. 'So, what are we going to do about it?'

Hours later, they were getting nowhere. Emma was stalking up and down the room, trying to adjust to this new reality. Mark watched her, having told the others not to interfere, to leave this to him. But they were worried; they were all worried. Mark drew a deep breath.

'A friendship you ignored unless you wanted something from him? A friendship you used for your own purposes, so you could have the life you wanted while confining him to the peasantry? He didn't even have his own name! And then you sent him away, on your whim, as if you could overturn your sister's death, as if you had a say in Otto's schemes. You set out, without King Boleslav's permission, to make peace with Saxony on terms to suit you.' Mark could not know how closely he was echoing words used by Blanik in his initial conversation with Podevin across the border in Augsburg.

'But to betray us like this,' Emma said.

'What choice did he have? Blanik was the one who proclaimed him duke of Bohemia. Maybe Podevin has to go along with it in order to stay alive.'

'But he's *my* ambassador.'

'But *not* Boleslav's—and he wouldn't be the first ambassador killed as a spy.'

Emma stopped pacing. 'I didn't want him killed.'

'And I presume he doesn't want to die.' Mark's comment was dry. 'But he's now in a situation, along with Blanik, where all they can do is invade us and try to take over. Or die at Otto's hand. And, for all Podevin might have been discontented with his lot pretending to be Krok, he didn't go to Saxony until you sent him!' Mark now put both fists down on the table, leaning forward but looking up at Emma, staring deep into her troubled eyes. Both subconsciously heard noise from outside the room; both ignored it.

'What a mess! I was only …' Emma stopped.

She had told herself she was trying to stop a war with Saxony so they could face off with the Magyars—confine them to their lands in the north-east. Boleslav might win skirmish after skirmish, but they always came back. But she knew that wasn't it. Not really. She had reacted to the news about Matilda. And that stupid idea to kidnap her, with its attendant worry her husband would have done nothing to save her.

The chamber doors crashed open.

'The king wants you.' The knight didn't pause long enough to hear a reply, or an admonition to address Emma correctly, before disappearing in the direction of the great hall.

⁙

Cesta was waiting for them outside the hall, the same Cesta who had hanged 'Podevin' a decade ago. There were a few extra scars, but the beetle brows still met in the middle of his forehead above dark, bleak, friendless eyes. The doors were closed.

'Wait!' he said.

'I beg your pardon?' Emma, at her most imperious, brushed passed the knight.

Mark followed as Cesta made to grab Emma's arm.

'I wouldn't,' Mark said, putting his own hand out to stop him, but not making contact. 'Your lack of politeness might cost you.'

The guards on the door, weighing up the relative merits of disobeying a knight (who wanted them to deny access to a princess) against disobeying a princess (who wanted them to open the doors), a princess who, moreover, had been their commander until very recently, opened the doors so Emma could process in.

'My lord!' Her voice loud enough to stop the murmured conversation around the throne. '"The king wants you!" and then "Wait!" Setting aside the country manners of your attendants, which is it to be? I cannot attend to both at the same time!'

'Country manners?' the king said. 'I sent a message, that is all.'

'Delivered with no deference to the king's daughter-in-law? Is she some peasant girl to be ordered left and right at any man's will? Or do you expect your attendants to take her, use her for their pleasure? And after all, if no deference is due to the king's family,' Emma carried on, despite the king rising to his feet, 'then sooner or later, no deference will be due to the king, will it?'

'Oh, I think Cesta will show me due deference,' Boleslav said as Cesta, who had sauntered in after Emma and Mark, smirked. 'After all, we are fellow warriors. Anyway—'

If the king was going to say something along the lines of 'you are my prisoner,' or 'you will do as you are told,' he did not get the chance. Emma strode up to another knight, who stood his ground. Moving to his left side, Emma grabbed his scabbard and removed the sword. It was an awkward move as she had to twist herself so the sword came out easily, but it was quickly in her right hand and she was slashing in Cesta's direction. A fighter's instincts kicked in and his own sword was out. Metal clanged against metal, but Emma was not to be denied and the two of them closed. The rest of them, both Emma's attendants and the group around the throne, looked to the king to intervene, but the king sat down to watch. This was a knight, a seasoned warrior she was taking on; possibly, the king hoped one of his problems might be solved by this clash of arms. So, why interfere?

Emma's dress impeded her, and Cesta's armour helped him as blow after blow pierced his defence. Emma soon had a cut to her arm, which bled but did not hold her up. Cesta went for his dagger, but, instead of also going for an additional weapon, Emma merely used her free hand to jab at his face. Cesta reeled back, the dagger dropping as he clapped his hand over his left eye. Emma renewed her attack, forcing Cesta back towards the dais, where he tripped. Emma put her foot on his sword arm.

'Yield—or die!' her jousting cry rang out.

Silence.

'Very well.' Emma raised her borrowed sword.

'Madam!' Mark started forward.

'Enough!' Boleslav was on his feet.

'Well?' Emma's sword was still raised, still dangerous, so not even the king approached any farther. 'Am I the daughter of a king, sister to another, and daughter-in-law to a third?'

Cesta swallowed. 'Your highness. And my lady.'

Emma stepped back, looked round for the knight whose sword she had borrowed, and flung the weapon at him. It landed at his feet. Shamefaced, he picked it up. Cesta was also on his feet, sheathing his weapons. Using his own knife, Mark tore a strip from the tablecloth, and, without asking permission, picked up a goblet of wine, soaked the strip of fabric, and roughly bound Emma's arm, while she took the goblet with her other hand. Apart from a slight wince, she said and did nothing, other than sip at the rest of the wine.

Boleslav was clearly waiting for Mark to finish. Mark stepped back a couple of paces. It was time to find out what the king had wanted in the first place.

'I will thank you, my lady, not to humiliate any more of my knights.' He held up a hand to prevent Emma's comment. 'My knights, in turn, all of them,' the royal gaze encompassed Cesta, 'will give due deference at every meeting—however short-lived.'

Emma inclined her head. 'Perhaps you will also remind them I too have been in battle. It was, after all, my introduction to this country.'

There were a few smiles at that; everyone knew a version of the legend about how the Anglo-Saxon princess's escort had been attacked by brigands on the road to Prague and Emma had been forced to fight for her life.

'Yes, and you saved Podevin's life.' King Boleslav watched her face as he mentioned the name of the man he had so recently declared an outlaw.

'And he mine.' Emma stared back. The fight had invigorated her; her cheeks shone, her chest might be heaving, but the deep breaths were not from fear.

'But it's a pity you did,' Boleslav replied. 'As Podevin, self-proclaimed duke of Budec, is now in Augsburg, and Otto is backing him to take my throne!'

'But "Podevin" is dead.' With her calm comment, Emma had the king's attention. 'And there's the man who can verify it.' She pointed at Cesta.

Even Mark had frozen. Emma focussed entirely on Boleslav. How much did the Bohemian king know? And how much could they surmise from their own knowledge? She knew she was playing a dangerous game. After all, it was no longer a secret who she had sent to Augsburg; but she had very few cards left.

'Yes,' said the king. 'We know all this. We also know you, my lady, saw the body and accepted it as Podevin. If I recall correctly, you were the one to inform us that the last of the rebels who was at large in our country, was dead.'

'But, if you also recall, I was going on what your knights were telling me. Is Cesta now saying he just picked on any passing peasant to hang in your forests—and then he made up a story to please me? He and his friends—there was a whole group of them.'

'Who maybe should have been helping you in the east?' Mark interjected, earning himself a glare from the king.

'Cesta's "help" as you put it, has been very useful for the past ten years. We are not worried about him, but we are concerned about reports that you, my daughter...' Emma tensed, the king never called her his daughter, what now? 'You called your ambassador by the name of Podevin before he left here. And it was under that name he visited Duke Radslav on his death bed.'

'I apologise if raising the name of Podevin has caused … concern. But I was, I assure you, my liege lord, only trying to sort out issues which had occurred while you were away. I had no desire to foment trouble or disorder. And nor, when he left, had my ambassador.'

For good measure, she sank into a curtsy. The pause grew into a silence, during which Emma dared not even look up.

Then the king spoke. 'We have already heard what Cesta has to say, but let us hear more from our messenger from Saxony.'

A man who had, up till now, kept in the background, stepped forward. He bowed to the king, to Emma; he even bowed, but from the neck only, in Mark's direction. He looked at the king, waiting to be invited to speak.

'This, Emma, is Sven. Your chaplain has met him before. He recognised Podevin—we have gone into that. However, Sven was in Augsburg with your man for a week.' The king turned to Sven, who eyes flickered from one person to another, as if he were not sure quite what was going on. But he spoke readily enough.

'I found it difficult to believe, sire, that this man could have been sent by the lady, especially without your own permission. I mean, what would one such as you have to do with someone like him? I could only think this "Podevin" was merely waiting his chance! Had I the authority to execute spies, I would have, but I had to wait for permission.'

'But that permission failed to arrive.'

'The lady, the princess Liutgarde, decided her father needed to consider the offer of peace. On the strength of the lady Emma's ring.'

'Which ring is that?' Emma said. She made to hold out her left hand until she saw Mark shake his head. Now what? Giving Podevin her ring had been Mark's suggestion!

'He said it was a ring belonging to Queen Matilda—that she'd given to Princess Emma when they parted. I do not know, I barely saw it, but it seemed to satisfy Liutgarde—along with the letter proposing peace,' Sven said.

'Peace?'

'Yes, sire. Peace. It was the talk of the court. Princess Emma promised to pay all outstanding tribute and put the entire kingdom at the disposal of King Otto. They could march in anytime.'

'Really? They believed I would say that? I, and not the king, had authority to say that?' Emma was shocked. She knew court gossip could twist information, but this was too much.

'No, my lady. They didn't. They did believe, however, that the bearer of the letter used it to gain access to the court at Augsburg, so he could reveal his own plans. Otto would never believe Boleslav wanted peace—'

'What we want is not to pay tribute! Quite different!' Boleslav interrupted.

Sven gave a nervous laugh, and the king gestured at him to continue.

'But he would believe that an exiled member of the family, who wanted the whole of Bohemia as his dukedom, would offer tribute to secure that throne. And then they could take on the Magyars together.'

Sven appeared to have finished.

'So,' the king mused, 'it appears Podevin is still alive.'

'Unless he is a fake.' Mark spoke out of turn.

'But I recognised him!' said Sven, and then retreated into silence at Cesta's glare.

Both of them could not be right.

'If I may?' Mark said, glancing at the king, who nodded consent. 'Sven,' Mark said, 'how long is it since you saw Podevin? And, if I may again, was he alone?'

'There were two of them, but the other was a cripple.'

'I didn't hang a cripple—I think I'd have noticed that!' It was Cesta's turn to interject.

Emma began to hope, but turned to Mark as he spoke again.

'Forgive me, Sven. I'm sure you acted for the best in all this. Your whole family arrived in Saxony safe and well?'

'Er, just me and my mother in the end. My father and sister died in the forest. They were both injured,' Sven said, to Mark's surprise.

Had he not been there when Sven had met Priby? Why would the man lie about his sister's death? He decided to let it go, for the moment, and asked his next question. 'And this was how long ago?'

'About twelve years, but I don't forget a face!'

'I'm sure you don't, but we do have conflicting information here. Again.' Mark started pacing, as he tended to do while trying to think things through.

Though it cost her to remain still, Emma waited. She knew, none better, that Sven was spinning a tale to make himself look good, but she also knew Podevin was in Augsburg, plotting. And Mark was trying to help her get out of the trouble her own plots and plans had got them into.

'Stop!' The king rose to his feet. 'It matters not whether this man is Podevin or not. His life is forfeit as a rebel to my throne and estate. However, we have been asked to send a delegation to Augsburg. We are thinking of sending the new duke of Kourim. You, madam, as you seem so reluctant to accept our view of so many things and we need to confirm the identity of this pretender to our throne, may send an observer if you so wish—an observer, not a delegate. Leave us.'

Emma, with Mark following her, exited the great hall, leaving the king to debate with Cesta and Sven. Though what the new forester could contribute when he, having declared his loyalty to Boleslav, could hardly return to Saxony, Emma could not work out. She also found she was dreading her next confession before Mark, but what could she have done? Accepted that both she and Podevin were traitors? No, that couldn't be right.

Chapter 29
Talking with the Enemy

Mark travelled to Augsburg with a retinue entirely composed of Boleslav's men. Both the older and the younger Boleslav had contributed gentlemen to the delegation but, Podevin was told later, there was, apart from Mark, not a single one from Emma's bodyguard, nor her retinue. King Boleslav was not pleased with her efforts to interfere in foreign affairs—even if the foreign person who had started this whole sorry saga was her dead sister. Mark was only here as an observer. An observer who was excluded from the private discussions between the new duke of Kourim, as head of the Bohemian delegation, and Kurt.

Podevin, for all the discussion must touch on him and his future, and despite his insistence on being involved in such discussions, was not invited to these meetings. Literally kept out of the room.

He was wandering the battlements again when Mark found him.

Mark glanced left and right and, noting the absence of anyone other than guards, said in Czech, 'This is a pretty mess, isn't it?'

'I don't see anything pretty about it.'

'And you're scheduled to marry a princess.'

'A young girl still in mourning for her mother. How fortunate I am unmarried.'

By this time, they were both leaning on the balustrade, staring out across the Saxon countryside: a vision of peace and sunny loveliness, early summer crops wafting in the breeze, vines on hillsides and verdant trees in the distance. The birds were still; the only fauna in sight domestic or farm animals. It was the midday lull before the sun drifted towards the western skies and lessened its heat for another day.

'You, "Brother" Mark, are apparently not licensed to perform marriage services. Lyudmila is merely a concubine, and my sons are bastards.' Podevin said the words in a dull voice. He turned to face the castle where the negotiations were taking place. 'It seems only when I rule Bohemia can I expect to be able to make them knights.'

If he further expected Mark to comment, it yet took a while for him to register the monk's silence, and his stillness. Podevin turned his head. Mark avoided eye contact, staring at the view beyond Augsburg's walls.

'There is no easy way to say this. Lyudmila is dead. Killed by the king's new forester in Prague.'

Perhaps it was fortunate that the guards did not understand what was being said, but the reports to Kurt would likely note the tenor of the conversation. It was obvious Podevin had received bad news. It was clear he was both upset and angry; at one point, the two of them nearly came to blows as Podevin's fist came within an inch of Mark's face before the monk was able to block it.

'You promised! It was the only reason I came here in the first place.' Podevin's voice rang across the courtyard despite Mark's attempts to quiet him down. 'You said, Emma said, they would all be looked after. They'd all be trained.' A sudden thought made Podevin wheel round to face Mark. He thrust his face near Mark's and grabbed the man's habit with both hands. 'Where are my children?' Each word was ground out with fury. 'Tell me!' He shook the older man.

'Is there a problem here? We generally respect men of the cloth.'

A Saxon captain had strolled up. Unlike the two Bohemians, he was armed. Podevin glared, but took his hands away.

'He was supposed to keep my family safe. He didn't do it.'

Podevin pushed his way past the captain and left for his rooms. He heard Mark calling after him, but ignored him. If he could not trust Mark and Emma, if he could not trust Blanik, who was there he could trust—apart from himself? He was being kept from the discussions about his future. He was stuck in a foreign land … and now, judging by the noises outside, the midday meal was being prepared. Podevin had been told he was to sit at the top table—for the moment, the Saxons were sticking to their notion he had a claim to Bohemia.

☙

That lunchtime, Mark was there, too. He hadn't even bothered to smooth down his habit where Podevin had grabbed him. Apart from the new duke of Kourim, the rest of the Bohemian party were sitting together at their own table, their negotiating, or sparring, partners from the Saxon side opposite them on the other side of the hall. No informal discussions here. Conversation at the top table was bland.

'Don't worry,' Kurt had muttered under his breath, 'we're not sending you back across the border.'

The duke of Kourim, Radslav's eldest son, nodded towards him as if he would be friends—or at least, friendly. He even raised his goblet in Podevin's direction, but Podevin did no more than smile and nod in return. Eating was becoming more difficult—he had lost his appetite days ago. The thought even crossed his mind that he should be planning another escape. But how and to where?

After the meal, Podevin sought to retreat out of the way, but none other than the duke of Kourim stood in his way.

'You need to apologise to Brother Mark,' he said, the mealtime friendliness lacking in his tone. 'And heed his explanation.' With that, the duke turned on his heel and walked away, leaving Podevin facing Mark.

There were many witnesses to what had just happened and, for good measure, the duke of Kourim had spoken in German. Podevin led Mark to a bench at the side of the hall, and sat with his arms folded across his chest.

Mark also folded his arms; he also sat. After a pause, perhaps realising Podevin was in no mood to apologise, he began speaking. He spoke in a low voice. He spoke in Czech, though they were being left alone. But he was going to say what he was going to say, and Podevin had to sit and listen to it.

Firstly, he had to listen to Mark's account of Podevin's stupidity in trying to demand entry to Augsburg at night. Hadn't Podevin been given enough funds to pay for an extra night's rest? Because of his penny-pinching, or general impatience, Geraint and several others were dead. The rest had only just escaped with their lives. So, yes, Emma knew all about it.

Secondly, because Podevin had made a mess of it, Emma's situation had gone from bad to worse. Not only that, but the king—by which Mark meant Boleslav, not Otto—had heard about it, and had taken his son's part. Emma was no longer castle constable in Prague, so she couldn't have helped Podevin's family even if she had wanted to.

Thirdly, Lyudmila was dead because Sven had arrived from Saxony, backing up the worst of what Boleslav already believed about Podevin, so Podevin had lost his job as forester, which had been given to Sven— along with the authority to evict whoever he found living in the king's forester's home.

'You should be grateful all four of your children are still alive. Even if they are hostages against your good behaviour.' Mark finally had Podevin's full attention.

'They do say the duke of Budec spends a lot of time with the hostages,' Mark mused.

'Why?' Podevin asked.

'Your niece appears to have caught his eye. She is, after all, descended from the Premyslid family. The same family as King Boleslav.'

'But I thought she was keen on her captain of the guard at Prague Castle—whoever he is.' Podevin's puzzlement grew.

'Ah!' replied Mark. 'That man was married. But the duke is a widower—his wife died in childbirth.'

'So? Are you telling me I can expect a wedding?'

'No. I'm not.' Mark paused. 'Actually, I don't know. All this has gone wrong in ways we did not imagine. I'm doing what I can.' Mark looked out at the sky. 'Come on, I think we should walk, before it starts to rain. Can I assume you will not attack me again?'

Podevin avoided the monk's gaze and peered out of the nearest window, but could see no clouds. It was an awkward move, as he still could not glance left.

'Your eye?' Mark said.

Podevin shrugged as if it didn't matter. Mark stopped him, made him sit on a convenient low bench. Podevin submitted to the inspection.

'You're going to have to learn to be careful of people coming up behind you on the left-hand side. There's a shadow in there.'

'But the doctor said it was fine. It could be fine,' Podevin muttered.

'I'd have said the same, and hoped. If it doesn't hurt, that's the best you can hope for. Head wounds, and wounds around the eye, are tricky.' Mark began strolling again, leaving Podevin to scramble to his feet and catch him up.

International diplomacy exhausted, and his wound examined, talk returned to Podevin's family. Specifically Maria.

'Come on,' Podevin said, 'tell me the worst. She is alive, I take it?'

Mark checked no-one was close enough to hear. 'She has persuaded my lord, the duke of Budec, that, as she is not your daughter and neither is Priby, the two of them do not need to be treated as hostages. He has even petitioned the court in Prague to that effect. As it was true—and we thought at the time, she would still be part of the foursome, and it was just a strategy to get them all released—Emma agreed with her husband and father-in-law that the petition be granted. You must remember Tugumir's treachery has been forgotten; his death has been added to your crimes.'

Podevin barely registered this. 'So, how is Maria seen, then?'

'As Tugumir's daughter, who was kidnapped by you, and should be treated with the honour and respect that any duke's daughter, any lady, would receive.'

'But she doesn't know how to be a lady! Where'd she learn that?'

'She is learning remarkably fast. The current duchess of Budec's mother has taken her, and her lady-in-waiting, under her wing. Especially given Maria's closeness to her son.'

'Oh, she has, has she? Let's hope Maria doesn't make a mess of it … Hang on. Lady-in-waiting? Who's that?'

'Priby.' Mark held up a hand to prevent Podevin's comment. 'And she should be grateful for that role instead of being a kitchen hand, given both her parents were peasants who'd been run off their land.'

'Don't tell me that's what you said?'

'It is a version of what I am told Maria said to Priby, when Priby remonstrated with Maria.'

'Why, the sneaky little …'

'Maybe she's just trying to stay alive.' Mark's comment was typically dry, but held the suggestion of a question.

'But to abandon her brothers, and downgrade Priby like that!'

'But Priby was always your favourite.'

'Don't be ridiculous! Priby was the one who did the chores without complaining.'

Mark opened his hands, a gesture of appeasement. 'I'm only telling you what I know. For all Maria kept her distance, your sons are being brought up as befits their station as part of—if a distant part of—the royal family. If Maria does become duchess of Budec, she will be in a better position to sponsor them.'

'And Priby? Will she sponsor Priby?'

'Ladies-in-waiting can marry well.'

'If their mistress permits it. And if she wants it.'

'You think Priby would prefer not to marry?'

'I think she might prefer the forest to a castle.' Podevin shrugged. 'But the boys? They'll be knights?'

'Are you sure that is what is wanted? That it's what *they* want?'

Mark's direct gaze troubled Podevin. Hadn't Lyudmila asked the very same question. He'd missed something. Something vital.

'Vaclav would—he's always rushing into a fight.'

'And …?'

'All right! Alexandr might want to do something else. But what?'

'A clerk? He's very sharp with his figures, as well as his letters.'

'I didn't bring him up to sit in some scriptorium, grubbing away for some lord.'

'I seem to recall a young man railing against having to do what he was told to do, rather than what he wanted to do. It wasn't that long ago.'

'He's too young to know his own mind.' The words were out before Podevin realised their similarity to what Wenceslas had said about a ten-year-old Mladenic, who was supposed to grow to love Emma.

'Alexandr's no fighter. Unless he has a real reason to get involved, he does not see the point. And too many times, the reason is provided by his brother—who will have to learn by himself not to be so impetuous.'

'A clerk?'

'Even a monk. It might work, you know.'

'I'll think about it,' Podevin said. As if he still had any influence over the matter.

Chapter 30
Podevin is Left Behind

'We're handing you over at dawn tomorrow.'

The Bohemian delegation was hardly through the gate on their way back home after the formalities of an early morning departure, when Kurt turned to Podevin and murmured that sweet nothing in his ear. After the previous day's discussion with Mark, Podevin had suffered a night of restless sleep at best, replaying every argument, every dispute, with Lyudmila. His mind had even replayed in relentless detail that first time he and Krok had gone hunting for deer and he'd behaved like the spoiled brat he was, and managed to injure Krok as well as leaving him with the task of killing a wild boar. A dangerous thing to do, even when you were not injured. It was not Podevin's finest hour and, in the fevered watches of the night, he wondered if he had changed at all. Ten years he'd spent in that forest; had he learned nothing? Still the idiot who charged in and thought later.

It was obvious to him now that it was too late. But if Emma had made it impossible for him to remain in Bohemia, he should, like countless others before him, have packed up his family, loaded the cart, and brought them to Saxony, or Poland, or anywhere there might be a bit of peace. He could have plied his trade as a forester. For heaven's sake, it wasn't as if there was a shortage of forests around that needed taming; it wasn't as if there was nowhere he could have gone.

But thoughts were futile. Lyudmila was dead. And he could not even show his grief. Although the ones inside the door had been removed, there were still guards outside his bedroom door. So his sobs had to be muffled by his pillow and his howls unhowled—kept inside until his ribcage felt as if it would burst open with the agony of his guilt and sorrow. He imagined his essence flying back to Bohemia, leaving the shell of a pretend diplomat, a pretend usurper, a pretend husband and father, to drift through the days and weeks ahead.

Therefore, when Kurt made his comment (which completely contradicted what he had previously told Podevin), all Podevin did was turn to look at him, his face a stoic mask. Kurt's smile faltered.

'I was making a joke; we would never get you to the border in time. And they have to get back to Prague to report.' Kurt gestured at the departing group of visitors, now all through the gate.

Podevin remained mute.

Kurt swallowed. 'I apologise. Heinrich values you too highly to barter you away just because a delegation came here making demands.'

'I take it there were other demands?' Even in his confused state through lack of sleep, Podevin saw Kurt's embarrassment as a way of getting him to open up. There might not be another opportunity.

'An alliance. A demand for support against the Magyars: "to crush them with overwhelming force."' Kurt shrugged. 'But with that, they expose their own weakness. If they cannot manage the Magyars by themselves, maybe we can beat them both. The rest of Heinrich's forces are on their way. We march out tomorrow. And,' Kurt added after a pause, 'that is not a joke. You need to be ready … general.'

❧

Blanik arrived at midday.

'Thank the gods for once I didn't have to force march everyone here!' he said on seeing Podevin. 'At least we're getting you sorted at long last.'

'It would have been nice to have been kept informed. Unlike some people, I was only told this morning.'

Blanik said, 'You knew we were looking after you.'

However, Podevin's former tutor did not look in his direction as he spoke. Podevin allowed the silence to lengthen before responding.

'For all I knew, you were preparing to hand me over to Radslav's son and his delegation, so Boleslav could kill me as slowly as possible.'

'Now you are being ridiculous. I mean, of course, if you think about it: the Bohemian delegation—what if one of them had managed to get to you with a knife?'

In his current mood, Podevin wondered whether or not such an attack might have been a relief. He shrugged.

'Come on, Podevin! This is your chance to get what you've always wanted,' Blanik said, as if he could not understand Podevin's reluctance.

'No, Blanik. It's your chance to get what you wanted. The Boleslavs, both father and son, might not be my favourite people, but, I say again, I had no thought—none whatsoever—of taking over from them until you started calling me duke of Budec. A title I can do without, thank you, given my children are residing with the current duke of that name.'

Blanik looked confused—or tried to. But Podevin had not finished.

'Did it never occur to you that, with my family back in Bohemia, Boleslav might do something about it? My sons are hostages against my good behaviour!'

'But they're peasantry. You don't have to worry about them. You,' this time Blanik faced him and put both hands out, one for each of Podevin's shoulders, so he could give his former tutee a gentle shake, 'are destined for greater things.'

Podevin reached out and removed the hands, one at a time. 'I think the cost, for me, is too high. Lyudmila is dead. Killed by Boleslav's replacement for me in the forest. And my sons—and my daughters— may yet die too, unless I give up this … foolishness!'

For a moment, Blanik looked stunned. His expression hardened, his eyes narrowed. 'Listen to me. Otto has bigger schemes than little Bohemia. He could hand that piece of land over to Duke Heinrich for him to do what he will. Heinrich has his own forces, and he's on his way. Would you prefer a Saxon in charge, living it up in Prague? This is our chance to have a proper say in how Bohemia is run. Your private concerns don't matter. If you don't play your part, it will be worse for everyone.'

'Including you, Blanik?'

'Boleslav killed my master. I have taken a vow. Nothing, *nothing*, gets in the way of that. Not my family, and certainly not yours. You no longer have a choice. Get yourself ready to claim a kingdom. *Now!*'

Blanik turned on his heel and left. Podevin had heard Blanik had a family. But now, he wondered what sort of life they led if their head was always out fighting, or simmering with frustrated revenge. Did he need this? Was his decision to go along with this whole plan, just in order to stay alive, the wrong one? Even as he readied himself, for the rest of the day, he was thinking hard. Would he end up facing Emma on the battlefield?

Chapter 31
Priby in Trouble

It was Priby's decision to try to see the duke of Budec, to put the record straight, that led to her whipping. The man, the widower who needed a new wife, was already infatuated by Maria's obvious charms. One of the girls was lying, and it was no contest as to which he would believe.

Priby made the mistake of claiming sisterhood, which she had to retract when Maria told the true tale of Priby's arrival at her forest home. To prove who was telling the truth, Priby was grabbed, her dress torn open, her naked, scarred back exposed. The duke decreed, in his mercy, that Priby should 'only' be whipped. Twenty lashes. He could, as Maria pointed out, have decided on a public hanging.

Nonetheless, the whipping was public. The rough wooden stake with its shackles at the top, for her wrists, and at the bottom for her ankles, stood in the centre of the courtyard. She was stripped to the waist. Cloth stuffed into her mouth so she could not cry out. The squires gathered, mostly in front of her so they could watch her breasts move every time she changed position. She saw Vaclav. He could not look at her face. The clerks were at the side, viewing the spectacle of a half-naked woman less obviously. Alexandr had to be held to make him watch. Senior people, important people, sat in the dais raised for the purpose and pretended to be unaffected. Maria was amongst them.

The first cut made her arch her back in an effort to avoid the pain. The whipper knew his art; he dragged the leather thongs through the cuts he had just made. After seven strokes, Priby could feel the blood trickling down her back; after twelve, she was beginning not to feel anything. By the time the last five were being counted down, her head was hanging, and she could take no more. She fainted. But water was thrown over her head, and she was slapped awake.

'You'll take your punishment, whore!' The man nodded in Maria's direction.

Maria was in the stand, sitting next to the duke. The remaining strokes brought Priby more pain than she ever thought she would have to withstand. At the end, when she was barely conscious, rough fingers gouged the cloth from her mouth.

'Now! Thank those who punished you for treating you so kindly.' And, when Priby hesitated, he screamed, 'Do it!'

'Thank—thank you.' She managed to get the words past her dry throat.

'And beg the duke for his mercy,'

For this part of the ritual, she was unchained and penitential sack-cloth forced over her head, making her cry out in renewed pain as it rubbed the raw flesh on her back. Maria's face swam into view. A face shiny with sweat. A face filled with triumph.

'Don't ever defy me again. Now, beg!' Maria said.

Given she was so thirsty, but no water was offered, Priby did not know how she begged for mercy. But she did it. She was dragged away, her mind only just hanging onto the idea it was her sister who had the energy, the will, to see the whole punishment carried out.

It was, Maria said, to impress the duke of Budec. Maria had shown she was unafraid to keep control of a household. Nobody would argue with that. They had all seen. Maria would decide what to do with Priby. That is, assuming she survived the 'light punishment' she had received.

❧

'I have to take this off, Priby. Do you need something to bite on?'

She'd been left alone. She recognised the room as the one she'd shared with Maria when they first came to Budec. However, there was nothing other than a wide bench, which could be a bed or table—or both—to lie on. So much pain. She'd kept her eyes closed for the longest time. She didn't know if she'd slept or not.

'I've brought some broth. And some water from the stream, but I need to clean you up.'

How she didn't scream again as the sackcloth was separated—with Alexandr's repeated 'sorrys' for hurting her—from her blood-soaked back, she would never know. She lay there as he dabbed at her wounds.

'I've got clean cloths, but I need to clean your back first.'

'Who told you what to do?' It was a new voice, one they both recognised. Alexandr paused for a second, before carrying on his careful stroking.

Maria sniffed. 'Well?' she said.

'Brother Mark.'

'He isn't here.' Maria stepped farther into the room.

'We talked a lot about healing.' Alexandr concentrated on cleaning Priby's back. Priby tried to remain conscious and not scream.

She didn't know what she would do if Maria took her anger out on Alexandr—he was much too young to have to deal with all this.

Maria paced.

'Right, once you're better, I am going to keep an eye on you. Tomorrow, you'll be moved to my antechamber and, when I decide you're fit enough, you'll take up your duties.' Maria then turned her attention to Alexandr. 'As for you, once you've done your job here, you can go. And don't come back.'

'I have a name. And we have the same mother.'

Maria moved. In two seconds, she had grabbed the hair at the back of Alexandr's head and forced him to look at her. 'You chose to be a cleric. Your name doesn't pass my lips again. Your mother was a peasant. Your father's a traitor. I'm part of the royal family—don't you forget it.'

She let him go and wiped the hand that had grabbed his hair on her dress. Priby twisted round, ignoring the pain in her back. Her torn muscles screamed.

'Leave him alone! He's just as royal as you are!'

For all Alexandr had refused to move, Priby saw the tears standing in his eyes from the rough handling.

Maria stopped, turned. 'You've been warned not to contradict me! Or do you want death? Both of you?'

'What about looking after all of us?'

'You don't deserve my help. However, you will note I have kept you alive—so far.' Maria swept out of what had been their room.

Priby lay down again on her stomach. Alexandr remembered to carry on dealing with the mess that was her back. For a while, they were both lost in their thoughts.

'Priby?'

'Yes?'

'Why has Maria become so horrible? Until she started going to the castle by herself, she used to be nice.'

'She went to the castle with me.'

'Not always.'

'What do you mean, Alexandr?'

'Remember when I was ill, so Mum gave me my supper before you?'

Priby nodded; just another childhood ailment. Alexandr often seemed to get them but, with extra food and extra sleep, seemed to get over them quickly enough. Alexandr carried talking in his calm, quiet way.

'Maria put something in the food. She told me it was to make it taste a bit nicer, but you all got tired.'

'Why didn't she give you any?'

'She did, but I picked it out.'

'Was that one of the nights Maria said she wasn't hungry?' Priby asked, already knowing the answer.

Maria had been brought up by Krok and Lyudmila before Krok's death and before Podevin had become their father. But Krok had needed so many herbs and medicines—and no-one had thought such knowledge had to be kept secret. Hadn't Maria been so interested in her, Priby's, arrival as a sick child? Hadn't Maria also asked Brother Mark about how he healed people? One thing she had not questioned in her brief visit, was Alexandr's treatment. Maybe her back would heal. But Maria's sickness would not.

'How often did Maria go out—she did go out that night, didn't she?'

'A man came, on a horse.'

Priby shook her head in disbelief. 'Did you ever see who it was?'

'No, but she called him her captain.'

It was becoming more and more clear to Priby what had been going on. If she was right, it explained why Maria was so unhappy about hearing her captain was a married man, and why she was so advanced in her pregnancy so early in the year. That part of it had always puzzled Priby. It still rankled that it was she, Priby, who'd been called a whore. It would have been a relief to have been able to talk with Brother Mark, and not just rely on his healing solutions processed by her youngest brother ... Talking of brothers...

'Where's Vaclav?'

'With his friends.' Priby could hear the hurt in Alexandr's voice.

'Anything to be a warrior, is that it?'

'They still laugh at him. They still...' Alexandr paused, steadied himself. 'They still know he could be killed any time our dad doesn't do what the king wants.'

'What a life, eh, Alexandr?' She tried to make light of it.

'But only Vaclav and me are really Dad's sons. You and Maria aren't.' His façade cracked.

The sobs, once begun, could not be contained. She told him to put the bowl aside, to lie down next to her so she could put an arm around him.

It was how both of them slept.

᧞

In the morning, it was clear Priby could not begin her duties until her wounds had cleared up—or at least had healed enough so that she could wear clothes over her stripes without that clothing rubbing the cuts open again.

The chamberlain reported back to them, that he'd asked whether 'madam would prefer it if her lady-in-waiting wore only blood red garments?' Priby had managed a smile on hearing this, barely registering that a chamberlain would not normally be bothering over someone, and a female at that, who had recently been publicly punished. But she was grateful when the man said Alexandr had been appointed as her carer, until she started her duties upstairs.

In that week, as Priby's young skin began to heal, she and Alexandr had many talks. They discussed what they could and what they could not do. She promised him she would not provoke Maria again. There were enough scars on her back already for her not to choose to add to them. She made him promise not to do more than keep his eyes and ears open—he was not to interfere. If, assuming he would be sent back to his duties in the scriptorium once he and Priby no longer shared a room, he copied something, no matter how bad, he was not to change it. They would meet; even as hostages, it would surely be considered unusual if they never saw each other.

Over the following months, as spring turned to the height of summer, Priby became used to pretending not to see the duke of Budec coming to visit Maria. It was said, the duke had started taking afternoon naps as he was sleeping less at night. By then, Priby realised she felt no surprise that Maria had no monthly flow. Without a wedding, Maria was playing a dangerous game. Lyudmila was not around to be asked about Maria, or anything else. Priby felt she had lost her sister, and did not know how to help her brothers.

Chapter 32
On the Battlefield

Summertime. A time when work is well underway on the farms, when farmers check their fields and hope can tentatively turn towards expectation that there will be a good harvest. However, summertime is also when kings go to war. The worsening relations across the border had mirrored an improving situation for Emma within Bohemia. Put bluntly, when faced with real danger from known opposition, King Boleslav's senior fighters had made it clear they preferred his daughter-in-law as a general to his son. The king, once he had taken the time to work out how much of the anti-Emma rhetoric had come solely from his own son, and how much he could give greater credence to, had conceded that evidence of actual treachery (rather than errors of judgment) was very thin on the ground. Also, much as it annoyed him to admit it, if she had not been present, on both previous occasions when he had faced a Saxon army ... well, the outcome might have been very different. And had he not seen only recently, how good she was at single combat? It was no good; she should have been the boy, and his son the girl. King Boleslav had shaken his head; there were things he could not change. Emma would have charge of Prague Castle, and the environs to the border.

On the border and dressed for battle, Emma paused. She looked across the valley to the flat, open plain where the Saxons' serried ranks marched and counter-marched on their daily exercises, where the black-plumed mounted brigades wheeled and cantered knee-to-knee in open display. For every fighter she had, they had a cavalryman, and an infantryman, with more to spare. If only she had a plan where she could ensure they charged across the brook at the exact spot where they would end up in the bushes, the trees and—most usefully—the marshy ground on the Bohemian side of the border. Where her lightly armoured, and lightly trained, troops might have some sort of advantage. For the present, all she could do was plan to cede ground as slowly, and with the least cost, as she could. She sighed, and ducked into her tent, hoping she could at least be polite to her visitors.

'Madam, shall we see what has arrived—and what we can do with it?' Mikael said, as he and Mark, her twin shadows ever since they had set up camp here, stood in the entrance to the tent.

Their intervention had come just as the right moment. Emma did not think, on top of everything else, she could stand the sight of her husband billing and cooing with his latest favourite.

He'd arrived with impossible orders: A dawn attack the next day. Daddy's orders—but, strangely, Daddy had forgotten to write those orders down. Then, her husband had gone into the 'I'm your husband, you do what I say,' mode of argument. Despite everything she had been through, despite knowing she could not rely on her father-in-law, on the battlefield, she was not going to be told what to do, what to plan, by an idiot. As ever, she had been about to say so, when Mikael's timely arrival had prevented a row which both Emma and Mladenic would have found difficult to back down from.

She strode out of the tent. The first sight that greeted her was a new fire, a new fire with little smoke, but lots of people round it. The lucky ones would be getting roasted horsemeat tonight.

'Madam! Would you care for some?' A shout from among the fire-watchers.

Emma smiled, despite her empty stomach. 'Thank you, but no. You all enjoy.' She waved and passed on, striding out to meet the bedraggled force that had followed Boleslav into the camp.

Whatever else they needed, they needed rest. She could not use these men in an attack tomorrow. Nor the next day—she needed time to see what their skills were. Some of them were clearly archers, but all the Saxons had to do was retire until they were more than a bowshot distant from the Bohemian lines and wait. None of them were knights and, apart from Boleslav's little coterie, there were few horses. Yes, there were pack horses, and there were some supplies. But—it was explained to her by the newly promoted captain—all he'd had time to do was strip the castle kitchen of food for the journey to feed all the men he'd removed from the defence of the castle.

'And I was in enough trouble for doing that. We're expected to live off the land, madam.'

Emma shook her head in disbelief; how could Mladenic be so stupid? Yes, armies lived off the land, they always had, but, if you could supply your army from elsewhere, then the local people did not resent you so much. And if you were camped in an area from which most of the local people had already fled, which was the situation she was in now after ten years of conflict on this very border, then there was less readily available food to start with.

The inspection of the tiny baggage train was swift. The stores they had brought with them would feed the new arrivals for a day or two, or her whole army could have a decent meal this one night. The pack horses were slaughtered, and any other horses—no matter how much affection they were held in by their masters—if they were unfit in any way, they were killed too. Horses, as she told her husband when he found out and tried to object, ate a lot of fodder and, unless they could be part of the cavalry in his dawn attack, she had no use for them other than as food for her soldiers.

Not that she had any intention of attacking at the next dawn. She had assumed, after her discussions with Mark and Mikael, they'd be fighting a defensive battle. Let the Saxons attack. It was more a brush-wood defensive wall, instead of shields, but even a nine-year-old lad can direct a spear into the body of a charging man, or horse, if its blunt end is propped against the ground. A lad that age certainly can't be expected to run into battle wielding … wielding what? A kitchen knife?

To stop any trouble between her army and the new arrivals, she ordered a share out of the limited food. Each troop could make its own decision about whether to feast that night, the next morning, or have two smaller meals. She abandoned her own tent to Mladenic and his friends. It still left them discontented, squealing for better treatment. She ate with her bodyguard, and her chaplain, openly discussing the new orders. Cesta and his friends were sent off to sort their own food—and, having been told Duke Boleslav was now in charge, he wasn't needed at Emma's counsels of war any more.

Despite everything, Emma felt good. She smiled as she looked around, even though she knew she would get no thanks for it once she was no longer needed to defend Bohemia, and they would be dispersed again. Once Mikael had got word out, her troops had been turning up—in dribs and drabs. Hilde had even turned up with her burly Anglo-Saxon. 'The farm can cope without us for a few weeks,' she'd said, lying (what farm can afford to lose two workers at the approach to harvest?), but taking up her own duties, helping Beatrice—the two of them would be sorting fires, cooking, seeing to any injuries. Hardly the stuff royal ladies-in-waiting were trained to do, but, in Emma's service, her ladies had learned to adapt.

'We can't attack. And certainly not tomorrow.' Mikael's blunt assessment of the military situation, for all it matched her own, was still not pleasant to hear.

'What is Boleslav playing at? If he's coming with his army from the east, why not wait and let him do the leading?' Brother Mark was referring to the elder Boleslav, but the question, Emma realised, also applied to the younger. And the younger avoided any sort of battle whenever he could.

'Maybe,' she said, 'just maybe he—the king—is thinking the Saxons know he's moving his army this way. They know his tactics are to take the battle to the enemy whenever he can. So, they will be expecting him to come up, perhaps wait a day or two—and then charge. What they won't expect is an attack before he arrives.'

'And they certainly won't expect his son to lead it!'

Emma never discovered who made the sarcastic comment, but she smiled as bitter laughter rippled round the tent. Her smile faded as a thought crossed her mind. Her husband had won no glory on the battlefield. The two times he had been expected to lead troops in battle, he'd been more a danger to his own side than the enemy.

'Madam?' Mark said into her silence.

She raised a hand, cupping it as if she were trying to grab at her thoughts.

'What if,' she said, 'what if—and, remember, Mark, my husband did not bring these orders with him—what if the king had ordered his son into battle? We know I'm not in good favour with the king. We know the king expects his son to be a warrior,' there were a few splutters from her bodyguard at this comment, but otherwise, they were all listening, 'and the king has sent no missives here.'

'That's true enough,' said Mark, 'and if he wanted a battle that much, he knows you're the better general. As well as mother to a son …' Mark's voice trailed off.

The tent fell silent. At different speeds, the gathered warriors grasped at the implications of the assumptions that had been spoken, too freely perhaps, in the last minutes. However, much as they continued the discussion, much as they looked for alternatives, there was only one option that made sense. Either the Bohemians won the battle, and Mladenic could be hailed a warrior-hero and secure his place as his father's heir; or they lost and, in all probability, Mladenic and Emma were killed—along with most of the people they had gathered here. In that case, Boleslav would appear with his army, prevent the Saxons from following up their victory, and he could declare his grandson as his heir. The boy was a mere child, but Mladenic had hardly been a grown man when he was declared heir.

With those sombre thoughts, the tent settled down to its council of war. A dawn attack, particularly a dawn attack in a handful of hours' time, was dismissed. Spending the next day pretending to go about their ordinary business, but overnight moving towards the Saxon lines—their cavalry horses were kept in makeshift stables behind the lines and the Saxons were not expecting to be attacked—might allow for a dawn attack the day after, if the Bohemians could coordinate their attacks from all sides to sow confusion.

It would be Emma's job to explain this to Mladenic, with Mark and Mikael in attendance. They retired to get a few hours' sleep.

❧

The following day started with yet another dispute between Emma and her husband. She woke him in her tent when the sun was already high in the sky.

'What are you doing here? I said you were to lead the battle at dawn. Dawn! And that's hours ago.'

'So why weren't you up to support and encourage us? Or,' Emma leant forward towards her still recumbent and heavy-eyed husband, 'lead us?'

At her last words, the young Boleslav's eyes opened in alarm, and he struggled to get up from the mattress on the floor. 'Who told you?'

'It was obvious—why else would you be here? So, my lord prince, what's your plan?' Emma's words, as she intended, received a sharp glance from her husband, but he said nothing.

'Guards!' Mladenic called. 'Guards!'

Nothing. Other than the sound of swords being unsheathed. Nothing. Emma sat. After all, it was her chair. She said nothing about her husband sleeping in her bed last night, while she slept with her troops on some straw. She waited until her husband realised no help was coming. She knew she was playing a dangerous game, but she had realised, whatever happened, her husband wanted her dead. That knowledge, the idea there was nothing she could do to change that, had, in an odd sort of way, freed her. Why did she need to be afraid? She looked death in the face every time she looked at him. Even in camp, he had brought a silk nightshirt to wear in bed. His clothes lay in a heap. Was someone supposed to have sorted them, washed them even, ready for him to wear today? This was a campaign, not an excursion into the countryside for a pleasure trip.

Mladenic stood on his still spindly legs. Tried to saunter over to the table. It was either a stool, or remain standing. He chose to stand.

'Where are my guards?'

'You don't have any. Your friends have been rounded up—they can walk back to Prague. And I have sent a message to your father, asking for clarification as to why he's changed my orders.'

'You did what? You had no right! And I'll be the one who decides what my father hears. And he will hear about you holding me captive here.'

Emma laughed, but there was no humour in the sound. 'What did I do, ride back to Prague, capture the castle, kidnap you and drag you here in chains?'

Mladenic stared at her. 'How did you find out? You were the one who was supposed to be kidnapped. I arranged it with—' He stopped, he attempted to saunter, to look at the food on the table.

Emma affected boredom. 'Oh, I know everything. You arranged it with the Saxons. But for now, I'll leave you to get dressed.' She stood. 'But I will leave my guards at the entrance. Do you need help?' The last question was asked in her sweetest voice, but Mladenic ignored the implied insult and shook his head.

Emma left, followed by Mark and Mikael. Mark suddenly stopped. The others looked at him.

'How long do we have?' Mark said.

'Before he's ready to receive us? An hour. Maybe more,' Emma replied.

'Where are your letters from your sister, madam, and the other information?'

'The information about the attack, the kidnap, is in Prague. My sister's letters are in my travelling trunk,' Emma replied, turning to the tent. The one Mladenic was in.

Suddenly in no mood to bother with his objections, she pointed to two of the bodyguard to accompany her, walked straight back to the tent and through the flap, ignored the squawk from a half-naked husband, gestured to the two men with her to pick up the trunk, and left. All without saying a word, nor glancing in her husband's direction.

҂

'"If this is my last letter to you, and the next you hear is my death, I shall have been murdered—I fear my husband is bending his ear to wild counsel telling him to conquer all lands—Frankish, Polish, Bohemian, even the Papal lands to the south—he can be a second, and better, Charlemagne. He does not see that, even as he does this, there is no guarantee his successors will hold it."' Mark looked up from his slow reading of Matilda's letter.

Emma was looking puzzled. The rest of them were blank. German, they could have followed, but that was Anglo-Saxon. Only Mark and Emma understood that tongue.

'Shall I read it again: "shall have been murdered"—why not, "I'll be dead," or "they'll have killed me"?' Mark looked up again as Emma's face cleared.

'She was my sister. Of course! She wouldn't use such formal language. About herself, or Otto—she loved the man! Besides, he is quite capable of being a second Charlemagne. We're witness to that. He's not turned up himself, but he can send all these forces to stop us in our tracks.' Emma was pacing, trying to work it all out. 'But why? Why set this up? And who?'

'"Who" is obvious, madam. The "why" is a little less clear. But we only have a little time left. We have to face him with what we know.'

'What we know is, I—yes, I, Mark—sent Podevin on a fool's errand. Matilda died young, and I'd still like to know more, but if that letter's false, we have no evidence she was killed by anyone.'

There was a sudden commotion outside, and shouts of 'Madam! Madam!' and 'He's getting away!'

With a 'Now what?' Emma wheeled away from Mark's deliberations, and dashed out of the tent, only to find herself in a storm of people milling about. Her bodyguard was among them. In the distance, she could see a party of men on horseback riding furiously down the slope towards the border.

Chapter 33
Mladenic Escapes—
And Is Returned

Thankfully, they were not making straight for the Saxon lines. Emma assumed her husband was aiming to bypass the enemy troops and make for—what? The nearest abbey? Anywhere he could find sanctuary against his father's wrath. He'd seemed scared enough this morning when she confronted him, but however angry she had been, she could not arrest her husband, condemn him, and have him killed. His father could. For that matter, Otto could.

She stopped musing. Practical steps needed taking. Firstly, how could Mladenic have got out of her tent? It was her guard, her troops—she had been very careful last night, when Mladenic had arrived, to make sure no soldier with potential loyalty to him was anywhere near him (though once she'd spoken to the captain about the supplies, she did wonder how loyal any of these reinforcements would be to him, rather than her). She strode to what had been, until last night, her tent. The guards were still there. They straightened to attention when they saw her approach.

'Why did you let Duke Boleslav escape?' she rapped out as soon as she was close enough to speak without shouting at them.

The guards gaped. 'But ... but, madam, he's not. He's still in there.'

She pushed past them, shoved the tent flap aside, and entered the tent.

Mladenic hadn't bothered to untie the back of the tent from its poles. He hadn't bothered to see if he could unstitch where the panels had been tied together. He had taken a knife—at least, Emma assumed it was a knife—to the back of the tent, and cut his way through the thick canvas. Perhaps it was the strength of desperation, though why he was so scared, Emma could not tell.

Mark and Mikael walked past her and out through the gaping hole. 'Oh, dear,' said Mark. 'He tripped over the peg on his way out.'

The monk pointed to the footprints showing Mladenic's stumble, and the peg that was no longer upright. However, the escapee must have managed to stifle any expression of pain or anger, as the guards insisted they had heard nothing. Once he was away from her tent, Mladenic would not have been stopped, as no-one else had been ordered to detain him. Emma had not thought he would have the initiative to try to get away. Where would he go?

'Now, what do we do?' asked Mikael, once they had worked out what had happened.

The captain of the Prague Castle reinforcements insisted he knew nothing of Mladenic's plans. The only people missing were Emma's husband and his seven special friends. It appeared they had decided, against her orders, to return to Mladenic rather than return to Prague on foot. The phalanx he kept around him so he could not be approached—particularly not by Emma. She was used to it. In one sense, it was explicable; had she not killed one of them in a duel?

Once again, Emma forced herself to consider the task in hand. The idea there would have been a dawn attack today, was farcical. It was suicide to consider such an attack—especially a frontal one—even tomorrow. What there would have to be was a parley. Somehow, she had to tell Duke Heinrich and his army, that on his territory, or Otto's territory, somewhere, there was an heir to Bohemia.

'If I may, madam,' Mark was only formal if the situation was serious, or he was telling her off, 'two heirs. Podevin's there as well.'

∽

They burst through the morning mist like men possessed, as if guided by divine purpose. They were right on target; a surprise attack on Podevin's position on the far left of the lines. He wheeled his horse to face the attack, but his western Franks—their blood up with the suddenness of the enemy's appearance—surged past him and ran towards the … eight men on horses, all yelling in Czech. Their leader's horse reared and the man on it, the one doing the most yelling, screamed, fell off, hit the ground and curled up into a ball.

Podevin's befuddled brain, his surprise at the 'attack' over, began to make sense of what was being yelled; they weren't demanding *his* surrender, they were saying, 'We surrender.' He began yelling too, but it was too late, battle had been joined. There were too many defenders for the normal advantage of charging cavalry to apply. Besides, the men did not fight as a cavalry unit; knee to knee, slashing down with swords. Only a couple had drawn their swords, so the pikes and spears stabbing upwards were instantly effective and, apart from the whimpering form on the ground, there was suddenly silence.

Podevin was reminded of an incident long ago, when Emma first made her journey to Prague, and the convoy was attacked by a band of ruffians. Then, Mladenic had the excuse of being ten years old. Now, he was a grown man. Fortunately, Podevin's men had heard their general's bellow of 'Enough!' It was over anyway. There was only Mladenic to do the explaining.

'It's easy,' Mladenic babbled, finally switching to German when it was too late, and not recognising Podevin, 'you just let me go to Rome. I'll renounce everything. My son can take over. He'll give you the tribute. You can do what you like to the others.'

'I'm glad "the others" can't hear you,' Podevin said. 'And shut up!' He spoke in Czech.

'You want to kill me! And my family—they're all going to die in your plans.' Mladenic's voice rose in pitch to a squeak.

'Will. You. Shut. Up!' Podevin repeated. 'And they are not my plans. I'm trying to keep you all alive.'

Well, he was trying to keep Emma alive. And, as an adjunct, her children. Mladenic was bottom of the list. So far, none of his troops knew who they'd captured. Podevin did not want to know why Mladenic had fled from his own lines. He hadn't even known Mladenic was there. Another lack of communication from Heinrich, or Kurt, or whoever was directing operations on the Saxon side. He had to think fast. If he could get Mladenic back to the Bohemians, with a message saying what he actually wanted—and it wasn't what Blanik wanted, nor what Otto and Heinrich wanted—then there was a chance. The message needed to get to Emma. He needed to tell her of the lack of information about her sister; the bloody flux is not a nice way to die, but as far as he could find out, there had been no murder.

He became aware of the silence around him. Even Mladenic had stopped whimpering.

'We're sending this one back. Under guard. With a message from me. You lot—get him ready.' Podevin strode away.

This had to be done quickly. If Kurt, Blanik, or any of the other commanders, got to hear about this, then he would be in trouble. But he was not going to kill Emma's husband. Not like this. Whatever his men thought, he could not have them wondering if he knew the prisoner. All he could do was hope their discipline was strong enough not to harm Mladenic, and their blood lust had been satisfied by the deaths of the rest of the men who'd charged into their midst. He went to his tent.

Some time later, shouts sounded from outside the tent, getting louder, disturbing his concentration. One word predominated: 'Pissenlit! Pissenlit!' He flung down his pen and strode to the tent flap. Mladenic was tied to the back of his horse, his backside to the sun. Podevin opened his mouth to remonstrate but paused. What good would it do? He still had his letter to finish and, if his Franks wanted to play by shoving some greenery into Mladenic's rear end and laugh about it, then all Podevin could do was hope Mladenic would remember that he could have been injured, or killed. He could not expect soldiers to pass up the chance of 'happening upon' some fine clothes—something to be bartered or sold once they returned home—so it had been inevitable that Mladenic would be stripped. Perhaps taking all his clothes so he was naked was a bit much, but Podevin had better things to do than remonstrate with his mercenaries just now. He ducked back into his tent.

He wrote his letter. To help, he even started with an Anglo-Saxon greeting. His limited knowledge of Emma's language preventing him from writing the whole screed in that tongue, but he had to hope the short opening would get the idea to her that he was not, and never had been, her enemy—or why would he have gone to Saxony on her behalf in the first place? He bent his head over the parchment and scratched away.

He folded and sealed his missive, inscribing the outside with Duchess Emma's name and title. Every inch the commander, he emerged from his tent. His captain was waiting outside, where it was now quiet. The troops had grown bored. It appeared even prodding Mladenic with the points of their daggers had produced little or no reaction. As Podevin approached, he could see they had stuffed his mouth with cloth—no wonder there had been no shouts or screams for Podevin to hear while he was writing. He handed over the parchment.

'Here,' he told the Frankish captain, 'put that in the saddlebag. The Bohemians can find it when this ridiculous person rides back to their lines.'

It would have been beneath a commander's dignity to do that sort of thing himself, and Podevin could not be seen to make too much of this missive. He wanted his troops to think it was merely a message of defiance, of provocation, not a plea for understanding.

Podevin went up to Mladenic. The man twisted his head, trying to make eye contact. His expression was difficult to read: Surly? Accepting? Resigned? Podevin bent down.

'Right. You're going back to your wife and your people. I hope you realise I could have had you killed?'

There was no answering nod, nor a change in expression. Podevin straightened. His captain was the other side of the horse. Podevin assumed he had obeyed orders and his letter to Emma was in the saddlebag. He could hardly check, beyond a surreptitious glance to see that it was no longer in the man's hand.

'Right, take him away.'

The last Podevin saw of Mladenic was the man's naked, lily-white rear end bouncing up and down on the horse's saddle as the selected troops, carrying a flag of truce, trotted away, leading him back to the Bohemian lines. The little party came to a halt within shouting distance of the enemy. In a practised manoeuvre, the escort began to peel away, leaving Mladenic's horse alone at the front.

Podevin now had to squint to see what was happening. One of the last remaining Franks slapped Mladenic's horse's rear, and it bolted. He was thrown about, but he was tied too tightly to fall off. He was on his way. Podevin could do no more.

ℰ෨

Not that she knew it was her husband initially, but his arrival back in camp, and the way he arrived, was sufficiently unusual to be reported to Emma. She was told it took several men on horseback to catch up with him, but even they were grinning as they told her about having to slice through the rough rope. It seemed they had not cared if they nicked his wrists and ankles.

She ordered a cloak to be flung over his shoulders, but he was still barefoot as they took him back to her tent. The rip in the back of it had been repaired, and she could see shadows prowling round. Good; he was not going to get out that way again.

'So. Why the posy of dandelion leaves?' Emma asked. She didn't remind him where those leaves had been.

'How am I supposed to know?' Mladenic replied.

'Madam,' Mark said, 'if I may?'

He was at the entrance to the tent, indicating she should withdraw, away from Mladenic's hearing. She took the few strides necessary to get outside.

'Well?' She was impatient. There was an attack to sort out—if it was still going ahead. The attack was one of the many things she needed to discuss with her husband.

'Dandelions are also known as "piss-a-bed" back home. Perhaps the Franks have a similar notion. Did we not hear an expression from them …' Mark paused as he saw comprehension dawn.

'"Pissenlit", wet-the-bed.' Emma nodded, but she was still puzzled.

'It means they are accusing this knight of being so afraid that he would, um, he would pass water … Dandelion leaves are a diuretic. Useful if anyone is having trouble, er …'

'Not like you to be embarrassed, Mark. Useful if anyone's having trouble pissing. Thank you. So, we know why the extra … vegetation.' Mark raised his eyebrows at Emma's own hesitation, but held his peace. She continued. 'My husband is a coward, who has got his "friends" killed.'

'Yes, I'm a coward.' The husband in question stood in the entrance to the tent, so he had heard their conversation. 'Yes, I got my friends killed. But, for your information, I was trying to outflank the Saxons. Only Podevin isn't leading Saxons. They're mercenaries from somewhere else, either the north or the west.' Mladenic paused. 'And, if you want to know, I was going to seek sanctuary until I could get passage to Rome.'

Mladenic turned, his back straight, and went back into Emma's tent.

Chapter 34
Mladenic's Confession

'And just where would that leave me?' Emma asked.

'That's irrelevant just now,' said Mark. 'We need to deal with what we have. And what we've got is Podevin leading troops, who could have killed your husband, but didn't.'

It took a second or two for the importance of Mark's words to sink in. She turned to him, open-mouthed.

'Ask yourself why. If he really wanted to disinherit you, to take your father-in-law's throne, why send his heir back to us? And why didn't he send any message?'

'He did send a message! But you lot were so bothered about me, you didn't ask—or look for one. Has anyone checked the saddle-bags?' There was a pause while Emma and Mark realised Mladenic was still listening in to their conversation. The young Duke Boleslav continued. 'They stopped my mouth, not my eyes or ears. Are you coming back in, or not?'

Emma and Mark re-entered the tent, but not before Emma sent a guard to search the saddlebags for a message.

'Perhaps you might need to read it in private?' Mark gestured at Emma's husband, who was sitting, eating a late midday meal.

He, however, unusually quiet, unusually calm and unusually—this was the oddest aspect of his whole demeanour—confident.

'Before you read that missive. You'd better know, my dear wife, I've been plotting your death for some considerable time. That party your lover-boy intercepted—oh, don't give me the rubbish you told my father, not that he believes it—was on its way to kill you. You see, I knew all about your correspondence with your sister. Brother Mark, here, isn't the only monk, or clerk, who knows Anglo-Saxon.' Mladenic looked up at Mark as the monk opened his eyes wide in surprise. 'I made sure my clerk had no contact with you. I had translations on my desk before you read the original, my dear.'

'Your desk?' Emma had been to her husband's rooms often enough over the years, but had never seen anything which could be called a desk.

'In the scriptorium.' The young Boleslav sighed. 'Much easier than explaining to my dear, delightful father, why I was engaging in such lower-caste occupations as reading and writing.'

'But that was part of your education—and mine, come to that,' said Emma, distracted for the moment.

A guard had come into the tent: the saddlebags had been searched and nothing found. She nodded her thanks—but could read nothing from Podevin. The question was, could she guess what he would have written? However, her husband was still wittering.

'Yes, I was supposed to know *how* to read and write, but not to spend any significant time actually *doing* it. That was a job for clerks. I know exactly who's cheating father on taxes, but it's not my place to tell him. However, aren't we wandering from the point?'

'I'd have thought you'd be happy to wander from the point, given you've just told me you've been spying on me for years.'

'And rather successfully, too. Not that it got me very far. Your Podevin saw to that.'

'But there were the letters—about a kidnap? And they were definitely Saxon. I saw the bodies too.'

'Duke Heinrich's men. He was in on it. Once you were dead, and I'd gone to Rome, he'd offered to deal with my father. He'd also offered to marry our daughter, provided Father stepped down.'

'What about our son?'

'Too young to worry about taking over the whole country, I think.'

'What!' Emma felt the fury course through her. 'Boys grow up! They'll want their inheritance—what did you expect him to do? Follow you to Rome?'

'When he grows up, he can do what he likes. This,' the young duke raised an arm to encompass the whole tent and everything outside, 'camp life, this charging backwards and forwards defending land and destroying it on the way. This constant battling for a spurious superiority. And you're as bad as my father as far as that goes!'

'If we don't have a country to pass onto our son, to our heirs,' Emma ground out the obvious, 'they will be killed. Not just us. Do you really think Heinrich and Otto would allow you to go to Rome? What if you changed your mind? Persuaded the pope to bless your efforts at reconquering your kingdom? Otto has interests in Italy, or didn't you know?'

'All right! I knew it had all gone wrong when I fell off that horse! Uncle Wenny couldn't get to Rome, you couldn't marry Podevin— though it might have been better for me if you had—and he had to settle for a peasant woman.'

'I didn't think you knew.'

'Let's just say it amused me to know Wenceslas's page had to live in a hovel in the forest and bow to me if he ever crossed my path. Besides, the reports were useful. Once I had my tame Anglo-Saxon, if you knew something, I knew it.'

'So why did you let me send Podevin to Saxony?'

For the first time, her husband raised his head and looked directly at her. 'So he could be killed.' He paused, but, before she could fill the silence, he carried on speaking. 'I did not expect him to charge the closed gates. I am sorry for Geraint's death.'

Emma scoffed.

'He was no friend to me, but he was a good fighter.'

'Was Sven part of the plan? Was Lyudmila's death? And was I really to be kidnapped? Taken to Saxony?' Emma asked.

'What would they do with you in Saxony?' Boleslav appeared to find the thought amusing. 'None of that. They were supposed to kill you—before Podevin started killing them.' Then, in a change of tone: 'We've never liked each other. You didn't want me, and I certainly didn't want you.'

'How many people like us "want" each other? It was my brother who sent me out from England.' Emma sat. Before today, Boleslav would have objected, but now he just kept looking at her, waiting. 'So,' she said, 'what do we do now?'

'Obey our orders, I suppose.' It was Mladenic's turn to pause. He glanced at Mark, who was standing at the side of the tent, watching the exchange but saying nothing. Reverting his gaze to Emma, Mladenic continued. 'Have you heard of the battle of Marathon?'

'Have I what?' she said.

'I'm not suggesting we do everything the Greeks did, but the Saxons—or their mercenaries—are behaving like the Persians. So we copy what the Greeks did. The first line charges them, they respond—they'll have to, especially once we're under their spear-throwing range. They charge—into that boggy ground. Their wings will come in to reinforce the centre if you charge at their wings to encourage them. We then retire and bring them onto your defensive lines.' Boleslav shrugged.

'That's all very well, but I can hardly lead a charge on the wings with the cavalry—not that we have many horsemen—if I'm also fighting in the front line.'

Boleslav stood. 'I thought that was clear. I'm leading the front line.'

Emma gaped. 'What?'

Her husband stood. 'While I was on that horse, tied there, I suddenly realised I had stopped being scared. Any one of them could have come up and killed me. I don't suppose I'd have been that sorry. In other words, I faced death today. Maybe, when it comes to it, I will piss my pants—or worse! But,' he shrugged, 'we've all got to die sometime. If this battle kills me, it kills me. If not … well, I'm hardly likely to be allowed to go to Rome, so I'd better learn how to be a king. However,' the look he gave Emma was, if not friendly, the most considerate he had ever given her, 'you will never be my queen. That's over. Even my father recognises that.'

'But England—'

'Has turned in on itself. You'll find out why soon enough.'

He was going to say more, but his wife stood up, approached him, put both hands on his face, one on each cheek, and kissed him on the forehead. For the first time in their marriage, she kissed him. She knew she had to take what he said about her, about England, seriously. But she also knew divorce was a serious matter that required the agreement of the pope in Rome, and the pope, in turn, would listen to other people, like Otto, and not just Boleslav. Maybe there was a way to … work together. She didn't know, but, if they were going to hold a battle by dawn the next day, there was still plenty to do. But first, she had a confession of her own.

The kiss done, but still holding his face, she looked into his eyes. 'And don't ever think I don't get scared before a battle. I do. But the nerves go once things get underway—too much to think about.' Embarrassed at her confession, she changed the subject. 'Come on, we have to get our troops organised. I take it you brought your armour?'

At his nod, she told him to fetch it and put it on while she rounded up her commanders to meet and discuss the battle plan.

Chapter 35
Battle Is Joined

It was before dawn the next day when Podevin was shaken roughly awake. And, once he was dressed, he was dragged—no other word for it—to see the commander of the Saxon forces. Once he realised what was happening, Podevin was not unduly concerned, at the summons to see King Otto's younger brother (the king himself was still, he was told, on his way). The blow fell as soon as he entered the tent to be faced with ten armed knights, all with weapons drawn. He hadn't been tied up, he had not been killed, but he had been forcibly disarmed.

The main camp was just behind the centre of the lines, plenty of preparatory work going on before the daily parades and inspections. Podevin could not imagine the same thing happening on the Bohemian side. Training happened, of course it did, but all this striving for perfection, for uniformity, was not something even Emma would have imposed on her conscripted army. There was, however, no time for anything other than a brief look, before he was compelled to duck his head to enter the commander's presence.

'The Anglo-Saxon was difficult, but the Czech—we understand Czech.' Duke Heinrich flung the scrap of parchment onto the table between them. 'You had the heir in your hands, and you sent him back to his own side.' The sneer was written all over the duke's face, and his cronies took their lead from him. 'What is the point in setting all this up, if you go and throw away your biggest advantage?'

'My children are hostages against my good behaviour. Am I supposed to be responsible for their deaths?' Podevin, erect but unarmed, stood waiting.

'How do you know your *illegitimate* offspring are still alive?' Heinrich was still clearly taking the official line.

'I'm sure you'd have told me quickly enough if they were dead. All the better to make me "behave" as you wanted.'

At Podevin's comment, some of the attendant knights smiled, until Heinrich glared at them and said, 'Unless their death means you'd have nothing left to lose? How would you have behaved then?'

With extreme care, unless you also told me Emma was dead, Podevin thought. However, Heinrich's comment confirmed Podevin's opinion of King Otto's brother: he was planning something not to Podevin's betterment. Podevin had a thought.

'Why is Blanik not here?'

'Oh, he's gone to plead your cause with Otto. After all, he is now your only ally.'

Heinrich paused. Podevin tried to work out whether he was pleased about Blanik's absence or not. He hadn't liked the feeling that Blanik had been playing his own game with Podevin's life. Perhaps, if Blanik had not immediately recognised Podevin as the duke of Budec and forced the idea of him taking over from Boleslav, then some, if not all, of this mess would have been avoided.

But what was the point of thinking about that? His message, his plea to Emma that he was not after her life, her status, her anything; his plea sent back with her living husband—even if his troops had done their best to humiliate him—just so that he could see what was left of his family again, just so he could ensure his children could survive his death, just so she would still love him—it had fallen into the wrong hands. Extracted by one of his soldiers and handed over to Heinrich.

Unbidden, while he stood there in the silence and watched the Saxon duke pretend to read the parchment again, the thought came to him of that first time they had been in a fight together. That first time when he had escorted her from Augsburg to Prague, when he'd been a surly youngster, and she'd been an equally uncooperative prospective bride for Mladenic. And they'd fought back-to-back against the brigands sent by Duke Boleslav. By the time they had arrived in Prague, he and Emma had been friends. Friends who became more than friends.

Podevin gave a mental shrug. Now they could be going into battle on opposite sides. How could he claim the Bohemian throne without it meaning death and destruction for Emma and her family? How could he lose the fight and not also lose his children? Just because the Saxons said they were illegitimate did not stop him loving them—no matter how much he'd got wrong. He hoped Maria and Priby were doing all right. That Vaclav and Alexandr could do some training, even if they were officially hostages. But how were they to show their support for the Boleslavs—father and son—given their father's supposed treachery?

How was he to get out of this crazy situation? What was Heinrich saying?

'I will keep this. And show it to anyone who says any different. That this "duke of Budec" is too much of a coward to be supported as a new ally in Prague. I will be the one to marry Duchess Emma. She's still young enough to make more babies. And if this brainless fool is so besotted with her as to refuse to fight against her, she must have something.'

'Be careful, my lord. What she has is a fearsome reputation as one who kills suitors she does not like!' However, the German knight was grinning as he spoke, and Heinrich laughed.

'So, you have heard the rumour about the Welsh outlaw, too?' he asked, rising from his seat and clapping the man on the shoulder. 'If she was that ferocious, she'd have made carrion out of that husband of hers years ago! Have any of you seen her in battle?' Heinrich looked around, but none of his knights seemed inclined to disagree with him.

'I have,' said Podevin. Why not, he thought, remind the Saxons he was here. 'And,' he continued, 'she is a formidable fighter.'

Laughter.

'She's a woman!'

'We knew her sister.'

'Women can't be trained to use weapons of war.'

Podevin shook his head. Maybe they would find out the hard way. And maybe now.

For there was a sudden blaring of trumpets.

'They're attacking! They're attacking! To arms! Defend yourselves!'

The shouts came from outside. Podevin could hear men running. The knights made a rush to leave the tent, pushing past Podevin as he stood there, facing a stupefied Heinrich.

'So? What now, commander?' he said. 'It appears the Bohemians will defeat you again.'

It was the wrong thing to say.

'If they defeat me, it'll be because they've got past you!' Heinrich snapped. 'Give him his sword.' He gestured to a squire, who leapt to obey. 'You,' Duke Heinrich's attention reverted to Podevin, 'will fight in the front line.' He looked the former, or pretend, duke of Budec, over. 'Good—nothing to identify you as a Bohemian.'

Given that all Podevin's armour, all his clothes, had been loaned to him, that was no surprise. He realised, of course he did, Heinrich's plan was simple. To have Podevin killed in battle would solve so many problems. For Heinrich, anyway. Podevin couldn't even be sure if his death would solve his children's problems. For now, the squire stood at the entrance to the tent, waiting to guide him to his allotted place in fighting off the enemy.

For the first time in his life, he was escorted to the front line. He shook his head. Was this it? From Heinrich's words, he could tell he was not meant to survive this day. If he took his helmet off, so he could be identified, it would be so much easier to kill him with a blow to the head. And who was to say being identified would help him anyway? Even if he was seen for who he was, he could think of some people (Mladenic for a start), who'd be happy to see him dead.

By the time he arrived at the lines, battle had already been joined. And it appeared the Saxons were getting the best of it. For the first few minutes, every time Podevin thought he had pushed through (being prodded and encouraged all the time) to the front, the Bohemians had retreated a few yards.

Had he the time to think about it, he might have recalled Wenceslas's tactics at his first battle—the one against the Saxons when his father was killed. The one that first pitted Wenceslas against Otto. However, the Saxons, having been surprised by the Bohemian charge, were not about to give up what they saw as their advantage. They pressed forward, taking casualties, but taking ground as well. Podevin moved forward. His blood up, the excitement starting to pump in his veins, he no longer needed the prods from behind. There appeared to be a Bohemian rally just in front of him.

He shouted, 'Come on!' and rushed forward, sword at the ready …

It was a trap. The Saxons around him had retreated. He was alone and surrounded. Before he could make the decision to fight, or try to yield, a blaring sound came across the battlefield. A long, loud trumpet call to 'Hold.' The sound came from behind, and in front of him. What was going on? The fighters hesitated, then stopped; then they stepped back—but only so they were out of range of their opponents' swords or spears. With his left hand, Podevin removed his helmet, so he could see. He turned to check behind him. Yes, there was the same sound. Everyone was to hold their position, but go no farther.

Silence. Apart from the groans and cries of the wounded. Then another trumpet blast. Again, as if it were coordinated, both sides heard their trumpeters sound 'Retire.' The wounded, those so badly hurt they couldn't move, would have to be left, but the rest—no doubt puzzled—obeyed their orders. Most, however, faced the enemy as they carefully, one step at a time, began to increase the distance between themselves and the person they had been trying to close with and kill only a few short moments ago. Podevin made to retreat.

'I think not, Podevin. You're coming with us.'

An unknown knight was addressing him. Padded jerkin, leather over that, but lightly armoured so he could still move freely. And he was clearly confident in his skills. So confident, he was barely watching Podevin's sword. However, he had his fellow soldiers with him. Podevin sighed. He hoped his would be a quick end once he was taken back to Bohemian lines—though he still could not work out why Heinrich had staged such a manoeuvre just to get rid of him: why not just have him killed?

The knight was still standing there. 'You don't recognise me, do you?' he said.

Podevin looked again. There was blood from a cut just under his eye, an arrow had grazed his arm, and there was a bigger gash on his thigh, but the knight looked very pleased with himself. Recognition slowly dawned.

'Mladenic?' said Podevin.

'I think you'll find I no longer go by that name,' said Duke Boleslav. 'However, we need to find out what is going on here.'

∽

Hands on hips, eyes blazing, Emma was furious. Too furious to bother with protocol. 'My husband is down there risking his life! And you're telling me to stop this? You're the one who ordered it in the first place.'

'And I reserve the right to change my orders. Otto isn't very happy.'

King Boleslav, freshly arrived from the east, just in time, as he put it, to 'prevent a bloodbath' (though he did concede later that his son and current daughter-in-law had concocted a plan that might have worked), had carefully omitted to tell his son that negotiations had been opened with the Saxon king. Negotiations that mainly concerned the Magyars, but also contained a certain amount of discussion over tribute (or the lack thereof) reaching Saxon coffers. It was his turn to appropriate Emma's tent and her seat, leaving her standing.

It appeared it was all very well for King Boleslav to beat the Magyars enough to send them back across their border with Bohemia, but not slaughter them sufficiently to stop future raids … into territory held by Otto. Otto, or his vassals, could also deal with the raids after a fashion, but the Magyars kept coming back. In order to beat them, in order to teach them a lesson they would not forget in a hurry, both Boleslav and Otto had come to the conclusion they needed to work together. Possibly, they needed a grand coalition with the Poles and others. This would, of course, take time, but what they did not need, was border skirmishes with each other.

Just as Otto had come up behind his brother's forces in order to impose his will, King Boleslav had approached Emma's position.

Emma had known about her father-in-law's arrival, but she had assumed he was bringing reinforcements, not a treaty. Hadn't he spent the last ten or more years, the whole of his reign, provoking Saxony? Hadn't Saxony taken Podevin's flight across the border as a ploy to advance their own agenda? Hadn't Boleslav given Sven Podevin's job and home when Sven came to Prague with his tale?

All this Emma poured out to an overly calm king. He waited until she stopped.

'My dear, with your actions of late, you ought to know you are expendable. You allowed Podevin to escape. You misidentified someone else as him ten years ago. You have been deceiving me.'

'I doubt that! If your son knew everything that was going on, I'd be very surprised if you weren't kept fully informed.'

'Enough! England is not the power that it was. There's another half-brother on your English throne, so be careful. I have my grandson. My son can marry again.'

Emma opened her mouth to spill news of his son's plots against her, but the Bohemian king was not paying attention. Podevin had been shoved into the king's presence. However, even the supposed traitor was ignored, as he was followed by the king's son, his wounds still unattended.

'Father.' Duke Boleslav bowed.

'Well, well, well.' The king looked his son up and down. 'What's this? You look like you've been in a fight.' He nodded. His son did not speak. 'You'd better go and get those wounds seen to. Actually, I'll come with you.' King Boleslav stood, then he looked over at Emma and Podevin. 'As for you two: make a decision. One of you lives.'

Chapter 36
Facing Death

There was silence in the tent. Emma paced back and forth in the narrow space. Podevin stood. Outside, they could hear orders being given, people coming and going. Presumably, the wounded were, by now, being collected and brought back to camp. Brother Mark, and any others with healing skills, would be busy. Emma wondered what her bodyguard was up to—whether they would take orders from either Boleslav, or whether they would try to get in touch with her. It had all been so chaotic.

One moment she had been in the role of general, trying to see how the battle was going between the front lines and ready to order the first arrows fired over Bohemian heads into Saxon ranks. The next, she'd been told to stop the fighting, and that the king wanted to see her. She knew—oh! How she knew—sending Podevin into Saxony had been a mistake, but she had thought she could trust him not to rebel so openly against the Boleslavs. And as for wanting the throne himself with a new wife … all she could think was that she was glad Lyudmila was not alive to hear about it. And then he had been captured—it beggared belief. How he could stand there and look so unconcerned was beyond her.

⁊

For his part, Podevin decided he might as well be comfortable and sat down. For the moment, he was still alive. How he had managed to get himself into the situation where he was hated by both sides in this petty dispute, he did not know. He knew it would be his life that would be sacrificed. For all Mladenic might want his wife out of the way, as an Anglo-Saxon princess, it would not be, he hoped, too politic to kill her—especially as her elder sister's death was still too recent to be out of everyone's thoughts. Never mind that the conversation had been a non-starter back at Augsburg; there was something Heinrich was up to, even if Podevin had never found out what.

Emma's voice broke into his thoughts.

'Thank you for humiliating my husband.'

'It would have been easier to let him be killed. But I thought, on the whole, that might make things worse.'

'Worse? Worse than this!' Emma's voice rose in her anger as she gesticulated round the tent—at the shadows of the guards. 'I could be following my sister to the grave very shortly.'

It's not like Duchess Emma to be melodramatic, Podevin thought. 'It's my life Boleslav's wanted ever since he killed Wenceslas. Do you really think he's going to let me go now?'

'How can you be so calm? Where's your fighting spirit?'

Podevin sighed. 'You know, Lyudmila always said I rushed into things. And she was right. If I hadn't rushed off to kill those Saxons, if I'd merely reported their existence to you, to Prague Castle. If I'd just watched them kill that poor farmer, then maybe none of this would have happened. And I would still be Krok, living in the forest around Prague, hoping you'd train my sons as knights.' He stood, so he could look her in the eye. 'That's my only worry, you know, what will happen to them after I'm gone. And the girls, of course.'

'Your boys would be better off living off the land,' Emma said, distracted. 'As for the young ladies, Maria's done all right for herself. Played off being Tugumir's daughter brilliantly. Whether Pribyslava is happy being lady-in-waiting to the new duchess of Budec is another thing.'

'What? How do you know all this?'

'I do get to know some of what happens in my own country! I was trying to keep an eye on your sons. You can be thankful they were not sent here.'

'Can I?' Podevin stood, took a few steps. She was aware he'd moved closer. 'Does the condemned man get a final kiss from a princess?'

'What's to stop her also being killed? Especially if she is caught kissing a traitor?' But she was facing him, their lips almost touching.

'I was never a traitor to you. I said so in my letter.'

'What letter?' She drew back.

'The one I tried to send with your husband.' Furious with himself, Podevin turned away.

They were both aware the moment was lost.

'Tell me what it said. Before it's too late.'

So Podevin told her about his doomed quest. The insistence by Liutgarde, along with any and everyone else he talked to in Augsburg, that her mother died of the bloody flux. The fact that he had never seen Otto. Otto was, however, in mourning for his wife. There can have been no plan by him to do away with Matilda. If there had been, surely by now the Saxon court would have heard rumours about who would replace her as queen? He told Emma about Blanik—another person mysteriously not around at the moment—and his recognition of Podevin as Tugumir's younger brother. And so, Podevin could fulfil the same role, couldn't he? Only this time, if Princess Liutgarde married him—'She's only half my age!' interrupted Emma—then that would tie Saxony and Bohemia together nicely.

'All she'd have to put up with is having her aunt, nieces, and nephews killed before she becomes duchess of Bohemia!' interposed Emma.

'You think I hadn't thought of that? You think *she* hadn't thought of that? You think I didn't try to get out of it?' Podevin pushed his hand through his hair. 'But Blanik made it very clear, it was either take over Bohemia, or die. For all Liutgarde accepted my story, I'm now wondering if Heinrich ever really went along with it. You know, I think he wants Bohemia for himself.'

'A lot of people want Bohemia for themselves. This land has caused an awful lot of deaths.' Emma moved to the seat and sat down, brooding.

Podevin gave a fleeting smile. 'And I was offered Bohemia—I didn't want it, because it meant not having you. It meant—' He couldn't say it.

For the first time, he realised, in the ten years he'd spent with Lyudmila, pretending to be Krok, he had also been pretending not to want Emma. Now she was here, both of them under threat of death. Emma had lived with that threat the whole time since she'd arrived in Bohemia—and she hadn't wanted the country either! He raised his hands in frustration, then let them drop. There was no way he could let her die. Yes, he would die for her. He would pray to any god, every god, to look after his children. But he would die for Emma.

'I'd never have done it,' he said. 'Even with your husband dead, I could not have done it.'

'Not even with a sixteen-year-old bride?' Emma smiled. She reached across, moved a stool closer to her own seat and patted it.

'Not even with a sixteen-year-old bride who reminds me of you when you and I first met.' He sat.

'Now there was a fight!' She leaned towards him.

'My first ... And there was all that time we spent together, pretending to be just friends.'

'I'm getting less good at pretending.'

Once again, their lips were close. This time, Podevin made no mention of a husband.

Their lips met; arms reached round bodies. Emma left her seat to sit on Podevin's lap.

Sounds came from outside. They were ignored.

'I have the king's permission! I'm hardly going to help them escape, am I?' The voice was cross.

The kissers leapt apart. However, Podevin realised their visitor had to be extremely unobservant not to notice the flushed cheeks, the overturned stool, and the resolute refusal of the condemned to engage with each other. He couldn't even glance in Emma's direction.

'The latest idea. He wants to set up a duel between you.' Brother Mark said as he looked at the two of them.

'Who?'

'What?'

Two voices, the words different, but the surprise was total.

'When he said only one of you will survive, Boleslav, King Boleslav, meant exactly that. It will be a public fight to the death. The charges against both of you have been resurrected—you remember Sven? He claims to have uncovered evidence hidden in your former home, Podevin, that shows you and the Duchess Emma had a child together. That child is being taken to Budec to join your other children. The king seems to think he can solve his problems in one go.'

'No! It's not going to happen like that!' Podevin reached for his dagger, forgetting he'd been deprived of it before he was allowed to enter the tent. He stopped, turned to Emma, pointed at her dagger. 'Kill me. You can say we fought. You can say we should not have been left alone, but kill me now because I shall never kill you!'

'And I will never kill you.'

Now they were gazing at each other. Mark coughed.

'It has been decided what will not happen, hadn't we better work out what is to be done? While you two have been murmuring sweet nothings to each other, some of us have been busy—and keeping our ears open.'

It didn't need any of them to keep their ears open to hear Mikael's entrance. His 'Out of my way if you want to live,' growled at the guards before they had time to react, was audible to all three of them. He pushed his way inside the tent, approached Emma, and knelt.

'Your bodyguard awaits your command, madam. We are armed and ready to fight our way out of here. Your ladies, Beatrice and Hilde, are with them.'

'But where do we go? And what about the children?' It was Mark putting the objection.

'Madam's son is safe. After all, he is heir to Bohemia,' Mikael said, still on his knees. Emma indicated he should rise. 'However, her daughter is not yet at Budec.'

'So, we have to find her, and my sons and daughters—if I'm to be killed, what of my offspring?' Podevin said.

'The king has said nothing about that—so far. Unless Mikael knows different?' Mark said.

It was Emma who posed the next question.

'Are you sure about this, Mikael? Are you all sure?'

'All those who objected to disbanding are. Warriors and knights tend not to like being downgraded to guards.'

'Is that what he said? You were to become guards?'

'At Stara Boleslav—not even in Prague. He wants us away from where we might cause trouble.'

'So, the king thinks you might cause trouble? Why are you here?' Podevin asked. 'I mean, why are you allowed to be here?'

'Who said anything about "allowed"?' Mikael replied. 'If I come anywhere near my "former mistress", I am a traitor. The king thinks the rest of your guards are packing to go to their new home and new duties.'

He paused, waiting for Emma's lead.

'We need to get out of here if we want our lives, that's obvious,' she said. 'Mark, you're the only one not immediately in danger. Can you find out what's going on with Podevin's dependants—and where Edith is? It seems my son is lost to me.'

Mark bowed his head and turned to leave the tent. He got as far as putting his head through the flap before turning back.

'Ah!' he said. 'I fear your presence, Mikael, or mine, must have been reported to the king. There are too many of them on their way here for us to fight off.'

'Quick!' Emma said, leaping to the back of the tent and the recently repaired exit Mladenic had used on his flight from the camp earlier.

Mikael was out first. A clash of steel and a groan caused Podevin's headlong rush out, but the guard was dead, and Podevin now had a sword to use. The others followed. So far, there were no shouts, and most of the ordinary soldiers still assumed Emma was in charge—had she not been the one to lead them ever since they arrived? It was just their leader taking another stroll, another chat, another inspection, wasn't it? For all Podevin would have run, they walked.

Emma's bodyguard had gathered by the horses. They were within hailing distance before they heard shouts of 'Escaped prisoner!' behind them.

'Keep walking,' Mark said. 'They haven't said who has escaped, yet.'

Within seconds, the party had mounted and was ready to move out.

'Budec,' said Podevin.

Possibly the nearest place, and no doubt Boleslav would regard it as an obvious place for him to go to, but, if they could get there first, round up his children, and … then they could think where to go from there. Besides, no-one else had a better suggestion.

The break out of the camp was easy: they just took the nearest pathway. It headed off towards Saxony, but that was all to the good. If they could disguise where they veered off the track, then maybe it would delay Boleslav long enough for them to get to Budec and leave again. They just had to ride, and ride hard.

℘

As they cantered along, Emma realised she had, in choosing Podevin, very few options left. Either they worked out how to live together (she even found herself wondering how many more children she had within her), or the best she could hope for was the nunnery King Athelstan had threatened her with all those years ago before he sent her out here in the first place. If they failed, it was that, or death. She doubted Podevin would even get that choice. She looked at him. All this was her fault, and yet he still loved her. He had not spent much time on a horse in the last ten years, but his old skills were clearly coming back to him. They had Brother Mark—who was, she must not forget, a former warrior before he took up his more peaceful profession—and Mikael. In her mind, Mikael was still so young. She felt the responsibility of care, even though her chief bodyguard had made his own choice to come to her. Then of course, there were her ladies. Beatrice and Hilde had been with her for years. Hilde she'd ordered back to her farm with her husband on sight—officially those two weren't even here—Beatrice was 'Not going anywhere without you, madam.' Emma had been too short of time to argue.

The sun was beginning to set before they came close to Budec. There was a brief discussion but, given Podevin's experience the last time he'd ridden up to a fortress after curfew, and the fact it was summer, they decided they could cope with a night outside the gates, and they would make their approach in the morning.

It was a mistake. As was their assumption that, because they'd heard no rider coming up behind them, they were ahead of the latest news from the border. At the time, Podevin and Emma were unaware, but while they were wasting time circling round from the Saxon side of the Bohemian encampment, supposedly laying a false trail, Boleslav had already sent his messengers off to any and every castle and fortification in his domains. They all carried the same message: 'Take them, dead or alive.'

Chapter 37
Preparations in Budec

That fateful morning, once she knew Podevin and Emma were due to turn up outside, and her brother Sven was inside ready to hand over his missive from the king, Priby knew she had to say something but had no idea what. Maria was now successfully, if hurriedly, married, and not bothering to hide her pregnancy. Nor was she hiding her increasingly foul temper. A wariness had crept into the castle; people had become careful about chatting to other people they met in a corridor. Would someone, someone willing to curry favour with the new duchess, be listening on the other side of a door or from behind a curtain? Even in the kitchens—a place Maria had never been known to grace with her presence—she was referred to as 'Madam Her Grace', rather than any other epithet: just in case word filtered back to the Duchess Maria.

'It needs to be thicker.' Priby brought the posset back to the kitchen, giving the message with an apologetic shrug. As the head chef turned towards her, opening his mouth to object that someone had disparaged his creations, she added, acting out a parody of a lady tossing her head and waggling her fingers, 'Madam Her Grace says so!'

The chef grinned in acknowledgement, took the bowl of thick, creamy, spicy posset, looked around, and handed it to one of the kitchen boys.

'Here,' he said, 'you've done well today.'

The lad took it, murmured his thanks and buried his face in the bowl.

'You won't get far if you treat your peasants like that. They take advantage.'

The languid voice, from the seat at the head of the table, made both Priby and the chef turn. For the second time they had met as adults, Priby recognised her brother. For the second time, Sven failed to, or pretended not to, recognise her. This time, he was wearing the badge of King Boleslav's messenger, though what he was doing here, in the kitchens at Budec castle, Priby did not yet know. His son, at least Priby assumed it was his son, sat, a silent shadow, by his side, picking at his plate, casting nervous glances at his father every time he put a morsel of food in his mouth. Priby noted the lad kept a box between him and his father—she wondered why.

'I'm not sure it's your place to tell me how to run my kitchen. As long as the duke is happy, then that is all I need to worry about.' The chef turned away to start on a new, thicker drink for her grace.

Sven shrugged, and turned his attention to Priby.

'And who are you?'

'You know full well who I am,' Priby replied, 'and what you did the last time we met.'

'It was all perfectly legal,' Sven muttered into the sudden silence of the kitchen.

A brief, thin smile crossed Priby's lips. So, he did recognise her, did he?

'Killing unarmed women is never perfectly anything. And, just to point out, whoever you may think you are now, I know you were born a peasant.'

'I think you'll find, as the king's messenger, it would be a mistake to refer to me as a peasant. I am here to destroy Podevin and his lover—on the king's own command.'

'I thought you were the forester?'

'The king's forester. Others can do the actual work. I keep the ear of the king.' With that enigmatic statement, Sven stood.

His son, obviously realising the supply of food was about to be taken from him, and that his father wasn't paying attention, began shoving as much as he could down his gullet.

'The duke's not here. Nor is his brother.'

The duchess of Budec, it was explained to Sven, would receive the message, via her lady-in-waiting. Priby wondered how the world had been so turned upside-down that one peasant, now a king's messenger, was giving a message to another peasant (whatever her father's rank), who was now a duchess? Via another peasant, who was acting as the lady-in-waiting.

Sven was 'only in the kitchen' because he'd already been told the duke wasn't at home. No-one had told him the duke, or dukes, weren't expected until the next day. And the king was already on his way. The king wanted the traitors, dead or alive.

'Oh, so we have traitors, do we?'

'Yes, we do!' Sven said. 'Your precious Podevin and his lover!'

'What? But surely, they'd run away—if that was true.'

Priby realised, as soon as she spoke, that Podevin would try to find his family. He'd not abandon his sons to be killed. But Podevin did not know what Maria had been up to. She needed her wits about her; somehow, she must get her own message to Podevin. And what, her startled brain registered, about Emma's children? She took a breath. One thing at a time. She needed to find out how bad things were.

'So, are you going to deliver the message, or is the king going to get here before anyone knows what he wants?'

Priby realised the new posset was all but ready for her to take to Maria. And Maria's mood these days was not something to be trifled with. If she found out there had been a delay in getting the message to her… Unbidden, Sven dogged her footsteps as she walked out of the kitchen.

❧

Placing the posset on the table well within reach of her mistress, Priby handed over the message. Sven, not being part of Maria's household, had been left outside the room. Sven's son, who apparently went by the name of Woden, had been left in the kitchen to guard the box. It would be up to Maria if she wanted to see Sven, but Priby reckoned she would not be interested in his son as well, even if he was learning his trade from his father. She hoped the boy would be allowed to fill his tummy while he was there. The Budec kitchens were one place Priby had been able to relax a little.

Maria left her standing while she read the message and read it again. Then the duchess smiled.

'It seems we might be expecting extra visitors. Fetch this messenger in.'

Servants rushed to open the door and usher Sven into the room. He bowed to Maria as soon as he crossed the threshold. He bowed again when she beckoned him closer, and yet again when he stopped within two feet of the duchess. The duchess waved a hand at Priby to instruct her to retire. She stepped back, moving out of Maria's line of sight, but not out of hearing.

'So, messenger. What do you know of this?'

Sven straightened. 'I think I can say I have the king's confidence. He will not punish any who kill them both; but I rather fancy he would prefer to interrogate them himself—before they die.'

'What about England?'

'We have been assured England will do nothing. It is not the country it was under King Athelstan.'

Who is this 'we'? thought Priby. Was her brother so close to the king—or had he acquired his information by listening in to conversations behind doors? It did not matter, since Sven appeared well informed. So well informed, he could tell Maria all about the latest developments on the border. Including the calculated humiliation of Duke Boleslav, the king's son, by the traitor Podevin. Sven spent some time, however, pointing out how well King Boleslav's son had fought in the next day's battle.

At the time, Priby did not know there was an alternative explanation for the battle, or about why Duke Boleslav had landed himself in such trouble in the first place—or what the alternative to his humiliation was. She reeled from the information, unable to understand what had happened to her family. Vaclav and Alexandr, for the moment, simply by not being mentioned, might survive. Certainly, she and Maria did not feature in the latest moves the serpentine king was making. However, Priby realised they must all tread carefully—and she knew Maria would do whatever it took to reinforce her own credentials as not being Podevin's daughter. Unless King Boleslav was going to be particularly vindictive, the duchess of Budec would be in the clear.

Priby realised Sven was departing, backing away, bowing repeatedly as he exited the room. Maria still had the message.

'So, what are you going to do?' Priby asked.

'Firstly, get a message sent to my husband and his brother,' Maria replied, sending a servant to find a scribe.

'But they'll be back tomorrow, won't they?'

'They plan to be back tomorrow. Plans change. Besides, it's not going to be said I did not make the effort to keep my husband informed.' Maria looked down her nose at the older girl. 'Now, leave me in peace to compose my letter to my husband.'

'Yes, my lady, no, my lady,' Priby muttered under her breath as she turned to leave. 'Whatever you say, my lady.' The gatehouse would be her next stop.

Chapter 38
Maria in Charge

They could never hope to take the castle—there were much too few of them—so simply riding up and asking for entry seemed the best plan. And, in so far as it got them inside the fortress, it worked. In so far as they saw Priby for a few moments, it worked. In so far as it got them an audience with the duchess of Budec, it worked. Just Podevin and Emma, with Mark in attendance, of course. The bodyguard would be given food and drink, so that was all to the good. Beatrice was also cared for. In so far as the three of them would be stunned by the outcome of that audience, then—their plan failed.

'So, you come demanding an audience, do you?' Maria's opening gambit made Podevin look up in surprise.

'Maria?' he said, then, following instructions to pretend they had not seen her at the gatehouse, 'and is that Priby by your side? This is wonderful.' He opened his arms, and began to walk towards them for an embrace. Priby had an answering smile, but Maria's words stopped them.

'Stay where you are, traitors!'

'But I'm your father. And you know Emma. Where are your brothers?'

'Your sons have been put under lock and key,' Maria said, clearly stunning Priby as well as the rest of them. 'Where you will shortly join them. Your companion will be held separately.'

'What is this?' Podevin tried to speak with authority. 'I raised you and Priby. All I want is my family, and we'll go. You could come too, if you wanted …' He faltered to a stop.

'Here, we obey the king's command,' Maria said. 'You held me, the duke of Budec's daughter, captive, so I did not even know who I was! You have always been a traitor to King Boleslav, with your life forfeit. And we now know his suspicions about you and the whore were true!'

With those last words, Maria burned her bridges, isolated herself from her family, and made an enemy of Emma. She even stood and pointed at the Anglo-Saxon princess, just in case anyone was in doubt over who was meant by 'whore'.

It was Mark who stepped forward. 'Madam, I trust you have proof to support your accusation?' He spoke quietly, reasonably, but somehow everyone in the hall, no matter how far back, heard him.

'The king is bringing proof with him. I understand she is known as Edith, after her aunt's Anglo-Saxon name.'

At this Priby started, 'But you never mentioned that—where will she stay?'

Maria turned her head. 'I thought I told you to keep quiet?'

Priby bowed her head and went very quiet. In the silence, Podevin found himself waiting for Maria to strike out at Priby. But instead, Maria turned back to her shocked visitors.

'As you can see, we have been well informed of your arrival and your plans. The king has out-thought you. Your daughter Edith is being brought to him for examination. I have been instructed to build a scaffold in the courtyard. For the moment, you are to be confined, to await the king's interrogation.'

Podevin briefly closed his eyes as he saw Mark approaching the chair where Maria sat. He ignored her glare, waved away her attempt to speak, leaned forward and spoke into her ear, but not so quietly Podevin did not hear the words.

'I do hope you are only following the king's orders, Maria. And adding nothing to them?' He didn't wait for a reply, but continued. 'Power is a deadly drug that feeds on itself and destroys all its servants.'

'Just be thankful, monk, you weren't included in the orders for confinement.'

Mark stepped back. 'Then you'll have no objection to me offering what peace and comfort I can to those who are confined, will you?'

There was a pause, as if Mark were defying Maria to make more of his impertinence. But she said nothing, merely gesturing to the guards to take the prisoners away.

Priby breathed a sigh of relief that the duchess hadn't decreed Emma and Podevin were to be summarily executed. Hearing her name made her start.

'Priby. You'd better accompany the female traitor to her cell. And keep me informed of what Mark gets up to.'

Maria picked up the king's message, which had lain in front of her. She had read it before, several times, so Priby knew this was a pretence so Maria could avoid any questions Priby had. Maria could have done everything so differently: she could easily have not officially recognised them, she could have kept the king's message secret until Podevin, Emma and the boys—and even Priby herself—were well away. But that was not to be.

Priby went to Emma. She realised, for all the Anglo-Saxon princess had, over her eventful life, had her ups and downs, this must be the first time she found herself without any servant. Her one remaining lady-in-waiting was to be kept 'out of harm's way' until the king made up his mind up who she was to serve. Emma's door was guarded, and the guards told to allow nothing and no-one in, except for 'the monk who came with them and my lady-in-waiting'. Further orders meant the guards were to keep watch all the time through the bars, 'or, if expedient, inside the cell'.

What, Priby thought, was the point of her being told to report everything back, if the guards were doing the same? But male guards can be embarrassed into looking the other way by females desiring to 'adjust their attire', nor do males wish to view women, of any rank, using a piss-pot!

'We all need to do this,' Emma called, before instructing them to come and take it away—and to make sure the next pot was clean. Perhaps because she was used to command and was, after all, born a princess, the guards did as they were told. After a little discussion, it was decided starvation had not been ordered, so food and drink could be brought to the prisoner.

All this Priby had helped with, pointing out that the king had yet to appear.

'But the dukes have,' said one of the guards, 'so you'd better enjoy it while you can.'

Priby and Emma were left alone. Thankfully, there was plenty for both of them, but they had barely settled down when the cell door was unlocked and opened, creaking on its hinges.

'Well, well,' said Mark, 'some are doing better than others.'

'How's Podevin?' was Emma's instant question.

'Other than being determined to take all the blame in the hopes King Boleslav will be satisfied with one death—surprisingly calm.'

'I shouldn't have sent him to Augsburg. You were right.' Emma stopped eating.

'Firstly, we've been over all this before. What's done is done. Secondly, if you don't eat that, then you'll not get any more. And you don't know how long all this is going to take, even if Boleslav arrives today.'

'What do you mean, "how long"? The king decides, the king decrees.' While Emma spoke, Mark sat down and started helping himself to meat and bread. Priby noticed. 'How can you be so calm?'

'Despite the circumstances, the king will have to appease England— you know that country your half-brother Edred rules, Emma—King Edred will need to hear there was a trial, there was a case to be heard.' Mark said, as if it was obvious.

'Edmund,' Emma interposed. 'King Edmund.'

Mark shook his head.

'Dead,' was the blunt comment. 'Killed by an outlaw in his own hall. Edred has only just taken over, not crowned yet, but I cannot imagine he will be unconcerned about his sister's welfare, especially as another sister has recently died.'

'What have you not been telling me, Mark?' Emma said. Priby watched silently.

'Where were you during the last days of May?' Mark replied.

'I was getting ready to go to the border. Why?'

'So, you were either officially banned from getting any news, or were too busy to react to it. Not that we heard immediately. But the news came soon enough.'

'May I ask,' Priby said, not following the conversation, 'what this has to do with us? How can it help?'

Mark gave her a small smile. 'If it was thought that Edred would be weak, that he'd allow the Vikings to take over, for example, or there were other claimants who'd start a civil war, Boleslav would not need to worry. But it appears the council in England are united. What we didn't know, until I had communication from your sister's chaplain…'

Mark ignored Emma's exclamation at this point, but he had the grace to blush at not telling her he had his own contact in the Saxon court. After a pause, Mark carried on speaking, explaining to both Priby and Emma.

'What we didn't know was that Edmund had already asked questions of Otto about Queen Matilda. All very diplomatic, and yes, even queens can die of the bloody flux. However, two sisters dying too close together might give rise to more, and less diplomatic, questions. And Boleslav also has to deal with the strange timing, especially as you've just held off an invasion force from Saxony.'

'But it isn't the only charge, is it?' Emma had sat and was chewing her food. To Priby's mind, the duchess appeared to be taking what Mark was saying very calmly. 'I am supposed to have allowed Podevin to flee to Saxony, so he could lead the rebellion against Boleslav.'

'But who instigated that?'

Emma thought. 'Blanik?'

'At whose suggestion?'

Emma shook her head. Priby decided to remain quiet and listen. She was supposed to report back, so she had better have something to report.

Mark was speaking again. 'Duke Heinrich. Didn't your husband let slip he was in communication with Saxony? It wasn't with King Otto. There's your defence. If you erred, it was at your husband's instigation. Your husband also fled the field of battle, didn't he?'

'After I confined him to his tent—my tent,' Emma said.

'Hmm,' said Mark. 'Let's hope that doesn't come up at the trial. I think we have enough to cause confusion.'

'Yes, but this all deals with me. It doesn't help Podevin!'

'What did he actually do in Saxony? He helped put down a rebellion in the west, he led some forces but, as soon as he could do anything, he sent your husband back to you and he was captured before he could do anything in the last battle. A traitor? Given he also took on a whole party of Saxons who were on a mission to kidnap you, madam, and killed the lot of them—and I can verify they were all very dead.'

Emma sat back and smiled. 'You know, Mark, I think I could look forward to this trial. Do we know who will be there?

'Everyone. The dukes of Budec and Kourim are back today. And the king and his son are due soon, of course. And I understand there's going to be a visit from Saxony—but that will be later.'

'You mean Boleslav will want us dead and buried before he has to be nice to Otto?'

'Something like that,' Mark replied.

ᴇ⃰ɔ

Priby, in the end, did not get much time to report back. It was the briefest of conversations with a nervy Maria—she always needed to look her best for her husband the duke—and she was only able to say Podevin and Emma intended to mount a strong defence.

'They feel confident of an acquittal, madam.'

Maria looked at her. If Priby's words had been intended to worry her about her previous actions, it did not show. 'My wimple. Is it pushed back enough?' was all she said, and Priby supplied the required assurance.

Chapter 39
A Case for the Prosecution

There was pomp: trumpeters trumpeting, drummers drumming. There was splendour: best, most colourful, uniforms on display. Despite the heat, velvet cloaks adorned the shoulders and the backs of dignitaries. The hall itself was decked with tapestries. Giving away the purpose of the meeting, there was a high table loaded with documents. There was a dais behind the table, with a throne, and other high-backed chairs for dukes to sit down on. There were stools for their wives and other lower-ranked persons, who nonetheless had to be there. There were guards. The king's bodyguard up by the thrones, the duke of Budec's forces being used around the hall. A screen of guards prevented the guilty from taking any steps towards the evidence on the table. It was perhaps fortunate they had their own dais to stand on so they could see and be seen.

Over to the left side of the room as the prisoners were escorted in, they could see a girl. She sat with her head bowed. Stern matrons sat on either side of her. She was dressed plainly enough, and her well-scrubbed face was uncovered. Every now and then, she would raise her eyes and stare around the room. Her hazel eyes, so like her mother's, taking everything in. Each time she did this, one or other of the matrons would admonish her in a fierce whisper. The look the matron was given by the girl was not subservient, but she would lower her gaze, until the next sound or entrance.

On the right side, the squires and clerks were gathered. One squire had been disarmed, and one clerk stood a little to the side. While

Vaclav and Alexandr were not on trial, what happened to their father would, no doubt, affect their futures—and all those who surrounded them knew it. Priby, on the other hand, was officially under the protection of the duchess of Budec—who was herself definitely not associated with the traitor Podevin, and his Anglo-Saxon adulterous lover.

Podevin had had plenty of time to think. Mark's visit the day before had been brief. The monk had tried to suggest lines of defence; that it was not Podevin's fault. Not all of it. What had General Blanik and Duke Heinrich been up to? Podevin had pointed out those two were not in Budec, that Blanik would deny everything and Heinrich was too important to accuse of anything. His concern was Emma, and his sons. After the meeting with Maria, apart from knowing there was no sympathy there, he could only hope she would protect Priby and the two girls would at least be safe. If he could get Emma, Vaclav and Alexandr out of this mess, what happened to him was of no importance. After all, hadn't Boleslav-the-Cruel been trying to have him killed ever since Wenceslas had been assassinated? Perhaps, Podevin thought, as he looked round the room, he should be grateful for the last ten years.

He didn't see Mark. Perhaps the monk had taken to praying, but Podevin had thought he might have stayed by Emma's side.

Over the last few hours, shut up in another dungeon, he had realised he still missed Lyudmila, his 'peasant concubine'. Her sound advice had been not to get involved with Emma's scheme, but Emma was the princess, the castle constable, and, back then, likely to be the next queen of Bohemia. All that was gone, of course, and now she was just Emma. She still held herself like a princess, and like a warrior—like a warrior about to go into battle. He leaned as close to her as he dared.

'Leave this to me. I'll take the blame,' he hissed.

'Don't be ridiculous! Didn't Mark tell you? We have a way out,' she whispered back.

'I wasn't about to listen to Mark! We can't blame Blanik, or Heinrich.'

'Why not? The first thing we need is time.'

'We have no time. Didn't you see the stakes out there in the yard? The noose?'

'Not like you to be so pessimistic, Podevin!'

There was no time to reply, as King Boleslav had stood. A small commotion occurred at the door. The king, seeing who it was, paused, indicated that whoever it was could enter, but then pointed to a far corner. Podevin turned his head, to see Sven and a boy scuttle to their designated place. The boy was carrying a box.

The king coughed. All attention reverted to him. He waited for silence.

'My lords, ladies and gentlemen of the court. We are here,' he began, in a staccato fashion, 'to establish, the guilt of the traitor, who goes by the name of Podevin, declared outlaw eleven years ago, murderer of his own brother, who has lived off our land ever since, before fleeing across our borders to raise the standard of rebellion against our crown, our throne, and our person. In this, he was given aid and instruction by our supposed daughter-in-law, who, as we shall see, provided him with documentation to facilitate his flight—she even sent her own force, her own bodyguard, to face mortal danger in support of this treachery.

'But why? Why should someone whose loyalty we counted on, ever since we came to the throne, behave in this way? Because, my lords, this was no master and servant relationship; this was no simple friendship. This was a more intimate relationship,' Boleslav paused, waited for the expected gasp (which duly came) to die down, then carried on, 'a *much* more intimate relationship. The results of which can be seen here today!' Boleslav moved his right arm to indicate the girl sitting quietly in the middle of the hall.

It must have been rehearsed. The two matrons rose as one, grabbed the girl between them by the arms and hauled her to her feet. The girl's mouth opened in protest, but, with everyone's attention on her, no sound came.

'Perhaps you ladies might like to place her between her parents?'

King Boleslav posed it as a question, but his words were a command, and were received as such by the matrons. The girl was all but carried across to Emma and Podevin with all the speed the old ladies could muster. She was thrust into the space between them and abandoned. The girl looked about her, her eyes red-rimmed. Emma bent down.

'Edith? Is that what they call you?'

The girl nodded.

'All right, Edith, we're going to look after you now.'

'But … who are you?'

'I am your mother. We haven't met much, but that's going to change.'

Podevin shook his head. Why didn't Emma promise her the whole world while she was at it? Why not say: I wish you long life and happiness? They were here as a prelude to their deaths.

'Well,' King Boleslav was saying, 'take a good look! Doesn't she have the appearance of her father?'

Murmurs of agreement crossed the hall but, given Emma was holding Edith to her so the girl's face was buried in her mother's dress, there was so little to see of the girl that nobody would be able to tell who she looked like. But court sycophants—all those whose position depend on being agreeable to the king, the duke, to whomever is the most powerful person in the room—can always be relied upon to nod at the appropriate moment.

'My lord,' Emma's voice rang out clear, 'you do yourself, this child, and us, a disservice. If she looks like your cousin, who is standing beside me today, then is that so surprising? A family resemblance is nothing unusual through the generations. And, if I recall, I fought a duel with a gentleman of my husband's court over the allegation of this child's paternity. What has changed since then? I say nothing has changed. And why is my husband not present? We could all then see if our daughter looks more like him, or does she look like me?'

Emma paused to look down at the daughter she had only just seen for the first time in ten years. Then she looked up.

'No? My husband, as with any occasion where "difficulties" might ensue, seems somewhat conspicuous by his absence. And,' Emma raised her voice as the king opened his mouth, 'as for me sending anyone to Saxony to rebel, as you know, and as my husband knows, I sent my emissary to Augsburg to find out why my sister died. My sister, who was queen of Saxony. My sister, who was young, healthy and full of life. You have seen copies of the letters I sent. If this is a proper trial, those copies should be on that table.' Emma pointed with her free hand, while the other was still round her daughter. 'Further, if this was a proper trial, there would be representatives from Saxony to speak to the truth of what I have said!'

'I wasn't aware you had been invited to speak,' the king replied.

'I wasn't aware there was to be no defence against these preposterous allegations!'

'Silence!'

The king's bellow got the desired result. However, there was some shifting in the hall. Not everyone was happy. Not that anyone would intervene, Podevin realised. Much easier to be safe, keep your head down. This was his mess: all he'd done in appearing to go along with Blanik's plans was postpone his own trial. After all, what had he done? Tried to save his own skin. Emma's former chief bodyguard had been killed through his own stupidity. Perhaps his sons would do better without him …

Having secured his required silence, Boleslav decided to pace round the table, looking at the documents on it. He turned to regard his daughter-in-law.

'A pretty speech. A very pretty speech. But it won't help you. Even if all the documents are not here. Yet.' He paused and addressed the far corner of the room. 'Sven?'

There was a stir as Sven swaggered forward. His son followed, staggering under the weight of the box he was carrying, and looked less self-assured—overawed at the company he found himself in. The box landed with a thud on the table. The boy looked with fear at his father, who was clearly holding himself in, his smile frozen as he looked at Boleslav. However, Boleslav indicated that Sven had the floor and returned to his throne.

'My lords! I am unused to addressing so many, so noble an assembly, so please forgive any mistakes, any errors on my—on our part. It is well known that I, too, have suffered at Podevin's hands. I lost my father and my sister because of him.'

'No, you didn't! You lost your father because of Tugumir and his thugs beating him up,' Priby shouted. 'You only lost your sister because, when she was injured, you left her behind. It was Podevin and Lyudmila—a woman you killed, Sven—who rescued me, healed me and brought me up!' Priby got no further.

Maria rose from her stool, turned and slapped her.

'I apologise, my lord. I dismiss my servant—who knows nothing about which she speaks. If she is so determined to stand with the traitors, let her!' Maria pointed to where she required Priby to move to.

Boleslav nodded. 'Yes, there have been too many interruptions! Let her be dismissed to know my displeasure! She can stand with the prisoners.'

Priby did not wait for the guards to escort her. Her face a blank mask, she walked over to where Podevin, Edith and Emma stood behind their screen of guards. She stopped, and waited until, at last, the guards realised they had to make space for her to pass between them. Still saying nothing, Priby walked round the dais until she reached the steps and took her position between Podevin and Emma. Edith looked up at her.

'Are you someone important?'

'Me?' said Priby. 'Not really.'

'For what it's worth,' Podevin interrupted, 'you're important to me.'

Sven was waiting.

He jumped when Boleslav growled, 'Get on with it.'

'As I was saying.' he stammered, 'I lost my family and had to flee to Saxony, where it is fortunate I happened to be at Augsburg when he,' a dramatic finger pointed in Podevin's direction, 'rode up to the gates, demanding to be let in as the rightful duke of Bohemia.' At this point, Sven interrupted himself, wheeled round to face Boleslav, bowed, and said, 'My apologies, my lord king, but the traitor would not have said "king" while he was in Saxony—and what he said in Bohemia, I am afraid I do not know.' Sven bowed again.

While this was going on, Podevin was ignoring Emma's pleas of 'Say something—this isn't true!' He knew it wasn't true. If it had been, he'd either have been welcomed with open arms and no fighting, or his whole force would have been annihilated—him included. However, if Sven's testimony could be used so it was just his fault, so only he would die, then what did it matter?

Sven had come to the box. The box had been found in Podevin's home in the forest. It was at the bottom of a hidden grain store—the fact the grain store was hidden was taken by Sven to mean Podevin was holding back on what he owed to the Bohemian crown. The crown, in the person of King Boleslav, nodded encouragement as Sven piled accusation upon accusation. The box was opened with all due cere-mony. It contained letters. Letters from Podevin, letters to Podevin, all detailing his adulterous relationship with Emma. There were letters asking how their daughter was faring. There were even letters—if the ladies present would cover their ears, please—describing the carnal knowledge they had of each other.

Chapter 40
A Case for the Defence?

'Just a minute!' Podevin began to say, finally provoked out of his stupor.

This implicated Emma too. He stole a look in her direction, and she was looking daggers at him, as if to ask why hadn't he said something earlier? Podevin was about to speak again when the door at the back of the hall opened. Mark arrived, showing two more people, a woman and a girl, into the already overcrowded room. He was also followed by a second man—wearing Bible black from head to foot.

'If you will excuse our late arrival, my lord,' Mark said, but carrying on whether the Bohemian king excused him or not, 'but may I introduce Father Luke? Father Luke was formerly chaplain to Queen Matilda and currently serves as King Otto's envoy.'

The last words arrested Boleslav. He had half risen, clearly to order Mark to be detained, but now he had a problem. Even Podevin turned to look; what now? And what had been said at the border between the two rulers? There were affairs in this trial that affected Saxony, whatever might or might not be going on as far as Bohemia was concerned.

'Well, my lord, how far can you afford to offend Saxony?' Emma called out. 'Given you have promised to work with Otto, help keep the peace with Otto, and you need his help to defeat the Magyars?'

Did she know, thought Podevin, or was she just guessing? Then he heard the king.

'How do you know that?' Boleslav was sharp.

'Oh, isn't it obvious?' Emma stepped forward, pushed the unresisting guards aside, and strode to the middle of the floor. 'You and Otto, having been absent from the border between your two domains for months on end, then suddenly you both turn up at *exactly* the same time? You both order your armies to fall back, even while the result of the battle is still in the balance. And you, at least, my lord,' the words were correct, the tone in no way subservient—but Emma was angry, or pretending to be so—'you order your generals away from the place, leaving you, and only you, to do the negotiating. And you expect me, my daughter, my friend and his daughter,' she pointed at each person in turn, 'to pay with our lives?'

'I think…' For the first time in the trial, German was spoken, everyone understood and heads turned towards the new speaker: Father Luke. 'I think, my lord, King Otto would regard that as a little excessive, given he has pardoned his brother. However, be that as it may, I am sure my lord the king of Saxony would have questions. Many questions.' At that, Father Luke stopped speaking. He waited.

King Boleslav sat down in his seat. He pointed at the box on the table. 'What about the letters? You can't argue with those.'

'You can, if they're faked.' The woman stepped forward, guided by Mark, supported by Mark. She was gripping her side as if she was in pain, and her words were gasped out. The child, her daughter, came up beside her. Father Luke merely watched.

'Mark,' said Emma, moving up to the box, where Sven tried, but failed, to stop her looking in, 'what do you know about this?'

'Only what I have learned this morning. Oh, my lord,' he addressed Boleslav, 'just so you know, I'd expect very little from the forests around Prague this coming autumn and winter. No crops were sown, so there will be no harvest, and very little hunting has been going on. It seems the castle has been supplied out of all the stores Podevin laid up before he left. Though I might question why a man about to turn traitor would lay up so many stores to help those he was about to fight.' Mark shrugged, then he, too, looked in the box.

Emma straightened. 'These are all written in German! Even the king,' she acknowledged Boleslav briefly, but she was addressing the whole gathering, 'knows that when Podevin and I resided in Prague before I was married, we spent our time learning each other's languages. These should be in Anglo-Saxon and Czech! And,' she peered closer at the scrap of parchment she was holding, 'it's not even good German: "I am desirous to tempt you with my body." This is farcical!' She held the parchment up to the whole court. 'This is what *he* is meant to have written to *me*! Allow me to assure you all that anyone writing such rubbish would certainly never come within a mile of my body—ever.'

There were a few smirks and titters at that from the ones who read the room, who could see which way this trial was now going. Most observers remained quiet, waiting for the breeze to build, or perhaps for a steer from King Boleslav.

'He burnt many a candle writing those,' the woman with Mark announced. 'Really, Sven, do you think my pain allowed me to sleep while you dealt with your "important business"?' As if to emphasise her point, her speech ended with a gasp, and her daughter, not minding, or ignorant of, protocol, guided her to the left side of the room where she could sit.

As Podevin approached the table, the guards finally deciding he, too, could move about, he noted one of the matrons offering a drink to the poor woman.

'That is not my hand,' he said, taking the parchment from Emma. 'As anyone who has dealt with the forestry accounts over the last ten years could tell you. I wonder,' he addressed the room at that point, ignoring Boleslav, 'if that's one of the reasons why this farce is taking place here in Budec and not in Prague? Maybe we should wait until someone can get here?'

'Or maybe we shouldn't!' The door to the room crashed open as yet another arrival entered.

Really? thought Podevin, as he and Emma turned, Emma open-mouthed in disbelief. *Can this get any more ridiculous?*

Young Boleslav, Duke Boleslav, Mladenic, entered the room. However, it wasn't his arrival that stopped proceedings, nor even its timing. It was the fact there was a girl, a young woman, probably not yet twenty, hanging on his arm. She was looking at him as if he were her saviour, her dream, her lover rolled into one. Emma could hardly restrain herself from rolling her eyes.

'Well, Father,' said the young Boleslav, 'you did say it would all be sorted by the time I returned. That I was free to marry into an alliance with the Bulgars. The duchess here,' he indicated the girl by his side, 'suits me very well indeed. Oh, my dear former wife, you may know her name: it is Emma. But that is all she shares with you.'

'I suppose if you're going to share your name with your father and your son, you might as well scour the world for wives who have the same name, too,' was Mark's dry comment.

'I think you had better tread carefully, my lord of Bohemia!' Father Luke's voice rang out, strong, overriding all the murmuring at the surprise generated by the new arrivals.

'I … I appeal to the pope in Rome!' Boleslav the Cruel had never looked more nervous. 'My son was simply sent to escort the lady to and through our lands on her father's behalf. We know the Anglo-Saxon alliance has not worked as it might. Therefore, the Anglo-Saxon princess,' the Bohemian king pulled himself together, 'we order to the nunnery at Tetin! I am still not satisfied about Podevin, but, for mercy's sake, I will not have him killed. But he is banished from our lands. If, after seven days, anyone finds him on any property owned by me, he can lawfully kill him!' Boleslav licked his lips before continuing. 'My son, and his new bride, will be escorted to Prague. Where we hope his holiness will allow him to celebrate his wedding.'

'But those letters are forgeries!' Podevin bellowed as renewed chattering broke out at King Boleslav's pronouncement.

'You'll never get him to believe that! Not now!' Sven, having kept quiet all this time, was making a bid for importance. 'I found these and, when I showed them to the king, he believed me!'

'Because he wanted to! And besides, even if I would have written in German, my German is better than that.' Podevin was face to face with the man.

Sven's son was tugging at his sleeve.

'But, Daddy, it's true! You did write them.'

'How many times have I told you to shut up!'

Sven's attack on his son was as sudden as it was vicious. His open hand caught the lad on the side of the head. The blow sent Woden reeling towards the table. Podevin saw it in slow motion. He had even started to move, shoving Sven aside as he could see the lad's head now coming into contact with the unyielding corner of the table. A sharp crack as the head bounced up again before the weight of the body it was still attached to dragged it to the floor, where there was another, duller, thud as final contact was achieved with the flagstones.

There was chaos. Woden's mother struggled to her feet and, with her daughter, dragged herself to her son, where she collapsed next to Podevin, who was already kneeling by the small, still form. She forced him to let Woden go, so she could comfort him. Emma, Priby and Edith arrived in the next seconds. But it was obvious the boy was beyond all comfort. Sven was left standing alone, talking, shouting even.

'It's all true. Podevin's the one who did all this! He deserves to die.'

Podevin, his anger building, rose from his knees, the young boy's blood on his hands. He turned, approached the still shouting Sven and slapped him hard across the face.

'Shut up! You're a liar and a fraud. You were born a peasant. You didn't lose your sister, you ran away from her.' He stopped to take a breath, and realised he had the attention of the court. 'You enrolled in the Saxon army—if anyone is a traitor here, it's you—and you saw your chance to create mischief when I arrived in Augsburg. You saw my papers, my credentials. You knew I was to ask about Queen Matilda, I was to ask about making peace between our countries, *and nothing else*. You fled again when your plan to kill me in Augsburg failed. *You* poured poison into King Boleslav's ears—not me! You have destroyed everything you've touched. Including your own son. And we all saw it.'

He did not know who started it, and, at first, it was no more than a low murmur, but it grew in volume: 'Death! Death! Death!'

In the end, it was one mighty shout. At first, Sven smiled at Podevin, as if it was Podevin's death that was being called for. Podevin stared back, realising the mood in the court had shifted. The truth only dawned on Sven when, on receiving the nod from King Boleslav, the guards reached in, grabbed him and dragged him away.

'No! No, it can't be me! I've done nothing wrong! Woden will be fine—he's survived worse! No!' The last was a scream as he was carried out of the hall towards the gallows.

'Perhaps, having been promised a death or two, they'll be satisfied with this,' Mark mused as the hall emptied after the struggling Sven and his captors.

For once, the king waited. Father Luke had a quiet word with him, though Podevin saw no more than a sigh from the king as he stood and made his way to the door. As the ruler here, he had to see justice done.

'My judgment stands,' Boleslav said as he passed Podevin.

~

Death by half-hanging followed by disembowelment, is neither pretty nor quick. Sven's screams rang out over the whole castle. The huddled group of women surrounding Woden's body in the hall heard it and reacted in different ways. Sven's wife and daughter looked at each other and shrugged. Priby shuddered; Emma shook her head; and Edith wept.

Podevin had not bothered to go outside. Father Luke and Brother Mark had left to offer what comfort they could to the one on the scaffold—which was precious little. It seemed a long time before the screams died away. Duty done, Luke and Mark reappeared in the hall.

Podevin raised his eyes to them, questioning—except he didn't know quite what he was questioning them about. Sven's soul? What about Woden—who'd had no chance to repent of his sins before he died? Him? Emma? What was left of his family? What was Edith's status?

'Boleslav wants a word—a quiet word,' Luke said as he and Mark approached.

'Why?' Podevin asked.

Even Emma looked up, puzzled.

'You cannot remain. You have to go far enough away to never trouble Bohemia again. Mark suggests England—and himself as the escort. Your sons will go with you.'

'And my daughters?'

'Your adopted daughters can choose, but Edith joins her mother in the convent.' Mark stopped Emma's protest with a gesture. 'It's a man's world, my lady. The pope won't listen to you, so you'll get your divorce—it probably won't even register in the history books ten years from now. And simply by having her birth questioned, Edith—I am so sorry,' Mark broke off to address the girl, 'but you won't be approached for marriage. All I can say is, they are used to high-born ladies at the convent.'

'And me?' said Priby. 'I have been publicly sacked from my job at … at the duchess of Budec's side, and I am not high-born.'

'As I said, you have a choice. Go with Podevin, or stay. There is an empty forester's hut in the forest by Prague—or it will be empty soon enough. However, I expect the king will want a man to be in charge …'

Nobody mentioned Maria.

Chapter 41
The King Stoops to Explain

For a second, Podevin thought he had gone back in time over ten years, and he was the page going in to see Wenceslas. But it was Boleslav standing at the window with the light behind him. They were in a small chamber, set aside for an exalted guest—the golden thread on the furnishings gave that away—but small. Intimate. Worryingly so for Podevin. He had been ushered in, and the door closed behind him. For the first time ever, it was just him and King Boleslav.

There was a table, with a pitcher of wine, a plate of sweetmeats, two goblets. Podevin stood and waited. The Bohemian ruler turned, smiled briefly, and moved to the table.

'Come on, cousin, come and sit,' he said, waving Podevin to join him.

Boleslav poured the wine into the goblets. Podevin hesitated.

'If I was going to kill you, you'd be dead by now. Drink.'

Podevin drank. It was good wine, but strong. He'd better not have too much of it.

'You're wondering why you're here, aren't you?' Boleslav said.

With a half shrug and a smile, Podevin acknowledged the truth of the words.

'You're here because Luke and Mark think you're owed an explanation. Though I'm not sure they thought I'd give it.' Boleslav paused and looked into his drink. He looked to the ceiling, then down again at Podevin. 'I don't know that I ever really believed the stories about you. Wanting the crown, that is. I couldn't see you putting Emma in danger—and, after all, for you to have the crown, you'd need to kill off my whole family, wouldn't you?'

Podevin nodded. He thought he would be better off not speaking.

'I have done a lot for my son—though he doesn't realise it. You did him a favour, you know, sending him back to his then wife the way you did. And in some ways, I'm sorry your missive was put into the wrong hands. Heinrich destroyed it, by the way, so I can't even check if your writing from that box is genuine or not!'

That was clearly supposed to be a joke, so Podevin smiled again, sipped more wine, and waited.

'My son will never be an instinctive warrior. But he will never be as afraid of death again. I'm told he actually chose to go into that battle. And he has the scars to prove it. But he cannot pretend to like your Emma.'

Podevin looked up sharply at the 'your', but Boleslav was just using it as a way of differentiating her from Mladenic's new bride.

'And, in some ways, I am sorry to lose her. It wasn't like her to be taken in by my son's intrigue with Duke Heinrich. And her unmasking you was a big mistake—you will get to be able to tell her this—I have called for your death too often to easily overlook it, just because you went on a visit to Saxony and then were embroiled in a plot to put Heinrich on my throne.'

Podevin nearly spilled his drink. 'What? You know it was all about Heinrich?'

Boleslav was openly laughing at his surprise. 'Of course I do. You were never going to get near. And, as for Princess Liutgarde ...'

'She's promised elsewhere?' Podevin guessed. He recalled his conversation with Blanik a few days ago now: he hadn't been so far wrong about his own fate.

'Duke of Lorraine—Otto's expanding westwards as well as every other point of the compass. Oh, and he's forgiven Heinrich because he wants his brother to stop rebelling and have Bavaria—also by marriage. It seems the current duke of Bavaria is not long for this world, and he has a comely, young wife.'

'How convenient,' muttered Podevin, wondering why he was being told all this. Then he started wondering how Boleslav knew all this.

'Otto and I will be meeting in person again soon enough. He's going to "forgive" my not paying tribute up till now, and I'm going to promise to start paying that tribute. And we're going to work together, with others, to destroy the Magyars. They're getting overconfident. Otto doesn't want them back in West Francia, or anywhere else in his kingdoms again.' Boleslav paused. 'But you won't be around to hear about that, even if it is happening in Prague. However, back to the point. As I say, I cannot have you in, or anywhere near, my kingdom. It might not be Blanik next time, nor Heinrich, but some idiot will want to use you to make you king. And if Otto would ask questions about me killing you on some trumped-up charges, I'm stuck.'

'Trumped-up charges?' Podevin asked.

Boleslav shrugged. 'It would not have been the first time. Though I might suspect Otto is more worried about his sister-in-law than he is about you; at the moment, I can't take the risk.'

'So, England? With a monk as an escort.'

'He can hardly be expected to live where Emma's going, can he?'

'Will Emma be happy with a divorce?'

'She'll sign to say she is, and that will be the end of it. They were always unsuited. Besides, I need a grand coalition to beat the Magyars. My son's new father-in-law is part of that. Much more useful than far-away England.'

Politics. That's what it came down to. Not even marriage can get in the way of kings doing deals. Podevin realised Otto would not make a fuss if it helped him to deal with his enemies. But if England, and its troubles, counted for so little, why had Boleslav, all those years ago insisted that Emma wed his son—who was a mere boy? Why, after all this, could she not have married Podevin? It was as if he'd spoken aloud because the king came up with his excuse, as if there had been no pause to sip at his wine.

'But, of course, if the Anglo-Saxon hadn't married my boy, she'd have to have married Wenceslas—and that would never have done. A second cousin like you has turned out to be bad enough, just imagine what would have had to happen if I had actual nephews to deal with? And, no, she was never going to marry you: Wenceslas was never going to put you on the throne.'

'Emma had to wed into the throne?'

'That was the agreement with Athelstan. He was a very powerful ruler. We couldn't know his successors were going to be more … insular. Too busy being Mercian, Northumbrian, "men of Wessex," than English. Their last king was killed by an outlaw.' Boleslav raised an eyebrow.

'I am unarmed.' It was true enough; he did not even have a dagger.

'We'll see you properly equipped before you set out. But that's as far as my largesse goes. My ruling was made in public.'

'I understand,' said Podevin.

He felt he did, at least in some ways, understand the Bohemian ruler. Having killed to be king, everything he did was geared towards both keeping the throne and passing it on to his son—and no-one else. He had gone as far as he dared with potentially annoying Otto; he could get away with annoying England—preoccupied as they were with getting their new king settled on the throne.

Podevin was going into exile. He would spend the rest of his life speaking a different language. Hopefully, his sons would adapt. The king made to stand, so Podevin stood. The plate of sweetmeats remained untouched, the rest of his wine undrunk. He would never see the king, or any member of the king's family, again.

Chapter 42
A Final Escape

Emma's use as a breeding machine was being overtaken by a younger princess; one who was prepared to fawn over Mladenic—and one who knew not to call him by that name. Anglo-Saxon Emma's use as a fighting general, castle constable, leader of men, was no longer required. That was not to say she looked forward to entering the convent at Tetin.

'What am I to do with "a life of contemplation"?' she stormed. Podevin had no answer. 'And I'm to lose both my chaplain and Beatrice.'

Beatrice had not been given much in the way of choice: she was off to help Hilde on her farm. The chaplain was already lost, in that he was tending to Sven's wife. At least he had found out her name; she was Birgit and her daughter Astrid. The older woman was very ill, and in a lot of pain. It had only been her determination at last to do something right, and Mark's inspired visit, that meant she had struggled her way to Budec. Mark had ridden overnight to get there and had found horses to ride back the next day. Emma was going to have to do without him until tomorrow, as, once he'd finished dealing with Birgit, he was 'going to sleep, madam, whether you like it or not!'

'At least we are alive,' Podevin said, an idea beginning to form, but not one he could give voice to yet.

Maybe, what Mikael had said to him, after finding out where Emma was being sent, might be useful after all. Mikael, being too closely associated with Emma to have any other realistic option, had also chosen exile. The rest of Emma's bodyguard had been forgiven their brief rebellion and ride to Budec and had been transferred to the duke of Budec's forces—on pain of execution, should they fail in their ultimate loyalty to Bohemia again. Relieved that there would be no more deaths, Podevin's mind reverted to Emma's troubles.

'But I have to stay in Bohemia, and you have to leave—with Mark,' she said.

'Your order of nuns has houses everywhere—maybe in England too,' Podevin blurted out, immediately cursing himself—what had he just told himself not to do?

'Oh, yes, and how long before I'm senior enough to ask for a transfer?'

'We don't know how these things work yet. All we know is that we'd better do as we're told if we value our lives!' Podevin paused. Him and his big mouth. 'Look, don't let's argue.' Now he was sounding like a child. 'If this is our last meeting, let us at least depart as friends.'

Conversation stalled. With no more than some brief hand-holding, Podevin and Emma silently bade each other goodbye.

༄

It had been a horrible week. Emma was only just beginning to learn how vindictive these brides of Christ could be. And how untrusting. Here she was, locked in her cell again. It was like a prison. Outside military campaigns, she had never risen so early, gone to bed so early, had so little to eat—and all in silence. At first, she had hoped for a visit, even if just from Mark. But seven days and six nights had passed without the hoped-for appearance. The seventh night had begun.

'Madam? Madam! Are you there?'

Emma shook her head. She was sure she'd just heard Mark's voice.

'Madam!'

It was Mark! Emma scrambled from her hard wooden pallet and crossed the wooden floor of her cell on bare feet to the window.

'Mark! What are you doing here? You're supposed to be gone by now.' Peering through the bars, she could see the top of his head

'I wasn't exiled, or outlawed. We're here to get you out.'

'We?'

'Never mind. Can you open your cell door and get to the wicket gate?'

'They're both locked—so, no.'

'Here.' A key flew through the window, almost hitting her forehead. 'It's the same key. You have one minute. Go!'

Without thinking, Emma flew to the door. The key was stiff but, using both hands, she forced the lock. She had gone two steps outside her cell when she was reminded how cold a stone floor could be. But she had no time to put her wooden sandals on! Instead, still barefoot, she ran to the small gate within the bigger one. The key worked better this time.

Outside, there was a small party. One of them held something large but immobile over his shoulder. Mark had another bundle. What were they trying to smuggle into her cell?

'What's going on?' Emma used her normal voice.

'Nothing if you don't keep quiet! We're getting you out of here, as I said.'

'But Edith!' This time, she kept her voice down, but her urgency made her stand in their way. 'I'm not going without Edith.'

'I'm here, Mother.' A small voice and a small form pushed herself to the front.

Emma snatched the child into a fierce embrace.

'Come on, you can do that later. Which is your cell?' Mark demanded.

Still on bare feet, Emma led them down the corridors, round two corners, and into her cell. The bundle was deposited straight onto her cot.

'What are you doing?'

'We have permission,' said Mark but, before he could say any more, Edith dashed in.

'Someone's coming!'

Only Edith was small enough to get under the cot. The rest pressed themselves against the walls, out of sight of anyone peering in through the narrow, barred window in the door. Emma frantically locked the door, and was left having to lie down next to the bundle.

'Sister? Did I hear a noise?'

'Surely not, Reverend Mother,'

'You are awake very late, sister.' The voice came from outside the door, a face very close to the tiny, barred window in that door, squinting to peer inside into the, at best, half-light.

'I am very sorry, Reverend Mother, but I have yet to get used to life here.'

The door rattled as the lock was tried. 'I'll expect you at confession straight after matins.'

'Yes, Reverend Mother. Good night, Reverend Mother.'

The footsteps retreated, and the blocks of shadow on the wall resolved themselves into Brother Mark and Mikael. Edith scrabbled out from under Emma's cot.

'You've got to dress her in your clothes, Mother. I'll help. I already helped Astrid.'

'What? What is going on here?'

'Please, madam, just do it, we haven't time and I promise we'll explain,' Mark said, passing over his own bundle to her.

Dressing a dead body is not as easy as a person may think—especially when one of those people isn't used to dressing even themselves. The Reverend Mother had taken it into her head that a former princess, a disgraced former princess, needed to learn how to be humble by starting at the bottom of the hierarchy. Hence the bare cell, the single blanket, and the lack of any creature comforts whatsoever. Usually, high-born novices, nuns who'd yet to take their vows, were not locked in, were afforded some comforts of home, including servants but, in this case, it was not to be.

With the men resolutely turning their backs, Emma and Edith managed. Mark's bundle was clothes for Emma—more merchant's wife than princess. Linen, not silk, sleeves reasonably tight, rather than flowing, but at least there were slippers, not wooden clogs, to put on her feet.

'Are you ready? Now, come on!' Mark said.

The key was failing. It took Mikael's strength to persuade it to turn in the lock, but they were out. Slowly, slowly, Mikael turned the key to lock the cell door behind them. They dashed down the corridors, round the corners, to the wicket gate.

Where someone waited for them. Emma came to a screeching halt. Who was this?

Then her heart lurched.

'Come on,' he said, 'the horses are waiting.'

'Podevin!' She flung her arms around him.

And found herself carried through the wicket and put down on the other side. The outside. There was time for one kiss, then holding her hand, he ran with her down the slope, to where the horses, and one pony, were waiting.

'We ride for an hour, then we can all rest. Priby has a camp set up. All right? Can you do that, Edith?' Podevin was encouraging Emma to mount, while also helping Edith onto the solitary pony.

The hour was a blur. At least, with it being the height of summer, it was warm. There was a moon, so they could see. Emma allowed that the plan took care of the fact that, if they could see, even at night, they could be seen.

The 'camp guards' were both asleep, with a smiling Priby watching over them. There was a paddock set up for the horses, a fenced area with plenty of grass. There was food—so much food—Emma, who felt she had been on starvation rations since she'd entered the nunnery, went faint just at the smell. Edith also appeared to revive for a short while, but soon she was too tired to lift the spoon to her mouth.

Priby helped her, but then said, 'Let's get you to bed. There will still be plenty to break your fast in the morning. And you can meet your brothers.'

Emma, on the other hand, was fired up, and thought she would never sleep again.

'When are you going to tell me? And what's Mikael doing here?'

'Let's do the last question first,' Podevin replied. 'Mikael's here because his sister is one of the sisters where you've just escaped from. He told me that as soon as he knew where you were going. I think he meant that you'd have a friendly face inside.' Podevin paused. 'But I had another idea. It seems the Reverend Mother's sight is failing, so she won't be able to tell it's not you in that bed when she unlocks your door. And, once she has decided you, Emma, are dead, no-one will be able to tell her differently. And Mikael's actual sister will look out for Astrid—who will identify her mother as her mother, who has died,' Podevin said.

Slowly, Emma understood that, before they had come for her, they had smuggled Astrid in, and Edith out, of the nunnery.

'We thought it might be more difficult to wake the child than the adult—and Astrid would not have to see us handling her mother's body,' was all Mark said in explanation.

It went without saying that Edith had been kept in a different part of the nunnery. If King Boleslav had kept Emma apart from her daughter, why should Reverend Mother treat either of them any differently?

'Do you mean I am to be officially dead? What will Otto say? And Astrid? Why should she be punished? What's she done?'

'Your Reverend Mother will not rush to tell him. She certainly won't tell him she lost you. She was paid an awful lot to take you on.' Mark took up the tale. 'And, as for Astrid, do you think that, for her, living in a nunnery, where she'll be fed, she'll be looked after— we've already said Mikael's sister will keep an eye on her—she will be allowed to grow up with no man beating her like her father did on a regular basis ... Do you think she will regard that as a punishment? She has no family, no country to call her own. Who'd look after her on the outside?'

Emma nodded her slow understanding at Mark's words.

Then Mark said, as she yawned, 'But before we go any further, can I point out one thing: if it wasn't for Podevin, none of this would have happened. His plan.'

'But you helped—you both did. And Priby,' Podevin put in.

'But won't someone work out we're here?' Emma said.

'We're going tomorrow. Besides, it's a winter hut, for when they bring the animals down from the summer pastures.'

Podevin pointed up; they were in the mountains. Of course, Emma realised, there would be summer and winter pasture.

'They've been well paid,' Podevin pointed out.

'Who provided the money?' This was Emma's final question for the evening, as she yawned again.

'Maria, Duchess of Budec. I think she is feeling guilty,' Priby said, a grimmer note to her voice.

'She's made her decisions,' Podevin said, also speaking seriously, 'and I am so sorry you suffered, but the rest of us are here.'

'And tomorrow, we head for the coast and find a ship to take us to England,' Emma said into Priby's silence. She stood. 'Where do I sleep?'

It would not be quite that simple, but they would all, bar one, end up in England, and all those having at least a smattering of Anglo-Saxon, before the first of the winter storms.

Acknowledgements

The second book in *The Premyslid Chronicles* series, has taken much less time to write than the first—less than sixteen months against sixteen years!—and I am very happy about that. It also means there are many people to thank for their encouragement along the way to keep my writing on track. Firstly, my sons, Alastair and Jonny, have been, as ever, a wonderful support: thank you both. And an especial thanks to Alastair for allowing me to use the illustrative map of Bohemia once again. I must also mention all the folk at Resolute Books, who have been unfailing in their help, support and encouragement: especially Sue Russell, Sarah Nicholson and John Stevens who, once again, performed the task of peer reviewing *Podevin and the Queen's Death* uncomplainingly—I hope you enjoy the final result. My editors, Amie McCracken and Annie Percik have worked very hard to ensure I corrected my mistakes and left no obvious plot holes! (Any that do remain are the sole responsibility of the author.) Thanks also to Liz Carter, who has come up with another brilliant cover.

My writing groups, especially the u3a one led by Marilyn Sands, have been an unfailing source of encouragement, as have folks from Lichfield Methodist Church—up to and including offering the church as a place where I could hold a book launch! Thanks go particularly to: Rev Mark, Alison, Rebecca and Sue.

Thank you one and all, and I do hope you enjoyed reading Emma and Podevin's second adventure.

About the Author

Originally a 'Shropshire Lad,' Nigel has long harboured ambitions to be a writer. However, life intervened, and the later 1980s saw him teaching Maths in Botswana. On returning to the UK, he continued teaching for a while before going to Durham to get a PhD in Theology and working for Durham Diocese as their World Development Officer.

Now living in Lichfield, Nigel writes a short story each month, some of which end up on his website www.nigeloakleywrites.com and is working on the third and final part of Podevin and Emma's story.

About Resolute Books

We are an independent press representing a
consortium of experienced authors,
professional editors and talented designers
producing engaging and inspiring books of the
highest quality for readers everywhere. We
produce books in a number of genres including
historical fiction, crime suspense, young adult
dystopia, memoir, Cold War thrillers, poetry,
and even Jane Austen fan fiction!

Find out more at resolutebooks.co.uk

for the joy of reading

Printed in Dunstable, United Kingdom

76356924R00180